The King's Quest™ Companion

Second Edition

The King's Quest™ Companion

##ABook
Companion

Second Edition

Peter Spear

Osborne McGraw-Hill
Berkeley New York St. Louis San Francisco
Auckland Bogotá Hamburg London Madrid
Mexico City Milan Montreal New Delhi Panama City
Paris São Paulo Singapore Sydney
Tokyo Toronto

Osborne **McGraw-Hill**
2600 Tenth Street
Berkeley, California 94710
U.S.A.

Osborne/McGraw-Hill offers software for sale. For information on translations, software, or book distributors outside of the U.S.A., please write to Osborne **McGraw-Hill** at the above address.

This book is printed on recycled paper.
This book was produced using Ventura Publisher Version 2. Design by Judy Wohlfrom.

The King's Quest™ Companion, Second Edition

Copyright © 1991 by Peter Spear. Portions Copyrighted © by Sierra On-Line®, Inc., 1983 through 1990. KING'S QUEST and the names of the KING'S QUEST characters are Trademarks of Sierra On-Line, Inc. All rights reserved. Printed in the United States of America. Except as permitted under the Copyright Act of 1976, no part of this publication may be reproduced or distributed in any form or by any means, or stored in a database or retrieval system, without the prior written permission of the publisher, with the exception that the program listings may be entered, stored, and executed in a computer system, but they may not be reproduced for publication.

34567890 DOC 91

ISBN 0-07-881671-8

Acquisitions Editor: Roger Stewart
Associate Editor: Laurie Beaulieu
Technical Reviewer: Chris Iden
Proofreader: Julie Anjos
Word Processors: Lynda Higham, Stefany Otis
Illustrations: Karen Minot
Diagrams: Judy Wohlfrom
Composition: Bonnie Bozorg
Production Supervisor: Kevin Shafer

Information has been obtained by Osborne **McGraw-Hill** from sources believed to be reliable. However, because of the possibility of human or mechanical error by our sources, Osborne **McGraw-Hill**, or others, Osborne **McGraw-Hill** does not guarantee the accuracy, adequacy, or completeness of any information and is not responsible for any errors or omissions or the results obtained from the use of such information.

Contents

	Read Me First	xi
	Introduction	xvii
1	The Eye Between the Worlds	1
2	Quest for the Crown	9
3	The World of Daventry	44
4	Romancing the Throne	59
5	A Magical Primer	91
6	To Heir Is Human	115
7	Grave Matters	159
8	The Perils of Rosella	167
9	Iconomancy: A Magic Without Words	217

10	Absence Makes the Heart Go Yonder	239
11	The Easy Way Out	317
12	An Encyclopedia of Daventry	435
13	The Final Score	525

Dedication

For my parents:

Alexander Spear

Josephine McCausland Spear

I love you

Acknowledgments

Oodles of people have played a substantial part in helping me put the second edition of this book together. My wife, Virginia Soper, was brutal and ruthless as she tore the unfinished manuscript to shreds—she remains the toughest editor I have ever had. I owe her also for her library of folk and fairy-tales, top-of-the-head knowledge, insight, patience, and Pope Sylvester. Thanks sweetheart—the check will be there any day now, real soon; it's in the mail!

Roger Stewart at Osborne/McGraw-Hill calmly withstood my months of telephone calls, bad puns, and missed deadlines. If his boss is reading this—he deserves better. Associate Editor Laurie Beaulieu has an exacting eye for detail that is awesome to comprehend. So few things slip by her that I'm astounded she hasn't been hired away by the Border Patrol.

I cannot praise nor thank enough Chris Iden at Sierra On-Line. When all was in hurry and scurry around him, he would always take my phone calls, correct my mistakes, or find me a corner in which I could work. In between, he put in his usual 36-hour working days getting King's Quest 5 out the door.

Karen Minot did the illustrations and cover. I like them a lot. She also deserves belated thanks for her buzzer-beating art in the first edition.

Dr. Magic himself, Larry Magid, got me into this book. If it weren't for him, Victoria Smith, Andy Goodman, Phil Dein, Gene Guerin, Alice Baro, Peter Jacobus, Ron Hesse, Debby Everett, Mary Lou Manalli, Gary Saxer, and Kevin Strehlo, I wouldn't have to work for a living. Thanks for the memories.

Bill Davis, Ken Williams, John Williams, and Kirk Green at Sierra made the way easier than it might have been. Ann Pharr at Osborne made my days brighter.

Derek Karlavaegen keeps sending me material. Obviously there would be no book without him.

Most importantly, though, there is Roberta Williams, the author of the King's Quest games. She has provided me with encouragement, support, and access to a work in progress. I owe her a lot. We all owe her a lot.

Read Me First

xii
King's Quest

*T*he gnome's name is IFNKOVHGROGHPRM, but lately he's also been answering to the name NIKSTLITSELPMUR. Of course, he only does that for certain people. You might be one of those people. Again, you might not.

There *is* a way out of the maze in Mordack's castle—just one, but it's there. All you have to do is discover which of the 64 different places it's located in, and how to get to it.

And it is possible to survive the endless desert of Serenia. You just have to know where to look for the few oases and safe spots that are there—and one important skeleton.

There are maps for both of those mazes in this book. You'll probably need them.

Oh, Daventry is a real place.

I hope all of that got your attention.

This book tells you everything you need to know to successfully play, and complete, the King's Quest computer adventures. This is not a hint book, it is a solution book. Unlike any hint book you have ever seen, the solutions and problems are given directly, clearly, and in narrative form. The narratives themselves are the main path through the games. Everything you need to know is right here in front of you, including real maps of the world of Daventry (not just the traditional box-type diagrams). There are no answers printed in invisible ink, none that you have to hold up to a mirror to read, no crossword puzzles to solve, and no riddle is ever answered by another riddle. It's all right here for your eyes to see and your mind to digest.

As of this writing there are five titles in the King's Quest series: King's Quest 1: Quest for the Crown, King's Quest 2: Romancing the Throne,

Read Me First

King's Quest 3: To Heir Is Human, King's Quest 4: The Perils of Rosella, and King's Quest 5: Absence Makes the Heart Go Yonder. The games are set in the kingdom of Daventry and follow the adventures of King Graham and his family—from Graham's initial quest to obtain his kingship to a time 20 or 25 years later. Within the games you encounter dozens of familiar characters and situations from the lands of fantasy, fairy tale, and myth. The player becomes, and controls, the hero or heroine, interacting with the other creatures and people in order to complete that game's particular quest. A wrong step can mean death...with a message asking if you'd like to try again. And people do try again, and again, and again.

The King's Quest games are outrageously popular and addictive; millions of people (one estimate claims more than 10 million) have played the adventures. They tax the player's brain and, occasionally, eye-to-hand coordination. Most of all they tax the player's problem-solving ingenuity and patience. Frustratingly difficult to solve at times, they have forced grown people to ask, beg, plead, and demand hints from whatever source they can obtain them.

The games' publishers, Sierra On-Line, located in Oakhurst, California, do everything they can to help. They give out clues and solutions by phone to people who call from literally all over the world. They have established their own electronic bulletin board service to give hints out by computer, sell their own hint books, and have hints published on the major computer on-line services. Clues and hints also appear in popular computer and game magazines. Still their switchboard remains jammed with stumped players, and the phone traffic has been so heavy at times that it's knocked out phone service to their community.

Thus this book.

Solutions to the toughest problems are given more than once—first, in the narrative history of the actual adventures, and again in the specific step-by-step walk-throughs of the games that I call "The Easy Way Out." The narratives give the complete story of what really happened to the main characters. When you play along with those, you complete the adventure, just as Graham, Alexander-Gwydion, and Rosella did.

What, you may ask, does this guy mean by saying, "...*the narrative history of the actual adventures....what really happened....just as Graham, Alexander-Gwydion, and Rosella did*"? Be patient; all will be explained in the "Introduction" chapter that immediately follows. In it you will learn how much of the material in this book came to be; how it was sent from Daventry to our world—where it ended up as the plots for the King's Quest computer game series. Face it—computer game hint books are not this thick. There is much more here than that. This book contains documents that detail real events that happened to real people. Or, so I and my editors are led to believe.

In the autumn of 1990, Sierra On-Line released a new and graphically improved version of King's Quest 1: the Quest for the Crown for IBM/compatible computers. Called the *SCI* version on the disks and Enhanced Graphics and Sound on the box, its main purpose was to upgrade the graphics and sound of the game to state-of-the-art levels by using the Sierra-developed "SCI Interpreter." Don't worry about the technical stuff, the result is sharper, more-detailed pictures on the screen—more like an animated movie than a clunky cartoon. This system had already been used in the Perils of Rosella and other of the company's newer titles to rave reviews.

Although King's Quest 1's graphics and animation were revolutionary when the game was first published in 1984, as is often the case in such matters, the revolutionary became old technology. It had become time to upgrade the older, but still best-selling, adventure. It was a good idea; it does look great.

In improving the look and sound of the game, however, Sierra decided to make a few changes in the game itself. Not many, just enough to make a few tough problems more logical and a little easier to solve. Thus, in the *SCI Version* only, the gnome's name problem can be answered in more than one

Read Me First

way, the condor doesn't appear until late in the game, and the pebbles by the river find a more visible home by a lake. These, and the fine tuning of other sequences, changed the game slightly. It's called "creative license."

The *SCI Version* of King's Quest 1: The Quest for the Crown is now the only IBM/compatible version on the market. Since the majority of all computer games sold are IBM/compatible, it is clear that almost anyone buying this game after October 1990 will be getting the changed version.

This book covers both versions of King's Quest 1 game. However, the changes in the game do not, and cannot, reflect what actually did happen to Graham as he quested to save Daventry and win its throne. Anyone with an older or non-IBM/compatible KQ1 can play the game along with the narrative in Chapter 2 and win through to the end. This is no longer completely true for folks with the new version.

It has been strongly suggested to me that I "rewrite" that particular court chronicle to reflect the game's changes. I have not. To do so would be to rewrite history, and thus reduce Graham's adventurings to a mere fiction. To do so would be to deny the reality of Daventry, something I am not prepared to do at this time.

The other reason for my decision to leave the KQ1 narrative the same as it appeared in the first edition of this book is a more practical one. The vast majority of KQ1 players have the original version—King's Quest Classic, so to speak. To modify the words of that nameless court scribe would be a disservice to those game players, as well as a misrepresentation of apparent facts. For the sake of verisimilitude, my editors and I have decided to leave the narrative the same as it was sent to me.

However, all of the changes to KQ1 have been included in Chapter 11, "The Easy Way Out." That chapter accurately reflects both "game realities," the old and the new, and can be confidently used by all King's Quest players. No matter which version of KQ1 you have, we've got you covered.

"The Easy Way Out," the chapter containing my notes on the games, does several things for you: it describes alternative ways to pass many problems, and it gives you some tricks for dealing with the more frustrating parts of the games—physical things you can do to avoid certain death, to find your way through mazes, and to get up and down stairs, paths, cliffs, clouds, one nasty beanstalk, and a couple of even nastier mazes. If you play along with "The Easy Way Out," you will learn these alternative solutions, pick up tips for easier play, and have an actual screen-by-screen, encounter-by-encounter, problem-by-problem path from beginning to end of all the King's Quest games. Use it as you see fit.

The chapter titled "The Final Score" lists all the ways to score points in the games. Follow these techniques and you can play to win.

The rest of this book is a guide to the world of Daventry. It is a true companion to the games, with backgrounds on the main characters, fuller descriptions of the many creatures, people, and beasts that you're likely to meet, a geographic atlas, and a general all-purpose reference. At your fingertips you have the information you need to survive and win at King's Quest. Keep it by your bed, on your desk, in your bathroom, or next to your computer. Use it to help you play or to enhance your game-playing experience. Even if you have never played King's Quest, think of it as a colorful fantasy universe to be explored and enjoyed.

I hope you have a useful, fun read.

Introduction

King's Quest

How I came into the possession of these documents is a mystery for which I have no answer. Words and sentences, paragraphs and pages that cannot, and should not, exist in the last clock-ticks of the millennium glow back at me. I keep telling myself that this is the final decade of the twentieth century, that we still live in an Age of Reason, a highly technological, scientific era where anything unexplained will have a rational explanation—if not today, then anytime now. Real soon, I hope.

I can describe the physical manifestations of the process, and I can read the words that are its end product. They flicker across my computer's monitor no differently than if I had typed them there myself or had received them from one of the many electronic mail or electronic on-line services to which I subscribe. But I've checked with those services also, and they cannot confirm any messages or mail transmitted to me at the times in question. I knock on glass. Yup, they're still there; the mundane and the fantastical crawling up and down the screen like some Kafkaesque bug. Because the context is so ordinary—a finger-smudged Macintosh monitor in an unfinished garage office—the unimaginable becomes metamorphosed into something more comprehensible, something almost normal. Almost normal, but very, very strange.

A much wiser person than myself once observed that the universe is not stranger than we imagine but stranger than we *can* imagine. Astronomers and theoretical physicists re-prove this adage with disturbing regularity. As soon as we learn that the speed of light is an upper limit that nothing can reach, much less exceed, we are told of the existence of particles that cannot move slower than light. It is also explained that the universe is uncounted billions of expanding light years across and would take billions of years to cross even if we could travel at light speed. Then we learn that there might be shortcuts through all that space by way of stellar "wormholes" or some such. Shortcuts through *what?*

Introduction

Whatever wonders the mind can conceive, the universe will have stranger ones hidden away just waiting to stub someone's toe. Wonders upon wonders! Puzzlements within puzzlements! We live, it seems, in the universe of the Cosmic Giggle.

In Daventry one of the great principles of magic states: "Nothing is as it appears." Keep that in mind as I tell you the following story.

In late 1984, I was working as a writer and producer for a television station in San Francisco. One of the projects I worked on was a multipart series about "the tenth anniversary of the home computer." In the course of research I began contacting the many publishers of computer "entertainment" software. (The computer "game" market had crashed a few years earlier. The product was the same, but the euphemism was different.)

It was in this context that I talked to John Williams, the head of marketing at a small company called Sierra On-Line, located somewhere between Yosemite National Park and Fresno, California. John told me Sierra was about to publish a new game that would revolutionize computer adventures. I had heard that line before, so I politely asked John to send it to me along with some stuff I was more interested in, forgot it, finished packing my bags, and headed out with a reporter and camera crew to cover the famine in Ethiopia—the real world.

The game that was waiting for me when I arrived back from Africa was King's Quest. Not King's Quest 1, not Quest for the Crown. It was just plain vanilla King's Quest. It sure was unique.

If you weren't into computers or computer games back then, you might not recall that computer adventure games (as opposed to fantasy role-playing games such as Wizardry or The Bard's Tale) were divided into two broad types: text adventures (no pictures) and graphic adventures (words and static pictures). King's Quest was an *animated* adventure. Its hero, Sir Graham, walked, jumped, swam, climbed, fell, fought, and got chased much like a character in a Saturday morning cartoon.

Cartoons, however, are passive—you just sit there and watch (and maybe cheer, jeer, or talk back). You don't just "veg out" with King's Quest. You become Graham, you control his actions, share his adventures, ponder his problems, and suffer his fates. Set in a land filled with monsters, magic, and fantastic creatures, King's Quest takes on its own life. Right from the start, people became hooked on Graham and Daventry, and the game became a runaway hit. As for myself, I played it a bit and then put the fantasy world away to plunge again into the real world of television, news, and computers.

Years and sequels followed. King's Quest became, and still is, one of the most successful series of computer games ever published. Unlike many other games that people buy, the digital reality that is the world of Daventry took hold and kept holding on. For many, the line between fantasy and reality blurs a bit; Graham, Gwydion, Valanice, Rosella, Manannan, Lolotte, Edgar, Genesta, Mordack, and Cedric become real. Kolyma, the Land of the Clouds, Llewdor, the shipwreck island, Dracula's Castle, Tamir, the dark forest, and Mordack's island seem real places. How do you get to the Land of the Clouds, how do you get off the shipwreck island, and how do you get out of Mordack's maze?

It's all good, clean, problem-solving fun. There are puzzles, perils, and predicaments—all the ingredients for a hit game, and all the ingredients for a reality, just as John Williams had predicted at the game's inception. I smiled smug and told people how I remembered when (but I didn't mention I had heard the line before).

In late 1988 I moved on to producing and writing a television show about personal computers called "The Computer Show." While we seldom covered entertainment software, I became, more by elimination than anything else, I fear, the entertainment editor for the program. One week we aired a brief segment on Roberta Williams, the creator and author of the King's Quest

Introduction

series. Roberta had been traveling around the country visiting shopping malls and bookstores to autograph copies of her latest King's Quest adventure, and she was sometimes getting mobbed. Since this is not your everyday occurrence, we covered one of her stops, and she and I spoke about it when we met in Las Vegas a few months later.

During the conversation Roberta talked about the land of her creation in a way that vaguely hinted the stories were not all fiction, that perhaps there might be more to Daventry than just imagination. She never came out and said anything specific; I may even be amplifying nothing into something via retrospect, but her body language, choice of words, the set of her head and that certain stare said "Pay attention, stupid! I can only say so much. Read between my words and read between the lines, if you know what I mean! (Nudge, nudge! Wink, wink!)" Her statements carried the possibility of a second meaning. They all hinted at a reality, a universe, so fantastic that I barely gave it even a first thought much less a second. In fact, it all went by so fast that I didn't even think about it again until after my computer started acting funny.

I started getting electronic mail from Daventry.

Normally I turn my computer off at night. Normally I don't imagine things mysteriously showing up on my computer screen, sent to me by a fellow journalist in another universe. The first time it happened, I assumed I hadn't turned off my Mac, and that somehow a computer virus or flu or something has caused the machine to dial into a bulletin board, which, in turn, had sent back the purported delivery from Daventry. It all had to be part of an elaborate hacker's hoax; I just happened to be one of the innocent victims. I checked it out. I checked it out a couple of times—no virus. It was strange, I agree, but I chose to ignore the incident and forget about it.

After the second incident several weeks later, I decided someone was breaking into my office at night and that the prank was somewhat more personal. I changed the locks on the office and double-checked that the windows were shut and secured. After the third time I confronted my more computer-literate friends, neighbors, and occasional co-workers. Everyone denied knowledge. I have no reason to disbelieve them; few of them, I suspect, have much talent in the field of breaking and entering. I never got any messages if I unplugged the computer before locking up, but I did receive them if I only unplugged my modem. I finally decided, hoax or not, to get into the spirit of the mystery, collect what appeared, and to see just where I ended up.

So far I've ended up here, both feet firmly touching ground. The problem is that each foot seems to be in a different world.

Daventry could really exist. Several of the messages I have received talk about how their universe *withdrew* from ours through the use of magical forces, driven by the desire of the various more fantastical inhabitants to exist apart from the scoffing of an increasingly rational and scientific world. That which cannot be weighed, measured, or stuffed inside of the laws of thermodynamics used its own curious, but no less effective, laws to escape. And where they escaped to, whether another universe or another physical dimension, is a place that our own scientific theories say is entirely plausible.

One explanation put forth by a number of reputable scientists argues that there exists in reality an unknown number of different universes. These could even be thought of as different regions of the same universe, but in either case, theory allows for these "pocket universes" to have their own unique sets of the laws of science and nature. Another theory states that the universe is not made up of individual particles, like atoms or electrons, but instead is composed of strings—strange things that are long, but not high or wide, and have no other dimension. This theory only makes scientific sense, however, if our universe has more than the 4 dimensions to which we're accustomed; 26 dimensions is one number given. The reason we don't see these extra

Introduction

dimensions is that they're all folded up on themselves, but they are there, nonetheless. Could these also be pocket universes? Is this what Alexander of Daventry means when he writes of the "multiverse"? Is Daventry one of these pocket universes?

What I have really collected in this book are a number of documents of varied types—histories, press clippings, maps, a magazine article, and the like—all selected from scores of messages I have received from the one who signs himself "Derek Karlavaegen." If you believe their content—and I would like to—then you will come to see the truth of the incredible reality that Roberta Williams may have hinted about that January afternoon in Nevada. What we see, buy, and play under the disguise of games are actual histories, translated into the medium of the computer game. If played successfully to the end, you get an almost exact transcription of what, supposedly, actually happened to the people involved.

Reality or fantasy? Roberta Williams says she gets her ideas from myths, fairy tales, and her own imagination. She'll give you a funny look if you suggest Daventry has a physical reality.

Fact or fiction? Get a copy of King's Quest 3: To Heir Is Human. Look at the bookshelves in Manannan's study. Notice what appears to be a computer screen sitting on one of the shelves. Derek Karlavaegen says he found a metal head there that he now uses to communicate with us—one he has been using for some time that he calls the "Eye Between the Worlds." Has Roberta Williams been getting the same messages as I have, silently appearing on her computer screen from where our universes touch? Or is she a great dreamer, one who travels between the worlds in sleep? Derek thinks the wall between our worlds is so thin that we sometimes can dream each other.

Truth or hoax? I cannot rule out the latter. Many people in this world believe that the more elaborate the ruse, the more satisfying the joke. It may very well be that I am being played for a fool. That's why this book is being published as a companion to some computer fantasy adventure games; a book of clues and solutions; an aid and reference work for people who like to spend their time trying to figure out how to escape from inside a whale or off a desert island, steal from a fire-breathing dragon, talk to mermaids, save their father's life, rescue their family, defeat wicked witches and evil wizards, win a kingdom, or win the hand of a kidnapped princess.

Harmless fantasies and adventures they all are. Fantasies that live only in the flickering light of the computer screen and breathe only in the imaginations of their players.

Seen in that light, it's all really rather clean and simple.

On the other hand...

This is the second edition of The King's Quest Companion. The first edition appeared in November of 1989. In it I mention that Derek Karlavaegen had moved into Manannan's house a few months after Alexander had turned the sorcerer into a cat. In his messages to our world, Derek claimed that he could find no sign of Manannan, or of any cat, in the place. Derek felt that Alexander's former master had fled in his feline form and "...may well be hiding someplace plotting new revenge." That's a quote. Those words of Derek's were published more than a year before Roberta Williams began writing King's Quest 5. The plot of that game centers on Manannan and his brother Mordack's revenge.

Seen in that light, things aren't so very clean and simple after all.

And I can't help remembering what they say in Daventry: "Nothing is as it appears."

1

The Eye Between The Worlds

Compiled from Messages to this World from the World of Daventry, as Sent by Derek Karlevaegen

2
Kings's Quest

*G*reetings and salutations from the world you probably never suspected existed! It is a place where sudden violence and death are never far distant, where the magical, mystical, and fantastic are commonplace, and where the greatest rewards come from bravery and cunning, not from killing. It is a realm where human and not-so-humanfolk spend their lives free from the constraints of disbelief. It is a place where anything is possible and everything could be true. We have no name for our world, our universe, but you may call it Daventry if you like. We think of it as home.

My name is Derek Karlavaegen. I am a writer here, scribing stories about the current events of the day, which are then published for the information and amusement of whoever cares to read them. I study the magical arts daily and, while I am not so practiced as to pass myself off as a professional sorcerer, I have achieved enough proficiency to have attempted to contact your world. I suspect an explanation is in order.

We here in Daventry are your own descendents—the sons of your sons and the daughters of your daughters from generations and centuries back. And that's just the humanfolk. We are also your dreams and nightmares, your myths, legends, and stories. We are the reality that much of humanity has rejected over time—the unicorns, centaurs, and demigods. We are the other races of beings who evolved alongside humanity—the dwarfs, elves, gnomes, giants, and fairies. We are the users of the magic that you say does not and cannot exist. We are the truth behind what you dismiss as mere legend, and we are the flesh that became your fairy tales.

Once you could see the other creatures that shared your world; once you too could create ointments of invisibility; once you too could talk with the animals, and they would talk back; and once, you too could mount a winged horse and fight the dragons of the earth. Now you say that if you cannot see, feel, touch, hold, measure, dissect, count, smell, taste, deduce, or duplicate something, it cannot be real. If you cannot find its bones, it never existed. You see yourselves as the center of the universe, the focus of all creation, and you see that it is good. In doing so, you miss much.

3
The Eye Between the Worlds

When the universe was younger and humanity less proud, giants did roam the earth and magic kept the forces of chaos and darkness at bay. All of the races of the earth struggled for their survival, sometimes together, sometimes against each other. In time it was the humanfolk who proved strongest, both by the force of their magics and the number of their people. Uneasy peace existed for millennia as the humans moved from their caves and their forests to build their first cities. The places they deserted—the wild and free places—were left to the others.

As the centuries passed, more and more of humanity condensed into its cities and towns, and the passing years saw less and less of the dwarfs, and elves, and other beings. Humanity was fruitful and spread its masses over more and more of the earth, squeezing the dragons, and unicorns, and other creatures into smaller and smaller places, remote from humans. As humanfolk saw less and less of these beings and creatures, they began to say that they did not exist, and that the stories told of them and their deeds and adventures were myth, legend, folklore, and fairy story. As humanfolk built more and more across the world, they began to place more and more faith in their numbers and philosophies and technologies than they did in magic and nature. The world went out of balance.

Magic, like mathematics, needs faith and belief to operate properly. Walled away in cities and towns, isolated from the natural world by roofs and ledgers, magic was scoffed at and dismissed as fantasy and deception. In time, humanity came to not only reject the magical, strange, unique, and different, but to fear and condemn them. True, in some areas belief did not go entirely away. True, many of the other folk and creatures of the world survived hidden in their secret places. And true, some did continue to practice the magical craft. But the weight of disbelief was upon them, and like ripe grain at harvest time, they could see the thrashers coming.

To survive we *withdrew*.

4
Kings's Quest

As the centuries passed, it became apparent to our ancestors that much of reality—the irrational and magical—was doomed to extinction. They had knowledge of the passing of the lizardfolk, who had owned the earth and roamed the stars before the evolution of the mammals that would become humanity. Our ancestors did not choose to follow those creatures into oblivion.

A great conclave was called—a meeting between representatives of all the colors of magic and all the kinds of little folk. Fairies, and elves, and demigods were there, as were the special folk who watched over the more magical creatures. They decided that their only chance for survival was to find a new home far away from the swaggering, doubting humanfolk—not just out of their sight, but outside of their constrained reality. All differences were to be put aside, and all efforts were to be made to create, through the use of magic, invocation, and elemental powers, an entirely new universe far away from that of humans.

In time the spells were forged as we learned how to create our own reality, our own new world. It was a one-way path; once gone, it would be impossible to return, for the natural laws would not allow it. Always forward, never back, is one of the elements in the spell casting. For that reason, not all chose to *withdraw*. Many also wished to remain for other reasons, and no one was forced to go. Most went then—the good and the evil, safe and dangerous, big and small, magical, fabulous, and ordinary. A complete world was populated in an instant with beasts and monsters and all the different kind of folk. In some cases, even the homes and possessions of the more powerful were transported. As a result of that first great migration, cataclysms tore at the earth. Earthquakes rocked and volcanoes spat their lava into the sky, such were the forces needed to *withdraw* so many.

Where those first folk went, and where I live now, is as real and solid as your world, the one we call the Other World. It exists as just one universe amid infinite others in the greater reality of (for want of a better name) the multiverse. Daventry exists just over your shoulder, if you could only turn around fast enough to see it. I sit writing this to you just around the corner

5
The Eye Between the Worlds

of an eyeblink. We are so close that you sometimes dream of us, as we do of you. And that is why I send you these messages.

Many other times over the centuries have folk *withdrawn* from your universe, forced to escape as the rational world fenced them tighter and forgave their differences less. Great eruptions and earthquakes are the signs of their passing. It is your great loss and our great gain for, over the millennia, each new *withdrawal* gives us fresh life and new wonders. Always we reinvent ourselves, because, in our world of magic, everything is possible. As you have rejected it, all magic eventually comes here.

Which finally brings me to the rest of the explanation I promised. As I have said, I am an investigator and writer of contemporary events, who hobbies in magic and travels much. Some time ago, after having talked to and written at length about Prince Alexander of Daventry's escape from lifelong captivity, and his subsequent rescue of his sister and kingdom from the terror of a fire-breathing dragon (that was a lot, wasn't it?), I decided to visit the scenes of the prince's adventures in order to better understand what the brave youth had been through. It was for this reason that I, at length, arrived at the house of the wizard Manannan, whom Alexander had turned into a cat. No cat though was to be found anyplace there. The house was in good repair, but no person or animal was anywhere near. I resolved then to spend some days there, using it as a base for my explorations around Llewdor. At night I took advantage of Manannan's large library, looking closely through his books on magic and magical lore. The days stretched into weeks, and still no one came to claim the large house with its well-stocked underground laboratory.

It was during this time that I discovered the Eye Between the Worlds.

There is a lever set into one of the library's bookcases that opens the trap door into the secret lab. On a shelf nearby I discovered a most curious object. It looks much like a metal head, but with only one very large glass eye and an open jaw containing near one hundred teeth. Each of those teeth has a letter, number, or symbol inscribed upon it. This thing must have been made by Manannan or some other very great sorcerer, for when I pressed a certain tooth, light appeared to fill the eye. Moreover, when I touched on other teeth, words would magically appear on the eye's glass surface. Wonderous indeed was this thing that I soon came to see as a talking head, and think of as the Eye Between the Worlds.

Yes it did talk, and it still does; not with sounds, but with words that crawl across it and with pictures that draw themselves before my very eyes. After much experimentation, I found that I could make my thoughts and words appear on the eye's surface. The thing is a machine, to be sure, although how it works I do not know, for it has no parts which move.

I have said before that our universes—our worlds—are so far apart that we can never touch, and so close that we sometimes can even dream of each other. We know a little about your world because folk still *withdraw* from there to here, although not so very often anymore. They bring us stories and histories and descriptions, which we record for all who might be interested to read. Not many do; the Other World holds few charms for us. You, on the other hand, know nothing of us except what your dreamers dream, and *that* you reject and dismiss as fantasy. The fact remains, however, that the walls between the worlds are thin enough to let folk pass through in one direction, and thoughts and dreams to sometimes pass in both. The Eye in Manannan's study is a hole in those walls through which dreams journey.

I am a curious soul; I have read the records concerning your world and know as much about it as any here in Daventry. Because of this, I soon came to realize that much of what appeared in the eye of that mechanical head came from the Other World. Somehow in this strangest of multiverses, our worlds touch together in a place shared by the head in this study and certain of your machines.

My story might have ended there, except for that curiosity of mine. One night, tapping upon the teeth with no particular purpose in mind, I was astounded to find mention of Daventry and King Graham's adventures.

7
The Eye Between the Worlds

Apparently they exist in your world as a sort of fantasy adventure—a made-up story intended as an entertainment for people.

Again, our worlds are so very close that we can sometimes dream each other, and even turn those dreams into stories. This must be true, for I have seen the evidence with my own eyes, transmitted back from the Other World. Who the dreamer is that could learn enough to concoct these stories is unknown to me, although the person must be a very great dreamer.

I have experimented for much time now with the Eye Between the Worlds, and I am convinced that I can send messages directly to you through it. Perhaps that is why the Wizard contrived it—to talk to your world, or perhaps to recruit allies whom he could help *withdraw* here so that he and his evil family might rule cruelly over our entire universe. On the other hand, Manannan might just have been as curious as I am.

I do not know if what I write here will ever arrive in the Other World, but I think I have figured out what to do to send the words on their way. I have nothing to lose, of course, and for you who discover this, perhaps I will have provided some wonder, knowledge, and enjoyment. To that end I will continue my solitary experiments and copy for you some of the histories and narratives of my time. Since there are those in your world who are somewhat familiar with King Graham, I shall send you, on this night and others, some of the chronicles of his court—stories of the adventures of the King and his family. You might compare them to the stories that have been written. Perhaps I will write of other things as the mood strikes me, or perhaps I will just copy some interesting words of others.

I will do all of this over some time, and more than once. Your world could learn much from us of the wonder, mystery, and magic of the multiverse. Maybe you could learn again that anything is possible and everything could be true.

Perhaps you will learn to believe your dreams.

2

Quest for the Crown

From the Chronicles of Daventry, Part 1

10
Kings's Quest

11
Quest for the Crown

*W*e live in a time of change and contradiction. The kingdom is in uproar, yet it is whole and united as never before. A land of poverty, famine, and despair is rich with hope and gold. We laugh and shout and rejoice in our grief. We weep, wail, and with sorrow beat our chests in our euphoria and jubilation. Tears of every type score every face. The kingdom has been saved and the three great treasures of the realm returned. The fat and happy and quiet days are back upon us. But there was a price. Ah, the price. There always is a price. Great indeed it was, mortally great.

The King is dead! The King is dead! Long live the King! Long live King Graham of Daventry! Long live King Graham!

It is for others, at other times and places, to decide the reputation of the man we called, during his own time, King Edward the Benevolent. Elsewhere we have recounted the stories of how he relinquished Merlin's Mirror, the Shield of Achille, and the Chest of Gold. He lost all through love and treachery. He was the kindest and bravest and most innocent of men. Though he built schools and universities, he was not the most brilliant of monarchs, and in the end it was his very humanity that doomed him, and almost doomed Daventry.

Today we look to the future with the young and brave King Graham. He is a man of wit, wisdom, and learning; one of undoubted courage and fortitude. I pray that our future is as bright as our prospects.

During this, the inaugural week of his reign, we have been directed by the King to set down on paper the events that brought him to the golden throne. It is a tale of daring and mystery that begins when Graham enters the very castle from which he now rules....

Graham opened the castle doors and began following the familiar red-carpeted halls toward King Edward's throne room. He tried to keep the armies of depression from invading his mind, much as he had been trying to keep Daventry free from the invaders that had been shrinking its borders since the loss of the magic shield. Both tasks were nearly impossible. The famine had reduced the population again and again, and few remained in Daventry. Even if an army could be raised, no gold existed to pay it. The moat with its flesh-eating beasts and the thick metal-clad door were all that guarded Castle Daventry. The weakening spells of long-departed sorcerers, backed by the sword-arms of fewer than 100 worn-out and battered knights, were the kingdom's final defenses. "Whatever the old king wants," Graham thought as he bowed respectfully in front of his aged and weary monarch, "it will probably be the last thing I ever do for him. It's unlikely either of us, much less the kingdom, can go on much longer."

Edward struggled to give a pleased smile at Graham's bow. "Always the proper and respectful one, aren't you?"

"Here it comes," thought the young knight. He listened as the king's still energetic voice echoed quietly through the throne room. Like Graham's hopes, the room was empty save for some tapestries—sad reminders of brighter days.

"I'm old, Graham. My end is near. Find the three treasures. I've searched for years without success. You are quick of wit, strong, clever, and are learned in all the subjects taught at the royal university. Use that knowledge. Use your mental faculties as well as your knightly skills. You alone among my subjects can do it. There is no time; you are Daventry's last hope. Go."

"Yes, sire!"

"This much I promise you, Sir Graham. If you succeed, the kingdom will be saved. In reward, you will inherit my throne and become King of Daventry in my place!"

"Thank you, sire!"

"Now get out of here, Graham. As you leave, I shall lock this castle's doors; it shall be my last stand against this kingdom's enemies. Locked they shall

Quest for the Crown

remain against all, including you, Sir Graham. They will only open again when you bring me the three treasures. Our wishes go with you. We can give you no more! I have spoken!"

Graham knew an exit line when he heard one. As the castle doors boomed shut behind him, all he could do was remark to himself, "Some days you eat yogurt, other days you step in it!" He checked his boots, straightened his hat, made sure not to step into the deadly moat, and crossed the bridge into perplexity.

Just west of the castle, Graham paused to consider his problem. He leaned against a large rock in the first clearing he came upon, a peaceful spot dotted with wildflowers and shaded by many trees. He was not a large man. His body's length was just at six feet, and his muscles were long and low. When forced to arms, Graham beat you with speed and skill, not muscle. He kept his dark brown (almost black, really) hair cut long to cover his ears. He had begun doing this during his first years in the palace school, on the theory that if the teacher couldn't see his ears, the teacher couldn't pull them. The theory didn't work, but the hair length stayed. Sir David of Bruce, a former classmate of his, once described Graham's features (with clever but undue harshness) as being "forgettable the moment you saw him." The truth is, Graham is pleasant and strong looking, in a vague sort of way.

It was his quickness that set the future king apart from the rest of humanity. Nimble and fast of both hand and foot, he was, and still is, even nimbler and faster between the ears. Graduating first in his class from the royal university, Graham had specialized in knowing a lot about a lot of things. No one subject could capture him, and he had devoured all the lore and learning he could listen to and read. As he leaned against that rock, he scratched his belly and began to think.

The only leads to the missing treasures the young knight had to go on were slim. One: the dwarf who had taken the magic Shield of Achille had been seen disappearing into a hole in the ground. Two: the shape-changing witch who had stolen the Chest of Gold escaped on her broomstick into the clouds that clung to the peaks above Daventry, solid-seeming masses that looked like snow cornices, impossible outcroppings poised out from the mountains with no support. Three: the nameless sorcerer who had absconded with Merlin's Mirror had said it would be kept in a safe place, guarded by some fearsome beast. There were no easy answers in this list, but that was all anyone knew about the mystery.

To these facts, as lightweight as fiction, Graham added some home-brewed observations. "My daddy used to tell me, 'Boy, if I have learned anything in my life, I have learned this: when in doubt, or in trouble, pick up anything that is not nailed down, and, if it is, check for loose nails or boards. Check carefully into, under, above, below, and behind things. Read everything; you might learn something. Wear clean undergarments, brush after meals, and always remember, nothing is as it appears.'"

With all this in mind, Graham took inventory of what he had. He discovered nothing. That meant he had to get some food, some gold or the like with which to buy things, and a weapon. He leaned forward harder and harder, as he set his plans and sorted out his situation. The rock rolled. Graham stumbled but a little and, as he recovered his balance, noticed that the rolling stone had revealed a hole. "Well, it's time to heed some of Daddy's advice," he said to the trees, and looking into the hole, he saw what appeared to be a dagger. So it was, and while taking it he breathed, "Thank you, Father," a note of respect in his voice.

"I sure hope this is an omen."

Food and treasure were next for Graham to obtain. Treasure, he realized, would not be particularly easy to come by, but food could be taken care of quickly in a vegetable garden that had been planted behind the castle. Graham headed north so as to arrive at the garden from behind the castle. Passing beside a large, lush oak tree, flushed with the confidence of one easy success, he decided to test his father's rule another time.

There was nothing hidden in the hole at the tree's base, so Graham started climbing up, the songs of birds surrounding him, until he reached a fork in the oak's branches. Within that fork a nest had been built; in it a lone egg lay surrounded by the dry twigs and grass. Graham looked closer at the egg and almost fell out of the branches so startled was he to find that the egg seemed made of gold.

"I guess it always pays to heed your father's advice," Graham told himself as he climbed down from the tree. He had taken the egg—a treasure to match a weapon.

He was still marveling as he turned east into the castle garden. Mostly carrots grew here in neat, tended rows; but none was large enough for picking. Only on the garden's western edge did he find anything worth taking. "I'll harvest just one carrot," he decided, shaking his head in disappointment. "I'm sure I can get more food along the way."

Leaving the walls of the castle behind, wondering if he would ever see them again, Graham wandered north, intending to skirt the small lake where he had played often as a child. Some call it the Lake of Maylie still, after King Edward's lost wife. It had been named that when Edward and Maylie married. They were often seen sitting in a small boat upon the lake late on summer afternoons. Shadow players against a setting sun, they were alone in their love for each other. The lake's name has lost favor since Maylie's death, and few ever float upon it or splash in its water, out of memory of happier days.

Graham's mind was floating in the past when his reverie was broken by the sudden appearance of an elf playing in the sunbeams.

In the interests of future understanding, it should be clearly noted here that many in Daventry don't hold much love for the little people—the short elves, dwarves, gnomes, and leprechauns. This was not always so, of course, for the little folk also *withdrew,* or were forced to *withdraw,* from the Other World. They too are partly responsible for the very fabric of our world. It was, however, one of the little people who duped the king into parting with the Shield of Achille. A dwarf, it was claimed, but that word never came from Edward's lips. He said it was a small figure bearing a root known only to dwarves. With the subsequent death of the queen, the populace pointed the fingers of hate, fear, and anger at all of the small ones.

Graham saw only someone who might offer him assistance in his quest. Feeling the dagger secure against his hip, he approached the gamboling elf and began to talk. "Hail, friend," he exclaimed. "I quest to save Daventry and hope you might be able to help me."

The elf stopped, stunned—surprised by Graham's sudden appearance. He listened as the knight explained his search for the treasures, tugged on his ear frantically as if to hurry up his thoughts, and replied in a voice of pure melody.

"Sir Graham, I know but little of the treasures, and I cannot much help you there. But there are some things I do know that might help you in your travels. Know then that there is much evil and danger now both on the ground and in the air. Ogres and trolls, wolves and dwarves, wizards and witches—all are about in the forest to the west. Take much care. Flee at first notice, or you are doomed. Giants and dragons patrol both above and below the earth. Weep for Daventry, the end is near! Know also that you, Sir Graham, are the first humanfolk to speak with me in years, and you have spoken without hate or anger. In return for that, I will give you something."

Holding out a tiny hand, the elf showed Graham a golden ring with an inset tiger's eye stone. "This ring is magic. Wear it and you will become invisible in a time of danger. There is a catch; it works but once and for only a short time. Use it wisely, just as you have acted wisely in speaking with me! Only through wisdom and courage might you succeed in your quest."

17
Quest for the Crown

In a blink, the elf was gone. Graham was so busy examining the ring that he noticed not if the elf disappeared or ran. He never had chance to thank him for either the ring or the advice.

Caution was a virtue Graham had cultivated since his father had first explained to him about things not always being as they appeared. He was neither a rushing fool nor a timid one. He believed that his head, for instance, better served his king and himself while firmly attached to his neck. He would give it in battle, if he must, but he refused to offer it around like the dark, warm top to a fresh loaf of bread. The elf's words made the kind of survival sense that Graham appreciated. With more care in his step, he continued his journey northward.

Maybe it was his lucky day, although no four-leafed clovers had crossed his path and the shadows were beginning to assert an argument for dusk. There, filling his path, was an empty bowl, appearing as unlikely to the eyes as his chances for success in his mission appeared unlikely to his judgment. Curiously he picked it up and examined it. A word was inscribed inside the red and yellow ceramic container: "FILL." The bowl appeared to be large enough to hold a dozen or so apples or enough stew to feed a family. It wasn't nailed down, so he took it. It would be a perfect wash basin in the morning, provided he could find a safe place to spend the night.

Graham didn't have to wander much farther north before he found a camping spot. Just beyond the clearing where he found the bowl was the River Fools. It screamed around a bend as it tore through the earth, much like it would tear apart anyone who attempted to wade or swim in it. It is said that only a fool would enter the river's waters, which is true; but it actually got its name from a time long past when a group of thrill-seekers tried to ride its waters. They inflated a number of pig bladders and connected them inside a piece of canvas. They called the thing a raft, though no one had ever seen such a raft before. They said it could not sink, that the breath that inflated the bladders would protect against the shocks of the ragged rocks, and that the river spirits welcomed them. They were dead wrong. If the spirits did welcome them, perhaps it was as a sacrifice that day or as a warning against trespass. Neither bodies, bones, nor bladders were seen again. Since then, all know it as the River Fools. To this day, all that stop by the river carry away pebbles to appease the river spirits, as if with each stone taken the river would have more room to grow.

Graham picked his pebbles from the small beach and then chose a dry, high place above the river. Laying his head on his pack, he was asleep in moments.

Dawn broke a ruddy orange color. It awoke Graham to the fact that all he had to eat was one carrot, and a carrot was not his idea of breakfast. He decided to save it for an emergency, and, putting his appetite away with the carrot, continued his journey northward. He was quite aware that he had made no apparent progress since leaving King Edward and that his prospects did not match the bright dawn.

He followed River Fools but a little way before he realized that further progress in that direction was barred by the very river he had appeased the previous night. Worse, a very large mushroom grew just on the other side. Almost close enough to smell, it was forever out of reach. He avoided the obvious comparison to his quest.

With the river to both the north and east of him, Graham was faced with returning the way he had come or venturing west. West was the direction the elf had warned him against. Rubbing the magic ring for good luck, and taking a deep breath for courage, Graham headed west into the unknown.

Distracted at the time, Graham had neglected to ask the elf just how the magic ring worked. He knew now. As he watched himself rub the ring, he watched his hands disappear. He also knew that this would be the only time

Quest for the Crown

the ring would work, the only time he could disappear from sight. In despair he realized that he had wasted his magic gift thoughtlessly.

Actually, the irony of the events that immediately followed was totally lost on Graham at the time. This is understandable. No sooner had his mistake struck him than something else almost did. Suddenly faced with an ogre—several hundred pounds of human-eating appetite, all claws and fangs, charging and slavering directly at you—you don't usually stop and chuckle, wryly noting that the ogre can't see an invisible person. Usually you run. Usually you lose. Ogres are over seven feet tall and run faster than people. You run anyway, if only to get away from the stench.

Graham turned and dashed south. Risking a quick look behind and still forgetting he was invisible, Graham almost collided with something short, massive, and ugly. It also seemed to have an ugly temper.

"Two hours gone in the day and I haven't found anybody to rob! Two hours and no treasure! The wife will kill me! Or worse!"

The sudden look was enough to tell the knight that he had now almost crashed into a desperado, a dwarf by its looks, and one out hunting for trouble. Continued flight seemed to be in order. Maybe the pursuing ogre would see the dwarf and forget about Graham. It sounded good in theory.

Only marginally curious as to why he hadn't been immediately jumped by the surly bandit, Graham burst back into a run, dodging boulders and heading south as fast as he could. His hope for escape lay in getting a quick, big lead and surviving on endurance. After a short sprint, dwarves usually just give up, their stubby legs moving them fast but not far. When that happened, maybe the ogre and dwarf would take their ill humors out on each other.

The dwarf, though, astounded Graham by not giving chase at all. Perhaps theory was working for a change.

Enlightenment finally came to Sir Graham as he leaned against a walnut tree, safe, he hoped, from further pursuit. Still gasping, trying to bring cooling air to his flaming lungs, he felt something bounce off his head. His eyes followed the walnut as it fell to the ground, joining dozens of other nuts scattered around the base of the tree. His first thought, now that the near panic had passed, was food—here was food! He'd been up for hours without breakfast, and he was surrounded by nuts. He realized he was ravenous. Eager to fill his stomach, Graham reached up to pluck a walnut.

This, of course, is when understanding number two hit the monarch-to-be. He could not see his hand. He could feel the walnut, he could lift it and see it float above the ground, but he couldn't see his hand! It was invisible!

Graham's laughter filled the little grove for minutes as he realized that he had been running like a madman from creatures that didn't know he was there. He might have been able to walk up to both and spit in their eyes with impunity; well, maybe not spit in their eyes, but perhaps check them for lice. Laughter roared again as he remembered cussing himself as a fool for wasting the power of the magic ring. "With a few more mistakes like that," he murmured, "I just might be able to save Daventry!"

In a moment, Graham quieted, and for a moment the future looked almost golden. Maybe today was his lucky day. Maybe.

Moments later that future shone still brighter, for upon opening the walnut clutched within his transparent hand, Graham discovered that instead of nut meat, the shell was filled with what looked like the purest gold. One bite confirmed it.

"I think I'll look for other nuts to breakfast on," thought Graham. And for the third time that morning, there was laughter.

"You were right, Daddy. Nothing is as it appears!"

Actually, Sir Graham tarried beneath that walnut tree for little longer than it takes to tell the tale. His breath returned quickly, as did his determination and his mirth, which went from hilarity to good humor. The sun was much higher in the sky than when he had rubbed the ring, and he remembered that

Quest for the Crown

the elf had warned the ring's spell did not last long. How long he knew not, but he did not want to be facing other dangers when he became visible again.

South continued to beckon Graham. This was the way he had fled, so it seemed his lucky path. That path soon skirted the edge of some mountains, the same cloud-crowned monsters that had climaxed the witch Dahlia's broom-borne escape with the Chest of Gold. This was a part of Daventry unfamiliar to the knight. He thought it a likely place to pick up clues to at least one of the stolen treasures, for some assumed that Dahlia had secreted the Chest somewhere within its cloudy shadows.

A huge door, girded with iron bands, seemed to be waiting for Graham as he explored. It was set into a wall of cyclopean stonework that itself had been inset into the living rock. The whole construction looked as if meant to repel armies—large armies. On the other hand, it could be the door to someone's home or fortress. If the size of the keyhole were any indication, the person hiding behind the massive door would be a very large person indeed.

The keyhole, while not so large as to provide entrance to even the smallest of little people, was ample enough to allow Graham to peek within. The scant light revealed what appeared to be a set of proportionately huge stairs that appeared to wind up into darkness. Without surprise, Graham confirmed that the door was locked as tight as it seemed, and no matter what he tried, he was unable to force it open.

Graham thought back on the words of the friendly elf who had cautioned him to be wary of giants and dragons—creatures who now roamed both above and below the earth. He suspected the stairs beyond led to one of the two, and that creature might someday be a stop along his quest. Stymied for the moment, the knight vowed to return and journey up the mountain.

Graham also noticed an inviting mountain lake, like emerald sparkles on the horizon, luring him from the west. He hadn't bathed in days. A short swim was one temptation to which he could succumb; it would both clean and refresh him, he rationalized. Anyway, as he was still in strange surroundings, one direction seemed about as promising as another. Fortune, however, continued south while Graham walked west because, as soon as he had entered the chill, fresh water, the magic ring slipped off of Graham's finger. He was visible once again and suddenly felt very alone, very mortal, and very exposed. The chill he felt was coming from more than just the lake's alpine waters.

"I think I'd better get moving," thought the vulnerable and now young-feeling knight. "North, south, or west? The lake's narrow and I'm already wet. Go west, young man!"

And thus it was that Sir Graham swam right out of the ice bath and into the fire.

Fortune is a mercurial lover—fickle and fast to flit away. Fortune never says good-bye; you find out it's deserted you just when you need it most. That's usually when you begin meeting the bad things. Bad things, it has been noted, often come in threes. This particular day, three big bad ones were just waiting for a lone wanderer.

Graham walked a few paces, shaking off as much water as he could along the way. The sun was sure to dry him out, and he was sure his edgy feelings would evaporate along with the remaining moisture. As he reached up to wipe some final cold trickles from his brow, he caught sight of something so chilling that he dashed back into the frigid lake. At that moment, Graham felt he had moved faster than ever in his life.

Bad thing number one was jetting across the sky, black robes trailing what could only be a broomstick. It was undeniably an evil witch. Graham had read histories that told of witches swooping from the sky so fast that it was almost impossible for anyone to escape. The few that had muttered of how they were imprisoned and kept caged, much like a dangerous pet. They talked of how some witches played with their new pets, and they groaned out details of unspeakable torments to both mind and body. Only a few of those that got away escaped with their sanity.

Graham was sure that the witch in question this day could only be Dahlia, for that wicked one was the only cone-crowned cackler reported in the realm for decades. As he carefully crept out of the lake and crouched under a pine tree, he was sure he had not been spotted. He also was sure that if he were captured, for him, at least, the game would be over. Death would be preferable, and he knew he wasn't that lucky today.

Bad thing number two came along just as Graham convinced himself that he had again escaped the terminal jaws of catastrophe. Turning south from the lake to avoid the witch, he had barely taken his first step into a clearing when he saw the hate-red eyes and drooling jaws of what could only be described as a very big, very bad wolf. How Graham pivoted before he finished his step, and how he was able to dash back into the lake before the jaws closed on him, he has never been able to reconstruct. But he won that dash, too, and the wolf, deigning not to follow him into the water, soon disappeared.

That cold, nameless, mountain lake was quickly taking on the warm feelings of home, a safe spot to retreat to when all seemed hopeless.

"It would sure be nice to have that ring back," Graham murmured wistfully as he crawled back under what, by now, had become his favorite tree.

"I could go back the way I came this morning, but there's an ogre and a crazy dwarf that way. I could stay here, but that wouldn't get me anywhere. Things have just got to be better to the north."

Bad thing number three was north, and it appeared just as suddenly as the prior two misadventures. It came in the form of a wandering sorcerer who was out looking to give somebody a bad day. Perhaps Graham was tired from the exertions of the past hour; perhaps so much had happened to him so quickly that his mind was unable to react in time. No matter. This time Graham could not flee quickly enough. In fact, after the wizard had made his mystic signs and shouted his incantations, the hapless knight was unable to move at all. He was paralyzed.

Looking at the result of his work with a knowing smirk, the sorcerer sneered, "Hope no hungry beasts or worse come this way, young fool!" He waved and laughed at Graham as he disappeared from sight.

Graham was still dazed when the spell finally wore off. Both his mind and his body were numb from standing immobile for so long, but the fact that he was still in one piece gave him hope that some sanity had come back into his life. He had stared into the west while he was spellbound, and during that time he had noticed the outline of a small house in that direction. Perhaps there he could rest and recover for a while.

The smell that surrounded Graham as he approached the ornate cottage was very familiar. He had quietly come up the path that led to the front door and sneaked around to peek into one of the windows. The glass was so cloudy that he couldn't see through it at all, and his fingers stuck to it slightly where he had touched. The slightest lick of his finger brought a taste much like sugar to his tongue. Since he couldn't see inside, he decided to try the direct approach. As he reached to knock on the door, it became clear to him that he really *had* tasted sugar on his hand and the aroma in the air was gingerbread.

The hunger hit him at once. Graham has always had a sweet tooth. As a child, he was the first to snitch particles of pie, pastry, and confection from sills and counters where they were left to cool after leaving the ovens. Knights and ladies all knew to have an extra dessert ready when he came to sup.

Graham started to eat the gingerbread abode; not a lot, but merely a small piece of the front door trim and a bit of a chocolate drop nail. He was sure the owner would neither notice nor mind.

He was wrong again, but eating part of the house saved Graham's life.

As he licked the sweet, aromatic crumbs from his hand, he heard a cackle from within.

25
Quest for the Crown

"Nibble, nibble, little mouse. Who's that eating at my house? I'll eat them, if I catch 'em!" Sir Graham had again blundered upon the evil witch.

For what seemed like the thousandth time that day, Graham sprinted for safety. Convinced that the crone would come out the door he had been consuming, the knight sprinted out the front gate and around the side, barreling north past the confectionary cottage. He kept going until he came to a long lake surrounded by moss-bedecked willows. He was sure the trees would shelter him from any aerial observation.

Sometimes the only way to keep moving is to stop. Take a few moments to watch the sun play with water and the breeze caress the trees. Sort through what has been happening too quickly to be assessed at the time. Breathe deep, slow your heart, and let your brain waft over what you have experienced, caressing facts and impressions like that breeze moving through the leaves. Take some quiet time.

Graham's unharried musings brought him to one firm conclusion: he must get into the witch's house. He was sure he had discovered Dahlia's home (if that truly was her name) and thought the Chest of Gold might be inside. If not, he was convinced a clue would be found, or some knowledge would be discovered that would aid him in his quest. He also knew that he had to wait until the witch was away, for he was no match for her magical powers.

"Tomorrow then," he thought to himself. "I'll scout around a little more today and spend the night here. Tomorrow I'll take on the wicked witch while she's away."

Continuing to move north, away from the gingerbread house, seemed the safest choice, although Graham's bones and bruises reminded him of the results of his earlier "safe" choices. North it was, however, and after an easy hike through woods untainted by any hint of danger, he found himself in front of a log cabin.

Red and yellow flowers grew happily near the open door. A woodsman's ax stuck out of a short chopping log, mimicking the handle on the house's water pump. It was such an ordinary scene that Graham was tempted to go inside immediately. "On second thought, check the place out, you dummy!" he chided himself. He had been both safe and sorry already that day, and he much preferred being safe.

A window on the side of the house seemed a likely avenue for snooping. Looking inside, Graham saw two sorry-looking, hungry people. They appeared to be a woodcutter and his wife, and they were so emaciated that it looked as though they couldn't do much damage to anyone.

He remembered his father's advice about things not being what they seem, patted his dagger, walked around to the front, and entered the cabin.

The years of famine and poverty that had attacked Daventry were quite apparent throughout the one-room hovel. The furniture was sparse and shabby, rotting where it barely stood. Holes in the floor made it a dangerous place to walk, and Graham reminded himself to watch his step. The only glimmer of beauty was a fiddle tucked into a corner.

As a knight of the realm, Graham was a man of privilege. Though not unaffected by the calamities of the hard years, he could still eat daily and sleep secure in his bed. The sight in front of him threatened to bring tears.

"Welcome to our humble home," the woodcutter greeted Graham.

"We'd like to offer you something to eat, but we have no food," volunteered his wife.

For Graham, the emotion of the scene demanded he do something. Again, his father's advice echoed in his thoughts.

"It's worth a try," he said as he took the ceramic bowl out of his pack. Despite the pounding of the day, there were only minor nicks in its finish, and the container remained in one piece. Looking at the word inscribed in the bottom, Graham breathed the word "Fill." At once, the air shimmered, and the bowl grew suddenly hot. Steam and savory smells filled the cabin,

Quest for the Crown

and the bowl magically filled with stew. Graham presented it to the starving couple.

Tears and wonder filled all eyes. "Please, eat," said the man who would be King. "This is yours. I hope it is enough."

"We can never thank you enough," cried the woodcutter's wife.

"Please, take my fiddle. It is our last possession, but it is now yours. Please take it in payment for your kindness!"

Graham knew he would insult the two if he didn't do as they asked. Gingerly he stepped around the floor's holes and retrieved the precious instrument. The finish was still good, and the polished cherry wood grew warm and friendly in his hands. Playing a few experimental notes, Graham discovered the fiddle was still in tune. With a merry "One, two, three, four!" he played the couple a happy song.

The melody still filled the cabin as he left. The sad pair had little information to help him on his quest, but they did mention a mysterious rock with a small hole in it. The rock was just south of the rear of their cabin and not far from where Graham planned to spend the night. It wasn't much and probably didn't mean anything, they said, but it was the only odd or mysterious thing they knew about in their vicinity.

Since it was not out of his way, Graham decided to pay the strange boulder a visit on his way back to the lake.

It really wasn't much to look at. The boulder was obviously ancient, covered with brittle green moss. The hole in its base was just as it was described to him, too small for any person to enter. Graham stared deep into the hole's blackness. He thought he noticed a faint, green glow, but wasn't sure. It was getting on toward dark, and the last light of the day played many tricks with color. It was time to leave anyway. Standing up, Graham walked west to his camp.

As promised, the rock was only a short distance from the tree-ringed lake. Sleep again came quickly, blocking out all aches and fears and doubts until the morning.

The second dawn of Graham's quest was overcast. It was the kind of sky that seemed unsure of itself, one that could just as easily turn gray and stormy as it could blue and warm. This seemed to be an omen to the knight. He had resolved to enter, if he could, the witch's house this morning. Like the weather, his prospects could not be predicted. They could be very good, or terminally bad. Graham decided not to dwell on the might-be's and planned on breakfasting on the gingerbread house. If he failed, he wouldn't need food anyway.

The cool air of morning muted the overpowering gingerbread aroma Graham had noticed the day before. It still smelled good, though, and he put his plan into action. Making sure the witch wasn't roaming around outside, he walked quietly up the front path, gently laid his ear to the delicious door, and listened intently for any sounds from inside. All was quiet, but he continued listening, hardly breathing, for several more minutes. It sounded as quiet as death inside, a comparison that did little to allay Graham's misgivings.

It was time to do something.

Graham grabbed a firm grip on both his courage and the door knob and opened the door. He did this, of course, very slowly and very quietly. If the witch were home, he reasoned, he might be able to slip in unnoticed. That was his theory, anyway.

Sneaking inside, Graham could see or hear no one. The room he had entered was furnished with just a table and a pair of hard wooden chairs. A second door led off to the right, and Graham quickly tiptoed to it. Still there was no sound, so he tentatively peeked around the corner. It was the witch's bedroom, and it had the off odor of someone who didn't wash very often. It was empty. In fact, the little cottage was completely deserted. Quickly Graham began his search. Disappointment hit him hard when all he could find in the room was a brief note on an empty bed table, a note that read simply, "Sometimes it is wise to think backwards."

The unexpected sound of Dahlia returning made Graham freeze where he stood, but the crone did not go to the bedroom. Soon he heard sounds of food preparation coming from the other room—the witch talking to herself aloud about cooking up something "good and human" to eat. Graham peeked out, trying to judge whether he could bolt for the door successfully. What he saw was the bent-over form of a figure larger than himself. The witch's attention was on stoking her cooking fire. Escape seemed problematic at best.

Sometimes we all do things without conscious volition and later explain it as something we did on the spur of the moment. In this case, the particular moment spurred Graham into sneaking quickly behind Dahlia and giving her a mighty shove. The momentum from the blow sent the witch headfirst into the fire, where her body immediately burst into flame. It was over so soon, the body might have been made of the driest parchment. Dahlia had returned to the skies from which she had wreaked terror, and an indifferent wind dissipated her ash and smoke to nothing. King Edward and Daventry were avenged.

Safe for the while, Graham ransacked the gingerbread house looking for the Chest of Gold or some clue to its whereabouts. Except for a piece of cheese he took from the kitchen cabinet, and the enigmatic note already acquired, there was nothing.

"Dahlia's dead, and I guess that's something," Graham told himself. "And maybe the note is a clue. Onward, dear boy! The day is young and you have already done one impossible thing!"

On the road south, the piece of gingerbread house he was munching tasted even better than the one the day before. The morning had decided to be as sunny as Graham's new mood, and he passed without encounter or incident through the territory formerly hunted by the wicked witch. About an hour later he came across an ancient well and stopped, thinking to cut his thirst with some water. Graham lowered the old bucket there into the depths of the well, but it reached the end of its rope without touching water. Drought had taken its toll here. Looking down, though, he could see a reflective glint, indicating there was still water down there.

Thirst gave the young knight an idea. Raising the oak bucket back up, he cut the rope and took the bucket. Lowering the rope again, Graham intended to climb down the well, fill the bucket, and climb back up. He was confident in his agility, having scampered up and down ropes for years as part of his martial training. He was always considered the best climber in the army. Carefully, he climbed onto the rope and shimmied down. As he reached its bottom, the best climber in the army's hand slipped.

It was a short drop to the water, and when Graham recovered himself, he found he could reach up and touch the end of the rope with his hand. Knowing he could get back the way he came, Graham dove back under the water, as much for sport as for curiosity. One bit of his father's advice had been to search over, under, around, and through everything. Diving to the bottom, he saw the usual assortment of old bottles and trash, but in one wall there appeared to be an entrance to a cave or grotto. Swimming into the opening, he immediately popped out of the water, and was able to crawl into a hot, dry cave.

King Edward the Benevolent had spent a score of years trying to recover the mirror that foretold the future. Countless people had searched, both in Daventry and elsewhere. And there it was, not more than a score of steps in front of Graham. One of the objects of his quest, one of the salvations of the kingdom, was in plain sight. All Graham had to do was get rid of a little problem.

31
Quest for the Crown

...Graham looked deep into the glass that told the future. His own face looked back, and on his head was a crown!

Kings's Quest

The problem took the shape of a 12-foot long, iridescent, green-scaled, fire-breathing dragon. The flames that blazed from its jaws had scorched deep the virgin rock. From across the cave, the heat of the sulphurous flames singed Graham's hair. The dragon made half-rushes back and forth at him, taking its dragon time before making a killer charge.

Graham tested the balance of his dagger, knowing he had only one chance to strike the dragon in its heart. He knew he could retreat safely back into the well, but his duty was clear; he must rescue the mirror from the beast.

First, though, he had to distract the dragon to give himself more time to aim and a clearer target. The oak bucket was still with him, now mostly filled with well water. Graham reasoned that, instead of extinguishing his own thirst, that water was going to extinguish the dragon's flame. It was the distraction he needed.

Hefting the bucket, Graham advanced as close to the dragon as he dared; a mistake would turn the knight into a crispy critter. Just as the dragon exhaled, he flung the water splat in its snout.

As a distraction it may have worked, but Graham would never know for sure. The liquid hit the dragon's flame full-on and put it out. The green-scaled monstrosity just stopped and sputtered, steam and bubbles gurgling from his nostrils.

It was the expression on that dragon's face that held the dagger in Graham's hand. He speaks in wonder when he says that he never knew a dragon could blush and show embarrassment. It could only have been that; dropping its head and tucking its tail, the beast pushed a boulder aside and pussyfooted out of the cave. Sir Graham was left behind, alone.

Graham spent many minutes just touching and looking at Merlin's Mirror. Its surface still shone, and the luster of the carved mahogany frame still glowed. Picking it up, Graham looked deep into the glass that told the future. His own face looked back, and on his head was a crown!

Quest for the Crown

"I hope this mirror doesn't make mistakes," he prayed. He put the mirror into his pack and followed the dragon's route to see if it would lead to open sky. It did.

It was a jubilant and confident Sir Graham of Daventry who walked out of the underworld as if reborn. He didn't recognize the cave he emerged from, and he paused to get bearings.

Above him, condors were soaring, sweeping steeply up and down, seemingly weightless. One unusually large condor made a few low passes at Graham in what seemed a friendly manner, as if inviting him to climb aboard and fly too.

A short distance to the west was another of the many lakes that dot Daventry. Tall cattails grew on its banks and trembled in the slight breeze. The lake was inviting to Graham, and after the singes and sulphur fumes of the dragon's cave, it was an invitation he could not refuse.

Graham bathed himself as he frolicked in the water. After a while, as he swam near the western bank, he thought he saw something growing in a nearby clearing—something he had wanted since the start of his adventures. He rushed out of the lake. There, just a little west of where he stood dripping wet, grew a patch of four-leafed clover. He knelt to pick one, and held it for a moment in front of his eyes.

"This just might be my lucky day!" he told himself and, sticking the clover into his hat, hurried back to the cave to complete his quest.

The big bird was still there when he returned, still seemingly inviting Graham into the heavens. Its curious behavior demanded attention.

"Why not?" he thought. "If the bird could carry my weight, I could see a lot from the sky, and I could figure out just where I am."

The knight began jumping up and down, trying to attract the bird's attention. Banking quickly, the condor swept low and plucked Graham into his claws. Rising into the clouds, the powerful bird easily carried Graham aloft, first in a tight and dizzy circle, and then in a wider, freer arc, swooping east on great wing-strokes.

The flight went quickly, though not smoothly enough for Graham's stomach. His nausea was soon forgotten, however, when the condor, perhaps tired or perhaps having served its own unfathomable purpose, just let go of the knight and soared away, screeching as if in triumph. Graham was too busy falling to notice the bird's departure. He hit hard and rolled with the impact. After a series of bumps and tumbles, he rolled to a dusty conclusion and finally arose with a thumping head to keep his clutching belly company. The scrapes and bruises would have to be ignored.

A rapid survey revealed that he had been dropped onto an island in the River Fools, within sight of the bank where he had camped two nights before. The fat, speckled mushroom still grew not far from the river, large and alone. It looked like no poison fungus Graham had ever studied, so he picked it; it could be food, or it could be useful.

What appeared to be the spires and turrets of Castle Daventry were outlined faintly in the distance, unreachable across the river. A large hole in the ground was his only companion, and a glance down into it revealed a faint, green glow coming from not far below.

Graham attempted to climb down, but the hole's sides were too steep. They crumbled at once and he fell, leaving him at the bottom of the hole with another aching bruise. There seemed no way back up.

So, Sir Graham pressed on, following the faint green glow farther into the gloom. The hole had turned out to be a fairly extensive cave, with the glow providing enough illumination by which to grope along. Scraping and scratching sounds grew louder as Graham padded deeper into the cave; rats, most likely.

He was wrong. It was one rat, a giant one easily his own size, that guarded a door at one end of the cave. Making soothing "Nice ratty, nice ratty!"

sounds, Graham crept as close to the rat as he dared. Reaching into his pack, he pulled out the piece of swiss cheese he had taken from the witch's house. Gently, he gave the cheese to the rat. The giant rodent practically bit Graham's fingers in his greedy grab for the morsel and dashed away with his prize, seeming to disappear into the rocky walls.

"That wasn't too hard, was it?" he congratulated himself. "Now, let's see what's behind that door."

There was no answer to Graham's loud rapping on the door the rat had guarded. It creaked inward, slowly, as he opened it. Waiting for him inside, however, were two more guardians, leprechauns to be sure. With their green clothing from tip to top, clover in their lapels, and silver-buckled shoes, there was no mistaking these little people.

There are few outside visitors to the Hall of the Leprechaun King, so the guards were idle, humming a tune (a jig, Graham recalls), when the knight entered the antechamber. At first they were startled by the surprise visitor, but seeing the four-leafed clover nestled in his hat, they respectfully stood aside to let him pass and went back to their humming.

"Top of the day to you, little folk," Graham greeted the guards. He was hoping to get some information as to where he was and how he could get back to Daventry. They were too involved in their music-making, though, and paid no heed to his queries. Graham decided to join in. Perhaps they would be more talkative after a song.

The cherry wood fiddle had survived Graham's series of bruising misadventures. Leprechauns are a musical people, and as Graham's first notes began dancing in the air, a look of ecstasy burst upon the guards' features. They began a frenzied dance, leaping and twirling, abandoning everything to the music.

Graham followed as they danced themselves right out of the chamber and into the adjoining throne room. There the rest of the emerald court joined in the delirium. Lost in the abandon of the moment, they all danced off, abandoning their monarch. Graham put down the fiddle as the Leprechaun King followed after his merry subjects, leaving behind Sir Graham, his royal scepter, and what appeared to be a shield.

Graham took the scepter and moved to the other side of the stone throne to take a careful look at the shield. It had been manufactured out of titanium; emeralds ringed its edge. As he picked it up, a surge of invincibility rushed through Graham. It was the Shield of Achille. He had found the second of the three great treasures.

A flight of stairs led out of the throne room, which still vibrated from the dancing bodies of the little people. Graham had no choice but to follow their path. The stairs climbed upward a short way and ended abruptly at a wall of rock. No door was there to aid his exit, just a hole too small for Graham to squeeze through. He could see the outside world on the other side.

Graham sat a moment to think through his problem. He could feel the slight draft of air that entered through the hole; it smelled of green, living things, of sunlight and open spaces. Sitting there, Graham was also aware of the fresh smell of the mushroom he had picked before he had fallen underground. It, too, smelled fresh and wholesome. It made him hungry.

He took a tentative bite of the mushroom, almost positive it wasn't poison, but giving it a taste test to be sure. A wave of strangeness overwhelmed him with that first bite, and the world rushed past his eyes in a blur. As his vision cleared he saw a large doorway ahead of him, leading outside. Graham rushed through, and a second wave of strangeness followed the first. When he had recovered, Graham recognized where he stood.

He was next to the old, moss-laden rock, the one with the small hole, not far from the woodcutter's cabin. Apparently, eating the mushroom had made him shrink, making the tiny hole a huge doorway. For the second time he had escaped from beneath the earth. Again he had come back with one of the objects of his quest, this time with the shield of invincibility.

Graham felt ready for anything.

Now began the final part of Graham's quest for the throne. First he visited the woodcutter and his wife to see if all was well, and then he continued north at a leisurely pace until he came to a large lake. He followed it, skirting its shore, sometimes swimming, always moving to the west. In the stump of a tree near a rotting log, he discovered an old leather pouch filled with diamonds. He took the jewels, found a soft piece of ground, and slept his last night as a knight.

In the morning his wanderings took Graham south, past another of the countless lakes that help make Daventry the fair land that it is, through a fertile field of wildflowers, fresh with their springtime smells, and on through tall trees. Here the countryside opened up again, and Graham passed the cave that led into the dragon's lair. He waited there a bit, scanning the skies for the friendly bird, but it never appeared. He would have liked to thank it, caring not if it understood the speech of humans.

Graham's path soon filled with the the unmistakable smell of live goat. The goat in question was caged in a pen large enough to hold a herd. Graham leaned for a while on the gate, smiling at the noisy creature's antics. The scene was so normal that he almost forgot, for the moment, his quest and the troubles that threatened the kingdom. Almost.

Just a little to the west of the goat pen lay another pretty meadow filled with wildflowers. While Graham paused to sniff and gaze a while, the air around him began to glow, a light floating within it. It soon materialized into an attractive woman who spoke as follows to Graham: "Gentle Sir Graham, I am your fairy godmother. Your quest is indeed noble. My small part to help you can be no bigger than this magic spell, protective but for a little while. I will be watching over you, Sir Graham."

Fairy dust filled the air and Graham was alone again. A moment of quiet seemed to own the universe.

"Thanks a lot, Grandma," Graham thought aloud and punctuated it with a sneeze. "I accept your gift with gratitude, but I sure wish you'd come around earlier!"

Turning north, Graham continued through fields of lucky clover until he arrived at a wooden bridge that spanned a section of the River Fools. Here his way was barred by nine feet of green, ugly troll. It appeared in a combative mood.

"Listen, buddy, this here is a troll bridge. Understand? Pay me a treasure or you will never cross alive!"

The troll looked perfectly able to back up his threat, so Graham, unwilling to part with any of his hard-won treasure, decided to find another way to the small island on the other side of the bridge.

In the next hour, Graham found two more bridges, but no matter which one he tried to cross, the troll was always blocking his way. It was time to teach this troll a lesson.

As he hiked back to the goat pen where he had lingered earlier, Graham grinned in anticipation of the prank he was soon to play. Opening the gate, he walked up to the goat and tried not to breathe through his nose. It worked in theory, but the goat stench was so strong he could now taste it. But, it was just something he would have to put up with for a while.

Graham got out the carrot he had never eaten. He knew goats love carrots and that they'll follow you anywhere if they know you have one, just to get a nibble. He showed it to the goat, being careful not to let it get a bite.

Quest for the Crown

"That's a nice goat, you rancid old beast. Nice goat. Come along with Graham. I have a juicy carrot for you!"

Graham really didn't have to coax the goat out of the pen; it wasn't listening. It just wanted the carrot, and it was in this manner, holding out the carrot as bait, that Graham brought him to meet a troll.

It is a well-known fact that goats hate trolls even more than they love carrots. Graham merely stepped aside when the threatening troll tried to exact his toll.

"Surprise!"

Old Billy needed no coaxing. At first sight of the troll he lowered his head and charged directly at it. The goat's blow sent the troll flying straight off of the bridge and into the river. The splash was quite large. The old goat just kept going.

It was the sight of a crude lean-to that had lured Graham to go through all that effort of crossing the bridge and exploring the small island. When he got closer, he realized that it was the residence of an old gnome.

"Hail, good sir! My name is Graham, and I'm looking for some help."

The gnome stared at Graham for a few seconds.

"I'll make you a deal, kid. I know all about your quest, and I can help you."

Graham's heart leaped in anticipation, and he listened closely.

"I've got something you must have to finish your tasks. I'll even give it to you. But first you must tell me one simple thing. What is my name? I'll even give you three guesses!"

There are perhaps a handful of people in all Daventry who might know the answer. Graham is one. He had studied our world's histories while at the university and knew that the gnome he was confronting could be none other but the one and only "Rumplestiltskin!"

"You're dumber than you look," snorted the old gnome. "What backward part of the realm are you from anyway? Wrong! Want to try again?"

Graham could not understand how he could be mistaken. "Unless, of course, the answer is not what it seems," he realized. "Or the gnome's reply isn't either."

The solution flashed in his brain like an old witch in a cooking fire. The gnome had accused him of being from a backward part of the realm; therefore, the name must be Rumplestiltskin spelled backwards.

"Nikstlitselpmur!"

"What kind of a backwards answer is that, you alphabetical imbecile? Wrong again! Want to bet you don't get it right the third time?"

Graham was stymied. If he couldn't solve the riddle, all would be lost. His wit had failed him; his brain burned in confusion.

He kept thinking back to "backwards." The gnome had deliberately used that word twice now. Graham knew the name was really Rumplestiltskin, but twisted backwards somehow. He even remembered the note he had found in the gingerbread house: "Sometimes it is wise to think backwards." Backwards? An alphabetical imbecile?

Maybe a backward alphabet was the answer. Change A to Z, B to Y, C to X. If that were the solution, then the answer was....

King Graham has confessed to me that he really wasn't sure about his final answer. He does agree, though, that when all other possible solutions have been discarded, whatever remains, however improbable, must be correct.

"Ifnkovhgroghprm."

The gnome looked at him for a moment with what might have been affection. If it were, it passed in a blink.

"Not bad. Here are some magic beans for a reward!" With that, the old gnome was gone. The beans lay on the ground where he had stood.

41
Quest for the Crown

Magic beans need to be planted if they are going to do any good. Graham suspected a nice, fertile flower patch might be a good place, and there was such a patch just past the troll bridge to the east. Picking up the small, dried beans, he set off to finish his quest.

More massive than any tree, the beanstalk disappeared into the clouds, its thick foliage offering precarious footholds. The magic beans had sprouted as soon as Graham planted them in the flower bed, and when the growth had stopped, it had become obvious what he had to do.
  Upward he climbed, slowly making his progress into the sky. Grasping and clawing around the twisted stalk, Graham lost count of the times he almost fell, but nothing, not even the cloud-slicked leaves, was going to stop him from saving Daventry.
  At last his head poked above the clouds, and he was able to step off the stalk. Looking around, Graham saw low clouds everywhere; like the heaviest of fogs, they obscured the ground, making it almost impossible to see where to place his feet. He had to be very careful, lest he step off into nothingness.
  Graham's direction, however, was clear. With patience he moved due east where, after a few hundred yards, the clouds broke enough to show him the floor of a forest. The woods extended a little to the south, and Graham followed them there until clouds obscured the ground again. He continued west, staying near the cloud edge, wondering at the strange trees that grew there. In a tree at the eastern edge of the cloud border, Graham discovered a sling for shooting stones, and he took it with him. North of the tree, he found a cave burrowing its way into the mountainside.
  After some minutes of searching the cave, Graham descended partway down some slick stone steps far enough to become convinced that this was the way back to Daventry. He was sure that these stairs were the very ones he had glimpsed early in his quest winding upward toward unknown dangers; the stairs behind the locked door set in the mountain.

Suddenly, from the clearing behind him, Graham heard noise—booming thumps that shook the ground and rattled his teeth. He hastened away from his investigation of the cave to find out what was making the giant sounds.

Ten or twelve feet tall it was, human in outward form and with bulk to match its build. The giant was carrying a golden chest under his arm, pacing wearily to and fro, silent except for the impact of his steps. It seemed weary, much like a guard who is asked to pace the same small area endlessly. Back and forth and around again the giant thundered, aware of nothing but its one small post.

From the magic shield that he was carrying, Graham felt a surge of energy engulfing and protecting him. The giant seemed uninterested in Graham. Perhaps that was part of the shield's magic.

Faced with the problem of getting the chest from the giant, the last task in his kingly quest, Graham took advantage of his being ignored. He stopped to think through the problem slowly, something he had seldom been able to do during the previous days' adventures. As Graham sat there, debating whether a stone in his newfound sling could fell the goliath, the giant dropped down on the ground, wriggled himself a soft spot in the earth, and fell fast asleep.

Snores—long, drawn-out explosions—filled the land in the clouds. Graham waited a while until they became regular, like the beating of a heart. Slipping from behind a tree, he hefted the golden chest from the ground, taking it from within inches of the giant's limp grasp.

The weight of the chest was not as great as Graham had feared, a property, perhaps, of its own peculiar magic. On the other hand, it was not light, and the knight's return trip to the cave and down its long, narrow, stone stairs seemed to last forever. He kept listening for the thud of the giant's following footfalls, but they never came.

Quest for the Crown

Graham's surmise about where the stairs ended was correct—the entrance into the mountain was indeed at the bottom of the stairs. He was surprised, however, that the door was open, but lost no time pondering his good fortune. Closing the heavy door behind him, Sir Graham headed quickly, and in singular triumph, back to the halls of King Edward.

The royal alligators seemed hungrier than usual, thrashing and snapping almost to his feet as Graham crossed over the moat's bridge. He made his way past them and up the few stairs to the castle door. Its locked doors opened at his touch, a sure sign of his success. He entered to greet his king, and to meet his destiny.

My telling of this history must end as it began; with both grief and rejoicing. As soon as Graham had bowed his respects to his monarch, Edward arose to greet the kingdom's savior. A smile crossed his face as he moved to embrace his successor, but the smile abruptly turned to pain as the old king clutched his chest, his face ashen in agony.

Tears ran down the face of King Graham as Edward's face became still. It was over quickly. Edward's last words were, "Well done Sir Graham...my kingdom is now yours!"

Thus you have it. I myself observed the beginning and end of the tale with my own eyes and ears, sitting as scribe in my accustomed place in the corner of the court. The rest was told me that very evening by King Graham himself, who was anxious to record his quest while the dust of adventure still clung to his body. I have done so, my Lord.

Long live the King! Long live King Graham of Daventry!

The World of Daventry

*Compiled from Messages to this World from the
World of Daventry, as sent by Derek Karlavaegen*

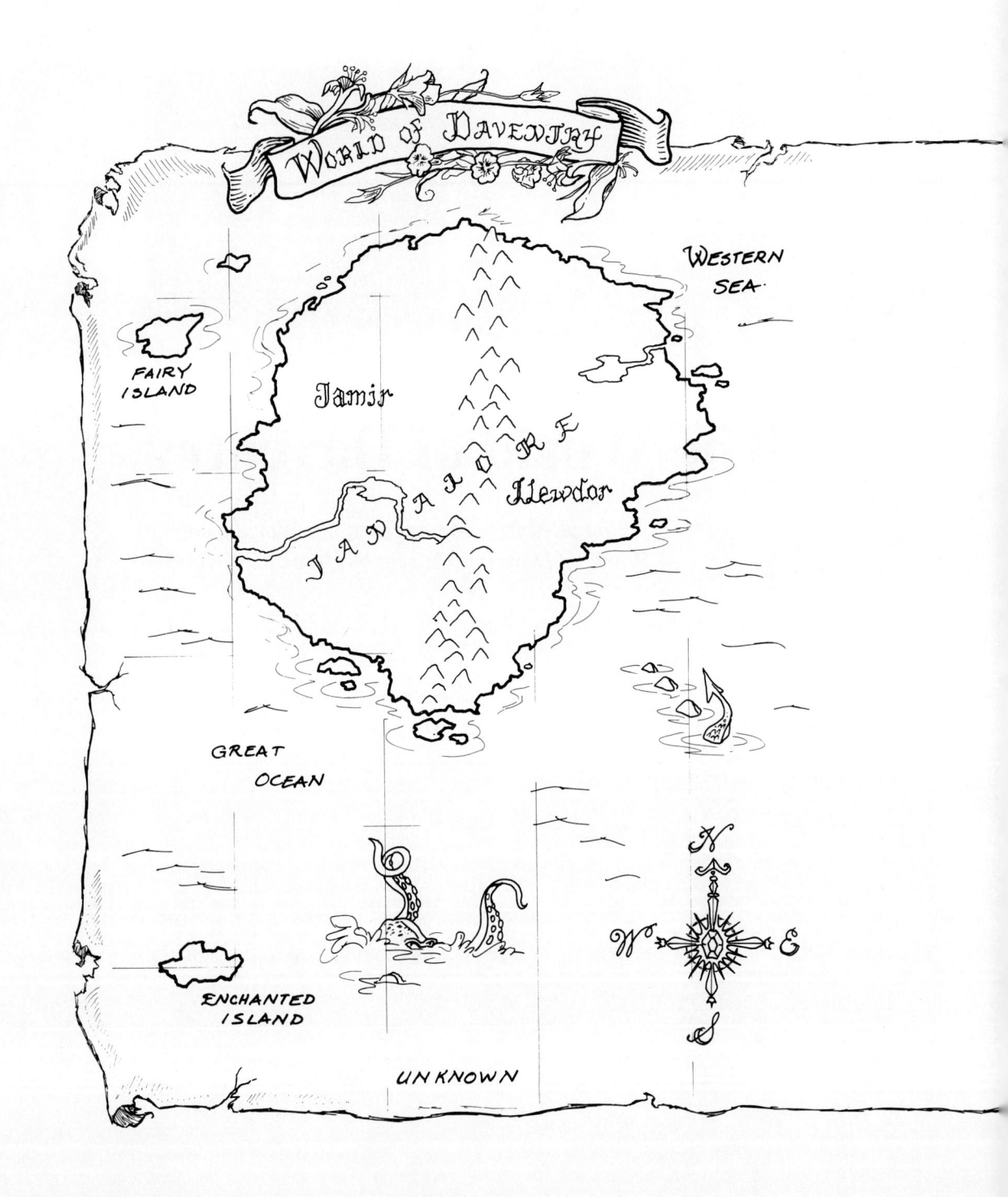

World of Daventry

- Western Sea
- Fairy Island
- Jamir
- Daventry
- Tanalorf
- Great Ocean
- Enchanted Island
- Unknown

47
The World of Daventry

To you, whoever you are, who read my messages sent between the worlds: Greetings! All is well here for the moment; the stars and sun and celestial bodies still revolve around the sky, neither falling down upon our heads nor failing in their appointed rounds across the heavens. Few are held in fear or bondage by sorcerers or witches of the evil persuasion. Ravaging flame- or frost-flinging dragons have been somewhat conspicuous in their absence.

True, some pirates still sail the seas, bandits prowl in forests, deserts, and other remote spots, and hags and their sisterly witches keep stewpots at the ready for the unwary. But I never did claim this was paradise; this is the real world. The normal cares and challenges of life fill our days. The occasional conflicts between people or kingdoms are seemingly woven into the fabric of reality, but the harvest seems good and this year's wines seem even better.

With that said, and with a glass of smooth, sweet red at my side, I've decided to give you, unknown friend, a quick tour of Daventry. I'm going to try to send some of my own crude maps along with this communication to further illustrate my world—what there is of it. Please excuse their artistic shortcomings; I am a writer and magician (of sorts), not an artist.

My universe is divided into many parts. How many, we may never know, for we are always reinventing ourselves, and today's count of the number of realms, and kingdoms, and deserts, and islands, and mountains to hold up the sky will be different tomorrow. It will be different again the day after tomorrow, and again the day after that, and again, and again. Today's fact is tomorrow's anachronism. In a world of magic and wonders, all is possible—if not inevitable.

As best as I can learn, the largest and broadest and most ancient of our sometimes fantastical lands is that of Serenia, named after the peaceful place where our people appeared when they first *withdrew* here. The exact spot of the arrival has never been marked by stone or statue or eidolon, for that is not our way; but many hold that the place is where the house of the great

The World of Daventry

wizard Chrispinophur now sits. It is said that the house has been there, never aging, since the beginning of time. It is also claimed that is was built in less than an instant by the same magician, who himself was already an old man when time began.

In front of that dwelling is an odd device of no apparent purpose. Chrispinophur is said to call it his "Universe Interpreter", and that he uses it to keep the stars in alignment, and the gears of the heavens greased. Others, though, claim that it is the magically constucted engine through which was focused the mystic forces that made our *withdrawal* from your world, the Other World, to our world, Daventry, possible. To me it looks like something to scare gophers away from the vegetable garden. It may very well be both.

Serenia, the continent, is divided into many kingdoms, most of them small and only a day or three's journey by foot in extent. These fiefdoms sometimes war or battle with each other for reasons only their rulers care about, and shrink or grow depending on their martial fortunes. They seemingly come and go with the seasons, and few are remembered after their passing. Two lands however bear special notice.

Greatest is the Kingdom of Daventry, a land of wonder and marvels. It is home to King Graham, his queen, Valanice, and their children, Alexander and Rosella. Twins these two are, and courageous beyond words, as are their parents. Here too abide monsters and magicians, giants and little folk, witches and fairies, cruel beasts and human people, commoners and kings.

Great troubles have beset this illustrious kingdom for years, pausing only to allow troubles that seem greater still to befall. Great too are the tales that have been told and sung of the struggles to vanquish those difficulties. Good King Edward gave his life for the sake of his people and kingdom, as King Graham and his children almost have.

Daventry is the most populated part of my world; it is renowned for its great keep, Castle Daventry, and its gentle lakes, which are so numerous as to be almost beyond counting. Many lakes are fed by that greatest of streams, the River Fools. Daventry's awesome mountains, the great mountains, punch upwards through the clouds to snowcapped summits daring to be scaled. Giants walk those clouds, yeti prowl the snows, and the great Rocs nest in its most inaccessible peaks. Dragons own the land's innards and share it with leprechauns; witches on their brooms fly the skies along with giant condors; and ogres and trolls and dwarves and elves and gnomes fill the secret spaces known only to themselves. Magic flows through everything.

At the moment, the Kingdom of Daventry still rebuilds itself from years of flaming terror caused by a three-headed dragon and constant earthquakes. These twin terrors destroyed much of the beautiful land, forcing many folk to flee to the western and southern kingdoms. Vast chasms appeared, ripping the earth apart much as one would open a ripe fruit. Whole sides of mountains have collapsed, burying some landmarks and creating others. Great walls were built throughout Daventry to contain the terrible beast so it would not maraud the entire continent. These walls succeeded, but they also magnified the damage done within the kingdom.

Now, though, the walls are being torn down and the stone used to build homes for the returning population. The rains have been good, perhaps in celebration of deliverance, and the natural world has begun to heal. The fresh greens of new trees and shrubs and bushes and plants are wiping out the blacks and browns of formerly burnt landscapes. Great magics have been unleashed; although unable to destroy the Dragon, they rebuild and reclaim the land. One might think that some dread technology were at work, so quickly goes the transformation.

Prince Alexander, a great scholar and magician himself, has even claimed that any magic, sufficiently advanced, is indistinguishable from technology. In this case, he just might be right, although I hope the two never merge. There is something too unnatural about technology for the taste of folks here.

To the north and west of Daventry, beyond the River Fools and the Great Mountains, is the other of Serenia's great lands. Indeed, the continent itself takes its name from the Sovereignty of Serenia, the first home of all my world's people. Despite being somewhat near to each other, commerce and communication between Daventry and Serenia is limited because of the physical barriers between the two lands. Nonetheless, the inhabitants of both places are similar, consisting generally of humans and the Little Folk. Most humans live in the one small town of the realm, a lovely place with the usual shops and places of business. The bakery is renowned for the goodness of its pies, as is the inn for its unsavory clientele.

Serenia, however, is generally a less violent land than most, an island of peace in a less tranquil world. This reflects both its name and its rulers' policies of harmony amongst all beings. While some of the more cynical persuasion quip that the first law of the land is "You will be happy—or you will regret it", the truth of the matter is that the people of Serenia believe peace to be the natural order of things and, in believing it to be true, ensure that it is. It is an innocent, though effective, magic which should be practiced more.

On Serenia's western edge is a great and trackless desert. Hidden somewhere within its northern wastes is an old and abandoned temple of some diety whose name is unknown to me. There, bands of desperate bandits store and hide their bloody booty, the treasure of caravans lost to their savage attacks. The boots and bones of the victims are often found in the sands, sun whitened skulls the homes to snakes and scorpions.

It is said that a magic spell has been cast over the temple by either the anonymous god or by the bandits. Whichever is the case, many swear that the temple eats those who are enraptured by its treasure.

Not all of the scattered bones, however, come from spendthrift gods or bandits' blades. The sun too takes many victims, those who have lost their way and have died of thirst. There are but few oases concealed among the baked sand and mirages, and it is quite easy to lose one's way in the desolation. One does not survive the heat long without water.

Serenia is bordered on the north by a dark and daunting forest so thick that Death itself is said to have gotten lost inside of it. It is known that some of the Little Folk, elves and gnomes mostly, have their own hidden ways in and out of the Dark Forest, but they guard their paths and tunnels well. Even the charmed smiles and honeyed words of the Gypsies have been useless in discovering their secrets. It is just as well, I suspect. Local rumor has it that a particularly nasty witch makes her home within the woods, protected by its thickness. I am assured she doesn't like vistors.

Finally, to the east hover the Great Mountains, an almost impassible barrier, and part of Serenia's border with Daventry. A great Queen holds thrall over the highest and coldest of the region's icy peaks. Known as Icebella, her heart is said to be as cold as the glacial ice from which her throne is carved. Her only subjects are the dire wolves. While harsh and moody, she is not considered an evil ruler. Little else is known of her.

Beyond the Great Mountains is the Northern Sea. Little is known of what lies beyond the horizon there, mariners seldom stray far from the sight of land in those rocky regions. The usual sailors' tales of great monsters and serpents large enough to swallow ships are told, but the same stories are told wherever strong drink and sailors mix.

To the south and east of the continent of Serenia, there is the tropical land of Kolyma, from whence Valanice came. It bathes in balmy breezes, and the Southern Sea laps its beaches with waves like warm, green tongues. Mermaids sun themselves here and sing the songs that capture people's souls and haunt them always with liquid melodies and the rhythm of eternal tides. The King of the Sea keeps his court and throne near its western shore, so the winds are always gentle here and the skies forever blue and clear.

Few inhabit the western part of Kolyma, despite its beauty. Simple monks give shelter to occasional travelers, lest they be caught outdoors after dark, for vampires hunt this land at night, with ghouls and ghosts as their grim companions. These undead are truly evil, not like the restless sort of spirit who sometimes haunts the living, seeking release from its torments. The vampires rule the dark from a cold castle on an island in the middle of a lake so poisonous that a stray splash is fatal.

For these reasons, most good folk make their homes on the eastern side of Kolyma, separated by a spine of high mountains and a great chasm from the greater horrors. Only a magic door grants passage from east to west, and even this will send one elsewhere if they have not the proper key. A great strangeness folds the western land back upon itself to both the north and south, forever bringing travelers back to where they started. All these barriers have, with only occasional exceptions, kept the Children of the Night isolated.

To the north and west of Daventry, across the western sea, lies the great continent of Tanalore. An eternal city of the same name is said to exist somewhere there, touching all of the realities of creation; but none has ever found it—or returned after having done so. The great middle of this continent is covered with deserts, swamps, and mountains taller and steeper than those of Daventry.

In the eastern part of Tanalore there is the land of Llewdor, where, until recently, the evil sorcerer Manannan ruled the countryside through terror and magic. He kept his home atop the highest mountain there, living alone except for a single boy slave. Through a long looking glass, the wizard was able to spy on all parts of the unfortunate realm, killing all who dared oppose him. I make my home there now in Manannan's place, but I will tell you more of that at another time, for it is why I am able to communicate with you who are reading this.

Llewdor is a compact land bordered by ocean on the west and deadly desert to the east. No one, residents claim, can walk far into the desert and live. Medusas dwell there—gruesome creatures with the ability to turn any who stare upon them to stone. At times, now that Manannan is gone, people sneak into the sands in search of statues that were once people. It is a risky business, but the merchants who do this are known to turn a great profit for their efforts. Some folks disapprove of the practice, seeing it as merely another form of grave robbing. If the medusas don't claim victims, however, the desert does. The sun, heat, and shimmering horizons conspire to rob travelers of their sense of direction. Lost, a person can perish quickly in such a place.

The bulk of the country is pleasantly wooded and dotted with occasional cottages. Other than bears and the seldom-encountered giant spider of Llewdor, it is altogether an entirely pleasant, if unspectacular, place. Its one major city, Port Bruce, is a healthy sea-trading town, where ships from all parts of the known world visit. Llewdor's chief products are rare ingredients for magic spells, such as toad spittle, stones of amber, nightshade juice, and mandrake root power. There is an attempt being made by the merchants of Llewdor to export the desert statues, but the sailors who might transport those items refuse to accept the cargo at present. They claim the bad luck of the stone people might somehow rub off on them. They may be right; stranger things than that are commonplace here.

Because Port Bruce freely welcomes all ships that visit its harbor, the pirates who roam the Western Sea are no problem to people on the coast. Other than the brawling, cussing, and drunkenness that seem to be as much a part of the pirate's code as shipboard cats and captains' parrots, they are more colorful than dangerous and provide needed gold for the local economy. Bandits, on the other hand, are a different story. These brigands, numbering in the dozens, prowl the woods beating, robbing, and sometimes killing those they can waylay. They were encouraged and supported by Manannan while he held sway in Llewdor for all those years, and efforts to get rid of them have been only partially successful. The problem is expected to be under control soon, however.

The World of Daventry

On the far western side of Tanalore lies the land of Tamir, the last of the great countries of our world. The Great Sea Ocean washes Tamir on its west, and it is here that the good fairy Genesta resides on her magical isle, attended by others of her kind, as well as by birds and dolphins—all of the most beautiful appearance. Many small islands dot this part of the sea, something for which many a shipwrecked sailor has been thankful. Sharks, whales, and other monsters of the deep are abundant there, and beyond Genesta's isle lies the Unknown. Fantastic rumors of yet greater monsters and wonders that exist there buzz about Tamir. Some must be true.

Tamir itself is much like Kolyma in that it is open and pleasing along its coast. The sea breezes, however, are much stronger and intemperate, which accounts for many of the shipwrecks that happen near there. Fishing is good in the sea, so the coast is home to many families of fisherfolk. Diamonds and precious metals are mined in the central hills by a race of sometimes sullen and dirty dwarfs. It is said that they get that way from their hard labors, digging from dawn to dusk, and they neither have time for hygiene nor humor. But they are good folk and are known to repay kindness with the same coin.

Two spectacular structures in Tamir are well known throughout the entire world, bringing sightseers and the curious to the country. First, a marble pool surrounded by tall columns lies peacefully in the northern part of the land. None alive now remembers how the pool got there, but legend says it came from your world, the Other World, when the magical creatures of Greece and Rome *withdrew* to Daventry. Strange melodies may be heard in the wind there at night, and Cupid and Pan are said to frolic in the waters. Second, against the Impossible Mountains to the west sits the eerie old house known as Whateley Manor, flanked by its twin graveyards—places not often seen here. This we know for sure was transported from the Other World. Haunted by ghosts and zombies, like Dracula's Castle in Kolyma, it is usually avoided after dark.

Also to be avoided is a small forest of cruel trees just north of the manor house. Indeed, this entire region of Tamir is inhabited by sudden death at almost any step. The trees reach out, grab, and kill all that walk into their grove. An ogre and his wife live at the trees' eastern edge. They like to eat people. If you're lucky enough to get past the ogres, and trees' deadly branches, you might meet three perfectly delightful hag sisters who also have an appetite for human stew. Almost all stay away from this part of Tamir; almost all who have ventured there have perished.

Hovering above all this are the Impossible Mountains, so named because of how hard they are to cross. Waterfalls thunder out of those mist-shrouded heights, which are the source of all Tamir's streams and fresh water. Some say vast sucking swamps exist on the other side of those peaks, but since no one is known to have crossed over the Impossible Mountains, who can know for sure? Perhaps someone went under the mountains as Rosella did; perhaps someone flew like an eagle over the peaks and returned to tell about it. We do not know for sure.

One lone, narrow path treks up into the crags. Its end is at a dark castle perched on the edge of a sheer precipice. The wicked witch Lolotte once lived there with her winged-monkey soldiers. She is gone now, and the lone human inhabitant is her son Edgar, a handsome youth who pines for the princess who rejected him. All hope that he will grow to be much wiser than his mother.

In any event, with Lolotte apparently dead, much of the despair that once hovered over Tamir has flown away. With her passing, the curious architecture and quaint places of the land have caught the imagination of folks who travel the world for amusement. Many tourists and adventurers are drawn there, so perhaps someday we will finally learn what really lies on the other side of the Impossible Mountains.

As for the rest of my world, little is known beyond the occasional strange tales of wanderers from unknown parts, the ravings of shipwrecked sailors, and the wild tales gasped out by those who have staggered out of mountains or deserts or the darkest of caves. I have heard tales of the Green Isles where the women are said to be the fairest in the entire multiverse. I have been told of a place where the oceans are red and the sands blue. Some claim to have seen islands that do not float in the waves, but hover above them; enchanted islands, perhaps the homes of great wizards. These I have placed on my map, convinced of their existence.

Kingdoms beneath the sea, jungles containing beasts the size of mountains, and cities containing people the size of peas. Of these I am not so sure. On the other hand, if they don't exist now, they will on some tomorrow.

This is the world of Daventry as I know it. I have spent some time writing for you this brief description of my world, my universe, as it appears today. Soon it will be different. This is a world of wonder and magic, and we constantly invent it, much like a tale that a storyteller creates over a thousand and one nights, never knowing what tomorrow's fancies will reveal. The unknown is always before us, but we do not fear it. We welcome and embrace it. It is the unknown that gives meaning to our lives and reason to our being. Triumph and tragedy, joy and fear, life and death, good and evil—all are but opposite faces on the dice of existence. One cannot exist without the other, just as perhaps we cannot exist without you—the Other World—or you without us.

4

Romancing the Throne

From the Chronicles of Daventry, Part 2

King's Quest

The Land of Kolyma

61
Romancing the Throne

Rejoicing, revelry, and carousing still roar from all the corners of Daventry this night. Our monarch, King Graham, has returned home to Daventry with a bride. They just arrived here yesterday after a slow voyage across the seas from Kolyma. Word of the royal wedding was immediately dispatched across the realm, carried in the claws of a condor that winged from town to town with the proclamation. The news set off spontaneous celebrations by all at first hearing.

King Graham, our most wise and beloved monarch, took to wife a maiden of the tropical land of Kolyma. Valanice is her name, and her beauty, wisdom, and goodness are beyond compare. The wedding ceremony took place in a small chapel in her homeland, our new queen wearing King Graham's bridal gifts to her, the diamond and sapphire jewels of Kolyma. At great and perilous risk were they acquired by our monarch, risks that he says were small compared to his bride's beauty.

Long live the Queen! Long live Queen Valanice of Daventry!

It is strange for me to see those words drying in front of my eyes, no less so for knowing that it was I, Gerwain, Prime Minister of Daventry and chief advisor to King Graham, who penned them there moments ago. Although I prayed in my heart that he would prevail, little did I expect my sovereign to survive the quest on which he embarked to find his bride, much less wed. I am happy beyond words for my king and his new queen.

I must confess, however, that I do not think it is proper for a monarch to go traipsing about the world by himself, questing in search of women and adventure. His duties are at home, near to his subjects. This is especially true if the king has no heirs, and Graham has none.

I must also confess that I do not think it proper for a king to wed quickly, without proper dowry or period of courtship. I do not think it proper that a king wed away from his own land, out of sight of his own subjects. I especially do not think it proper that a king marry without seeking the advice and approval of his own prime minister!

I suspect my objections might be judged by some as petty. Graham has heard my thoughts on this. He says I should continue speaking my mind, especially when it is contrary to his thoughts.

"A king," he says often, "needs 'nay' sayers more than he needs 'yea' sayers."

King Graham today recounted to me the details of his adventures since leaving Daventry—his quest: to rescue Valanice from her bondage in the Crystal Tower. He has directed me to rework his words to finer form, both for the sake of readability and for the historical record. He has also given me permission to add commentary of my own if I feel disapproval of his actions. He says it matters not; the deeds cannot be undone, and if they must be questioned, let the objections be raised now.

Here then is what befell our king. It begins with his search for the keys to the three doors....

King Graham had decided to travel light. He adjusted his favorite cap, setting it snugly on his long, brown hair, and made sure the red feather and four-leafed clover tucked into it were still there. His travel pack was empty, but he planned to change that as he went along. Graham knew that his strongest assets were agility and speed, wit and intelligence; he expected to live by the latter and survive by the former.

He knew also that the "fairest of all fair maidens," as he described her, was imprisoned in a tower somewhere. She had been put there by her kidnapper, a witch who called herself Hagatha. To rescue her, all he had to do was find three keys, presumably use them on three doors, and find the Crystal Tower. And survive.

The king looked around the beach where he had been deposited, which stretched apparently north and south. Graham knew this was part illusion; the geographers he had consulted had informed him that the magical law of "containment" operated in this western part of the continent. For reasons now forgotten—or perhaps it was whimsey on the part of the multiverse—movement to both the north and south in this part of Kolyma eventually turned back upon itself, contained as if inside some transparent cosmic doughnut. East and west, one could travel at will until confronted by more physical barriers—the sea or mountains, for instance—but he knew that if he journeyed far enough north or south, he would always get back to where he started.

The Southern Sea was at his back. Warm waves lapped at his heels, reflecting the tropical sun in sparkles of diamond and sapphire. The waves seemed to be telling him to move along or he would find neither fair maiden, food, nor anything else. Seeing a sandy trail leading away from the beach and into the trees, the king moved forward.

The path soon disappeared into the midst of a thick wood and then vanished altogether. The world seemed to close around Graham, and the king hoped he would find a clearing or a new path soon. Within minutes the trees thinned, and he was able to glimpse what appeared to be a white fence in the distance. Walking toward him was a girl. She appeared to be no more than a dozen years of age, short and slight in form, with blond tresses peeking out of her red hooded robe. She was in tears.

"Sir, you must help me, please," she bawled. "Someone has taken my basket of goodies! I was taking them to my Grandma and had stopped to pick her some flowers when a large wolf, with the biggest jaws, jumped me and ran away with my basket. I was so afraid he was going to eat me! Please, sir, will you help me get my basket back?"

Graham tried to comfort the near-hysterical girl, but she wriggled from his embrace and dashed into the woods.

I must, at this moment, take pause to praise my lord king. Undertaking his quest for Valanice was rash, and undertaking it unarmed and with no provisions was foolish. However, King Graham is a true knight, noble of heart and sworn to aid the helpless. His determination to help the child in the little red riding hood was correct; to do anything less would demean him.

Graham followed in the direction from which the girl had come. The white fence enclosed a snug cottage of the same color. Flowers spilled from boxes in the lace-curtained windows. On a mailbox by the front gate were the words, "Grandma's House."

He had already suspected that much, so Graham opened the mailbox in hope of getting some useful information. Inside he found a wicker basket covered by a red and white checked cloth enclosing some bread, jam, and cold meats. This must be the basket of goodies that had been taken from the girl. The picnic smelled delicious, but something else smelled very suspicious.

Graham walked to cottage door and knocked. A muffled "Come in!" sounded from the other side. The king entered and found a pale, ancient woman sitting propped among dozens of pillows in a massive brass bed. Dressed warmly in a cap and flannel nightgown, wool shawl pulled around her shoulders, she smiled and bid him welcome.

"Grandma, obviously!" Graham thought.

"Good day, kind sir. Welcome to my house. I'd offer you some tea, but I'm not feeling well."

Graham chatted with the woman for a few moments, but she seemed somewhat delirious, and all she would talk about were her grandchildren. Grandma also refused the basket Graham had found hidden in the mailbox, saying it belonged rightfully to her granddaughter and that he must return it to her. Then she closed her eyes and began snoring.

King Graham left the cottage intent on finding the little girl so he could give her back the basket and continue his search for the maiden. Moving east into the forest past the cottage, he began hearing the tolling of bells ahead of him, a rolling tintinnabulation that seemed to be a call to prayer. With the sound as his guide, Graham walked until he came upon the adobe walls of a good-sized monastery, its bell still swinging back and forth. By its door was a small brass plate that read, "Welcome, Travelers." Below that was hung another small sign, "No Vacancy."

Romancing the Throne

The door was thick, but it opened easily. Graham wanted to rest for a few moments and collect his thoughts; perhaps one of the monks there might have some news for him. So far, it seemed, he had made no progress.

A round, brown-robed figure, tonsured head bowed, was kneeling at the altar at the far end of the chapel. Graham quietly approached the altar and, kneeling next to the monk, joined him in a short prayer. The two men remained motionless for several moments. After a time the monk raised his head from his prayers and seemed to notice the king for the first time.

"What is your name, traveler?"

"King Graham of Daventry, brother."

"Yes. King Graham, I have heard of your quest, and I would give you something to protect you from evil."

The king was speechless as the monk took a long chain, bearing a small silver cross, from around his neck. As Graham took the gift from the monk and placed it around his own neck, he listened to the holy man tell him of a door that had appeared recently, not far from where they stood. This door seemed to float in the air, an aura of magic surrounding it. It was located on the far side of a bottomless chasm and could be reached only by crossing an old rope bridge immediately north of the chapel.

Having finished his tale, the monk returned to his prayers. Graham joined him for a moment longer.

"The door I have been searching for!" he thought in triumph. "The way to my heart's desire!"

He whispered a short prayer of thanksgiving and left. The monk remained, absorbed in his prayers.

The heat of the tropical day blasted at Graham as he left the monastery and a harsh glare struck his eyes. They combined to convince the king to pass the hottest part of the day near the cool water of a small lake, which he could see just a little south, beyond the chapel door.

A large boulder in the shade of a tree reached out a bit into the lake and appeared to be the prime point from which to relax and swim. Approaching the shoreline, the king noticed a small hole in the rock.

The king has often told me that he tries always to remember advice given to him by his father. The words are engraved in my memory, so often has he repeated them. They are "My daddy used to tell me, 'Boy, if I have learned anything in my life, I have learned this: when in doubt or in trouble, pick up anything that is not nailed down, and if it is, check for loose nails or boards. Check carefully into, under, above, below, and behind things. Read everything; you might learn something. Wear clean undergarments, brush after meals, and always remember, nothing is as it appears.'"

Graham looked into that rock. Inside lay a glittering sapphire brooch dripping with encircling diamonds. He took the brooch, intending it as a gift for a bride he had yet to woo. Then he sat down, out of the sun, dreaming of love and thanking his father.

Chasm it truly was; bottomless it truly appeared. The bridge that spanned it seemed as old as time and as feeble as the little girl's ailing grandmother. The ropes that held it suspended were frayed, reaching out from the body of the fragile cables like the hairs of a very frightened, very skinny cat. The planks that were left were as much air as wood.

"Okay," the king muttered to the wind, "I'll go over as quickly and as lightly as I can. I'll breathe deeply, pretend I'm floating, and I definitely will not look down."

The king has this annoying habit of talking aloud to himself when he ponders a particularly difficult problem or situation. I have told him countless times that polite people just do not do this, and that people look at him strangely when he does it. Usually he just gives me a patient look and walks away, still murmuring. In this case there was no one to hear, so no offense was given, nor taken. Nonetheless, it is an unseemly habit for a monarch.

Moving with his lightest steps in the exact center of the bridge, Graham held his breath the entire crossing, as if with his lungs full of air he was made lighter. "I hope I don't have to come that way again," he thought, looking back at pieces of the bridge spinning into the depths below.

The door was there, floating as predicted a few inches above the meadow. He could easily walk around the thing; it had a back and front, but no sides

Romancing the Throne

at all. The smell of magic threatened to overpower him. He was sure that the woman he sought to rescue, his heart's desire, was behind it.

An inscription was carved into the door's front: "Whosoever chooses to seek the key for this door will undoubtedly make a splash." That was all.

Oh, yes, the door was locked. No matter how hard the king tried to open it, the entry remained firmly locked. Graham realized that he needed a key. Not that this fact surprised him much; he had known since the start that he would have to obtain three keys for three doors.

"If that be so, so be it!" he decided resolutely (if not a bit redundantly) and breathing even more deeply than before, he returned across the shaky bridge.

He still had the goodies. Graham had been carrying the basket in hopes of returning it the the blonde girl of the red hood as he had promised. "I am honor bound to do this before all else," he chided himself. "Let me find the girl, give her the goodies, and get back to what I came to Kolyma for!"

Grandma's house, or somewhere in its vicinity, seemed to be the most logical place to find the child. With that in mind, Graham decided to zigzag west from the bridge, continuing until he could turn back south to the cottage. He reasoned that he would be able to do some exploring, search for the girl, and get to Grandma's, all at the same time. Another of the king's annoying habits: he much admires his own cleverness.

This route led him straight into the gloomiest forest in which he had ever ventured. Menace and misfortune seemed to surround him. Looking from side to side, alert to any possible encounter, noting every possible place to hide—whether it be bush, tree, or rock—Graham carefully began to press through the threatening trees.

Immediately, almost before his first step had touched the ground, he spotted the dwarf scurrying furtively about, as is the way of such folk. Graham moved quickly, but he was overtaken by the dwarf anyway and knocked to the ground by the force of the thief running into him. Over and over they tumbled, until the dwarf was able to strike a strong blow to the king's head, knocking him senseless long enough to escape with the sapphire brooch.

When King Graham finally recovered himself, he discovered but minor cuts and scrapes along with his throbbing head. "Never again," he promised the bandit, "never again!"

Graham walked a little north of where the dwarf had robbed him, hoping to avoid another encounter before his head was clear. Groggily he stumbled into a pine tree, tripping over a large rock near its base. As he picked himself up, he noted that this tree had a hole in it, and inside was a stout wooden stick with something metal attached. When his eyes unblurred, he saw that he had found a mallet.
"Two holes, two treasures—not bad. And now I have a weapon," Graham encouraged himself. "Now, let's go find that dwarf and get the jewels back!"
Moving west, even more cautiously now, the king soon came upon a large rotting log. In his quest to become king, he had once found a bag of diamonds near a log such as this. This time there was nothing.
"Come on now, Graham," he told himself, "you can't expect to find something under everything, can you?" With these words still on his tongue, he continued his way west to where a fresh, clear lake blocked his immediate way. There lay yet another hollow log.
"I'm going to prove something to you," he exclaimed to his own person. Enunciating each step clearly, he began to demonstrate to himself the truth of his previous observation. "See...log. See...hole in log. See...no treasure!"

I must admit a certain level of amusement when the king recounted this episode to me. There he was, playing the buffoon, talking to himself and reveling in his own cleverness. Of course there was treasure in the log; how could there not be, as my lord strutted pride to the heaven? Inside lay a necklace of diamonds and sapphires with a large sapphire pendant dangling from it. It should have been a tub of rancid yogurt or moldy cheese. I love my lord king, but that day he deserved much less than he received.

Graham decided to wend his way south to the old woman's cottage. He hoped that he could arrive there and return the basket to the little girl before darkness fell and he'd have to camp for the night. He much preferred to do his sleeping in less ominous parts.

The forest quickly opened up to a clearer though more rocky landscape. His feet stopped, frozen in stillness, as he heard cackling nearby. The smacking of hungry lips and the sound of tuneless humming brought back dread memories of the wicked witch Dahlia stirring her loathsome cooking pot. A hurried glance gave a partial glimpse of someone who looked remarkably like his now dead adversary. It was definitely time to be somewhere else.

Graham trusted his instincts, and his feet swiftly began bearing him east. Perhaps he could find a hiding place in the forest, someplace out of sight of the old hag he had just spied—the witch whose name, he was sure, was Hagatha—the same witch who had kidnapped the object of his quest.

The king does not know if the witch did spot him, gave unsuccessful chase, and then merely gave up. More likely he escaped before being noticed at all. In either case, he ended up in a part of the forest he had not been before.

This fact, though, was secondary to what he ran into therein: he ran into a door. The door in question was built into the living trunk of an enormous oak tree whose branches spread dozens of yards in every direction. A stovepipe poked an arm out of the bark just a little below the tree's lowest branches. Like the tree, the door was oak. It opened from the weight of Graham's rush upon it.

Now King Graham normally prefers to knock upon any door before entering; he says that you never know what you might meet upon the other side. In this case, he felt that the other side could be no worse than Hagatha. Most any other fate would be better than a witch's stewpot.

What Graham entered was an empty chamber in the hollowed-out tree, a sort of anteroom at the top of a ladder that went down through a hole in the floor. From below he heard no sounds, and the smell of food floated up into his nose. Graham waited some more, and there were still no sounds beneath him, so he began to climb down the narrow ladder.

A passageway led from the bottom of the rungs into a fragrant and cozy room. A fire blazed, working its magic on a pot of what looked like chicken soup. On a table next to the hearth lay a pair of stocking caps; one of them seemed familiar. Across the room sat an old chest, its hinges hanging loose. Graham opened the chest in order to find out something about the inhabitant of this unique home; what he found brought a revengeful smile to his lips.

First a pair of delicate diamond and sapphire earrings sparkled back at him. As he gently picked them up to admire them, he noticed a second item of jewelry, the piece the earrings had been nestled upon. It was the brooch that had been stolen from him by that "dirty, low-down, rotten, stinkin' little dwarf!"

Graham took both jewels. "No wonder that hat's familiar," he thought. "I think I'll climb back up and see if Hagatha has gone, and then I want to get away from here!"

A prankish thought bloomed in the king's mind as he started to leave. "In return for the honor of having separated me from the brooch, I think I'll separate Citizen Bandit from his supper!" With that, Graham took the pot of soup and climbed up the ladder toward the front door.

A quick peek out revealed to Graham that all was clear; there was no sign at all of the witch nor the soon-to-be-hungry dwarf. With a quick, deep breath he headed out the door and to the south, in the general direction of Grandma's house.

King Graham's plan to zigzag back to the cottage had been a sound one all along. Shortly after zipping into the woods from the tree house, he spotted the low white fence around the old woman's cottage. Pacing next to the fence was the blond girl, still distraught. Hurrying up to her, the king held out the basket.

"See, here is what you had stolen from you by the wolf. Take it back, please."

A transformation came over the girl's face, like sunlight through a thunderhead.

"Oh, thank you kind sir! Thank you! I will always be grateful for what you have done."

Romancing the Throne

The girl handed Graham the bouquet of flowers she was carrying. "Take these as a gift of appreciation from me. Please." Then she dashed off.

Glancing at the lovely flowers, still fragrant with the afternoon warmth, the king remembered that he was carrying the dwarf's soup in his other hand.

"Chicken soup! It is chicken soup, which means it has the magic to heal common ailments."

Graham set off in the direction of the cottage's front door.

Inside, the old woman looked even more pale and weak, her white curls drooping out from under her nightcap, her hands trembling slightly. Graham gave her some of the soup.

As is the way with chicken soup, the effects were immediate. Color returned to the woman's cheeks, and a weak smile crossed her face. She pointed a finger towards the floor and told the king that she had some things to give him in thanks for his kind act. They were hidden under the bed.

Dropping to the floor, Graham peered under the old woman's bed and, reaching under, pulled out a large ring with a fine blood-ruby stone. It seemed to fit Graham's hand well, and as he it put it on, the king noticed the initials "C.D." carved on the inside. There was also an oversized elegant black cloak, lined with red satin, and although it was somewhat large for Graham's frame, he decided to wear it anyway. The king always will attempt to cut a dashing figure, when the opportunity arises.

A few last pleasantries were exchanged at the end of their impromptu meal, and Graham was satisfied that the woman would recover soon. Wishing her his best, he departed, heading back to the sea.

It was the king's idea to spend the night by the ocean, lulled by the music of the waves. On the very spot of beach where he had commenced his exploration, Graham drifted off onto the sea of sleep, a speck lost in the breakers of infinity.

Mornings come with spectacle on tropic Kolyma. The gold, cream, and indigo of the dawn sky pulled the ocean back into the world from the dark dimensions of night. King Graham considered the sight and found it good.

"A perfect day to win a bride!" he proclaimed to the world as he set off. "Now I just have to find her!"

North was the direction Graham chose to move that morn, following the fluid border of sea and sand until he came back to his own footprints.

He had been traveling but a short time, climbing over and between surf-washed boulders, staying true to his course, when he spied a pointed object glinting in the grass. In truth, there were *three* points on the artifact. Rusty and corroded, it looked much like an elaborate pitchfork. Graham had come across what appeared to be a trident, symbol of the ancient gods of the sea. Ancient indeed did it appear, and out of place, as if it had been washed upon land by a thieving wave and left to be ravaged by the other deities of earth, wind, and fire. How long it had lain uncovered there he could not guess. Its age was great; it even felt ancient in his grasp. Graham carried the trident with him as he moved on; it hadn't been nailed down and would make a weapon if necessary.

The grassy dunes continued to precede the king, step by step, under the cloudless sky. They returned to sand as his march north paced on.

Graham chose as a resting place a log half-buried in the sand. He did check, but the giant driftwood was still solid, with no treasure buried in or under it. He neither felt nor played the fool while looking.

He did spend a moment picking up, admiring, and listening to the shells that dotted this particular beach. Conch, mussel, scallop, and clam—these and more lay scattered. One clam shell, larger than any of the others, seemed a special prize. Indeed it was! The king lifted it from the sand and found, lying beneath it, a piece of jewelry—a diamond and sapphire bracelet. It matched exactly the brooch, necklace, and earrings he had already collected. Graham wondered at the beauty of the assembled treasures and saw in them a royal gift—a gift fit for a queen. How they had come to be scattered about Kolyma was a mystery for which he had no answer. He played the problem in his mind as he resumed his northward journey.

73
Romancing the Throne

Mermaids are unknown in the Kingdom of Daventry, our waters are too chill perhaps, but travelers' tales of them are common, and all rave of their beauty and their beautiful songs. For this reason the king knew upon what he was gazing when he discovered her not long later. Stretched out lazily on a large rock rising out of the waves, with long green hair covering her breasts and sunlight bouncing rainbows from her scales, the mermaid seemed a vision shimmering in the rocky surf. Graham knew he must talk to her, but his shouts did not carry over the sound of the ocean. Swimming out to where she was, the king was overwhelmed by the mermaid's loveliness. Taking the bunch of flowers the blond girl had given him the day before—only slightly faded and not wilted at all, or so the king recalls—Graham presented them to her as tribute to her beauty.

A smile, for which a man might die, crossed the mermaid's face as she took the bouquet. She raised her voice in song, and a bridled seahorse suddenly swam up to the king's side. The mermaid then disappeared under the waves.

Left alone in the ocean with the creature, Graham chose to attempt to ride, instead of merely looking the gift horse in the eye—or the mouth. The moment he mounted, Graham was carried down under the waves, the horse of the sea bearing the monarch with a speed that would have taken his breath away if they had been above the waves.

I have asked King Graham how he was able to breathe whilst under the sea. His answer was, "Through my mouth. No water entered as I inhaled; air seemed to come in its place. I was under the protection of King Neptune, and that's the only explanation I can come up with." Mysterious still are the wonders of our world!

King Neptune, the monarch of all the world's seas, was waiting expectantly for Graham at the end of that watery ride. Neptune was physically magnificent, as one would expect of an ancient god. His green beard was touched with gray, like the whitecaps on waves, and his crown was made of shells and corals and other gems of the sea. He looked silently at Graham.

Our monarch, as has been often and correctly observed, is noted for the breadth of his learning and intelligence. Neptune seemed to be expecting something from him, and the king was sure he knew what it was. Taking the ancient trident from his pack, Graham presented it to the god.

A moment passed. And then another moment passed. When Neptune finally looked at Graham again, it was with gratitude. He waved the trident, and a giant clam that was balanced next to the god's throne opened. Inside lay a brilliant gold key.

Neptune gestured to the key, indicating that Graham should take it. At the same time he handed our monarch a bottle with what looked like a piece of cloth inside. Graham took both. The second wave of Neptune's trident was a gesture of dismissal. The king knew it was not wise to spend much time around gods, even friendly ones. He turned the seahorse away and was carried back to shore.

The king sat for a moment on the sand, letting the sun dry him, pondering all that had just befallen him. He took the piece of cloth from inside the gift bottle. It appeared to be just a plain piece of essentially colorless cloth with no inscriptions, pictures, or writing. He carefully put it away anyway. Turning the gold key over and over in his hand, he was reminded of the message carved into the magic door and how it described making a splash. Chuckling, Graham headed back to the rickety bridge.

Lightfooted, the king continued north, and it was a journey of not undue length that brought him to the site of his former camp. Heading east ran the familiar road past Grandma's house and the monastery. This he followed, the key weighing heavy in his hand, anxious to be used.

The bridge, if anything, looked less stable than when he had crossed it the second time. But cross it again Graham did; he knew he had no other choice.

The door, if anything, looked the same, taunting him to open it.

The key fit.

Graham smiled anxiously as he unlocked the magic door. What would the other side hold?

Romancing the Throne

Another door, another inscription, that is what. Graham had resigned himself to the possibility, so he read the words there and seared them into his memory: "Whosoever chooses to seek the key for this door should set their sights high." Graham lifted his eyes to the heavens and wondered how he was going to get there.

Mountains in the eastern part of Kolyma are unscalable, Graham soon discovered. So steep were they that all climbing was impossible. After he had lightly scooted back across the bridge, he was sure that it had sagged some more beneath his weight. He prayed it would hold for his next crossing.

King Graham chose to explore to the south, venturing past the little lake where he had previously stopped to cool himself and where he had discovered the jeweled brooch. The monastery bell continued its peaceful tolling, inviting all to prayer and succor, and the lake still invited a cooling dalliance. As he traveled past these familiar sights, however, the air began wavering and dancing before him. A fairy, a tiny one, dissolved into the sky and began sprinkling fairy dust in his direction.

"Good King Graham, I am here to help you. I give you a protective spell against evil, but it lasts for only a short time. Goodbye."

The fairy was gone as quickly as she had appeared.

Good King Graham had had experience with fairies before; his fairy godmother had dusted him the same way once in Daventry. He had learned four things from the experience: one, the spells lived up to their reputation for protection; two, they lasted a moderate while, but not long; three, they had a tendency to be cast *after* he really needed them; and four, fairy dust made him sneeze.

On the other hand, the king realized, maybe this spell *hadn't* been cast after his need for it had vanished. Sure he'd been mugged by the thieving dwarf and he had escaped from Hagatha, but the protection should last long enough for him to get close to the hag—if he could locate her or her den again. If he could do that, he might be able to find another key.

The king, of course, will always rationalize. "Hey! Maybe I'll just stroll over and peek in on a witch. Maybe she'll even invite me for dinner." That is how he thinks. Someday he is going to rationalize himself directly into somebody's cook-pot as the main course. I hope not.

Having decided to find the witch, Graham hiked back to the bridge. "I saw her just past the dwarf's hideout," he remembered. "That should be west of here. Let's go!" And talking to himself, as is his wont, the king reentered the dire forest.

A faint but discernible path slowly took form, leading away from the bridge in the direction Graham headed. Normally he would have welcomed a path of any kind through woods, but this one disquieted him, making him think of a string leading a cat into an ogre's cooking pot. Once he spotted the dwarf skulking in the distance, but he was easily able to avoid his notice. Perhaps it was the spell's protection.

Again Graham noticed the terrain opening out into rocky hillocks. It was right there that he had come across the crone before. The king shrugged his shoulders, looked back over them, and pressed on. What he arrived at shortly made him wonder about the wisdom of his coming.

Skulls were arrayed around a clearing in front of what appeared to be the entrance to a cave. Human skulls. Not attached to necks, attached to the tops of stakes. From within the cave came the unmistakable aroma of witch cuisine, ghastly to smell and even more ghastly to contemplate.

Inside, the odor hung so heavy as to stop one's breathing. The lack of sound from within the cave had convinced Graham that it was relatively safe to enter. His decision was sound, but it was difficult to keep from gagging. Most of the stench originated from a black iron cauldron bubbling on top of a wood fire. Floating in the stew pot were pieces of what once had been flesh—human flesh from the evidence of the limbs to which the meat now barely hung. Lined around the floor, and above, were scores more human skulls. Piles of human refuse littered the darker corners. The entire scene screamed death and decay—all except the incongruous song of a nightingale.

77
Romancing the Throne

Normally he would have welcomed a path of any kind through woods, but this one disquieted him, making him think of a string leading a cat into an ogre's cooking pot

Perhaps one full shaft of sunlight penetrated the shadows, and it was spending this moment lingering on a bird. The nightingale was enclosed within an ornate gilded cage and was swinging merrily on a perch. As Graham approached closer, the bird burst into a song of joy.

The king could not bear to leave such a creature of life behind when he departed Hagatha's charnel house. He placed the piece of cloth he had been given by Neptune over the cage so that the bird's happy song would not betray them to the witch. Then he grabbed the cage and carried it out with him into the sunlight.

The witch was waiting when he got outside.

She stood not ten feet away, staring at the cave as if she suspected intruders. Graham had walked out directly in her view, but she acted as if he and the bird, were not there.

"Thank you, little fairy!" breathed the king soundlessly. The nightingale, covered, cheeped not a sound.

Not daring to be near Hagatha a moment longer lest the spell wear off, the bird chirp, or the crone blunder into him, Graham turned noiselessly north. He kept moving as fast as he dared until the witch was left well out of sight or hearing.

King Graham paused only briefly on the western shore of the small lake. It appeared to be the same one near which he had discovered the necklace whilst mocking himself. This was no time for more searching, he realized; the time was for putting miles between himself and Hagatha. His wind returned, and immediately he continued his escape north, back into the forest.

After an hour or so of quick stepping, the track seemed to end in a dense grove. Progress was still possible in the direction he was heading, but the trees did begin to open somewhat to the east, and Graham thought he saw a faint splash of sunlight on water there.

Against one of the trees in the grove leaned a short, pointed piece of wood. Examining it, Graham saw that it appeared to be an ordinary tent stake, perhaps left behind by a traveler who had rested a night there. With a shrug,

Romancing the Throne

the king put the stake into his pack, readjusted its weight, and started moving downhill, east to the water.

Swimming is one of the king's passions, and he indulges in it often for sport, exercise, and relaxation. Lakes, especially, he favors with their deep, still waters warmed by the sun.

It took no genius, though, to observe that there was something wrong with the lake on whose edge he was standing. Festering incrustations fouled its banks, dead trees and brush ringed its shore, and it smelled only slightly less foul than Hagatha's cave. Sick green mists stuck thickly to its surface. Graham guessed the water was poisoned, or worse.

"I think I'll just pass on a dip this time," he mused.

Stopping seemed pointless, so he began following the shoreline to the south, looking for a way around. A dirt path gave him direction.

The mists cleared for awhile, and the path led Graham around to the southern tip of the stagnant waters, a level spot that looked north upon a small island in the lake's center. Two ghostly towers groped out of a decaying castle that sat atop the island. Could this be the kidnapped maiden's prison? There seemed no boat near that might take him across for a close look, so the king moved on, intending to return and explore this particular mystery further. The lakeshore had turned north, and he continued to follow it.

Follow it he did. North, north, and further north he trekked. There appeared no way across to the mysterious island. What did appear, though, was a sorcerer looking for trouble.

The king was peering across the lake when the short, robed man wearing a pointed magician's guild hat appeared in the corner of his eye. For a moment Graham thought it might be the same mage who had temporarily turned him to stone in Daventry the year before. He wanted no part of more prestidigenous pranks.

Evidently, though, the fairy's dust still clung to the king. The sorcerer paid no notice to Graham, who watched the stubby man sniff the air and snort in disgust. Disappearing in a puff of smoke, the sorcerer left Graham alone.

When the shore of the poisoned lake began to turn back to the west, Graham could see that there was nothing to be gained by following it any longer. He could also see a clear, pure-water lake just to the east. Maybe there he could rest a bit and clean himself.

Combining business with pleasure, the king explored this lake to its southern shore. He viewed its calming waters from beneath a tree and saw that it was the lake he had stopped at before, just to the south of the monastery. His view took in the rock where he had discovered the sapphire brooch.

"At least I know where I am now!"

With that thought, he took his pleasure of the lake.

The antique store in the glen was, in its own way, as incongruous as a birdcage in a witch's den. It stood by itself in a clearing just south of the swimming lake. No other buildings could be seen anywhere. The king walked up the steps to the small porch and saw a sign in the window. It read "OPEN," so he walked on in the door. Inside, old pieces of furniture, ancient brazen pots, and knickknacks of all kinds were displayed for sale. A gray-haired woman sat knitting and rocking behind a counter on the far side of the room.

"I have been closed until just now. What can I do for you?" she asked cheerily as Graham entered. "Would you like to look around, or do you have something you wish to sell?"

The king was happy for a chance to be rid of the bird and its cage. He had been carrying it as a gift for the old woman he only knew as "Grandma," as much to give the nightingale a safe home as anything else. Removing the cloth with which he had covered it, Graham offered it now to this woman.

The result of the offer startled the king.

"My precious!" declared the woman. Racing around the counter, she snatched up a brass lamp from its display and handed it to him. Taking the cage and cooing to the singing bird, she showed Graham out.

"Take this," she told him, as she locked the store. "It might help you in your quest!"

Romancing the Throne

With those words, she pulled down the shades and disappeared into the interior of the building. Graham was left standing outside with a lamp in his hand and a question on his lips.

"What do I do now?"

Rubbing tarnish off of the oil lamp with his sleeve was what brought the Djinn. Shirtless and turbaned, with nothing but smoke below the waist, he poofed out of the lamp's spout and hovered in front of my king.
"Master, I have a gift for you. A flying carpet!" the high-pitched voice intoned. Poof! It vanished back into the lamp.
"Not bad!" exclaimed Graham as he looked at a fringed Persian rug.
"A magic carpet, eh? Let's see if I can get the genie to come back." Rub. Squeak. Rub. Two more times did Graham rub the magic lamp, and two more times did the Djinn appear bearing gifts. And with the third disappearance of the magical messenger, the lamp itself poofed into nothingness.
Graham looked at the treasures bestowed upon him: the carpet; a short, sharp sword with a snake carved in the handle; and a leather bridle, adorned with silver. Putting the sword into his belt and draping the bridle over it, the king sat down to see if the carpet would really fly.

It did.
All the king had to do was sit on the magic carpet and it flew. As a method of aerial movement, it much surpassed hanging from the claws of a condor. The king also tells me that his journey was smoother, to the soothing relief of his stomach.
The rug soared to the highest peaks of Kolyma, the very mountains he had unsuccessfully attempted to climb. As he looked over that tropical land from the small mesa where he had landed, Graham imagined he could see to the ends of the earth. Well perhaps not that far, but the lakes and trees were spread out below him like the woven pattern on a carpet. This time the obvious comparison had not escaped him.

Not far from where he had landed, he came to a narrow passage that focused between a pair of steep cliffs. A serpent at least ten feet in length sat there coiled, hissing warning and ready to strike, as if guarding the path.

"Sssssstaaaayyy awaaaaayyyy, sssssst...," it seemed to be saying.

Graham knew that he must pass the serpent, although what was beyond he knew not. He recalled that the sword he had been given had the image of a snake engraved upon it. That weapon, he decided, should rid him of the menace.

Our king is amongst the most agile of people, and his sureness of both hand and foot have preserved him in several near-fatal situations. As a swordsman he is more the fencer than the hack-and-slash type who triumphs through brute strength. To dispatch the snake would take only a flick of his wrist, a flick of a moment.

Of course, he had forgotten about the bridle he stupidly had draped over the sword's hilt. It is through mistakes just as that that dynasties change. But not this time.

With one swift motion King Graham made to grab the hilt and swing the blade through the air, so to slice the head from the serpent's body. His hand grabbed the bridle's silver bit instead, and still thinking he held a sword, he flicked it through the air. Graham's hand opened in its surprise, and in result, he threw the bridle at the snake by mistake. But instead of the serpent slaying our monarch with its own quick kiss, the bridle magically transformed the serpent into a winged horse.

Silver white the horse was, the reins of the leather bridle now about its neck. Pawing the ground and bobbing its head, it neighed to Graham, "Thank you, kind sir, for saving me. To repay you I will give you a sugar cube to guard you against poison brambles." With that the silver steed flew away.

Still surprised even to be alive after his blunder, the king could only grasp the gift and watch the horse wing away.

"People sure do come and go quickly around here, don't they?"

Romancing the Throne

The rest was simple. The snake had been set to guard a small, damp cave. Within it lay a second golden key. Graham squeezed it in his hand purposefully, now knowing what to do next.

"Now back to the door. It's time to see just what this unlocks."

With that he sat on the carpet and flew away.

King Graham would have liked the carpet to fly him to the floating door, but this was not to be. Soon our monarch found himself back on solid earth, standing next to the closed antique store. Moreover, the carpet now refused to fly again.

Disappointed, the king turned in the direction of the sagging bridge and began his long trek north.

"Feet," he mumbled aloud, "don't fail me now!"

Door number two opened to reveal door number three, which also had a message carved into it: "Whosoever chooses to seek the last key must have a stout heart!"

"At least it says the next key is the last," reflected the king. "I'm sure that the castle in the lake holds the key to that key. I didn't say that, did I?"

I know the king too well. He did.

Ghouls in shrouds are not comforting sights. It was such a figure, though, that King Graham approached as he arrived on the south shore of the poisoned lake—shrouded, silent, waiting.

He had traveled north from the bridge until his progress was barred by a large, picturesque lake. From there, he had estimated, it was a short jog west to his destination. The king mused that the pretty sight might be his last look at beauty for some time.

Those disquieting thoughts were confirmed the instant he saw the skeletal figure lurking silently within the boat. Hands like claws gripped a long pole; silence, like death, gripped the dusk.

Graham approached the grim boatman to beg for passage. Neither movement nor sound stirred the apparition's frame. Graham entered the rotting boat anyway; perhaps the shade would transport all who approached. As he did so, the king thought he noticed a spark of recognition flash through the boatman's eyes, like the will o' the wisps that sometimes flash from tomb to tomb. Perhaps his nerves were just overexcited. Or perhaps he had been mistaken for someone else—a someone else who also wore a large black cape and ruby ring.

Still and silent, the shrouded figure moved the boat into darkness, stopping finally at the island's brambled shore. Graham carefully left the boat, but the apparition remained, never moving, never breathing.

Thorns and brambles overgrew the dirt path that led up to the castle. An unhealthy glaze seemed to drip from the thorns, and Graham took a moment to find the sugar cube the winged horse had given him. The king popped the cube into his mouth, eating it before beginning to inch his way between the baneful branches. A tingle of magic shivered down his spine.

It wasn't a long path, just a scratchy one to the castle door. As he reached the entry, graveyard wails assaulted the king from all sides. Several ghosts floated out of the sky, threatening in their approach. Guards they were to the dreadful denizen who inhabited the castle, but they allowed Graham free passage, much as the phantom boatman did, as if they, too, believed he belonged in the castle.

The thought did little to put Graham's mind at rest. Wrapping the large black cloak more tightly around him and rubbing the ring for good luck, he took his first steps into the haunted keep.

Although oil lamps blazed in the entrance hall, the castle was chill; it felt as if no one *lived* there. Graham took the passage to his left, through a cobwebbed stone archway, to a narrow staircase winding its spiral way up a tower into gloom. One torch halfway up was the only illumination for his slow ascent. He arrived at last at a vacant bedroom that overlooked the foul lake. This, too, seemed unlived-in, musty with the smell of mildew and

Romancing the Throne

disuse. A bare cot, sagging and unslept-in, and a nicked dresser were the sole, dismal furnishings. A brief search revealed a candle in one of the dresser drawers, but nothing else of any interest cluttered the tower room.

The way down was as perilous as the climb up. Graham took each step carefully, and when he came to the one burning torch, he used it to light the candle he was carrying. The torch refused to come off the wall, but the candle's added light made the rest of the trip seem safer than before.

Passing back through the entrance hall and through a second stone archway, the king entered a large, draft-filled dining hall. A massive carved table dominated the room. One place was set on that table, and a partially eaten ham sat lonely on its platter, inches above a black sea of foraging ants. Its wave had not yet touched the food, and Graham rescued the ham for his own personal consumption later.

"A king does not live by luck alone," he told himself, well aware that he might need more than food before he left the creepy castle.

Another stone arch seemed to plunge down into the castle's bowels, but Graham chose to first explore through the curtained doorway that also led out of the room.

It led to yet another damp stone circular stairway, twisting up into the castle's second tower. The room he found at the top of the stairs was even more barren than the cold bedroom. Here, only an old chest filled the space. It was locked and too heavy for the king to move, so he returned downstairs and entered the archway leading into the black depths.

In these days of oil lamps, we often take the lowly tallow candle for granted. Graham became aware of this fact as he slowly made his way down the long, steep, slick stairs. Any false step would have plunged our king to his sure death. That candle was all the illumination he had. It gave both scant light and comfort, but it did give some of both. At the edges of the light, the king caught glimpses of bats and rats hurrying on their nameless errands. From within the darkness came sounds that he did not wish to identify, coupled with the stenches of blood and death.

At the bottom of the long descent was a stone room. The candle flickered on the faint image of a doorway there, and Graham's nose reported that it was from there the charnel odor originated.

There came no sound at all from within; even the vermin seemed to shun that room. Breathing shallowly, the king peeked inside, paused, and then entered.

An ornate coffin lay on a stone bier. Closed it was, although the foul aroma passed from it as if there were no barrier at all. Carved upon the lid were the initials "C.D." As much as it repulsed him, King Graham knew he must open the lid.

Count Dracula, lord of the vampyres, is well known in the legends of Daventry, legends brought by some of our folk from the Other World. Never has it been mentioned, however, that the Prince of the Night had, himself, *withdrawn* here. But the creature revealed when Graham finally did open the lid of the dungeon sepulcher, the dead-white complexion and life-blood red lips, the tips of his stained fangs reflecting the sputtering flame, the initials carved in the lid—the same as the initials in the ruby ring he was wearing—all together whispered the name "Dracula" to the king.

Graham wasted no time in fright; he knew he must rid the world of the infernal fiend, and he must do it before his candle extinguished. King Graham killed Count Dracula there again, although how can one be truly sure the undead will remain so? The tent stake, driven through the thing's still heart by the mallet Graham had found, turned the creature in the coffin to a pile of dust. The dust still stank.

Within the dust Graham saw a key, silver it seemed, resting on a background of red satin. He took it.

A red satin pillow was the only other thing left within the coffin, and beneath it Graham found yet another key, this one gold, in all particulars exactly like the other keys to the magic doorway!

Graham lingered in the crypt for less time than it takes to tell the tale. Swiftly he moved out, up the stone stairs, lest his failing light die before he left the darksome depths.

Romancing the Throne

The flame expired as he reached the ant-covered table, but by then the castle's torches lent enough light to see. The king returned to the chest in the bare room in the second tower. Knowing that was where the silver key fitted, he unlocked the chest and, when he lifted its lid, was dazzled by the sight of another piece of jewelry. This time it was a diamond and sapphire tiara, its brilliance destined for a queen!

With the third gold key in his hand, King Graham was sure he would soon be with the maiden he wished to be that queen.

"If I can first make it past Hagatha, sorcerers, mad dwarves, decaying bridges, and who knows what else!"

Suffice it to say, the king did safely return to the floating doorway. For the seventh time he crossed the swaying span and, looking at it from the security of solid earth, was sure neither he nor it would survive an eighth trip.

We will never know if the king's suspicion was correct, for when he unlocked the third door, it opened to reveal not another door, but what looked like another world. He left the bridge and Kolyma behind when he stepped through it.

Such a world! To see such marvels myself would be worth most any price!

Astonishing pink sky reached down to meet the cobalt blue beach. A tempest sea raged rainbow colors, changing with the waves. Unclimbable rock-faced cliffs towered above and below the narrow strand. A lavender waterfall plummeted over them to reach unswimmable waters.

The doorway had disappeared as soon as the king stepped out, and his quick survey had emphatically confirmed that he was between the rocks and a hard place. He appeared to be stranded.

Near the waterfall, though, lay abandoned what looked like a fishing net, although the material was as unusual as the sky's color. Graham considered the net and his predicament for a while, then cast the net into the sea. Several times he did this, hoping to catch a flying fish or seahorse, or perhaps a mermaid to help him on his way. What he did finally net was none of the above. Oh, no!

The fish was as golden as treasure, and it flopped upon the blue beach gasping for breath. No words did it speak; its beautiful form writhed to and fro in agony. Unable to let the creature suffer more, the king mercifully picked it up and threw it back into the sea.

"Perhaps I'll have better luck next time," he told the waves.

But before he could pick up the net again, the wondrous fish lifted itself back out of the water and spoke to Graham!

"Kind sir! In return for saving my life, I shall give you a ride across the waters."

With little to lose by trusting the fish, King Graham jumped into the rainbow sea to be carried to another shore.

An island awaited King Graham at the other end, with more blue beaches, yellow earth, and oversized vegetation that was grotesque in its appearance.

"Curiouser and curiouser!" he breathed, and then headed inland in search of further marvels.

Inland, in this case, was east of where the fish had flung him. He had walked but moments from the beach when his eyes came across something metallic on the ground, just steps away from a miniscule lagoon. Picking it up, the king found it to be an amulet, tarnished, but with one word etched in its back. The word was "HOME."

"Just where I'd like to be right now," he thought. "But, there is a maiden to be found and her hand to be won. Then I'll work on getting us back to Daventry." With that said, he looked to the south and saw the Crystal Tower.

Creamy quartz, its blocks reflected the strange sunlight in rainbow waves. Tall it was, reaching thirty feet or more above the enchanted island. Near its peak a tiny window opened, and from it a delicate hand waved.

"Help me! Please, help me. I'm a prisoner here. Will you please free me? Help! The door is unlocked. Quickly before Hagatha returns."

Romancing the Throne

The voice, although desperate and pleading, was like melody to the king's ears. In his now heated brain, that melody became a martial tune impelling him toward the tower door.

Unlocked it was, the witch perhaps trusting the isle's remote and peculiar location as prison enough for the kidnapped princess.

It could be no other but the maiden; the king had passed the three doors and come to the Crystal Tower. The object of his quest was at the top of the the stairs.

Love—people just love to capitalize Love, for reasons that are beyond my understanding. I have often been told by the king, and others, that Love conquers all. Perhaps it does, and it did this time, but Love can turn the most composed and serene person into a sweating fool. Our king is neither.

Slimed and narrow, the stairs caused our excited monarch to slip and fall several times as he began his mad dash up. Finally his overworked emotions slowed enough for him to return to his senses. With more care this time he made his progress to the tower's top.

The lion there looked hungry. It also looked large. And it was looking at King Graham as if it were looking at supper.

"Maybe it just wants to be fed," the king reasoned in a moment of gargantuan understatement.

"Maybe he'll let me by if I give him something other than me to eat."

The king prefers never to kill, although he has. The sword he carried could very easily have dispatched the beast, he knew, but he chose a kinder alternative.

The ham had been with him since the vampyre's castle. Events had carried along so quickly that the king had had no time to stop, much less eat. He gave the food to the lion, knowing that if it did not distract the big cat or satisfy its hunger, he could always strike with the sword.

Lions snore; even I had never known that until the king told me.

Gratefully, the lion had taken the savory ham and, having devoured it and washed himself daintily, in the manner of the king of beasts, curled himself into sleep. At last Graham was able to step by the contented guardian and unlock the door to his heart's delight.

I shall spare you the more lurid details of the meeting, although the king raved on to me about it for what seemed hours, convinced, I think, that he and Valanice are the world's first lovers.

He looked at her. She looked at him. They talked. They sighed. They embraced. They kissed. Boring, isn't it?

In the end Valanice asked Graham if he would take her, and where? The king whispered, "Home."

With that word, the amulet transported the blissful couple away from the tower.

The tale of how King Graham found and won Queen Valanice is now finished, just as their marriage is beginning.

Perhaps now the king's adventuring days are over, except for that of the sweetest quest—the quest for an heir. It is an exploration that he and his queen embark on together. Gladly.

May their marriage prosper and may they have many fine children, strong and good.

May the Kingdom of Daventry prosper along with the royal family, it too growing strong and good.

Long live King Graham!
Long live Queen Valanice!
Long live King Graham and Queen Valanice of Daventry!

5

A Magical Primer

*By Alexander of Daventry
(Gwydion of Llewdor)*

Magic and magical encounters are part of the very fabric of our universe. Without it Daventry itself would not be, could not be. It was to preserve Magic, mystique, wonder, and enchantment—the nonrational aspects of existence—that Daventry *withdrew* from the greater multiverse. Indeed, it was only through Magic itself that we were even able to *withdraw*. And it is only through the continued practice and use of the arcane arts that we are able to preserve and protect our very being. From the simplest charms and trivial spells, the plucking of a four-leafed clover or the knocking of wood, to the cosmos shattering invocations of the most fearsome of paradimensional deities, Magic is not just part but the very fabric of our reality.

What is Magic? Pick a grain of sand from the palm-kissed beaches of Kolyma and pray that it answers the question. Then query the next grain, then the next, again the next, and when all the sand on all the beaches in all the realms of Daventry have answered you with their different answers then know that there are as many different explanations as there are "Once in a lifetime offers" in the Other World. In that light, here is *my* explanation.

Magic is that which actually binds the universe together. It encompasses not just the connections all things have with each other, but includes the aether through which these relationships flow. Magic is the essence, belief is the glue; all is connected each to the other. These connections may not always be clear to the mundane senses of sight, smell, and the like, but that does not mean they are less real. Cause and effect, action and interaction—all occur through the correspondences of nature. In conjunction with the elements of air, fire, earth, and water, all act to produce a desired result. The great principles are "As above, so below," and "Nothing is as it appears." The minute is attached to the mighty. The flame of the candle and the flame of love are one, and they too are one with the flame of life. We can learn the principles of these connections and how they are joined together. Then, by use of the proper words or actions or magical tools, the relationships implicit in the aether are made explicit. Together the essence, the elements, and the principle both create and control our reality.

A Magical Primer

It is through the art of Magic that we know, understand, and manipulate these connections. Through the studies of the practitioners of the magic arts—the wizards, witches, warlocks, sorcerers, seers, alchemists, necromancers, mages, and others—these relationships have been traced and to some degree understood. It must be admitted that these practitioners do come in the flavors of good and evil, and the shades of black and white. They also are known to follow both the Left-Hand as well as the Right-Hand paths. However it is through their use of the various magics that Daventry continues to exist at all. Evil follows good as night follows day and goats follow carrots. We suspect if the Magic were to go away, so would Daventry. To be as if we never were—that would be the greatest of evils.

With this said, let us concentrate on matters of a more practical nature. The practice of Magic is both an art and a craft. To practice Magic at all is to practice it exactly and correctly. It is perhaps too facile to say there are really only two kinds of magicians: magicians and dead magicians. However, it takes little more than a casual stroll through any of the realms to find odd statuary, pillars of salt, mounds of dust, or half-human half-insect abominations that were once users of the arcane arts who made a simple mistake, ones who did not follow their craft to the last letter. If my personal nemesis, the wizard Manannan, taught me anything between punishments during my years of ignorant captivity, it was to "follow the instructions exactly, boy!" At the time I thought he merely meant how many carrots, potatoes, and how much salt he preferred in his stew. It was only during the last part of my servitude, after I had stumbled upon Manannan's secret laboratory and began studying his hidden grimoire, his spell book, that the true import of his words became evident. For the art of Magic to work, the craft of Magic must be carried out with no substitutions, exceptions, or shortcuts. Nothing must be taken for granted and no factors may be fudged. On that fateful day in the wizard's laboratory it could very easily have been myself that was turned into a fluffy furry. I still tremble when I recall the awesome forces and formulae that I manipulated in that dungeon. If I were any less ignorant, I would have fled from that place in terror and gladly accepted whatever fate the evil wizard planned for me. As it turned out, I'm glad I didn't.

Now, because the craft must be practiced with concentration and precision, it is in the obvious best interests of the individual wizards and their ilk to record in some manner the proper route to the completion of the various mystical processes. To this end there arose over the eons a fabulous library of magical books—books that collected and explicated the great spells and conjurations devised and duplicated throughout the ages by the greatest of sorcerers. As a result, many general provisioners stock on their shelves a myriad of manuscript titles covering all areas of the mystical arts, snug against vials of generic toad spittle, eye of newt, beetle juice, and the like. Today hobbyists, apprentices, and even graduates of the various academies of Magic can find all they need to know and all their basic supplies in virtually any town.

However, so powerful are the contents of other certain volumes that they have remained secret even to the majority of serious magicians. These books themselves are often magical in their own right and are so rare that their very existence is doubted by the very few who have even heard of them in whispered fable. Indeed some, such as the near-legendary *Al Azif,* more commonly known as the *Necronomicon,* penned by the mad Arab Abdul Alhazred, contains knowledge so terrible that a mere glance at the illustrations and illuminations in the text drives many to madness. Perhaps it is just as well that few, if any, copies of such works as the *Necronomicon, The Key of Solomon, The Book of Dyzan, The Principia Discordia,* and *The Book of the Damned* remain, or even exist at all. The *Good Housekeeper's Book of Common Spells and Potions, A Field Guide to Enchanted Gems and Minerals, Understanding the Undead,* and *Housebreaking Dragons in 7 Days* are all inexpensive guides that have been on the bestseller charts for ages. They cover more magic than most folk will ever need and carry no possibility of apocalyptic catastrophe.

A Magical Primer

The Sorcery of Old was once considered one of the lost and legendary books of terrible power. Within its gold trimmed covers of leather ghastly to the touch were said to be compiled many old and powerful spells. It was whispered that many of these formulae were written in languages unknown since before the ascent of humanity. These stories have turned out to be true, with one exception. *The Sorcery of Old* is neither lost nor legend. In my fright I made scant note of it at the time, and it has only been since I have made sufficient progress in my own studies that I have come to fully realize just what that spell book was in the secret room beneath Manannan's study. The book was obviously old, the pages brittle to my shakey touch. The ink may have been made of blood and was so faint upon the yellow pages that it could scarcely be read. Of the scant pages legible in that copy of *The Sorcery of Old* most were written in symbols and languages that still have not been deciphered. A few pages, though, were scribed in my own tongue, and because of that I was able to escape the clutches of my captor, rid Llewdor of his tender little mercies, and after perils, pirates, and predicaments of every kind, return to the family, home, and kingdom I had never known.

Here then are transcriptions of the spells I found in *The Sorcery of Old*. I publish them for inclusion in the court chronicles and for the general knowledge of all who inhabit Daventry. Used properly they will not shake the cosmos and should prove as useful for others as they did for me. As with all Magic, use these spells wisely. Again, note well: It cannot be stated too often that the practice of the craft of Magic demands precision, exactitude, concentration, and the negation of distraction. Compose yourself, even if you are rushed. Do what is necessary to ensure your focus is upon the task at hand, lest a mispelled step or an unclear word becomes your final mistake. Often was I forced to deliver the swift boot to an underfoot cat at a critical moment. It was no act of needless cruelty, but necessary for my own survival. Mark my words: Once you have opened a book of Magic to the proper page, do naught else but that which is prescribed. There are some things that are worse than death!

Fragments from *The Sorcery of Old*
(Author Unknown)

(Note: To use the spells contained herein, have the proper ingredients and tools at hand, open the book to the desired page number, and follow the directions to the absolute letter. You might note that some of the spells have directions and information enclosed in parentheses. Let me clarify this matter. There has been a convention used by the more human-like authors of magical volumes throughout the ages to enclose comments, observations, and certain intermediate steps in parentheses. Anything so enclosed helps in the proper working of the spell, but is not essential to the proper casting of same. If the proper ingredients are used, and in their proper order, and if the proper directions are used, and in their proper order, the effects enclosed therein will happen. The rest is technique and equipment that the caster is assumed to possess. This is perhaps the only place in the practice of sorcery where rigid adherence to detail might be relaxed. This can most correctly be termed the "fudge factor." Magic making and candy making have much in common when it comes to following exact directions, although a flawed batch of fudge seldom turns its maker into an insect or a piece of statuary! I considered not even transcribing this information, but included it in the interest of historic and academic completeness.)

Page XXV *Transforming Another into a Cat*

Obtain the Following Ingredients:

1/2 cup of mandrake root powder

1 small ball of cat hair

2 spoonfuls of fish oil

A Magic Wand

To Prepare the Spell:

1. Put mandrake root powder in a bowl
2. Put the cat hair in the bowl
3. Put two spoons of fish oil in bowl
4. Stir the mixture with a spoon (dough will be oily)
5. Put the dough on the table
6. Pat the dough into a cookie (let harden on table)
7. Recite this verse:
   Mandrake root and hair of cat
   Mix oil of fish and give a pat
   A feline from the one who eats
   This appetizing magic treat
8. Wave the Magic Wand

(Note: The cookie thus created will turn whomsoever eats it into a feline (felis domesticus) forever; however, this is a difficult assertion to prove. No records have ever been discovered, though, indicating the spell has ever worn off. It should also be noted that adepts familiar with the spell can easily recognize the cat cookie. For this reason mages disguise the cookie in some way or crumble it into some other food when planning to use it on a rival sorcerer. The wizard Manannan did just this to a former rival and then kept her as a household pet for both his amusement and the eradication of vermin. It can be assumed that the victim was not amused.)

Page VII *Teleportation at Random*

Obtain the Following Ingredients:

1 spoonful of salt grains

1 sprig of dried mistletoe

1 smooth rounded stone of unusual color

A Magic Wand

To Prepare the Spell:

1. Grind a spoon of salt in a mortar (with a pestle)
2. Grind the mistletoe in the mortar
3. Rub the stone in the mixture
4. Kiss the stone
5. Recite this verse:
   With this kiss, I thee impart,
   Power most dear to my heart.
   Take me now from this place hither,
   To another place far thither.
6. Wave the Magic Wand

To cast this spell: Rub the stone. In a blink you will disappear from where you are and appear in another place. This spell may be used as often as one wishes provided the stone is in your possession.

(Note: This is a powerful and most useful spell. It has been used to avoid danger and peril, and legend claims that it has been used on occasion in the exploration of unknown lands. Be warned, however: that which snatches away from one predicament can just as well deposit into another. The spell has been known to leave one where they started. There is one fable that talks about a poor bumpkin who came into possession of such a magic stone. Unprepared to face the dangers of the wilder parts of the world, he rubbed the stone at will, poofing himself from place to place in search of wine, women, and easy gold. The purveyors of luck were with him for the first few times or so, and the stupid boy, whose name was Bob Jack, flitted from town to beach, across mountains and over the seas. Then the purveyors of luck seemed to say "All right Bob Jack, you've won a few; now it's time to lose a few!" When he rubbed again, instead of vista, panorama, or treasure, Bob Jack was faced with a hungry lion. Quickly he rubbed the stone again. Oops, he was in a magician's chamber and the mage looked not too delighted with the intrusion. Rub again quick, Bob Jack. This time, up a roaring stream without a paddle. Thus it went. Having used up his good luck, he used up his bad luck until he had no luck left at all, and he perished. The moral of the fable is: "Even when you rub things the right way, soon you'll rub them the wrong way, and if you do that too often, you'll eventually get rubbed out.")

A Magical Primer

Page II *Understanding the Language of Creatures*

Obtain the Following Ingredients:

1 small feather from a bird

1 tuft of fur from any animal

1 dried reptile skin

1 rounded spoonful of powdered fish bone

1 thimbleful of dew

A Magic Wand

To Prepare the Spell:

1. Put the small feather in a bowl
2. Put the fur in the bowl
3. Put the reptile skin in the bowl
4. Add a spoonful of powdered fish bone
5. Put a thimbleful of dew in the bowl
6. Mix with hands (mixture will now be doughy)
7. Separate mixture into two pieces
8. Put dough pieces into your ears
9. Recite this verse:
   Feather of fowl and bone of fish,
   Molded together in this dish,
   Give me wisdom to understand
   Creatures of air, sea and land

10. Wave the Magic Wand

(Note: Creatures see and hear much in this world, and they understand more than we give them credit for. Knowledge may be gained by one who keeps ears and mind open. Of course you also hear a lot about worms and nuts and the everyday life of mice. As you may have guessed, spells have both good and annoying aspects; this one won't let you talk back so you can't tell those chattering chickens to shut up.)

Page IV *Flying Like an Eagle or a Fly*

Obtain the Following Ingredients:

1 tail feather from any eagle (to become an eagle)

1 pair of fly wings (to become a fly)

1 pinch of saffron

Rose petal essence

A Magic Wand

To Prepare the Spell:

1. Put a pinch of saffron in essence
2. Recite this verse:
   *Oh winged spirits, set me free
   Of earthly bindings, just like thee.
   In this essence, behold the might
   To grant the precious gift of flight.*
3. Wave the Magic Wand

To become an eagle: Dip the eagle feather in the essence
To become a fly: Dip the fly wings in the essence

You can cast this spell as long as you have some of the essence left. You should get at least two, possibly more, uses out of a single batch.

To return to your own form before the spell wears off recite this verse
Eagle begone! Myself, return!
   or
Fly, begone! Myself, return!

(Note: I have always wondered why anyone would want to become a fly, although people have done so in both Daventry and the Other World. You could use the fly spell to spy on others, literally becoming a fly on the wall, but while you might not be spotted, you might get swatted or caught by a spider. Eagles have beaks, talons, and the ability to swoop down on prey. Swooping in sunlight or soaring on a thermal, the eagle's appearance is seldom greeted with revulsion. Eagles almost never sit on windows, walls, or drinking cups, so the literature contains no reports of them being smashed to a pulp by a casual swipe, or of being prey for arachnids—giant spiders.)

Page CLXIX *Becoming Invisible*

Obtain the Following Ingredients:

1 jar of lard

1 cactus

1 spoonful of cactus juice

2 drops of toad spittle

A Magic Wand

To Prepare the Spell:

1. Cut the cactus with a knife
2. Squeeze the cactus juice on spoon
3. Put the cactus juice in a bowl
4. Put the lard in the bowl
5. Add two drops of toad spittle
6. Stir the mixture with a spoon
7. Recite this verse:
   Cactus plant and horny toad
   I now start down a dangerous road
   Combine with fire and mist to make
   Me disappear without a trace
8. Wave Magic Wand
9. Put ointment in the empty lard jar

To cast spell: Rub the ointment on your body.

This spell only works in a place where there is both fire and mist. Also, because of the scarcity of toad spittle, much less two drops of it, the quantity of ointment produced is barely enough for one use.

(Note: One thing is immediately obvious with this spell: the ingredients are relatively easy to come across, almost any desert and a general store will provide what you need (assuming, of course, you have access to a magic wand and the store has the very seasonal toad spittle in stock). It would seem, therefore, that this spell is too good to be true, allowing one to move unnoticed amongst friend or foe, spy on lovers or would-be lovers, steal from the rich and give to the poor, or vice versa, sneak out of the castle for a midnight tryst, or anything else your heated imagination might devise. Remember, therefore, one of the major nonmagical laws of the universe, "If it's too good to be true, it's too good to be true." This very powerful spell has two small drawbacks: it only works in a place where there is both fire and mist (and there aren't a lot of those around), and it only lasts for a short time. A very short time. Whatever you do after you cast it, you've got to be quick. The spellcaster's rule of thumb for this spell is contained in the following ancient verse:

A Magical Primer

How long is fast
How short is quick?
Enough to cast another spell
And make it stick

If you keep the shortcomings in mind and know when to use this spell, it can be of great use to its caster.)

Page XIV *Causing a Deep Sleep*

Obtain the Following Ingredients:

3 dried acorns

1 cup of nightshade juice

1 empty pouch

A Magic Wand

To Prepare the Spell:

1. Grind the acorns in a mortar (with a pestle)
2. Put the acorn powder in a bowl
3. Put the nightshade juice in the bowl
4. Stir the mixture with a spoon
5. Light a charcoal brazier
6. Heat the mixture on the brazier (boil the mixture until the nightshade juice is almost gone, then remove from heat)
7. Spread the mixture on a table (wait until dry)
8. Recite this verse:
   Acorn powder ground so fine
   Nightshade juice, like bitter wine.
   Silently in darkness you creep
   To bring a soporific sleep
9. Wave the Magic Wand
10. Put the sleep powder in the pouch (for safekeeping)

A Magical Primer

> *To cast spell:*
> Be in a dank, dark space
> Pour the sleep powder on the ground (or, floor)
> Recite: *Slumber, henceforth!*
>
>
> *Use only as directed!*
>
>
> *(Note: This spell will cause anyone within about 50 paces in any direction of the sorcerer to fall into a deep sleep. How long it lasts I do not know. I have used this spell but once and didn't stay around long enough to see my former captors recover from the narcosis. It is claimed in some texts that the spell was revised into its present form by a priestess of Isis attached to the court of Cleopatra, Goddess and Queen of Ægypt in ancient times. Cleopatra appears to have been extremely fond of revels and feasts on her royal barge, she and her guests floating on the Nile in fogs of forced gaiety. Although Cleopatra was famed through all the quadrants of the world for her beauty, wit, and passion, likewise was she also famed for throwing terrible and tawdry parties. It was to escape one of these sad and sordid debacles that the great sorceress began work on the spell. When her experiments were complete, she prepared her ingredients, concealed them within a pouch, and secreted them aboard the boat. Not wanting to remain on the barge a moment longer than necessary, fearing both the loss of her mind and her virtue, she*

hastened to the supply hold as quickly as she could sneak below deck. After murmuring a soft prayer, she cast her sorcery and escaped. It is also said that when the royal yacht returned to Memphis from whence it started, all aboard were fulsome in their praise of the excursion saying, "Ye and verily, a wondrous and funfilled time was had by all. We must have, since we can't remember anything at all of what happened!")

A Magical Primer

Page LXXXIV *Brewing a Storm*

Obtain the Following Ingredients:

1 cup of ocean water

1 spoonful of mud

1 pinch of toadstool powder

1 empty jar

A Magic Wand

To Prepare the Spell:

1. Put a cup of ocean water in bowl

2. Light a charcoal brazier

3. Heat the bowl on the brazier (heat slowly, but not to boiling; then remove from heat)

4. Put a spoon of mud in the bowl

5. Add a pinch of toadstool powder

6. Blow into the hot brew

7. Recite this verse:
   Elements from the earth and sea,
   Combine to set the heavens free.
   When I stir this magic brew,
   Great God Thor, I call on you.

8. Wave the Magic Wand

9. Pour the storm brew into the jar (to store)

To cast spell: *Stir the storm brew with your finger.*
Recite: *Brew of storms,*
 Churn it up!

To stop the storm:
Recite: *Brew of storm,*
 Clear it up!

(*Note:* It is not known who was the first to devise this particular bit of magical pyrotechnic, but it was obviously someone with a distinct flair for the dramatic. It is significant that the god Thor, the god of thunder, is implored in the concocting of the potion. The inhabitants of the hamlet of Bruce in southeastern Llewdor have an oral tradition that Thor once visited there and cast a spell much like the one described above. At the time, Bruce was being threatened by some sort of monster (the legend is not specific as to just what kind) and when Thor was unable to defeat it in hand-to-claw combat, the god of thunder invoked certain words of power, turned day to night, roared for rain and wind, and cast a lightning bolt that fried his adversary. The people of Bruce were grateful and gave praise to Thor and begged to erect a temple to his honor. The God said he had no need for another place of worship and that a simple flag marking the site of the battle would be praise enough. Thus was born what became known throughout the lands as the banner of Bruce or, to some, the Bruce banner. The banner flew for scores of years until another hulking monster (the only thing we know about this particular one is that is was green) pillaged the village. So sudden was the rampage and destruction that there was no time to call for divine intervention Bruce was destroyed and the banner to Thor ripped beyond repair. Still, the villagers blamed Thor for not coming and when the town was rebuilt, it was without the banner.)

6

To Heir Is Human

(From the Chronicles of Daventry, Part 3)

King's Quest

117
To Heir Is Human

PRINCE ALEXANDER'S OWN STORY!
EXCLUSIVE INTERVIEW

Captive for 17 years, kidnapped prince escapes evil wizard, Medusa, monsters, bandits, and pirates. He crosses deserts, mountains, and the Western Sea to return home.
And that was the easy part.
In this *Daventry People* exclusive, the Prince tells us how he rescued both his twin sister, Princess Rosella, and the kingdom of Daventry from the very clutches of the fire-breathing dragon.
Daventry People reporter Derek Karlavaegen caught up with the prince as he relaxed in Castle Daventry,
the home he had never known.

To look at Prince Alexander today, it is hard to imagine that he is the same person as the bawling babe who was snatched one summer's evening from the rocking cradle on the shores of Lake Maylie, all those years ago. Lean of body, he is taller than his father, but his eyes and the firm set of his jaw are the same as King Graham's. His mother's fairness of face also is there for all to see, and Alexander's resemblance to his sister, Princess Rosella, is quite pronounced. One only has to look at them together to know they are twins. Even without the evidence of the small birthmark on his right thigh, his ears alone would mark him as the king's son. His voice is soft, mature beyond his young years. As he spoke to me, it held me with its intensity as if reliving his experiences for others might exorcise the daemons of his past.

Our interview was conducted over several days and was interrupted frequently by the queen's reports on the king's improving physical condition, and by their spontaneous hugs and tears. At these times of family emotion,

I would withdraw discreetly; some emotions demand their privacy. I have edited the prince's words somewhat for brevity and style.

Question: *Prince Alexander, can you tell us something about what it was like growing up a slave to the wizard Manannan?*

Actually, I still have a lot of trouble with the name Alexander. The wizard named me Gwydion. It is the only name I have ever really known, and I suspect that I'll always think of myself by that identity.

Chores and punishments, work and sleep; this is all that I knew while growing up. And reading; Manannan did allow me to read books from his library, although he never allowed me to find them for myself. He would tell me that reading kept me quiet and out of trouble when I wasn't doing something useful. Manannan always fancied himself a scholar and kept books on all sorts of subjects on the shelves in his study. From them I learned of the existence of magic, although no books on how to practice it were given me. I read from the histories and legends of our world and the Other World, poured over maps, studied drawings of the beasts and creatures who roam and soar and swim, and imagined myself free of my master, roaming and adventuring throughout the fabulous world that I knew only secondhand.

Most of my time was spent doing whatever task Manannan set me to—cleaning the chamber pot in his bedroom, dusting his office with the feather brush that he kept atop the cabinet, feeding the chickens, preparing his meals—whatever he desired. He didn't like me to dawdle, either. If I did not get my job done quickly, he would point a finger of punishment at me. At those times I considered myself lucky if he only materialized me into my locked room. At least there I was safe; never did he enter my poor room. Manannan always warned me if I messed up my chores once too often, it would be the last thing I ever did.

To Heir Is Human

He was both evil and cruel. I knew Mannannan kept a keen eye on the countryside of Llewdor by way of a looking glass he kept in the house's tower; and from there he could terrorize the people who lived in that country. He said that if I ever attempted to escape, he would be able to find me at once through the device. My penalty for such an act would be death, and when he told this to me he spoke as if he enjoyed the prospect. He delighted in telling me of the other boys who had served him and of how they had died for their various transgressions. He would tell me this in lurid detail.

Death too was threatened me if he ever caught me in possession of his personal things, or in posession of anything that might have any magical use. He would tell me, between threats, "Keep your hands clean and your pockets empty!"

Obey Manannan I did, although try as I might, he always found a petty mistake for which to exact a punishment. In the final weeks of my captivity, it was as if he were looking for an excuse to terminate my existence. It was at this time that I determined to be free of the wizard's tyranny. The worst he could do was kill me, and I suspected he was ready to do that anyway. Often had my master spoken of how none of his prior boys, for whatever reasons, had survived past their eighteenth birthday. On other occasions he promised me release when I turned that manful age. My own eighteenth birthdate was just weeks away, and I suspected—from Manannan's words and the hateful look in his eyes—that I would do my last chores that day, my last *anything* that day. I truly had nothing to lose and prepared myself to act at the first opportunity.

A few days later, soon after I had fed the chickens outside, Manannan materialized to inform me he was leaving on a journey and to warn me to stay out of trouble while he was gone. The moment he disappeared from view, I sprang into action.

My plan was to first make a thorough search of the house. I knew the wizard had a laboratory hidden somewhere below his study. It was a place I had never seen, but knew existed because my master occasionally spoke of going there to perform some magical experiment or other.

I also knew that he must have secrets hidden in his bedroom, because I was only allowed there to empty the chamber pot and only then for a very short time.

Question: *Why hadn't you done this before?*

Fear had kept my courage in check, and now desperation had given me daring.

Manannan didn't like me poking around in his study except when I dusted. In one corner was the locked oak cabinet upon which the feather duster lived when it wasn't being used. A huge oak desk, chair, and wastebasket filled the rest of the space, and bookshelves covered two walls. As I looked at the books on the right wall, I noticed a metallic glint I had never seen before. I moved the books at once and discovered a brass lever. When I pulled it, a trapdoor rose from the floor, showing me a set of stone stairs leading down. I was sure where they led.

The stairs were slick, so I had to be careful going down. Manannan's cat, the one with the name I refuse to pronounce, attempted to trip me as I descended. I'm sure I'd have broken my neck if she had, so I gave it a quick, soft kick with my foot. I am not cruel to animals, but this one and I were far from friends. There was only enough force in my blow to move the feline, not harm it.

Torches lit the laboratory at the bottom. What they revealed were shelves bearing jars full of strange things such as toad spittle, nightshade juice, mandrake root powder, and the like—ingredients for magical spells. A large oak worktable was set in the middle of the room. Upon it was a massive book bound in a curious leather, and it bore the title *The Sorcery of Old*.

To Heir Is Human

The ink and handwriting within the book were very faint. Most of of the writings were in languages with which I am not familiar. Some, I suspect, were not written with a human hand. From the few pages I could read, I surmised the book was a spell book. The spells had names like, "Causing a deep sleep," "Flying Like An Eagle," and "Transforming another into a Cat." Ingredients and required tools were all listed. A glance at the shelves proved that they contained many, but not all, of the ingredients listed in the spell book. The worktable had much of the needed apparatus. Here, I rejoiced, was the means of my escape.

Question: *And was it?*

Alas, no! It would be eventually, but at the time it wasn't. Search as I would, I found I had not the complete makings of any spell.

I decided that my best course would be to memorize all that I could from the book and then to leave the laboratory the same as if I had never been there, lest the wizard become suspicious. I would return again with what I needed to cast a spell on my evil master.

And I knew what that spell would be; the underfoot feline had given me the idea. If I could come up with a little cat fur, some fish oil, a bowl for mixing, and a magic wand, I would be delighted to turn Manannan into a cat.

When I returned to the wizard's study, I carefully pushed the lever to close the trapdoor and moved the books back into place. The room was now exactly as I had found it.

Question: *You must have been scared that Manannan would return and catch you redhanded, weren't you?*

Of course I was! I may be self-taught, but I'm not stupid. But at that point I wasn't too worried that he would return just then.

Question: *Oh? Why was that?*

My master was a man of extremely fixed and regular habits. He would rise at exactly the same time each day. Likewise he would retire to bed each night at the same time, accompanied by the same three fingers of the same awful brandy that his taste favored. When Manannan slept, it was for precisely the same period of time, and when he traveled, he always returned at the same time. It was as if he were a clockwork person with gears that repeated himself eternally.

Manannan kept in his house a magical clock unlike any I have ever read about. It was similar to an hourglass in that it would measure a certain short period of time and then begin again, then again and again and again, for as many times as you might count. The sorcerer kept the device, he would say, as a curiosity, for it measured the passing of time in an interval unknown to our kind. He told me once—why, I do not know—that it was created by another race, one that came before the human, or after—he was not sure which.

Over time I came to see the strange clock as a way to measure the man himself. His bath always took two measures of the odd time, his studies eighteen, and his sleep twenty-five— the same as his travels. It was because I knew this of Manannan that I wasn't worried that he would return just then. I knew that if I could keep track of time, as measured by the unhuman device, then my master could not catch me unawares.

Manannan would not return for some while yet. I used what time I dared to continue my household search. From the kitchen I took my favorite clay bowl from a shelf, and a wooden spoon and sharp knife from the rack next to the fireplace. As I passed through the dining room, I retrieved an old cup

To Heir Is Human

from upon the table. Manannan's dining room is large enough to accommodate a score of people, yet my master always ate alone under the eternal gaze of a stuffed moose head. I will always consider that a most curious sight.

I took what I had gathered to my sparsely furnished room, and I hid it all under my bed (a cot really). I was sure the wizard would not search for them there, even if he noticed them missing. Then I went to catch the cat and get its contribution to my future.

She was in the wizard's tower; she could have been just about anywhere, but she was on the third floor playing with a dead fly. It took several attempts and many more scratches before I got her, but I was able to hold on to her long enough to take some fur. The unnameable cat gave me an extra scratch as she squirmed out of my hands, but the spell ingredient was mine.

As were the fly wings. I recalled that the spell for flying like a fly called for a pair of those wings, so I took the fly to get the wings. Yuk, but it was for a good cause—saving my hide. I hid the fur and fly wings under my bed with everything else.

The rest of the time I spent searching Manannan's bedroom. Large and ornate it was, with an oversized canopy bed dominating it. In one drawer of a small vanity, which held the large mirror where the wizard groomed his dark features each day, I found a hand mirror. This I replaced, but noted for later use. In the back of another drawer, in the low dresser, buried beneath unmended hosiery and soiled undergarments, was an apparently forgotten bottle labeled: Rose Petal Essence. For me this was treasure; I remembered it as an ingredient also, although for which spell I was unsure at the time. I took it, praying my master would not notice it missing.

Manannan's tall closet was unlocked. Within were velvet robes, silken gowns, and some pointed hats of the magicians' guild. I searched the closet further and turned up a rolled piece of dusty parchment. I could see nothing on it except for some faded lines. I didn't know it at the time, but I had discovered a magical map, one that would return me to someplace I had been while carrying it. As I say, I didn't know that then, but I took it on the assumption that it might be helpful later and that my master probably wouldn't know it was gone.

The discovery that made my risks worthwhile, however, came when I stretched up and searched the top of the closet. There I found a small brass key. It didn't fit the bedroom closet when I tried, so I resolved to see if it would open the small locked closet in the wizard's office down the stairs.

It sure did! Inside was an ivory wand, not too ornate, smooth and cool to my touch, with an oaken handle. I had not seen a magic wand in the underground laboratory or in his bedroom, so this must be it. (Actually, I had never seen a magic wand before, but I knew such things did exist, and combined with the fact that it was kept under lock and key, it made the identity of the wand somewhat self-evident.) Manannan's magic wand—any magic wand, actually—was needed to cast all of the magic spells, and I had it! However, I wasn't ready to do any spellcasting at the moment, and I was sure that I would be just another dead slave if the wizard found it missing. So I put it back and locked the door.

Next, I headed outside to the chicken pen. I loathed the place you know. Twice every day I was forced to feed fowls. The rooster disliked me, and the hens pecked at my feet. I had to muck the coop, and chicken coops thrive on most unpleasant smells. All this plus killing an unlucky bird for the wizard's weekly chicken supper! As I said, it was not my favorite place, but it was quick work to catch one of the hens and pluck a feather to put away for a spell. With this done, I ventured down the mountain for the first time ever.

Question: *That must have been quite an experience. What was going through your mind as you were doing this?*

125
To Heir Is Human

You must understand that Manannan's house sat on the top of a lone mountain overlooking much of the land of Llewdor. From that perch I was able to see a world I had never experienced. So at first an overwhelming elation came over me, one of freedom and abandon. I came very close to terminal stupidity in those first few minutes, imagining myself able to run completely away from my master and to disappear into the vast world that was absorbing me. But then I discovered why the wizard always teleported himself to and from his home.

The path was a killer. It was narrow, steep, and twisting. The footing was treacherous and threatened to pull my feet out from under me at any step. Often on that walk I could easily have plunged to my sure death. If there were an easier way down to the world below, I would gladly have taken it.

When I did reach the bottom, though, I immersed myself in the colors and smells and sounds I had only been able to imagine before. Birdsongs I had never known filled my ears. Above me an eagle soared slowly—in all my life I had only seen eagles soaring below me as I viewed them from atop the mountain. In the trees chipmunks and squirrels chattered to each other in a language I did not understand. I drank of the world I had never known, turning my face to the sun, spreading my arms, and letting the feeling of the unknown enter through all my senses, through all my body.

I didn't stand there too long because I knew I must soon return back up that dreaded path, and I wanted to explore a little before that time. I had an idea where some things were because I had been gazing on them all of my life, but I needed to experience the great desert and put my hand in a flowing stream.

As it turned out, the desert began a very short way west of where the path deposited me. I knew deserts were hot and desolate places, but I had never expected the sand to shimmer like water, making waves in the air. In the distance I spied a figure moving quickly. At first I thought it was human, the first entirely new person in my life, but I changed my mind as it came closer and I spied things squirming around its head, as if under their own power. I had read of mirages and dismissed this as such, turning my back and returning to the path where I had descended. As I discovered later, that act saved my life.

To the east of where I had come down, the country was much different. A blue and white stream sparkled through an area of occasional trees—birches and pines, I think. Just across the small stream was a large black opening in the side of a hill. I spent a moment listening to the stream's liquid sighing and dipping my hands therein, tasting the water, cold and sweet. Upon closer inspection the opening appeared to be the entrance to a cave, somewhat deep, with a faint glow barely visible within the blackness. A huge, thick spider web was stretched across the cave's front. I would have attempted to enter the cave at that moment, but I was stopped by the sound of something large moving in the tree above me. A quick glance in the sound's direction alerted me to the presence of a giant spider lurking in wait for something to get stuck in the web. My hand stopped inches from the sticky strands, and I retreated again to my main landmark, the path.

The path down from Manannan's house continued south into the trees. I wanted to follow it a ways, but the time I had allotted myself was almost used up, and I had to return to the house before the magician's arrival. As I turned to tread my careful way back up the mountain, I gazed on the eagles still winging in joyous flight through the air. I was sure they had no cruel master to take away their freedom.

A feather tumbled slowly down as I watched, doubtless lost by one of the great birds. I rushed to it as it touched the ground and took it, for I recalled an eagle's feather to be an ingredient for one of the spells in Manannan's great book. I brushed it against my cheek and hoped it would help bring me the freedom I was seeking.

To Heir Is Human

Then I turned and set my steps toward home.

Question: *You made it back OK. I assume. Did Manannan discover what you were doing during his absence?*

I made it back sweating, both from the perilous climb and the fear that I had misjudged the time of my own absence. The curses that escaped my lips as I arrived would sear your ears if I repeated them. I hated my master even more for that mountain path.

Manannan was still a little time from returning, however. I went at once to my room to conceal my treasures and take stock of my situation. I unrolled upon my cot the parchment I had taken from the wizard's closet so that I could use it to list what I had and as a reminder of that which I should try to obtain. You might imagine my surprise when I found the blank sheet was now a map showing the places I had explored during my brief outing. This filled only some of the parchment. As I moved my finger across it, a luminous arrow seemed to follow, and the word "TELEPORT" hovered above the page. I reached and touched my other hand to the magically floating word.

I had come close to death several times during my trip down from Manannan's mountain stronghold, but at this moment I faced complete disaster.

The map was magic, of course, but I did not know that my action would transport me elsewhere. Poof! In a blink I was standing on the path at the foot of the mountain once again, the same place where my finger was resting on the parchment I still held. I was amazed, yes. But I was also terrified that I was not in my master's house and it was nearly time for his return.

I performed the same actions again, only this time my finger pointed to Manannan's house. Nothing happened: I stayed at the foot of the mountain. Several more times I tried, but I did not move. Panicked, and with time—and my life!—running out, I raced back up the path. How I survived that mad dash was a miracle. Cuts and scrapes covered my hands and elbows by the time I was in my room, but I succeeded in arriving before the wizard. The map went under the bed, and as I finished dusting myself off, I heard my master returning.

So, to finally answer your question, no. Manannan did not notice anything amiss when he returned; he merely demanded to be fed. I went to the kitchen and brought him a piece of fruit, and he just gobbled it and went about his business. I don't even think he noticed my knees shaking.

Question: *Were you able to get rid of the wizard then?*

Oh, not at all. I only had the ingredients for two spells, neither of which would dispose of my master.

As I performed the chores Manannan demanded of me, I realized I had what was needed to turn myself into an eagle or into a fly. I resolved to attempt making the spells as soon as the wizard retired to his sleep.

After some time he announced, as he did at the same time each evening, that he was going to sleep. I went straight to my room, prepared to make the best use of the time I would have to work.

His snores greeted me at the top of the stairs, so I took all that I had hidden and went straight to my master's study. There I retrieved the magic wand and opened the trapdoor down to the secret laboratory.

I took some saffron from one shelf, made sure I had all else that was needed for the spells, and opened the massive book to page IV. I read the directions carefully and followed them exactly. I recited the verses clearly and distinctly and waved the magic wand with only a slightly trembling hand. From what I knew from reading about magic, I would be the first to know if I had made a mistake. It would not be a pleasant experience.

To Heir Is Human

Nothing bad happened to me, so I took a close look at the vial of magic essence. Only a slight glow from within betrayed its magic property. So far, so good.

Next, I looked at the map and pointed to the bottom of the path. Hoping its magic wasn't a one-time deal, I touched the word "TELEPORT." Poof! Success. Now to find some more ingredients, if possible, and go back to get my revenge on Manannan.

Question: *It couldn't have been that easy, could it?*

I should have been so lucky!

First I wandered south, following the path that extended down the mountain. I moved through a sparse forest, looking everywhere and listening to the sounds of the birds and other animals. In a short while, I stumbled upon a trim cottage with a thatched roof and smoke wafting out the chimney. A small flower garden was abloom in front. I thought someone in the house could help me, but my repeated knocks brought no reply.

Unwilling at the time to enter without permission, I turned east and walked until I came to the top of a tall, steep dune overlooking the ocean. A beach stretched below me, and as my eyes followed it north, I saw outlined a pier reaching into the sea, and a small town.

"There," I thought, "is where I want to go."

An old oak, covered with moss, shaded me where I stood. As I made to leave, I noticed a dried sprig of gray-green hanging from one of the branches. It was mistletoe. I recognized it from pictures in Manannan's books. This I took, for it was an ingredient listed in Manannan's spell book.

The town was the same small seaport I had been looking down on for years. It was not much more than a general store where people could get food and supplies, a tavern where sailors might go to drink and swap tales, and a few houses.

I entered the store and there met the only other person I had ever seen in my life. Short of stature and of hair, the shopkeeper smiled at me with an emotion I had never known until that time—humor. Upon his shelves were many of the things I had come down the mountain to obtain, but the shopkeeper would part with none of them unless I gave him gold. My course was now clear—get some gold!

A dog lay sleeping in one corner of the shop. During my bondage I had had scant experience with animals other than chickens, bugs, and vermin, so I took the opportunity to touch the dog— his name was Kenny, I believe. As I petted the beast, a tuft of fur came off on my hand. I started to wipe it away, but realized that this, too, could be used in making magic. So I kept the dog fur and left.

The tavern I entered next. Its occupants were bottles of wine and rum, a pair of evil-looking men who were bragging about hurting people, and a large person with long, blond hair, wearing a dress that left most of the chest exposed. I had met my first woman. All looked upon me as an intruder. I moved into the shadows of a corner and tried to eavesdrop on what they were saying, but I could make out no distinct words.

This was as good a chance as any to try out my magic potion. I dipped the fly wings in the essence. Zip! I turned into a fly. The magic really worked!

Buzzing right up to the men, I sat glued on the wall and listened to them talk about robbing and looting travelers, and how they hid their ill-gotten gains high in a big tree. They mentioned a hidden ladder for getting into the hideout, and how one of them always guarded the treasure.

Not knowing how long the flyspell would last, I buzzed out. Perhaps I could find their loot and get some gold for myself. Rob the robbers, so to speak.

To Heir Is Human

Question: *Well, did you?*

Eventually. You see, I didn't know where the bandits' treehouse was, so I had to go find it. At the same time, I had to be mindful of how late the hour was getting. I didn't want Manannan to wake and not find me at home.

North from town took me back to the stream I had been to before. The spider's web that covered the cave was still waiting to catch the unwary, and the mysterious glow was still beckoning in the darkness.

Flush with my first magical success, I decided to take care of the waiting spider and explore the cave. An eagle, I knew, should be able to take care of a big spider.

I dipped the eagle feather into the essence. Whoosh! I was flying! Unfortunately I knew I had but a few moments in this form, so I swooped down on the big bug, grasped it in my beak and dropped it into the ocean. No sooner had I returned to the cave mouth than I returned to my real form. I was exhilarated from my flight; the freedom of the skies made me crave my personal freedom even more.

Inside the cave, the faint light became much brighter. It came from a giant crystal ball that pulsed with all the colors of the rainbow. As I stared, strange music filled the air, and I noticed a figure standing behind the ball. At that moment, my entire life shattered.

The person in the cave was an oracle, one who told the future. As she spoke, her words were reflected by visions in the glass. She spoke of the kingdom of Daventry, and how it had been invaded by a three-headed dragon years ago. I heard of how the land was devastated and the people terrified. And I learned that each year a maiden was sacrificed to the monster, and that this year the sacrificial one was to be my sister, the Princess Rosella! Time was running out for her, my parents, and Daventry!

I slumped to the ground in astonishment. Parents! A sister! In an instant I was a new person, one with a family I did not know. My sister was a princess! All were in danger! Was I a prince? I was the only one who could help them. Could I? Could I even save myself from my current predicament?

Even as I pondered these thoughts, the oracle handed me something. "Here is a small stone of amber. Use it wisely, my friend!" With that, the oracle slumped into a sleep-like trance, much like death.

Question: *So, one moment you were Gwydion the slaveboy, and the next you're Prince Alexander of Daventry?*

No, not really. The oracle never told me my true name. I didn't learn that until later.

I was in turns elated, depressed, and most of all confused as I continued searching for the bandits' den. Too many new ideas and too much excitement had come upon me in too short a time. I wandered past the mountain path, west again to the desert's edge, and then turned south. It was here the bandits found me.

I don't think I had gone more than five paces when I was set upon by a group of thugs. They beat me and kicked me. Then they robbed me of all I had while I was on the ground. In an instant, all was lost—my map, the amber stone, the magic-making ingredients, the magic essence—everything. All was lost! Why had I brought all of those things with me? By the time I had recovered my senses, all I could do was press on. It mattered not to me if I were caught and punished by Manannan. I was doomed already, and so was my family, and so was Daventry!

133
To Heir Is Human

I dusted off and continued south, and as quickly as my fortunes had changed for the worse, they reversed themselves yet again. This time it was in my favor.

Evidently the bandits had caught me as they were leaving their hideout. I had staggered but a short way south when I came across a large oak tree with a good-sized hole in its base. The bandits had spoken of such in the tavern as I listened in on them disguised as a fly. At once I knelt and reached into the hole. A rope was there as they had described it; I pulled it down and a ladder tumbled down out of the giant tree's branches, stopping a hand's width away from touching the ground. I rushed over to it in order to climb up.

As I did so, I noticed the ground around the tree was littered with acorns, dropped to the ground, perhaps, as a result of the cutthroats' constant comings and goings. I scrambled around and was able to find a few dried ones for later—if there ever was a later—magical experiment. Then it was time to visit the thieves' den.

As always, I had nothing to lose; sure death waited in Manannan's hands. Up the rungs I climbed and arrived at a house built in the branches. I peeked inside, looking to find the guard. There was one, so I ducked out before he saw me. Waiting outside the door to the thieves' den exercised my patience and courage but, as I have said, I was desperate and had nothing to lose. After awhile, I peeked again. This time it appeared the scruffy guard had taken to sleep. His head rested in his arms on the table, and his breathing was deep and regular.

On tiptoe I crept in, hoping the floor boards would not squeak. Looking about I saw a pouch on the table near the sleeping desperado's hand. I lifted it from near his fingers. It was heavy—later I would find the purse to contain eight gold coins.

In the far corner there was a large bin. I opened this carefully and found inside all of my stolen possessions. They must have hidden them there right after leaving me for dead.

It was but a moment's quiet work to retrieve my things and creep back outside. Turnabout being fair play, I had indeed robbed the robbers. Back down the ladder, I fled to town.

Question: *I hope things went more smoothly after that.*

Things never went easy for me. Remember, while all this was going on, my master was getting closer to waking from his sleep. Anyway, Llewdor is not large, and the town was due east of the hideout. I was able to get back to the store without incident.

This time the shopkeeper was more talkative. He saw the color of my gold and extolled the quality of his wares. I spent four of my coins buying salt, lard, fish oil, and a leather pouch. On the way out, I gave Ken, the dog, an ear scratch. Things seemed to be looking up a bit.

Anyway, I felt I had stretched my luck a bit on that trip down, so I looked at the magic map and tried again to teleport home.

Question: *Nothing happened, right?*

Wrong. I did get teleported, but not to Manannan's. Where I ended up was at the bottom of the path. I guess the magic map just didn't want to go up the mountain, or something. Anyway, I had another slippery trek ahead of me.

When I finally made it inside—after another harrowing, slow, and painful climb—I rushed straight to my master's study to see if I had been discovered. All was as I had abandoned it, so I closed the trapdoor, moved the books back in place, and then put the magic wand back in the cabinet exactly as I had found it. Then, I locked the cabinet securely.

Back upstairs I peeked into my master's bedroom to find him still snoring, sounding much like the pig he once had me slaughter. Moving to my room,

To Heir Is Human

I hid everything I had under my bed. The wizard would be awakening soon, and there was no time to do anything else. So I composed myself and waited for him to make his presence known, which happened soon enough.

"Gwydion, empty my chamber pot!" came the shout, and life temporarily returned to normal again in the wizard's house.

Question: *You obviously couldn't do much for yourself while Manannan was at home. What was going through your mind as you performed your duties?*

Having tasted freedom and knowledge, I was even more eager to be done with my master and be gone. I had all I needed to make what the grimoire—the spell book—called a "cat cookie," and I was determined to prepare the concoction during the wizard's next absence and hide it in his next meal. If I served it to him plain, I was sure he would recognize it and probably terminate my life quite painfully. This was something I was trying to avoid.

A quick trip down the mountain to obtain anything else I could find would come first; second, back to the laboratory to fix the cookie; third, I would fix Manannan, good and proper. If all worked out as I planned, I would have the time to create as many other spells as I could and then head off to Daventry. How I would get home I still wasn't sure. Perhaps a ship might be sailing there from the port, or maybe I could use the teleportation spell. Whatever, Manannan had to be eliminated first.

I was just returning to my cot after doing my chore when the wizard appeared in front of me. He announced he was taking another journey, and that he would be hungry when he returned. Poof! Gone again. It was time for me, too, to make a journey. This time I decided to take Manannan's hand mirror with me in case I had to go looking into any more small dark places. Quickly, I was in his room and removed it from its place in the vanity drawer.

Next into my room to collect my things. I opened up and used the magic map. In an instant I was outside the oracle's cave.

Question: *Why there? And why did you haul all those things with you when you left?*

As for the second question, I was never sure what I might need. Remember, I had never been out into the world before. It just seemed right at the time, and my bag had room for it all.

Why the cave? There were blank squares on Manannan's map, places where I had not yet ventured. Included in that unknown—the "terra incognita"—was the desert where I knew I must go to collect a piece of cactus. My plan was to enter the desert at its northernmost point and travel south, looking for the plant and anything else that might be helpful. It was a straight walk west to that part of the desert from the cave.

I teleported to the oracle's cave, also, because of the stream that flowed in front of it. Another thing I needed to collect was a spoonful of mud, and near water would be a good place to get mud, one would think.

Well, there was none at the cave, it was too rocky. But, just a little west of there, in the direction I was heading, the stream's bank finally did turn to mud. Using my kitchen spoon, I was able to scoop it out and leave my fingers clean. Then, it was on to the desert.

At the very point where the grass disappeared into the sand, I looked deep into the desolation. To the west it stretched as far as my eyes could see and gave every indication of being a place in which one could easily get lost. The sun blinded me as I looked in that direction, although when I squinted I thought I could make out a silhouette in the distance.

"Another mirage. Just take a few steps in, then go south," I told myself. "It's better for the eyes and I won't get lost." With that thought, I stepped into that harsh place and turned immediately south.

137
To Heir Is Human

...Averting my eyes, I quickly showed the mirror to Medusa

I mentioned earlier that turning away from the desert on my first trip had saved my life, although I didn't know it at the time. This time, as I moved south, I could notice the "mirage" again coming closer to me and closing quickly. The moving mass on the head of the figure resolved itself in that instant—snakes. I could hear them hiss and glimpse them writhing their separate bodies. All this I saw in a flash from the corner of my eye and heard through the evidence of my ears.

I might say that Manannan twice saved my life at that instant. In the books he had allowed me to read, I had learned the story of the medusas, foul creatures with snakes instead of hair. Their faces were so hideous that one full glance would turn someone to stone. Thanks to my master, I now knew what I faced, but I couldn't face it, so to speak!

A hero, once, had defeated one of the creatures by showing it its own fatal reflection in a polished shield. I had no shield, but I did have Manannan's mirror. Averting my eyes, I quickly showed the mirror to Medusa. My master's mirror won the day. Her scream was as hideous as her face must have been, but it lasted just an instant, cut off as she was turned to stone by the sight of her own image. After a few minutes of hearing no sounds—no sound of movement near me other than rocks cracking from the sun's heat—I dared look.

Even as a statue, the creature was appallingly ugly. The snakes had frozen with venom still hanging from the tips of their fangs, doomed to spend eternity without falling. The less I say about the face the better, although I did speculate that she would make a fair mate for my master.

On the ground, not far from the new statue, I saw something dry and crumpled. Looking closer I realized it was the skin of a snake, although it did not look as if it came from one of Medusa's pets. Another victim of the desert most likely. Gently I took it, for it could easily crumple, and carried it with me.

139
To Heir Is Human

Praying that no more of the serpent-headed creatures prowled the sands, I continued my southerly course. I trudged that way for some time, looking at every cactus in my path, but all were too thorny for me to take. At last, growing in the shade of a large rock, I noticed an unusual cactus without all the stickers, juicy and succulent in the parched land. This, too, I added to my anti-wizard collection.

Snakes and lizards were my gabbering companions as I finished that part of my trek in the southernmost desert. A glance at the map told me I had covered most of Llewdor except for the eastern seaboard. I thought I would walk there, paying another visit to the cottage in the woods on my way.

Dew glistened on the charming flowers planted in front of the house when I arrived, but I had no way to take any of the liquid. Disappointed, I walked to the door. A small sign hung there:

> The Bear Family
> Papa Bear
> Mama Bear
> Baby Bear
>
> Welcome! Our Home Is Your Home!

I knocked as I had done before. As was the case the last time, there was no answer. This time I decided to let myself in.

Question: *Why this time and not the last?*

Experience I think. I had been through a lot since I had come there last, so I had more confidence. Then there was the dew on the flowers. I needed something to collect it with, and maybe that something was inside. Also, I hadn't known about Daventry and my family before; I was now in a double rush both to rid myself of the wizard and to rescue my unknown homeland.

Inside, a fire burned away cheerily in the fireplace. A plank table in the room's center was flanked by three chairs, a huge oversized, overstuffed easy chair—easily large enough to comfortably seat a bear—a regular straight-backed chair, and one baby-sized chair. On the table were three bowls of what tasted like porridge. I shouted "Hello!," but still there was no reply.

Upstairs was a bedroom with three beds—giant-, normal-, and baby-sized. The place was a bit untidy, as if it had not been swept in a while. Coarse reddish-brown hair was all over as if some large animal, or animals, had been shedding their winter fur. Bears perhaps? Things were beginning to look ominous.

The only other thing there was a dresser in one corner, so I opened a drawer to look inside. A thimble rested among some mended clothes. Now I had found something in which to collect dewdrops!

As I ran back down the stairs, the steaming bowls of food gave me an idea. Porridge would be a perfect dish in which to conceal a magic cookie. I took one of the bowls from the table as I left; the smallest one seemed just right and easiest to carry. Then I was out the door.

Outside I knelt by the flower patch and collected as much dew as I could. Keeping my thumb firmly over the thimble's opening to prevent the drops from spilling, I hurried toward the sea. All the while I thought of what I had taken from the house. Necessity had prompted me to do something that I am not sure was right. Someday, after everything settles down here, I intend to go back and repay those folks in the forest. I, my family, and Daventry owe them much. I hope that my thievery is a burden they can bear.

141
To Heir Is Human

Question: *Why go to the ocean?*

I wanted to complete the map. I wanted to see if I might find something I could use against Manannan. I wanted to collect some seawater that I needed for one of the spells in the book. And I wanted to see if there was a ship that might take me to Daventry. Are those enough reasons?

Anyway, I followed north along the top of the steep dunes, passing through town until the country began to level. Where the small stream wiggled out of the woods and poured itself into the sea, I was able to make my way to the edge of the surf. There I filled my cup with seawater, and elation overcame me. All that I had risked my life to obtain was now mine, and all I had to do now was get back to Manannan's house and make the cat cookie. Then I would get back at him, good and proper.

On the other hand, I had to get back up to the house with a cup of seawater in one hand, and a thimbleful of dew in the other.

Question: *I'm sure that's easier said than done.*

You might say that. I was fortunate in that my adventures hunting and gathering had not taken too long a time; it gave me the opportunity to inch up the slippery path with the extra care my burden needed. To anyone who might have been watching me making my snail's progress up the slope, I must have looked a comical sight. With one hand cupped over the container of seawater and the other tightly squeezing the thimble of dew, I was forced to hold my arms straight out from my sides to keep my balance. The more treacherous portions found me crawling, using my bleeding elbows for leverage. But at last I did get back.

As soon as I entered the wizard's house, I made directly for his secret laboratory. Through the trapdoor and down the steps I went. Putting aside all that I did not need, and making double sure of having what I did require, I took the mandrake root powder from the back shelf. At Manannan's worktable, I opened the book to the indicated page and followed each step to the letter. After reciting the verses, and waving the magic wand, I was left with a round, flat cookie with cat hairs sticking from it. I know that if someone had offered it to me looking like that, I would not have eaten it.

Actually, I had time to cast two spells. While creating the magic stone for teleporting at random, I began to notice that time itself seems to stop when the magical craft is being practiced. It seemed I could stand there working for the longest while and find later that but little time had gone by. I thought this was very curious. Helpful, but curious.

With the two spells finished, I left the laboratory as I found it and went back upstairs. For the last time, I pushed the lever to close the trap and moved the books into their proper place. For the last time, I put the magic wand back into its cabinet and locked it away. For the last time, I hid my loot under the cot in my bare room.

I crumbled the cookie into the bowl of porridge. In that form, at least, it looked edible. This alone I carried to the kitchen, where I waited for Manannan's return.

I may have dozed a bit as I waited for my master in the kitchen, for his voice and sudden appearance startled me.

"I have returned, Gwydion, and I am ready to eat."

"Yes, master."

He disappeared from the kitchen as quickly as he came. Taking the porridge, I found the old wizard sitting impatiently at the table.

"Hurry with my food!"

"Anything you say, master!"

To Heir Is Human

I held my breath as I placed the poisoned porridge in front of Manannan. He snatched it from me before it had even touched the table, and he began to greedily devour all that was in the bowl. My late master's table manners were atrocious. Slurping and grunting and picking his nose, he shoveled down his gullet anything that was put in front of him.

Some sweat, I'm sure, beaded my forehead as I waited to see if the magic cookie worked. As he finished, Manannan gave me another of his cold, withering looks. Poof! My master was gone as usual, whisked from the table.

No sooner had I begun to think that I had failed than I heard the sound of a cat yowling at my feet. There stood what could only be Manannan on all four furry feet. I was sure it was he from the smeared porridge still on his whiskered face.

I was free!

Question: *Can you describe your feelings at that instant?*

I think I had no really strong feelings at that moment, except happiness, of course, and relief. I felt as if I had been holding great chains my entire life, and they were now gone. I didn't cry, or laugh, or scream to the heavens with joy. Some things, I have learned, are just too large to encompass the moment they happen.

I kicked Manannan once to get him out of my sight, not too hard, but firmly enough to convince him as to who the new master of the house was. That was about it. I had no time to reflect and celebrate because I had a sister and a family and a kingdom still to save.

I must admit that I walked *slowly* back to my room to retrieve my things. There was no threat of being punished for dawdling, and I savored the moment of returning there for the last time. And I also walked slowly down to the the secret laboratory in order to prepare all of the other spells for which

I had ingredients. When I left there, I had no intention of ever returning. I still don't.

With the cactus and its juice I was able to create an invisibility ointment; with the dog fur, chicken feather, and snake skin I made a magic dough that allowed me to understand what animals had to say; with the ocean water and mud I made the brew of storms. Soon all was finished. Using the magic map I teleported straight to Llewdor, ready to take on the world—and a three-headed dragon.

I was not prepared to take on pirates.

Question: *Pirates?*

Oh, yes. There were pirates all right, but I didn't meet them at first. First I explored around the countryside again, looking for any more stray bits of information, weapons, tools, or people who might help me. People, tools, and weapons were in short supply that day, but I did turn up more information about myself in places I would not have suspected.

Birds and animals see and hear much in this world, much more than we ever credit them. They talk about these things amongst themselves, much as people do. When I put the magic dough that I had made into my ears, it allowed me to overhear the conversations of many of the creatures of Llewdor. Much of what I heard was on the order of catching worms or the winter's nut supply, but some concerned me directly. From a pair of birds singing in a pine tree I heard, once again, that I had a sister. But they went on to mention that my sister was my twin. Scurrying about a large rock, one squirrel told another that it was too bad I didn't know my real parents were King Graham and Queen Valanice; indeed, they thought it sad that I was a prince and didn't know it.

A lizard in the desert told another that it looked as if I were running away from Manannan and they wondered how long it might be before I was caught

To Heir Is Human

and punished by the wizard. In all, my plight was well known to the birds and beasts of the land. They pitied me and hated Manannan.

I used one other of Manannan's spells as I wandered the countryside. At first I used the magic map to move me about quickly; all I had to do was point to someplace I had been and I could teleport myself there. Then I thought to try the wizard's "Teleportation At Random" spell. Perhaps it would take me somewhere I had yet to discover.

Whenever I rubbed the magic stone—poof!—I would be somewhere else, but *where* that somewhere else was to be, I could not predict. Once I ended back in the laboratory; another time, on the mountain path. After one rub dropped me in the middle of the desert, totally lost and afraid another medusa might appear, I decided to put the magic stone away until I might need it in an emergency. Of course, I prayed for a scarcity of emergencies and continued my way by map and foot.

In the end, I arrived at the Western Sea, although it is only called that in Daventry. In Llewdor, the Western Sea kisses the easternmost coast, but then there are stranger things in this world than how we name our oceans.

In the distance, a sailing ship sat tied up near the pier. I walked up to it, seeing firsthand the planks and riggings I had only read of before. She had the smell of the sea about her; not just the smell of seawater, but also of tar and spices and rancid oils. The aroma of sailors, too long unwashed, drifted from one porthole. A short gangway connected the ship to the pier, and an old seaman had been set to guard it. His skin was like ancient, cracked leather, and his voice was cracked also, as if the man's throat was entirely used up. Few words and less time did the sailor have for me. "Scram" was about the extent of his reply when I asked about passage.

That's why I walked into the town tavern again. The loud sounds of bawdy songs and tall seatales shivered the timbers of the establishment, punctuated often by shouts of "More rum!" aimed at the blond barmaid. They were a rough-looking crew, bearing much resemblance to the bandits I had met there before. They were different individuals, to be sure, but they seemed the same kind of men.

I didn't know they were pirates. There was no way I could tell; my experience of the world was still greatly limited at the time. I approached the largest man of the group, the one wearing the gaudiest clothing. He and his men were talking about setting sail later that day for a distant land across the ocean. They may have mentioned Daventry, but the noise was too great to make out all the words being spoken.

The captain looked at me through drunken eyes, and it was the same expression Manannan wore when he was thinking up some particularly foul punishment to inflict on me. He promised that he could provide passage for me, for a price.

"Let's me see how much ya got," he slurred. I took out the purse to count my remaining coins, but the captain snatched it out of my hand before I had finished.

"Aye, lad, I'll gives ya passage," he said, fondling my gold. "We'll wait for ya at the wharf, but not fer long!" With that the whole drunken crew drank up and left. The barmaid looked at me with alarm on her face, but I rushed after the men. They were my only way home.

Question: *When did you find out they really were pirates?*

The moment I set foot aboard ship, they raised the gangplank and grabbed me, twisting my arms behind my back. All of my possessions were taken, and I was thrown into the cargo hold. It hurt when I landed.

Despite this, things could have been a whole lot worse. For one thing, although I didn't know it at the time, the ship *was* heading for Daventry; it could have been going elsewhere. Also, while I was a "guest" in the ship's hold, I learned where the cutthroats had buried their own treasure. This came about as I was exploring my prison.

To Heir Is Human

The cargo hold extended the entire length of the ship. It was broken into three areas, all connected, filled with crates and boxes of different sizes, none of which I was able to open. The part of the hold in which I had landed was directly under a rope ladder that dangled down through a hole. It was the only way in and out of where I was. One of the larger crates was set directly under the ladder, but too high for me to get up on so I could reach the ladder.

Forward from where I had been pitched were the other two compartments, and in the middle one I found a small crate light enough for me to lift and carry. My idea was to use the small crate to get high enough to get on the larger one. As I was picking the box up, I disturbed a number of mice, which along with rats, I have read, infest all sailing vessels. Two of the vermin were chatting about how the captain and his mate were talking about where they had hidden their ill-gotten gains.

"Five paces east of the palm tree where they put ashore in Daventry," one said. "I sure wish we could do something about it!" replied the other. Their conversation then turned to fear of cats, and I heard nothing more of any interest to me, although I suspect the mice might disagree on that point!

Question: *You found out about pirate treasure from mice?*

Magic dough in my ears, remember? At the time, the information was interesting, and tempting, but I had no idea I'd eventually be able to put it to some practical use.

Anyway, I took the crate, dropped it beside the taller one, and then jumped on it. From there I was able to jump on top of the big crate, and from there, jump up and grab the ladder. Hearing no noises above, I climbed up and stuck my head through the opening.

The ladder continued up above me to the top deck. I was on the second deck by the ship's wheel. No one seemed to be about at the moment. In front of me, on the other side of one of the ship's large masts, was a lifeboat with a shovel beside it. Beyond that were the crew's berths. There was no luxury there; the crew's quarters, with their thin blankets and hard cots, reminded me of my accommodations at Manannan's house. Even as I peered inside, I could see fleas jumping furiously from cot to cot. Lice, I'm sure, also found a cozy home there.

As I moved back to the rear of the ship, I came upon the captain's stateroom. The furnishings were almost elegant—a comfortable bed, a large sea chest, and a desk and chair. Above the desk was a chart showing the route the craft was taking. We were to land at the foot of a mountain range on the northern coast of what appeared to be a small continent. We were heading toward Daventry; the chart agreed with maps I had seen at Manannan's. I was going home, if I could survive the journey!

A quick search of the captain's desk turned up nothing, but when I opened his chest, I discovered all my stolen posessions hidden within. I took them all and made sure the chest was closed after I finished. That's when I pushed my luck too far.

I climbed up the ladder to the deck. The bright sun and the reflections from the waves dazzled me as I popped through to the open air. For a moment I thought I might escape detection. I crept to the ship's rear and looked into a doorway I had noticed earlier. The ship's cook saw me though, so I fled back into the sun. Just as I reached the ladder going down, a couple of rough sailors caught up with me.

"Back down belows deck, ya go, me matey. If we catches ya again, ye'll walk the plank!"

Once again I found myself in the cargo hold. Once again my body hurt from the fall. And once again my belongings had been stolen from me. This was becoming a habit that I didn't need.

Question: *So, there you are stuck below deck, threatened with death if you're caught again. How did you escape?*

149
To Heir Is Human

Patience is an art that I was forced to learn in order to survive my late master, and it was patience that carried me through my crisis. All I did was wait, and think.

Upon reflection, I realized that if I could get back to the captain's trunk, I had a pouch of powder that would put people to sleep. With the crew sleeping, I might be able to swim ashore. First, though, I had to wait until we got near our destination, and then I had to get the powder back. I ignored the possibility of turning myself into an eagle and attempting to fly, because I didn't know how far from shore I might be. Eagles may be mighty birds, but they cannot fly forever.

So I sat and waited. And I waited. And I waited some more. I waited until the ship's lookout cried "Land ho!" I had figured that the crew would be so busy preparing to make landfall that they would have no time to keep an eye out for their prisoner. I also figured the captain would be on deck with them at the time. My assumptions proved correct.

I had waited the endless hours on top of the large crate directly under the ladder. Pausing but a few moments to allow the crew to get on deck, I hurried up the ladder to the captain's cabin and retrieved what the pirates had taken. Then it was back down the ladder into the hold—the dank, dark place necessary for casting the spell. Moments after reciting the magic words, complete quiet came over the ship. Up, again, I went. It turned out that there was no way I could move the lifeboat by myself, so I took the shovel instead. Maybe I'd have a chance to dig for that buried treasure.

The ship's deck was littered with slumbering sailors. Stepping over their bodies, I walked to the front of the vessel where I could see land not too far off to the east. Overboard I jumped, and began swimming as fast as I could toward the shore. I had almost made it when the shark showed up.

It was a race I could have easily lost, but an extra burst of speed, followed by a quick zig, and then a faster zag, brought me to land before I became the shark's supper. Breathing hard, I collapsed for a moment and let the sun dry my body and calm my soul. The escape had been much too close.

Question: *Frightening, to say the least. You looked for the treasure, I assume?*

It really was but a moment's work. Only one palm tree waved on the beach where I was, and it seemed the same beach as the one marked as the pirates' destination. I put my back to the tree and marched off the five paces. Then I began digging.

The small wooden chest was not buried very deeply in the soft sand. It was warped and tarnished on the outside, but inside were gems and pearls, and gold and silver. It wasn't very light, but I decided to haul it with me anyway.

Daventry! I was finally home. Not really, of course. I still had to find the castle, and I had no idea where that might be. Nonetheless, the excitement of being where I was, and the realization of what I had done to get there, shot through me like lightening. With a burst of energy and enthusiasm such as I had never known, I began hiking toward the giant snow-peaked mountains that lay in front of me.

It took a little searching to find the path that started me up the slopes. It began a little to the northeast of where I dug up the treasure and immediately moved west, straight to a stop against a large boulder. I climbed the face of that boulder, slowly because of the weight I was carrying, and because there were not many hand- or footholds. Up and over I went until I was back on the path to my destiny.

The mountains seemingly continued to march as if moving forever in front of me. Higher and higher I climbed, the air getting colder and thinner as I went. Soon traces of snow drifted, breeze blown—not much, but enough to put sparkles in the sky. Below, a great and beautiful valley began to reveal itself. It was a very long way down, and the footing had become as treacherous as the path back to Manannan's castle. Because of this, I forced myself to move as slowly as I could and still stay warm.

Just past a small waterfall, the path ended in an eternal drop, straight down to the valley below. To advance I was forced to climb up the falls, up into the deep snows. I discovered another narrow path there, packed down as if something large had been stomping through the snow. Soon I was to discover just what that creature was.

Do you know what is tall, wide, hairy, and ugly and lives in the snow on tall mountains? Since that time, I have discovered that the creature is known to some as the Abominable Snowman. The name, I think, comes from its smell, which makes the aroma of dirty sailors seem as sweet as that of rose petal essence.

At the time I didn't know what I spied there in front of me on the path, but I knew I had to get past it. I squatted in the snow and dipped the eagle feather into the essence I carried. There was enough left to turn me into an eagle for the second time. The creature had noticed me by then, and you should have seen the look on its face when I changed form. Anyway, it left me alone as I soared by it.

This time the spell lasted for a much shorter time than it had previously. I changed back to my own body not far past the monster, and right on the edge of a precipice. I had no choice but to clamber down the south face; it was that or face the Snowman.

The short, dangerous climb down to the small ledge immediately below was merely a taste of what was to follow.

Question: *It got worse?*

You should have been there. I could have used some help.

I had deposited myself on the sheer side of a cliff that was dotted with caves. Below my ledge and to the side, other openings beckoned. The problem was that from where I was, I couldn't get to them, so I explored the cave in front of me. It was extremely dark there, as you might imagine, but after a few minutes of groping about, I emerged back into sunlight. I was on one of the other ledges, high on the far east side of the cliff! I almost fell off as I emerged, and told myself to be more careful—that brought me a chuckle!

I had no choice but to brave the cliff face this time. Moving to the far left of my ledge, I began creeping my way on a diagonal to the ledge in the center of the rock wall. There were just not enough holds for me to get there, though, so I had to crawl straight down past it to the centermost of the three bottom caves. Here I was forced back into the darkness, for I had barely enough room to stand on the ledge, much less move.

This cave also was connected to another—the one on the far west of the cliff. Here, too, the drop was abrupt. After some consideration I began rock climbing yet again. Yet again I tried for the center ledge.

This was the hardest climb I have ever made. Straight up I went, the places where I put my hands and feet so shallow that they may have only been wishes. Straight up, and then away from the safe spot, and then up, over, and down to it. From there, I went through the cave, emerging at a path heading down in an easterly direction. Despite the slowness of my movements, exhaustion from exertion began to overtake me. I sat there for some time waiting for my strength to come back. After a bit, I began to descend from the clouds in the direction of my true home.

As I journeyed down the eastern flank of those mountains, descending through that land in the clouds, I became invigorated by the slowly returning warmth that the lower elevations brought. The snow and rocks soon turned to green grass and trees, and the path broadened into a veritable highway compared to what I had just been over. It seemed as though the closer I came to the valley floor, the more I became convinced that the worst of my journey was over.

Question: *And it was, of course. But surely you knew there might be a dragon in your future?*

A lesson we all learn in life, I suspect, is that when things start coming to you too easily, then it's time to watch where you're going. In my case, I wasn't watching, and when the road surface abruptly changed to air, I found myself falling head over heels.

It wasn't a great fall. Indeed, most of it was rolling and sliding down the slope, but it was nasty enough for me to be reminded about how quickly death can come when you start getting smug. I had finally arrived in my father's kingdom, and I hoped no one had seen my entrance.

Question: *What thoughts went through your mind when you realized you had finally arrived here?*

Obviously I was shocked and depressed. I had expected a beautiful country, a land of cool woods and blue lakes. Instead I was overwhelmed by the devastation and destruction all around me.

Cracks had been torn in the earth, boulders were strewn all around as if quakes had pulled them down from the mountain. A large, black cave was at the mountain's base with what appeared to be the remnants of door hinges still hanging from the raw rock. I could see stone stairs leading up into the cave's interior, and I wondered where they led.

King's Quest

To the west the country looked as if it had once been beautiful. Now the landscape was dotted with blasted trees and charred vegetation. A well stood amid this sad scene, filled with rocks. I followed a stone wall north, passing through more scenes of what I now assumed to be signs of a dragon's wrath. Topping a short rise, my heart soared when I saw the spires of a grand castle in the distance. I knew this must be the home of my true parents, and I moved toward it as fast as I could.

At once I came across a run-down old shack—the first sight and sound of life I had encountered since coming down the mountain. On the shack's collapsing porch sat an incredibly ancient little man. "Wizened," I think, is the proper word to describe him, like the ragged pit of a fruit set to dry too long in the sun. He was rocking away on a chair that must have been as old as he was, and was tooting a happy melody on a tin whistle. As I approached closer, I was surprised to find a merry twinkle lighting eyes that still shone with both life and intelligence.

"It's about time you got here, Prince Alexander. Welcome home!"

At that moment the universe froze for me—I had finally learned who I really was. I would have wept with relief and exhaustion, but the gnome would not let me. Staring at me with a gaze that demanded respect and attention, he went on to tell of the great dragon who was responsible for the devastation I had encountered. The three-headed beast had demanded the sacrifice of a maiden, and my own twin sister, Rosella, had been offered as the kingdom's ransom. Even as we spoke, she was in the clutches of the fire-breathing monster, and her time was running out. She would be cinders by sunset.

I listened to all the little man had to say. The king and queen, my parents, were so overcome by grief and responsibility for their actions that they had locked themselves away in the castle. All were turned away from there. Only I, he told me, could save Rosella and Daventry, and if I didn't get up the stairs in the mountain to her soon, there would be no princess to rescue at all.

To Heir Is Human

Like vengeance itself, I flew to the cave with the stairs. I wasn't sure how I would set Rosella free and kill the dragon, but I hoped I would think of something. Up those rock- and pebble-strewn stairs I raced to their very top. There a large opening gave way to an expanse entirely surrounded by clouds, strangely hot and moist at the same time. This place, too, was scorched, the charred trunks of trees reaching to the sky like the arms of the dead begging salvation. The clouds were so pervasive that I cautioned myself to pay attention to where firm ground ended and clouds began.

I could hear the sounds of a large body moving not far from me to the west. As I crept there, I could see the massive beast, smoke drifting out of its six nostrils, circling a girl who was bound to a stake. A corrosive fluid dripped from all its maws and sizzled the earth when it splashed. Its scales were covered with moisture, and where its claws gripped the ground, great gobs of earth were ripped out.

Rosella was struggling to free herself. I could see her muscles straining against the ropes, the veins and tendons of her neck quite visible from the effort. She was screaming in terror, as would anyone faced with the sure knowledge of being scorched to death at any moment by a reptile the size of a large house. I realized I couldn't get closer to the dragon at all because its three heads allowed the monster to see in all directions at once.

Invisibility was the only answer, and I possessed the means to disappear from sight. Rubbing the invisibility ointment on my body, I saw my arm fade from sight. Intending a major diversion, I then took out the jar containing the storm brew. If this spell also worked, I should have enough time to rescue Rosella, and the rain would douse the dragon's flames.

I was half right.

Invisibly, I crept right up near to the beast's tail. I wanted to be very close when I performed the spell, so the monster would get the full brunt of the deluge. Stirring the storm brew with my finger, I recited the words to the sky and waited for the rainstorm.

The spell calls a lightening and thunder storm; rain is secondary. The sky blackened to night at once. CRACK! CRASH! BAM! BLAM! and a lot of other explosive noises tore through the heavens. The lightening was harrowing in its ferocity. Deadly, too, for the bolts shot straight at the green monster as if mating with it. Moments later it was dead, thundering the ground as its bulk collapsed. The rain washed over me, and with it came the knowledge that I had saved Rosella and, presumably, all of Daventry.

Wasting no time, I walked around the sizzling bulk, making sure to avoid the unsure footing of the clouds, and untied my now-sobbing sister.

"Who are you?" she muttered.

"I am Prince Alexander, your twin brother," I announced. She looked as if she didn't quite believe me, something I could surely understand. But she kept staring at me, trying to see her own face reflected in mine.

"I'll explain it to you later," I told her. "Let's get back to the castle." With that, I gave Rosella a great hug of happiness and a kiss of vast affection on the forehead.

"It's so good to be home," I sobbed. "It's so good to be home!"

I think that's when Rosella believed me.

Question: *And your first meeting with King Graham and Queen Valanice?*

Other than hate and fear, emotions had been entirely absent from my life. I had been living in a void, ignorant of love, joy, and triumph. That day I experienced those emotions, fully and for the first time. With joyous shouts we were met by the old gnome as we made our way to Castle Daventry. Gleefully he ran ahead of us to announce our return to my parents. Around us the aura of doom and oppression seemed washed away, as if by the great, cleansing storm.

Banners waved as I entered the castle for the first time. I stared in awe at the grandeur of its interior. The throne room, however, faded in front of my

To Heir Is Human

eyes when I saw my parents for the first time. My father stood tall and proud, every inch the way I had always imagined kings. My mother seemed the most beautiful woman ever to have lived. Tears were in their eyes—and mine, too—as we just looked at each other for a few moments. The first words came from Mother, and they seem almost funny in retrospect. Note well: they were not at the time.

"Alexander, where have you been all these years?"

"Rosella, you're safe!"

With those words we all broke down in tears and began embracing each other until all were exhausted from emotion. Merlin's Mirror, which had been dull since the night I was kidnapped, shone again, ready to foretell the future. Miracle upon miracle seemed to descend upon us. Joy and happiness reigned unbound.

At last, my father took an old hat with a bright red feather from a peg by the throne and announced that, with his family together again finally, his own adventuring days were over. In ecstasy he tossed the hat to Rosella and myself.

For a brief, shining, wonder-filled moment, the hat floated in air, slowly soaring to our outstretched hands. It was the happiest moment in my life.

It should have lasted longer than it did.

7

Grave Matters

Excerpts from: Ten Days in Tamir—Vacation in Paradise. First published in the "Telltale Traveler" section of the Bruce Banner, whose motto is "If we see it or hear it, we print it. It's up to you to figure out what's real!"

Graveyards are far from common anywhere in this world, and to find one as extensive and full of authentic atmosphere as the one in east-central Tamir is worth a detour for any traveler. As always, bring along some food and drink, wear sturdy walking shoes, and be prepared to spend the day. For hardier souls, especially those with a taste for being frightened, be prepared to spend the night.

Cemeteries change much when the sun is gone; what seems normal and mundane by day turns supernatural and ghastly by night. Then the restless dead haunt between the crypts and moan their ways between the tombstones. Zombies search for fresh flesh and human brains. In all, it is a most enchanting chance to experience death without having to cross over to the other side yourself.

If you are intrigued by a darkside sojourn, do remember to carry along some protection. Garlic, religious symbols, or prayers offer good security for many, but if you have none of these, black scarabs can be obtained occasionally from witches, hags, or other magic users. These too offer sufficient protection from the undead, but at some price. Prices vary from gold coins or simple tasks to various parts of living anatomy, so do be careful to know the price before you agree to buy. In any event, heed this warning: Do not enter the cemetery at night without protection. Zombies, ghouls, and ghosts may be fun and exciting to watch, but you wouldn't want to become their dinner. If you have no protection, leave before dark.

Nonetheless, even if you can't stay for the evening's festivities and color, there is plenty to see and do during daylight. Your first stop should be the old Whateley Manor, which broods over and dominates the entire neighborhood. This massive edifice was not built in Tamir; it and the two adjacent graveyards were transported to their present location complete and entire—exactly in the decayed state we see them today—from the Other World. They somehow were carried along when certain inhabitants of the town of Innsmouth *withdrew* to this universe.

Not often do inanimate objects make the transition here, so the folk of Innsmouth must have been very powerful sorcerers. We don't know much about them; most apparently ran into the sea and disappeared immediately upon arriving in Tamir. They spoke little; they left no tales. The ones who stayed on land gurgled what little information has been passed down and locked themselves within the mansion. They disappeared from sight, and soon the eerie glows and rays which stabbed from the house at night vanished also. In time the hauntings began.

No living creature inhabits the house, and the spirits who haunt it speak of little except their own torments. Nighttime visitors have been known occasionally to be rewarded for listening to the ghostly pleas and performing some slight service to aid in putting the poor creatures' souls to rest.

Inside the creaky house can be seen the remains of a once grand private library; many of the original furnishings still remain to give us a sense of its former grandeur. Above the cold fireplace hangs a large oil portrait of an unknown young woman, not overly pretty, with a somewhat mischievous expression on her face. Her twinkling eyes do not look at you directly, but sneak off glancing at some prank somewhere to her right. If you follow that sly stare across, you will find a little latch that helps conceal a secret door in the wall. Local legend claims the mischief is that you will never, ever, see that latch if you don't look at the mystery woman first. You might like to experiment to see if the tale is true. Through that door a secret passage leads up to a tower room dominated by a massive and ancient pipe organ. Those few who know how to play such an exotic instrument say its tone is as eerie as its environment demands.

Much more time can be spent admiring the furnishings in the other parts of Whateley Manor. The bedrooms, though dusty, still seem to wait for their owners to return. In one of those bedrooms there is even a secret ladder ascending into the old attic. All in all, one could not ask for a more perfect haunted house.

For this reporter and traveler, the real highlight of a visit to the area is exploring the graveyards. There are two: one to the east of the manse, the other to the west. A large, locked crypt dominates the eastern cemetery. Built into the very rock of the mountains, some say the tomb was there even before the manor appeared. Priestesses of Aegypt are rumored to have hidden their own mystic treasures within and sealed the gate with Words of Power. There is a keyhole, however, so while no one has been able to force their way inside, the finder of the proper key might be able to discover the crypt's secrets.

Many are the people who have been buried in the Whateley graveyards. Nobles and commoners alike rest near each other beneath the earth. How easily they rest is their problem. For tourists, however, reading the gravestones can prove both informative and sometimes amusing. These stones sum up a person's life in just a few words, yet one cannot help but be moved to some emotion by many engravings.

Consider this epitaph on the northernmost grave on the western side of the East Yard:

> **1546**
> **Reader, here lies—but forbear**
> **To read more without a tear,**
> **One—I cannot speak the rest,**
> **You may weep. I'll smite my breast,**
> **Grief preventing, and this stone,**
> **Too small to be written on.**
> **Only this—a little boy,**
> **Willy - in Abram's bosom's laid.**

A boy, it seems was laid to rest by his grieving parents, perhaps with a favorite toy grasped in his small hands.

Here is another:

> **Betty Cowdon**
> **1650-1669**
> **Here lies the body of Betty Cowden,**
> **Who would live long but she couden;**
> **Sorrow and grief made her decay**
> **When she lost her lover at sea one day.**

163
Grave Matters

Somehow the mix of the poetry and the image of a pretty young woman grasping a locket containing the image of her lover tells us more than the few words declare.

I've made copies of most of the other stones in both parts of the cemetery. Here are some samples, again from the eastern plot:

1634-1672
She done her best.

Randolph Peter
1575 to 1629
Whoe're you are,
Tread softly, I entreat you,
For if he chance to wake,
Be sure he'll eat you.

At length, my friends, the feast of life is o'er,
I've eat sufficient, and I'll eat no more;
My night is come, I've spent a joyfull day,
'Tis time to part, but oh!—what is to pay?

Within this grave do lie,
Back to back, my wife and I;
When the last trump the air shall fill,
If she gets up, I'll just lie still.

Rebecca Freeland
1598
She drank good ale, good punch, and wine
And lived to the age of 99.

Here lies a poor woman who was always tired.
She lived in a house where help wasn't hired:
Her last words on earth were: Dear friends, I am going
To where there's no cooking, or washing, or sewing,
For everything there is exact to my wishes,
For where they don't eat there's no washing of dishes,
I'll be where loud anthems will always be ringing,
But having no voice I'll be quit of the singing,
Don't mourn for me now, don't mourn for me never,
I am going to do nothing for ever and ever.

The graves are more numerous and densely packed in the western plot. Here too a child lies buried, an infant this time. The tiny tombstone is partially obscured by tree branches and is in the back of the plot, on its western edge. I imagine a tiny rattle accompanying him in his rest:

To the ever living memory of Hiram Bennet,
baby son of Edward and Sarah Bennet,
who by a sudden - surprise fell asleep
the 11th day of November, 1553
Aged 6 months

Compare that epitaph to this one, written for a man in his strength:

Strong and athletic was my frame;
Far from my native home I came,
And manly fought with Simon Byrne;
Alas! but lived not to return.

Reader, take warning by my fate,
Lest you should rue your case too late;
If you have ever fought before,
Determine now to fight no more.

Grave Matters

By now, I think you get the idea of the variety of emotions and sentiments expressed in tombstones. It really is a pity that we do not often bury our dead here. It is this fact alone, though, that makes a trip to Tamir, and especially to the Whateley Manor and cemetery, so rewarding.

When you visit, bring along some parchment and chalk or charcoal. Hold the parchment over the stones and then rub gently. When you are done, you will have a reproduction of the tombstones to keep as a souvenir of your journey. Remember, if you want to watch the undead, wear your protection! You could end up like them...or worse!

Here are some more engravings from the west yard:

Lord Coninsby: 1559-1626
Sleepeth here in peace:
an honorable man,
a valiant soldier.
He served his country well.

I plant these shrubs upon your grave, dear wife.
That something on this spot may boast of life.
Shrubs must wither and all earth must rot;
Shrubs may revive: but you, thank heaven, will not.

1643
Here lies Newberry Will,
His life was finished 'cause he took ill,
But none'll miss him, he should've been wiser,
'tis his own fault, for bein' such a miser

Here lies the body of Mary Ann Lowder,
She burst while drinking a seidlitz powder,
Called from this world to her heavenly rest,
She should have waited till it effervesced.

Kings's Quest

Here I am!

Here I lie with my three daughters,
Who died drinking Chelt'nam waters.
If we had stuck to Epsom Salt,
We should not sleep in this cold vault.

Thorp's Corpse

Six feet beneath
This funeral wreath
Is laid upon the shelf
One Jerry Jones,
Who dealt in bones,
and now he's bones himself.

Beneath this stone, a lump of clay,
Lies Uncle Peter Daniels,
Who, early in the month of May,
Took off his winter flannels.

He done died

Dr. I Letsome

When people's ills they come to I
I physics, bleed, and sweats 'em;
Sometimes they live, Sometimes they die;
What's that's to I? I Letsome.

Dentist Brown

Stranger! Approach this spot with gravity!
John Brown is filling his last cavity!

8

The Perils of Rosella

(From the Chronicles of Daventry, Part 4)

168
King's Quest

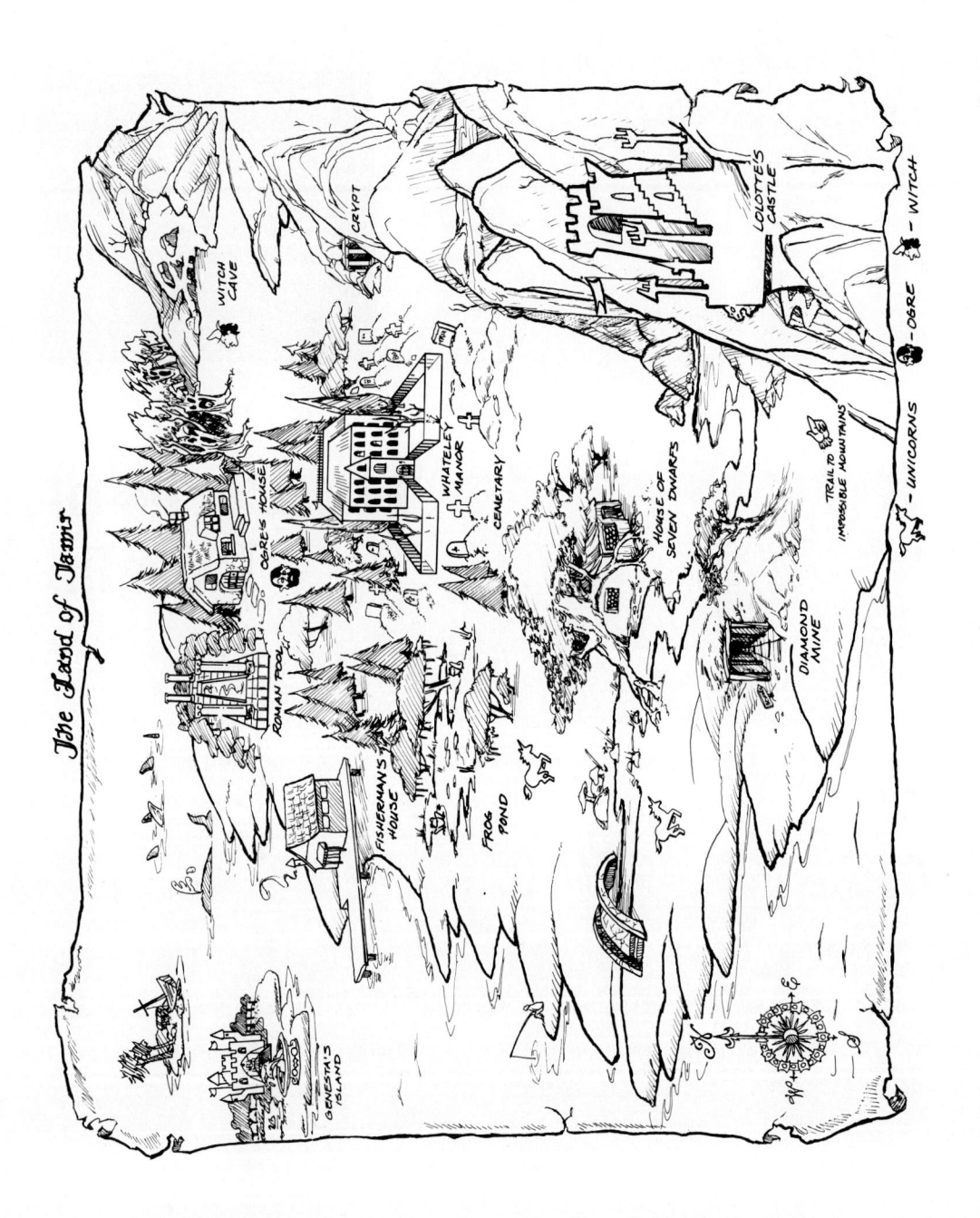

The Perils of Rosella

This is Rosella's story, although to tell it I must begin with myself.

Rosella lies quiet now, recovering from her ordeals. She has told me her story, again and again, trying to purge many of its horrors from her mind, to make them less real for the retelling. She begs me to record her recounting, ink to parchment, before the facts grow cold and distant. This I do gladly for my daughter who risked all, again and again, for love of her father.

My children are finally safe and my husband is again well. Daventry is rebuilding. A peace seems to be settling on the land like a weary warrior home from the wars sinking into a comfy chair. The fit is good—the fighter and the chair, Daventry and peace. All want and pray for the end of the troubles, and release from the weariness that steals people's strength and souls. We pray the peace does not pass as quickly as the almost- remembered dream of a quiet night.

I am Valanice of Kolyma, daughter of Coignice, who was a miller's daughter, and Cedric, a prince of that fair and tropic land. Now I am wife and love to King Graham of Daventry, who rescued me from the Crystal Tower of the Enchanted Isles, and who is father of our twin children, Alexander and Rosella. I have some small reputation as a scholar versed in the history and folklore of our world, but I am more comfortable as a teacher of young minds, getting joy from the smiles of discovery beaming from children's faces.

The pleasure of seeing those smiles on Alexander's face was denied me, as was his childhood and youth, after he was stolen from his cradle by the shores of Lake Maylie. But Rosella—ah, my darling Rosella—she I taught, both as student, daughter, and heir to the throne of Daventry. All I knew, and all I learned, I offered her, as did my husband. Histories, geography, folklore, common sense, and rules of thumb; swimming, running, riding, shooting, and fighting; stories of honor, courage, valor, humor, and humility; tales of love, death, and hard choices—all these she devoured, as if hungry to learn enough for two. She also learned to climb trees and clean house, sing, play the flute, the lute, and all the keyboards, speak politely, listen quietly, and survive alone in wilderness.

All of our love we gave to our princess, and when the dragon—Oh, vile beast!—demanded her as sacrifice against the total destruction of all Daventry and its people, she returned that love by willingly going to meet that flaming doom. She had learned well about hard choices, and marched with sure, firm steps, back straight and head held high, to the appointed place. Only one small, quiet tear glistened on her young face as she kissed us farewell for what we all thought to be the final time. As she disappeared into the mountain, Graham and I were devastated with loss.

I think it was the immensity of emotion, combined with the sudden and complete change of fortune, that brought about my husband's collapse. Rosella was gone but two or three hours when the gnome came shouting to the castle's gates that she was safe and well. We went from the pit of grief to the pinnacle of happiness in the time it took to hear "Rosella is safe, the kingdom is saved!" This news, this happy shock, left Graham and I so weak-kneed that we literally could not stand after hearing it. Thus it was that we were sitting on our thrones to greet the daughter who came back to us as if from the dead. She was leading her long-lost and presumed-dead brother, our only son, Alexander, by the hand.

It seemed hours, but 'twas only minutes that we laughed and cried and hugged and cried and cried and cried some more. In a world where miracles often happen, where the impossible sometimes only takes a little longer, that for which we had given up all hope stood embracing us. After almost eighteen years, we were a family again.

It lasted less than an hour.

171
The Perils of Rosella

In the euphoria of the occasion, Graham went and took the old hat he called his "adventurer's hat"—the rumpled one with the red feather—and tossed it to the children, offering them their future. It was still drifting down towards their outstretched hands when my beloved Graham dropped to the floor, clutching his chest. As I said, I think too many strong emotions in too short a time are what felled him.

With all haste he was taken to our chambers and the royal physicians summoned. They could do no good. Nothing helped my husband; neither their healing herbs and ointments, magical invocations, nor laying on of hands. Death seemed certain and certainly soon.

Rosella, who had just so recently stared at her own death, could not bear to witness her father's imminent end. New tears burst from her as she rushed to the throne room so as to grieve alone. "If there were only something I could do!" she demanded of the empty air, knowing that no answer could come. But one did!

A soft voice whispered to her from nowhere, "If you really want to help, look into the magic mirror, for help is there." Unbelieving and startled, Rosella quickly turned to face Merlin's Mirror, which tells the future and tells it true. She watched it shimmer and saw a woman's face appear. The image was that of the fairy Genesta who some say is the queen of all the fairies. Genesta told Rosella of a magic tree that bears just one fruit every hundred years, and how that fruit cures all ills, bestowing perfect health for many years upon the one who eats it. Genesta offered to take Rosella to Tamir where the tree was, even then, bearing its unique fruit. Genesta's magic would carry her to the far land.

There was something in the way Genesta made the offer that caused my daughter to refran from elation. "There's something you're not telling me, I think. I would accept the fruit gladly for my father's sake. But, why can't you simply bring it here? Why do I have to go there?"

Genesta nodded. "Life is never simple, is it? If you come here, I will explain. But you must make up your mind quickly, for my powers are fading and, once here, I might not be able to help you return. It is King Graham's only hope, and you must decide now if you truly wish to help your father!" Rosella says that doubts and indecision crossed her mind at that moment. They crossed her mind and then faded away behind a courageous and determined, "Yes, I will go!"

"What should I bring? Oh!" Rosella had continued speaking following her vigorous nod of agreement. These words were not spoken in the throne room of Castle Daventry, however, but on a lonely beach by an ocean. Genesta's magic had carried her there in the time between words. Rosella assumed she was now in Tamir. "I never expected to get here this quickly," she murmured in her amazement.

It seemed a fair place. Looking around, she saw a golden beach stretching north and south and a small river flowing out of the east through flower-filled meadows. The ocean filled all of the west, although Rosella thought she could barely see the faint outline of an island in the distance. On the other hand, it just might have been clouds or fog; she wasn't sure. As she stared across the waves, three dots appeared flying towards her, soon resolving themselves into the forms of Genesta and two other creatures, fairies of the tiny race. They all floated noiselessly to the ground in front of her.

Rosella was stunned by Genesta's beauty, but the fairy queen carried a sad and desperate expression upon her face. "Welcome to Tamir," she said. "Yesterday, while I walked through the nearby woods, an evil fairy by the name of Lolotte attacked me. She stole a magic Talisman from around my neck, leaving me, I think, for dead. I was not, although I will be soon, for the Talisman is the source of much of my magic. My powers have already diminished, and if the Talisman is not recovered within twenty-four hours, I will die! Lolotte is evil and hates me. She will use the Talisman for evil purposes and contaminate the land. Only you can stop her."

Genesta went on to say that she thought Rosella could get into Lolotte's castle, which lurked above Tamir in the Impossible Mountains. To help, she waved her wand and transformed my daughter's gown into the simple dress of a peasant girl, saying the disguise would help if Lolotte captured her.
"But, what about my father? What about the magic fruit?"
"The fruit is on a tiny tree, on a tiny island in a swamp. The swamp is on the other side of the mountains, on the other side of a waterfall, and on the other side of a dark and fearsome cave—the lair of the troll. That is where you must go to find it. However, I will not be able to return you to Daventry unless I have the Talisman, so you must get it back from Lolotte and bring it to me on my island. It is the only hope for me, Tamir, and your father!" With that, Genesta and her fairies flew back over the waves and out of sight.
"Thanks a lot!" my daughter grumbled. "But then, I'm not tied to a stake, face to snouts with a three-headed, fire-breathing dragon! My father, mother, and brother all have done impossible things; it's my turn to show them up!"

Lolotte and the Impossible Mountains lay to the east, so Rosella set her steps that way, following the cold river. She had not gone far when she was surprised by the sight of a unicorn standing in a fragrant meadow next to where the river turned north. Some say the unicorn is a mythic beast that does not exist in fact, but there it stood, spotted-gray in color, its head nodding and sunlight glinting off its long, golden horn. The great, magical horned horse grazed among the wildflowers. Startled at the sound of Rosella coming close, the beast bolted away.
Saddened at not being able to gaze longer upon the unicorn, Rosella continued following the river north, then east, until she came to a stone bridge crossing the stream. As she came closer to what she thought a charming span,

a sparkle caught her eye where a stray ray of sunlight slipped under the bridge. Kneeling, she got a good look at what appeared to be a ball—a golden ball the size of a large button. Rosella admired the ball's luster and hefted it. Heavier than it looked, it must have been made of pure gold. She put the treasure into one of the many pockets of her peasant dress and followed the stream east.

The river meandered calmly through the trees, on and on. Soon it even flowed directly through the roots of an oak so large that a small two storey house was built between the giant branches on the river's bank. A red door beckoned her to knock; perhaps here she could get help on her dual quests. Three knocks brought silence. Rosella thought someone should be home because a thin trail of smoke drifted out of the chimney. Gingerly, she opened the door and shouted, "Anyone here? Yoo-hoo!" Still there was no answer. So she started looking around. The place was an absolute, abysmal mess. In the sink were dirty dishes that looked as if they had been unscrubbed for weeks with crusty remains of half-finished meals stuck tight to them. Yuk!

It looked even worse to Rosella upstairs. Still calling for anyone who might be there, she discovered one large bedroom containing seven small beds. At least at the time she thought there were seven. So bad was the mess there—with dirt-caked clothes and boots strewn everywhere, stiff socks with odors that brought her close to retching, and filthy bedding that appeared to move under its own power—Rosella was sure no one who lived there knew just what the debris hid. There could have been an entire village there that she couldn't see. It was beyond yuk!

Down the stairs and outside my daughter ran, hoping to get some fresh air. Breathing deeply, she crossed the gentle river and walked to the hilly woods just south of the house. The scent of pine and fresh earth soon cleared her head. "I thought my room was messy," she told herself. Before long, Rosella spotted a door in one of the hills, apparently the entrance to a mine. The sound

The Perils of Rosella

of people digging came from within, and she thought perhaps these folk might be able to give her some help.

Inside she found seven stocky people, dwarfs by their appearance, digging what looked like diamonds from the earth. They were so dirty from their labors that she was sure that these were the folk who lived in the tree house. The mine even smelled much the same. "Hello!" she cried, trying to get their attention. Their attention she got allright. The dwarfs looked up at her, but their looks weren't very friendly. Grumbling, they went back to their work, but one especially grumpy looking one told her gruffly, "Scram!"

Rosella scrammed—right back to their filthy home. While not exactly hot-headed, my daughter does not take insult lightly. She felt her treatment by the miners was insulting and some retribution was in order. She cleaned their house.

I know it seems like a stupid idea: she has a little less than a day to accomplish two life-or-death quests and she spends some of the precious time getting even for some imagined insult. That's my daughter; she has always been her own woman. It's hard, but we must always remember that we cannot live our children's lives for them. Not that anyone could have stopped her at the time.

Why clean house, though? She tells me that in her messy room, she knows exactly where everything is and figured the same must be true of the seven dwarfs. By cleaning the filth and clutter, they might never find anything again, and this would be sweet payback. And it was a small house.

The dwarfs walked in just as she finished. Rosella heard them coming, but all she could do was hide in a corner and hope they'd just kick her out when they found her. She would not lie. She would admit to what she did, but she didn't have to tell them why. Anyway, they probably wouldn't hurt someone for cleaning, would they? They wouldn't.

One by one they filed into the kitchen and poured themselves bowls of steaming soup. Perhaps they were too tired from their labors, but they didn't see Rosella and they didn't see the cleaning. Finally, one by one, their bowls full, they sniffed and looked around. Grins burst out on their tired faces as they noticed both the clean state of affairs and my daughter. So delighted were they with what they saw, they actually thanked Rosella and asked her name, and would she like to sit with them and join in supper? Rosella smiled back. She too was no longer angry, and hungrily she ate some of the soup. It was surprisingly good.

The dwarfs had never heard of Daventry, but they were well aware of Lolotte and held no love for her. Such was the conversation while all finished the brief meal. They could offer no news or information to aid her. "Well, it's off to work we go," groused the grumpy dwarf from the mine. With a hearty "Heigh Ho!" they pushed themselves away from the table and started back to their mine. Rosella could hear them singing a marching song as they disappeared.

Clearing the dishes from the table before she too left, Rosella saw a thick blue pouch lying amongst the empty bowls; one of the miners must have forgotten it. Opening it up she discovered a large handful of sparkling diamonds, a fortune for miners such as these. She quickly hurried after them to the mine, to return the precious stones. I did raise her to be honest.

Inside the mine, diamonds sparkled and glittered from the walls. The dwarfs were already busily working; Rosella stopped the first miner she saw and offered him the pouch. "Thanks. Keep 'em," he said. "I don't want 'em!" And that's the way it was from all of the dwarfs. She walked deeper into the mine, and each one gave her the same answer: "Nah, you keep it. We got plenty."

At the very back of the mine, the grumpy one looked up and gently told her that he didn't want the diamonds either; anyway, the mine was no place

The Perils of Rosella

for a girl like her. "Here, take this," he said, handing her an extra lantern. "It just might come in handy sometime. Now, skedaddle!" Rosella did just that, being careful not to fall down the narrow path out from the shaft.

When she had arrived at the tree house the second time, Rosella caught a glimpse of another house beyond the trees somewhat to the north. Any help she could get she wanted, so she turned her steps north past the dwarf's place. She now thought of it as the home of friends.

The trees got thicker as she moved north, and they led to a graveyard just a little west of the large house she had seen. Graveyards are not common, I know, but it is said that they are creepy even in the harshest light of day. This one, shrouded by trees both alive and dead, seemed that way to Rosella. She stopped briefly to read the inscriptions on a few of the tombstones. At the back there was even the grave of a six-month old infant who had died in its sleep—Oh, so sad it was!—but she kept her legs moving mostly east to what now appeared to be an old manor house. Rosella kept looking over her shoulder, sure someone, or something, was following her, and that the cold breeze she felt on her neck blew from some unwholesome place.

The manor house wasn't much more comforting; ancient and falling apart, it too sent shudders up and down Rosella's back. No smoke left its chimney; it might well have been abandoned. Nonetheless, Rosella walked the few stairs to the door and knocked loudly. As was the case at the dwarf's house, no reply came to any of her repeated knocks and shouts. With a deep breath for extra courage, my daughter opened the creaky door and entered.

Rosella was not at all surprised at the many cobwebs she had to wave through. Abandoned houses grow them much as we grow nails on fingers and toes; they always grow back. She found herself in the entryway where a staircase led up to several open doorways. A mirror stood at the foot of the stairs, and in it she saw the reflection of a pretty peasant girl. With a start

Rosella realized that the girl was herself. A grandfather clock showed the only sign of life—the steady ticking of time reminded her that both her father's and Genesta's lives would run out of ticks the following dawn.

To her right, Rosella found the dust-incrusted dining room, and past that was an utterly cold kitchen. Rosella imagined it had been many years since it had been used. Indeed, it must have been many years since the house itself had been occupied by anything other than mice and spiders. To the left of the entrance hall she found an equally cold parlor; no fire in the hearth, but a few moldy books still sat on the dusty shelves. A large portrait of a young girl hung over the fireplace, its eyes seeming to stare at the parlor's left wall. Rosella's eyes followed that gaze and noticed something. Examining the left wall, she discovered a little latch where one of the bookcases and the wall met. She flipped the latch and it opened a secret door into the wall. On the other side of that door, Rosella looked on a narrow staircase going up, and a shovel leaning against one stone wall.

Shouting "Hello!" yet again, my daughter went up those stairs that were so narrow, twisty, and slick with damp that she was ever in danger of tumbling down to the stone floor, perhaps to her death. At the top—Oh, endless climb!—she found an old pipe organ and nothing else. The organ played well and had good tone, but there was nothing to keep Rosella there—other than her displeasure in having to climb down those treacherous stairs wearing a long skirt. There was much to be done so down she did go. The climb didn't change her mind about skirts and stairs at all.

My daughter loves books. She sometimes would rather read than eat or sleep, and this is a good habit that Graham and I have always encouraged. On her way through the parlor, Rosella spent a moment to look at the few books that remained in their abandonment. There was but one of any note, "The Compleat Works of Shakespeare," but it was one of her favorites. The Bard's works are rare but not unknown in our kingdom, and my daughter

The Perils of Rosella

had taken to memorizing many of the better passages and reciting them with dramatic flair. She always played the heroine. Rosella decided to take the book with her for when she returned to Daventry—if she ever returned, she reminded herself!

Atop the main staircase were three bedrooms in as much disrepair as the rest of the manor. The room at the top right of the hall had what looked like a trapdoor in its ceiling, but there was no way to reach it; the ceiling was too high and no rope hung down. The second door led to what must have been the master bedroom; it was dominated by a massive canopy bed. A baby nursery led off from this room, and Rosella sneezed several times from the amount of dust her passing raised as she walked to it. Once love must have filled it, but all that now remained amid the dust were a small wooden horse, a cradle, and some furniture. Even the memories were gone.

Rosella left the spooky old manor house and continued her journey east. It turned out that another graveyard lay there, butting into the sheer face of the mountains. A crypt was built right into that mountain, with a locked door to bar entrance to anyone without the key. Rosella looked around her and, though the sun shone bright above the overhanging trees, felt overwhelming gloom and despair oozing from the entire cemetery. She looked around, thinking movement might loosen the mood, but to no avail. Near the back part of the place, she came across the gravestone of yet another child, a young boy. This was too much for my daughter; so sad was the inscription, Rosella could stay there no longer. Weeping, she walked back the way she came, past the manor and on through the other part of the graveyard, knowing her steps should soon bring her to open country.

Sunlight bounced merrily on the still blue and green of the little pond. Rosella shares her father's love of water, and even though the pond was too small to swim in, it offered a clean, open, sunny, *healthy* place for her to rest a moment. She sought calm by looking at the water lilies that floated serenely on the surface, idly rolling the gold ball she had found earlier between her hands. A frog—something not at all unusual in a lily pond—sat on one of the floating flowers. The crown on the frog's head, however, was a trifle out of the ordinary. Rosella was immediately pulled out of her glum mood by her youthful curiosity—Ah, to be eighteen again (well, almost eighteen), with all the wonders of the universe waiting to be discovered!

My daughter quickly rushed to the other side of the pond to get a closer look at this remarkable frog. As she did so, however, the ball fell from her hands, and she watched it disappear into the pond. Flash! The frog was in the water, following the ball under. Moments later the small creature popped back up with it firmly in its mouth. Before retrieving the ball, Rosella reached over and picked up the frog. She was so happy to get the gold ball back that she held the frog firmly, leaned over, and gave it a kiss of gratitude. Yuk!

It gets yukkier. First the frog turned into a young man—a prince, actually. Rosella says her heart went pitter-patter when she finally got past her surprise at the sudden transformation. "Maybe he will help me in his gratitude," she told herself. "I hope so. He sure is good looking!"

This was the day my daughter finally learned the lesson that looks are not everything. The prince looked at her, once, twice. Twisting his face in disgust, he scowled at my princess and spat out, "You're just a peasant, you peasant! I don't want to be around you. Take this thing; you might look more pleasing as a frog, anyway!" With that, and not even a polite thank you, he threw the little crown to Rosella, turned up his nose, turned his back, and sauntered off. Even I hope that that nameless twit eventually said the wrong thing to the right monster! He was more disgusting than kissing a dozen dirty old frogs.

The Perils of Rosella

He didn't take the gold ball, so Rosella picked it up and put it in her pocket along with the tiny gold crown. Still fuming, she headed west toward the ocean.

Rosella found herself wandering through another wildflower meadow, the scents of summer hanging delightfully heavy and replacing all memories of damp earth and tombstones. What sounded something like a melody joined the perfume of the air as my daughter walked. It got nearer and more distinct as she journeyed. It also began to sound less and less like good music.

Rosella eventually encountered the musician, sitting on a stump in the middle of a glade. He dressed like one of the minstrels who had often entertained in the court of Daventry. He strummed upon a lovely cherrywood lute and even sang with a strong voice, but he wasn't any good. His fingers would miss the notes often, and his voice kept missing the melody. Rosella listened politely for a few minutes, but the man seemed to enjoy an audience and, smiling with the confidence of self-perceived talents, continued enthusiastically into another song.

When he finished Rosella attempted to talk to him. Instead of an answer, she got yet another untamed melody. This time it was "Greensleeves," the anthem of her father's court—at least that is what he was trying to play. This was quite enough to her offended ears. "Here, take this! she said as she handed the man the book of Shakespeare. Perhaps he would stop playing. If he did she felt that she would have done the world a large favor. Her idea worked. He did cease his playing to turn the pages. In a few moments, his face burst again with creative fervor as he began to recite one of the plays aloud. He was as good an actor as he was a minstrel.

"I shall become an actor!" he exclaimed loudly and proudly to the world. "I shall become famous throughout all the realms of the world, and all shall sing the praises of Frankie of Avalon! Oh, thank you for your gift, sweet peasant. As my gift to you, dear girl, I present you with my lute. It is precious, but you have given me something more precious still!" Waving his arms dramatically and reading aloud to the heavens, he wandered off. The direction he chose was the same as that of the the frog-prince. Rosella wished them upon each other.

Lute under arm, my daughter continued west to the sea. It was still there. To the north of where she stood watching the waves, Rosella could see smoke rising out of the chimney of a small shack. When she got there, she could see it was so rundown as to be falling apart. For a change, a woman's voice answered her knock. "Come on in!" she heard.

Inside was in as bad a shape as out. An old woman stood preparing food in the one-room shack. She was neither polite nor friendly. Taking one look at Rosella, she waved her hand towards the still- open door. "Yer not who I was expectin'," she growled. "Git out! I ain't buyin' anything! I ain't got no gold. Git, I say. Git!" Rosella got.

Outside, a long pier stretched its way out into the ocean. At the end, an old man sat fishing, although the complete lack of fish beside him suggested his luck had not been good. He totally ignored Rosella, rose and walked quickly back to the old shack as soon as she approached. He swung the door closed behind him, right in Rosella's face. "People sure don't seem to like strangers around here, do they?" she told herself. Scratching her nose, checking it for splinters from the door, she walked east past the fisherman's hut, considering what to do next. Time was passing quickly, and she seemed to be getting nowhere just as fast.

What-to-do-next had horns, hooves, and was playing a flute. Rosella recognized the creature as a half-man, half-goat satyr, if she remembered her natural history correctly. Possibly it was Pan himself. These rare denizens of the open woods love music and can sometimes be seen playing and dancing among the trees. In complete contrast to the wandering minstrel, now turned

The Perils of Rosella

actor, the satyr played beautifully. It was a lively tune—a Maytime dance—that it played; one that Rosella knew well. Plucking the lute strings with her sure, practiced fingers, my daughter played along with the creature's melody. This seemed to fascinate the satyr; after a few moments he ceased his own playing and watched Rosella, never taking his eyes off of her instrument.

As soon as she finished, she gave the lute to the silent creature, hoping he could play it as skillfully as he did the flute. His eyes lit as the lute was handed over and, with a great smile, he offered Rosella his flute. The creature spoke not a word, but the offer was obvious and my daughter was too polite to refuse the satyr's gift. As Rosella took the flute, the satyr danced away happily, fingering a new tune, one she had never heard before.

The river was the best place to go, Rosella decided. She finally remembered that Genesta had told her the magic fruit lay somewhere on the other side of a waterfall. Following the river to where it came out of the Impossible Mountains might just bring her to that waterfall. And that's just what she did, traveling back past the small stone bridge and the dwarf's house, farther and farther to the east. At last the river reached the mountains and—Good thinking, Rosella!—there tumbled a waterfall, straight down out of the heights like an exclamation point at the end of a shout!

Try as she might, Rosella could not swim under the falls; the current and the force of the water were just too strong. She thought she had seen a faint opening on the other side of the plummeting water, but her efforts to get there were proving, shall we say, fruitless.

"There just has to be a way through," she kept telling herself loudly as she sat drying herself on the grassy northern edge of the stream. "I bet I could do it if I were a fish." Pause. Pause. "Or, if I were a frog!" she exclaimed, enlightenment washing over her. Reaching into her pocket, she took out the frog crown. "The idiot said this would turn me into a frog. I wonder how it works?"

It worked the moment she put the tiny crown onto her head. Ribbit! Ribbit! Rosella was a frog. Diving into the water, she was able to go under the waterfall and emerge on the other side, on a small beach outside a dark cave. The moment she left the water, she returned to her own form. It felt good to be herself again, and she was sure she wasn't nearly as attractive while a frog.

"Gee, that was fun, and I think I might be going in the right direction," she congratulated herself. Looking around, Rosella noticed an old board lying next to the cave's opening. She also discovered that she was still holding the dwarf's spare oil lantern in her hand. The transformation spell had allowed her to bring her possessions along with her.

Let us pause for a brief moment. I have written that both my husband and I had tried to teach Rosella all we knew. During that moment under the waterfall, our daughter remembered advice that Graham had given her often: "Girl, my daddy used to tell me; 'Boy, if I have learned anything in my life, I have learned this: when in doubt or in trouble, pick up anything that is not nailed down, and if it is nailed down, look for loose nails or boards. Check carefully into, under, above, below and behind things. Read everything; you might learn something. Wear clean undergarments, brush after meals, and always remember, nothing is as it appears. Nothing.

Rosella took both the advice to heart and the loose board by the cave. Then, using the flint attached to the lantern, she was able to light it. Ever so slowly, she inched her way into the dark opening.

"Grrr!"

Rosella was out again before the troll's growl had finished reverberating. She waited a few minutes, getting her breath and courage back under control. She double-checked that the lantern was lit, and firmly told herself, "This is

The Perils of Rosella

for Daddy." Walking quietly and listening intently, she returned to the darkness.

The troll didn't get her, of course, otherwise this account would have no further to go. But Rosella swears that she never once breathed until she got to the other end of the cave, and she thinks she felt the troll's talons touch her neck once. I suspect she did hold her breath, but if the troll had touched her, she would be dead. Oh brave, brave Rosella! I too would have died of grief!

Her lantern gave just the barest of light, and she made much of her progress by feeling her way. Wary for any sight or sound of the troll, Rosella followed the cave east as far as she could and then as far south as was possible. From there she moved again to the east, shortly spotting the faintest glimmer of light. At that moment, her lantern revealed just the hint of a great, wide crack that slashed through the center of this last part of the cavern. Rosella almost, almost, missed noticing the drop. But see it she did, and by the slim light of the dwarf's lamp, she laid the narrow board across the chasm. It just crossed the span to the east, and so did my daughter, still not breathing. Taking the improvised bridge with her lest the troll follow—clever girl!—she followed the dim light, soon crawling out to find herself at the edge of a muddy swamp.

With perhaps the exception of the troll, problems did not follow my dear Rosella on her adventure. They waited for her, daring her courage, taunting her mind and body. In this case, the swamp just moldered there patiently with no breeze at all to ripple its shallow waters, waiting to suck her in.

Rosella pondered the problem and saw a solution in a series of tiny dry mounds—high spots—that peppered the swamp. Hiking up her long skirt to give her long legs their freedom, a quick jump took her safely to the first tiny island. Again, she jumped to a second and then a third. With one jump after another, she made her way through the muck until she came near an island larger than the rest. A little tree grew upon that small piece of land, a single golden fruit hanging from its limbs. My daughter silently rejoiced; she was looking at the magic fruit that could save her father!

She was also looking at one long final leap to the island, one she was sure she couldn't make unaided. She was also looking at a very large poisonous snake, a cobra, that seemed to guard the tree. The board she carried was long enough to get her to the island; the snake posed a sharper problem.

It is written that in parts of Daventry people are known to charm snakes, causing the reptiles to go into brief trances induced by the rhythm of music. Rosella had heard this story as part of her studies, so she put her knowledge to the test. First she laid the board across the final piece of swamp and crossed slowly to its other end. Then, before she actually stepped onto the island, she took the flute out of one of the deep pockets of her dress and nervously played a slow, hypnotic melody to the cobra. The snake's hard eyes appeared to fuzz over, and its body began swaying along with Rosella's tune.

Knowing that the charm might not last very long, my daughter rushed past the king cobra and took that single magic fruit from the tree. It was shaped much like a gourd, but she didn't take the time then to examine it. As quickly as she had rushed onto the final isle, Rosella hurried back to the board bridging the water. Carefully she stepped back on, for a single hasty misstep would send her splashing into the sucking slime. She heard the snake resume hissing almost as quickly as her feet stepped onto the makeshift bridge. As soon as she reached the other end, she stooped and picked up the board. The cobra hissed and spat even louder at its loss of the magic fruit.

Rosella left the swamp as she had entered—jump, jump, jumping her way across the water. On the shore she crawled back into the cave (she had forgotten to extinguish the dwarfs' lantern) and began her cautious way back

The Perils of Rosella

through the blackness. Again, she laid the old board across the chasm and carefully crossed. Once safely over, Rosella retraced her steps exactly. She was ready to dart backwards at any sight or sound of the troll, but this time she came through the cave without incident.

As she reached light again at the cave's entrance, Rosella saw something that had escaped her notice when she had entered: a large pile of gnawed bones, many of them showing fresh tooth marks. Remembering her father's advice, she took a bone to carry with her; it might come in handy as a weapon, although she hoped things never came to a desperate state.

The light at the end of the tunnel refreshed her soul; the air refreshed her body. She was out, alive, and carrying the fruit that could restore her father's life and health. A slight swell of pride coursed through her body. She revelled in her feat for a few moments, knowing full well that she still had a wicked witch to deal with and a Talisman to return. She also knew that she didn't have much time to do it in. Then Rosella dived into the water and lets its force sweep her back out from behind the waterfall—no frogging around for my princess that time! She wanted to meet Lolotte in her own form.

Rosella let her search for Lolotte's castle move her south along the wall of the Impossible Mountains. She was wondering how she would get the Talisman from the witch when a narrow path came into view. It was the first path she had seen that went up—the direction she wanted to go. My daughter put her planning to the back of her mind and began to climb, always paying close attention to avoid getting her feet tangled in the long dress. She didn't have to climb far; around the path's first bend, the black twin towers of Lolotte's keep shuddered into sight. They did not look inviting. Worse, though, were the two small, sturdy forms flying from there directly at her. Before Rosella had time to even think about eluding them, the two flying monkeys—that's what they looked like up close, but she never did find out exactly what they were—snatched her into the sky by her arms, and turning upwards, winged my poor darling straight to Lolotte's throne room!

Lolotte's castle was a cold, hard place, much like the witch herself, only more pleasant. Her throne stood upon a high dais, which permitted her to gaze down like a carrion bird on any who stood before her. Long and gaunt in form, Lolotte was dressed all in black, which gave her greenish complexion an even more diseased pallor. Her voice hissed from her throat like a sick snake; her eyes were tight and red, not quite as soft as a cobra's glare. Her hands gripped the arms of her throne so tightly that her long nails gouged deeply into the wood. A stooped, deformed man stood near her, scratching his armpits.

"What were you doing, coming here?" she demanded of Rosella. "You look like a spy sent by Genesta!"

"No, your majesty! I'm just an ordinary peasant girl. I was lost when your creatures grabbed me."

Real fear clutched at my daughter as she stood under Lolotte's gaze. It was obvious that the witch did not believe her story, and she waited fearfully for the full force of Lolotte's wrath.

The witch ordered her monkey guards to take Rosella to a grim cell—a torture chamber by its looks. Instruments of pain filled the stone room, the bones of unlucky victims hung in manacles from the walls and ceiling, and the place smelled of ultimate despair. Rosella glanced around at what would be her fate and shuddered. She had stared sure death in the eyes before; it still did not look inviting.

My baby was kept there for some time; not long in minutes, but long enough to make a firm impression. Then the guards came back and returned her to the throne room. Pointing to the misshapen figure Rosella had seen earlier, the witch announced that he was her son Edgar, and that he believed my daughter and had taken a liking to her. Rosella swallowed hard as she

The Perils of Rosella

saw how Edgar stared at her; it was like the dumb-love look a dog might give its mistress. At least, she thought, his stare wasn't evil. But that was small consolation.

"Bring me the unicorn that lives in Tamir. Then I will set you free and give you a reward, peasant girl. You can never escape me. Now, go!"

Lolotte called her flying henchmen and ordered them to take Rosella back to the foot of the mountain.

Rosella stood there, watching her captors disappear into the sky. She knew she needed help and advice, and Genesta might be the one who could give it to her. Having made the decision, she started walking straight west to the sea, intending to reach Genesta's island. As she hurried she came across a robin pecking at the ground, pulling up at a plump worm. Seeing this gave her an idea, and she decided to gather what worms she could to carry with her to the home of the gruff fisherman and his wife. Bait was her idea. Maybe the man needed more bait; that was why he hadn't caught any fish, and that was why he was so gruff. Maybe he could tell her how to get to Genesta. It sounded good in theory, but, in practice she was only able to come up with one worm. She carried it anyway, knowing she had to come up with a better plan.

Unicorns are shy and bashful beasts, magical in both fact and appearance. Rosella's westward course brought the animal into view a second time that day, but as before, it bolted the moment she approached. Although she didn't want to, she had to capture the creature, and she needed Genesta's help to do that. She moved quickly from the unicorn's meadow and soon arrived at the seaside shanty.

The man was not on the pier fishing; both he and his wife were inside and answered her polite knock with a surly "Come in!"

The man didn't want the worm; one worm would do nothing to change his luck, he said. Fishing had been so bad lately that he was afraid his wife and he might starve. If nothing else, that explained their mutual bad temper.

We have here in Castle Daventry a magic chest. Full of gold, it never empties, always replenishing what is taken from it. Because of this, we have no need for the normal material wealth of the world. So, reaching into her dress, Rosella brought out the pouch of diamonds the dwarfs had insisted she keep. "Here, take these, they should help you."

They both fell quiet when they saw the gems. Rosella insisted they keep them, so the man told his wife to give my daughter his fishing pole. "Thank you," they gushed. "We won't be needing this any more!" Pointing west, they told her the island on the far horizon was Genesta's. They had no boat, they said, and they hoped she was a strong swimmer.

Fishing is said to help relax, calm, and organize the mind. Rosella walked to the end of the long pier, baited the pole's hook with the worm, and cast her line into the sea. She cared not if she caught anything; she just needed a few moments to think of alternatives to swimming to the island. I have always told her that, when puzzled or in doubt, it is wise to stop and think a problem through; patience pays great rewards. This time it didn't pay her way across the waves, but after several casts, she did catch a fish. Rosella looked at it. "I'll be hungry soon," she thought. "Now I've got dinner." For want of a better place, it went into the pocket that had moments before held the worm. Then, fixing her eyes firmly on the hazy island in the west, she dove straight from the pier and stroked directly at it.

My husband Graham, as I have noted, taught his love of swimming to my daughter. She is a strong swimmer, and her sure strokes swiftly shortened the distance to the fairy's island. Once, a whale started to surface not far from her, but she quickly and briefly changed her course to avoid it. The same

The Perils of Rosella

with the one shark fin she spotted; a quick swerve, a burst of speed, and the shark disappeared.

At last my wet daughter stood on the golden beach of Genesta's isle. Birds of all kinds sang in the trees; a magnificent peacock strutted in the sand. She followed it in the direction of the dazzling turreted palace that stood in the island's center. It seemed made of ivory. As she followed the proud bird, a tail feather dropped from the peacock. It continued on its way without noticing the loss. Rosella picked it up; it was pretty, and it wasn't nailed down.

Marvelous gardens surrounded the ivory palace with fragrant bushes, herbs, and flowers. Small paths wandered throughout; a marble statue of dolphins playing in the waves graced one of the garden's corners, and a small pond, home to a pure white swan, adorned another. Hovering above the doors to the palace were two tiny fairies, perhaps the same ones who had accompanied Genesta to her meeting with Rosella. They made no sounds at all, their tiny translucent wings beating in silent strokes. They made no effort to hinder my daughter from opening the great doors and entering.

Inside, Rosella was greeted by two locked doors and a set of stairs leading up through an archway. The two tiny fairies had followed her inside and now fluttered ahead of her and up one of the palace's ivory towers. Rosella followed their lead to the top of the staircase and Genesta's bed chamber. On the marble floor a snow leopard sat guarding the fairy queen, who lay in a seashell bed.

Genesta lay there silently sleeping; pale and thin, she looked close to death. No sound but shallow, labored breathing came from her, and her fairies tried to back my daughter away from their mistress. Rosella was crushed with sorrow; Genesta was losing her hold on life and asleep—perhaps in a trance— was unable to offer her any aid or advice. All Rosella could do was return to the mainland and survive by her wits. Slowly, she left Genesta's chamber, never expecting to see the good fairy alive again. Her steps took her to the beach where she had arrived, and she started swimming back to the mainland.

Fatigue from the first swim had now caught up to my daughter. Following that came another whale. This time Rosella was too tired to elude it, and blackness swallowed her.

In truth it was the whale that gulped her down, but that distinction meant nothing to Rosella at the time. All she knew was that she was alive, in the belly of a whale, breathing noxious, deadly fumes, and swimming in digestive juices. Some ghostly red light, its source unknown, gave meager illumination. Rosella knew she had to get out soon, before the leviathan digested her. Ugh!

The whale's flesh was slimy and slippery. The only place Rosella was able to climb out of the stomach soup was on the far side to her left. From there she could see up the beast's gullet. This became her goal: somehow she would get out the whale's mouth, but first she had to climb up there.

Of course, it wasn't easy, especially in a wet dress that insisted on tangling her knees and tying her ankles. Up and over, up and over; a slip would skid her into forever. So very slowly she crept on that slick flesh, every inch momentous victory. Up and over, up and over, and then success; she could stand!

Looking up, Rosella saw part of the whale's gullet dangling above her—a tonsil, or something like that—it didn't matter. Whatever it was, she determined to tickle the whale with the peacock feather she was carrying, hoping to make the giant beast gag and vomit her up. She was wrong. The leviathan didn't gag, it sneezed.

The less said the better. Moments later Rosella was back out in open air, swimming in a sea of whale snot. But she was alive and could see an island nearby. She swam there as fast as she could.

The Perils of Rosella

Having cleaned herself as best she could and drying in the hot sun, Rosella took quick stock of her situation. She was neither in the dark belly of the beast, breathing poisonous fumes, nor up to her chin in stomach acid. That was good. On the other hand, the island was small, deserted, and without water. Numerous hulls of wrecked ships, mostly submerged, were decaying on the reefs that ringed it. On top of all that, she still had a dead fish in her pocket.

My daughter did not cry, would not cry. She did not shout her frustration to the heavens, she did not curse her turn of fortune. Instead, she took the previously forgotten fish from her pocket and threw it at the only other living thing there, a raucous pelican that seemed to be mocking her. Squawk! Greedily, noisily, the bird snatched the fat fish from out of the air, and as it did so, something fell from its beak onto the sand. It sparkled as it lay there, shiny and metallic. As the bird flew away, Rosella went to see what had fallen. She took it. It was a whistle made of silver, although how the bird had come by it will always be a mystery.

Her curiosity getting the better of her, my daughter searched the rest of the island. Looking on the ground inside the remains of a wrecked rowboat, she saw something else glisten. Picking it up, she marveled at her discovery of a golden bridle and again wondered how such a splendid thing came to be in that desert place. Perhaps one of the wrecks had once been a great treasure ship, dead now, the victim of a forgotten storm.

As Rosella was growing up, climbing trees and playing in the nearby woods, Graham and I had always told her that if she were ever in trouble or needed help, just whistle and we'd come to her aid. The silver whistle reminded her of those happy times of childhood. She walked to the edge of the island and blew on it.

We didn't come, of course, but a dolphin did. Perhaps the whistle brought it; perhaps it was loyal to Genesta and knew Rosella to be her friend and in trouble. It matters not why it came, only that it did. Many times have I read tales of these gentle, friendly creatures helping human folk in distress; I thought the tales to be fables. I have since changed my mind. Flipping and dancing in the shallow water near shore, it seemed to be gesturing for Rosella to ride it to safety. My daughter grabbed hold of the dolphin, and it bore her back over the waves to Tamir. Safely on shore, Rosella looked back to see the dolphin leaping into the air and flipping its shiny tail to the sky. Then it dived, disappearing under the waves. Rosella waved good-bye.

Where was she? That's what Rosella needed to know. Looking south, she could see the fisherman's shack, so she must be a little north of the fishing pier. With that settled, she began walking east looking for the unicorn. She could see stone pillars in that direction, so she decided to look for the unicorn there. If she could get near enough, she would use the bridle to capture it.

Her eastward trek brought Rosella to an artificial pool made of marble. Carved columns, also marble, flanked it on two sides. They looked to be waiting to hold up a roof; perhaps they were just keeping the sky from falling. On another occasion, Rosella might have swum in the pool's inviting waters, but not this time. Too many lives rested in her hands.

As she stood there thinking, a small figure fluttered down on stubby wings and began its own leisurely dip in the pool. At first Rosella thought it might be one of Lolotte's flying monkeys coming to look for her. That impression passed quickly; this being was smaller, chubbier, had no fur, and was completely naked. Her learning served her well; Rosella knew that she was looking at Cupid, the god of love.

Here, she was sure, was help for her. Rosella rushed from the shadows that had concealed her and swiftly walked to where Cupid was bathing. The god looked up at Rosella, surprise on his baby face. Quick as a hummingbird, his

The Perils of Rosella

...That's when she discovered the little key that had been concealed in the rose's leaves.

wings blurred and Cupid flew away from the pool, leaving Rosella with a face full of spray and nobody to talk to.

"Drat! It's so hard to talk to people around here!"

Cupid fled so quickly that he abandoned his tiny bow on the side of the pool. Next to it was a quiver with two arrows— love darts, as Rosella well knew. This discovery wiped all disappointment from her mind; with one of cupid's arrows she could enchant the unicorn, and with the golden bridle, she could take the proud beast to Lolotte. Once there, she would have another chance to get Genesta's Talisman.

With new confidence, Rosella decided to go where she had seen the unicorn before. She ran swiftly south until she reached the river, and followed this west until she came to the meadow. No unicorn. Perhaps it sensed she was there. Quietly she left, waited a few minutes and then returned, slowly and silently. This time the horned horse was there, moving through the meadow, its majestic head held high in the air.

The bow was strung, the arrow ready. Rosella moved as close as she dared and then shot the unicorn a true hit upon its flank. Instantly the magic creature stopped, shook itself, and then turned to face its attacker. Much sadness dwelled in its eyes as it looked to Rosella, but it did not bolt away. Instead, it stood waiting, nickering softly and pawing the ground. Slowly my distraught daughter walked up to it, patting its nose gently and putting the the bit in its mouth. Rosella mounted the unicorn and, sobbing, pointed it towards the Impossible Mountains. All is for the best, she told herself, all is for the best.

Three of the witch's goons set upon them as Rosella and the unicorn started up the path to Lolotte's. Again Rosella was grabbed and flown into the sky, at the mercy of flying monkeys, straight to the throne of the wicked witch.

The Perils of Rosella

Edgar still stood beside his foul mother, his puppy eyes moist as if with tears of relief at Rosella's return.

"I'm still not convinced you are telling me the truth, my ugly little peasant girl!" the witch snorted. At this Edgar flinched and glared at Lolotte. "Bring me the hen that lays the golden eggs, and then I will give you freedom and the promised reward. Fail and you shall die the death of a spy. The hen is kept by an ogre and his wife in the great forest. Go there now and bring it to me. Away with you!"

Rosella was roughly snatched by the flying monkeys and dropped again at the foot of the mountains. Again she felt anger and frustration at herself, having been so close to the witch twice but unable to figure a way to steal the Talisman from her. She hadn't even seen it!

Rosella's fury passed quickly. When her temper flashes it sears with intensity, and then focuses into determination. "All I have to do is steal a precious, golden-egg-laying chicken away from a family of ogres, and probably right out from under their noses. But if I do that, I'll have another chance to get the Talisman from her. Okay, girl; stop talking about it and do it!" At least she had an idea where the ogre's house was.

While she had been looking at tombstones in the graveyard, earlier that day, Rosella had seen the silhouette of a large hut in the distance north of the cemetery. The forest seemed to get more dense in that direction also, so my daughter deduced there was a good chance that that might be the ogre's home. If she were wrong, she was at least in the forest, and Lolotte had said the house was in there somewhere.

Rosella found the hut she was looking for rather easily. "Hut" is the wrong word for it, however; two stories tall, built solidly of large stones with a great thatched roof, it was a large and substantial house. From the look of the oversized doorway and the enormous flagstones leading to it, she felt confident that an ogre could live there. She'd find out soon enough if it did.

My daughter could see nothing by peering through the house's windows. They were set so high off the ground that she could not see into them at all. She decided to walk boldly up to the massive door and simply knock. If she heard anyone inside, she would bolt for the trees; if there was no noise or answer, she'd steal inside and look around.

There was no answer, but there was a very large, very unfriendly watchdog inside. Leaning against the heavy door with all of her weight and strength, Rosella had been able to open it. As she pushed, she heard the dog's growl and, peeking around the door's edge, was able to see it before it saw her. Reaching into her peasant dress, Rosella took out the bone she had been carrying with her for protection—Oh, what good that did!—and threw it inside to the dog. The growls turned to woofs at once as the grateful watchdog snatched the old bone, and then took it to his spot in the corner of the room, gnawing and licking contentedly. The beast stopped paying any attention at all to my girl.

Some tall tables and chairs were all that furnished the room she had entered, and the only decoration was a stuffed dog's head set high on one wall. A doorway opened on the far side of the room, and from within Rosella thought she could hear humming and someone moving around. Stairs went up; so did Rosella, on tip-toes. At the top was one room, filthy, containing a huge bed. Tattered curtains hung on the windows, and a gaping hole yawned unrepaired on the floor. There was a closet in the room, but it was locked and Rosella could find no key. A sharp ax leaned against the right wall. She thankfully took it, thinking it might come in handy if the dog got tired of the bone.

Back downstairs, Rosella saw another closet just by the open doorway. She crept past the dog and discovered the closet was unlocked. The sounds coming from the other room were now loud, and disgusting smells drifted

The Perils of Rosella

out. Evidently someone was cooking food there, but judging from the odor, she didn't want to know what was planned for the next meal.

Rosella quietly opened the door of the closet and slipped in, closing the door noiselessly behind her. A quick search uncovered nothing, especially no golden-egg-laying hen. That's when she heard the second ogre come home, slamming the front door, moving around the house, humming as it went. She was trapped!

Willing her thumping heart to be still, Rosella peered out of the closet through the door's keyhole. The ogre was huge, at least twice her own size, tall and broad with a huge black beard, huge black teeth, and huge muscles. With no idea of what to do next, Rosella decided to wait silently until they left the room, perhaps to go to bed. She prayed that they had no need of her hidey-hole. She watched them eat, and at one point the man started sniffing the air, telling the woman he smelled something. She assured him it was only the decaying deer she was preparing, and this seemed to satisfy him.

When the meal finally ended, the bushy ogre roared to his wife, "Bring me my hen!" Through the tiny hole, Rosella could see a small white hen placed on the table in front of the ogre.

"Lay, I tell you! Lay!"

Soon an egg began to appear from beneath the poor chicken. It was indeed golden and metallic in color. The ogre weighed the egg in his hand a few times, and then put it in a pocket. Moments later he laid his head next to the bird and fell into a contented sleep. His snores rattled the windows.

Rosella knew this might be her only chance to escape with the hen. As soon as she was sure the ogre's wife had returned to the kitchen, she opened the closet door knowing the snores would cover any sounds she made. Quickly she picked up the hen from the high table, only inches beyond the greedy grasp of the sleeping giant, and rushed to the front door. Just as she got there, the hen began to squawk. The noise woke the ogre and brought him roaring after her. Without hesitating, Rosella flung the door open and raced outside, the irate ogre screaming after her.

Speeding out the door, feeling the ogre's hot breath on her legs, Rosella turned left—east—and fled deeper into the forest attempting to elude the enraged creature. Finally, despite the hen's constant squawking, she did escape the ogre and ran right into the arms of even more danger.

I do not know how my daughter endured all she did that day. I am sure I would have gone mad, leaping from danger to danger to near death to sure death to even more danger, one shock following the other so close that it should plunge even the stoutest of heart into gibbering insanity. The young are strong and resilient; they don't think but *know* they are invulnerable and immortal. Perhaps that is what kept her going on. Whatever it was, I will always be grateful!

Rosella found herself in a thick grove of the oddest trees she had ever seen. All around her their branches drooped like zombie fingers eager to snare anyone that came near. Dim, strange lights seemed to glow dully from within them, vampire eyes by firelight. She stopped short; the ogre had ceased giving chase the moment she entered the strange trees. Hefting her newly acquired ax in one hand, the hen snug in the other, she wondered why. In the corner of her eye, she thought she saw a branch move and begin reaching for her. Startled, she swung the ax at the trees, yelling at the top of her lungs as if trying to frighten them. A sudden stillness descended over the odd grove, and the sense of evil she had been feeling lifted. No branch stirred there. All was still and calm again. Rosella wondered if it had been just her overwrought nerves playing tricks. "Probably," she told herself, but not believing. "That must have been it."

The Perils of Rosella

Whatever the truth, she met no more menace in the wood and kept her feet rushing further east towards the Impossible Mountains. There she discovered the skull cave.

At least, that's what it looked like to Rosella, a huge human skull built into the rock of the mountain. The rocks overhanging the entrance hung like teeth, giving the impression that to enter was to enter the maw of death. Smoke twisted up out of the cave through a small chimney, so somebody must be home, she thought. Wrong. Nobody was there, but a black cauldron bubbled over a fire in the middle of the cave. A quick search revealed nothing to Rosella. It was a relief.

Leaving the cave, my daughter sped swiftly south along the edge of the mountains. The afternoon shadows had become very long; night would come soon and she wanted to be through the graveyard before that happened. She was, and Lolotte's monkeys were waiting for her in the usual place.

That Lolotte was evil made flesh is beyond question. If Rosella had any doubts about this truth at the time, they were cleared up as soon as she was dragged into the wicked witch's presence. The hen had been taken from her by the guards, as had the unicorn.

"Poor peasant girl, if that is what you really are, I still don't believe you!" As Lolotte taunted her, the guard held Rosella tighter lest she try to attack their mistress.

"I demand of you a final task. Complete it and all I have promised is yours. Bring me Pandora's Box; it contains the purest evil in the universe, and with it I could—dare I say it? Yes, I dare!—I could rule the world! Find it and bring it to me. Take her away!"

Poor wretched Rosella! To find the box for Lolotte might doom the world to enslavement by the witch. To not find it would surely doom her father, Genesta, and herself, and still give no certainty that Lolotte would be vanquished. The choice was between sure death or barest hope. Rosella chose hope, however slim, resolving to get Pandora's Box and try to overcome Lolotte. She hoped she wasn't making a mistake.

Rosella decided to start her search for Pandora's Box back at the skull cave. There she had seen a number of containers there containing the raw materials of spell casting: weirdly twisted roots, rare herbs, unnaturally colored fluids, and assorted preserved body parts. Chances were it was the workshop of a wizard or perhaps a witch. If she had no success there, she would revisit the old manor house, and if that proved fruitless—well, she hadn't thought the problem through past that point.

My daughter was incorrect in her assumption that a witch might reside in the cave. Not one, but three dwelt within, and by the way they eyed Rosella, she wasn't too sure entering the skull cave had been a good idea. First of all, they were witches of the dark variety, followers of the lefthand path who used their magical art for evil. Then there was their welcome, cold and cackling, like a spider asking the fly to come into its web.

"Hello, little girl. Would you like to join us for dinner?" One look at their boiling cauldron was enough to tell Rosella just what they intended by that invitation.

Lastly, there was the matter of the eye. The three crones were blind except for one glass eye which they were able to pass back and forth between them, cupping it like the rarest of jewels in the palms of their hands. The eye was pointed directly at Rosella, held by one of the weird sisters furthest away from their cave's entry. The woman began giving directions to the witch closest to Rosella, and that one started after my daughter, arms outstretched, fingers writhing, trying to grab her.

Rosella knew at once that if she could take the eye from the dark sisters, she would have no troubles from them. With their sight as hostage, she might

The Perils of Rosella

find out the location of Pandora's Box. All she had to do was avoid the one who was clutching at her.

Because of her youth, Rosella was sure she was quicker than the blind witch. She took a position near the left wall of the cave, slowly moving back and forth a few steps in each direction, enticing the hag to rush her, back and forth, back and forth, keeping a safe distance between them. Rosella's movements were mirrored by the two witches in the rear; back and forth, back and forth they passed the eye, always directing the third. Finally, the witch near Rosella made her move, rushing past the cauldron straight for the girl.

Rosella darted as quickly as she could away from the hag across the cave, past the cauldron and then straight back, almost hitting the great pot, so close did she pass it. Her rush took her to a spot directly between the two hags passing the glass eye. Rosella reached out as quickly as she had run and snatched the eye from them, closing her hand tightly around it.

The three witches screeched, blind and lost; the pursuing one stopped and stumbled, unable to see her prey.

"Give us back our eye!" they demanded, falling on their knees.

"Give me Pandora's Box!" was my daughter's reply.

"We do not have it! Give us back our eye!"

Rosella searched the cave for the second time that afternoon, but did not find the treasure. The hags had been telling the truth. She kept the eye clutched tight so they couldn't follow, and left the cave. Outside, her heart softened; she couldn't leave the witches in blindness forever. With that thought, she went a little way back inside.

The intensity of their pleas increased as the three weird sisters heard her return. One of them threw something in Rosella's direction; it rolled to a stop at her feet.

"Take this, it will protect you from the undead!" one cried. "Look for the box among the undead. Give us our eye!"

Rosella looked to the ground and picked up a scarab—an obsidian charm carved in the form of a scarab beetle. She admired its workmanship and then placed the cool stone against her cheek. She could feel it warm to her touch.

"Thank you for the loan of your eye," she told the witches, her business in the cave done. Rosella walked to its edge, then threw the eye to the cave's floor, away from the three crones. She was out of there before the glass hit the ground, sure they would have revenge if they could get close to her again.

In that part of Tamir the dead walk at night—the restless dead, the uneasy souls, the tormented ones. Zombies that tear the flesh and then devour it prowl among the tombstones. Ghosts, the ephemeral ones, haunt the world seeking peace. Night gaunts, dholes, and ghouls lurk in the darkest places. They wait. They hunt. They feed.

Darkness was beginning to take its daily dominion of the world. Rosella moved swiftly south to the graveyard. She was not particularly looking forward to the prospect; the night chill was about her, and the sounds of the world scratched claws up her back. The scarab, now in one of her pockets, began to vibrate softly.

Zombies smell of damp earth and decaying things that are best left nameless. That's how my daughter remembers them, and she shivers some when she does. They exploded out of the ground, grabbing at her ankles, holding her legs as they pulled themselves from their graves. Rosella screamed, and the undead backed away in fright. At first my daughter thought it was her scream that did it, but when she took the scarab charm from her pocket she could see it glowed with a strong, healthy light. The stone's vibration produced a low hum that had been muffled by her skirt. Rosella thanked the witches under her breath and was glad she had returned them their eye.

Other than the zombies groping hungrily among the tombstones and the locked crypt built into the mountainside, Rosella found nothing in either part of the graveyard. There were no signs anywhere of Pandora's Box. She moved on then to the spooky manor and found that this too had become haunted after dark.

A baby's cry startled her as she stepped inside the front door. It was coming from upstairs. Rosella rushed up the steps, wondering how an infant could have come to the deserted house. The smaller bedroom was as she had left it, as was the master chamber. There, however, the cries came much stronger; their source seemed to be the nursery attached to that room. She quickly entered it. The nursery was still empty, but the old cradle was now gently rocking back and forth. It was empty, but the cries were definitely coming from it. Rosella was sure she could feel a ghostly presence, that of a dead baby seeking comfort. Perhaps the ghost wailing in the cradle was that of the baby whose tombstone she had read before.

Rosella had come across the graves of two children, one in each part of the graveyard; an infant had been laid to rest on the western section. Evidently, it wasn't resting very well. Why the child's spirit had returned to the nursery, Rosella didn't know. Perhaps it was looking for something, or someone. The sound of its crying was heartbreaking.

Rosella walked downstairs to the parlor. The secret door in the wall was open, just as she had left it, and inside that door the shovel still leaned against the stone wall. Rosella took the shovel and left the house. The hags said she might find Pandora's Box amongst the undead, so she intended to open the infant's grave and see if it were there. It would be grim work in the darkness.

The child's tombstone lay in the northwest corner of the western graveyard, partially obscured by the low branches of an overhanging tree. The stone said the child's name was Hiram, and he had died at the age of six months. Rosella read the tombstone and then began to dig. After digging for a few moments, her shovel turned up a small silver rattle mixed with the dirt from the grave; it must have belonged to the unfortunate child. Rosella took it, thinking she would place it in the empty cradle. Perhaps it would quiet the crying ghost.

She returned to her digging, and reached the tiny, pine box holding the baby's remains. She forced herself to open it. It contained the sad remains of the child's burial clothes and his bones, which had been undisturbed until now. That was all she found; she closed the coffin and left. She would refill the hole later.

Rosella returned to the house with the silver rattle, dodging zombies all the way. With the scarab protecting her, they were more nuisance than real danger, but their touch was cold, unwholesome, and thoroughly disgusting. Like too many cats in a house, they were always underfoot.

The cradle continued its ghostly rocking, side to side. The crying still filled the air. Rosella polished the tarnished toy as well as she could with a corner of her skirt, and carefully put it into the cradle. In an instant, both the rocking and the crying ceased completely. Peace returned to the deserted room. It was replaced by terrible noises from downstairs.

Thus began a series of nocturnal huntings and diggings as Rosella sought to quiet the ghosts of that haunted house, all the time searching for the box she must return to Lolotte.

From the landing at the top of the stairs, my daughter spied a second ghost—a stooped old man who trudged from room to room, walking through the walls. He moaned loudly, wailing loss and despair. It sounded as it he were howling the word "gold" over and over and over. Rosella thought the

The Perils of Rosella

wails would drive her insane if she stayed there much longer. She went grave-hunting again in self-defense.

After a search of both parts of the cemetery, Rosella dug up the resting place of one "Newberry Will." She chose his grave because his tombstone branded him a miser—one who valued gold and treasure above all else, doomed to spend the after-life shackled with the chains of greed. The grave was on the southern edge of the western graveyard, and after she had dug there a bit, she discovered a bag of gold coins—nothing else. When she returned to the manor and offered it to the ghost, he snatched it from her and drooled. Then the ghost disappeared, taking with him his wails and moans. They were replaced by the weeping of yet another of the undead.

The third ghost had once been a beautiful young woman, tall and slender, with hair the color of midnight. She didn't appear to be much older than my daughter. She was sitting, rocking, in the small bedroom, her face buried in her hands. The ghost wore a large wedding band, now wet from her crying. Only once did she lift her face to reveal a large pair of gray eyes, flush with tears. Those eyes looked as if they had stared into infinity and had found it wanting. Then the woman's head sank again into her hands and the ghostly weeping continued.

Rosella found her grave in the eastern burial ground. She knew it was the correct one the moment she saw it. A nineteen year old girl by the name of Betty had died of a broken heart after her lover had perished at sea. Rosella dug and found a little locket attached to a thin gold chain. Engraved on it was the image of a black-bearded sea captain—her husband. Again she had not discovered Pandora's Box; again she took a small treasure to the restless dead.

I never knew a ghost could smile, but my daughter says this one did. The young woman's weeping ceased the moment Rosella offered her the locket. She took it, held it up, looked at the picture, smiled, and vanished—rocking chair and all. Rosella felt sorry for the girl and her lost love. Of course, that's when she heard new cries of anguish from downstairs.

Ghost number four looked much like the man etched in the locket; older though, and a soldier from the look of his uniform. He paced despondently in the parlor, peering into corners, under furniture, and behind the few remaining books. Searching, pacing, wailing, the ghost made his futile rounds. One of the ghost's legs had been lost, perhaps in battle, and had been replaced by a wooden one. The sound of his walking was uneven and wrong. Rosella went to the cemetary to find whatever he was looking for.

It turned out to be a medal in the form of a golden cross. Engraved on it were the words "For Valor and Bravery." It had been buried along with Lord Coningsby in the western graveyard where he lay next to his wife. Their graves were closest to the house they must have once lived in. Rosella took the medal of honor back inside and presented it to the apparition. He took it from her reverently and slowly faded from sight.

The last ghost made all of Rosella's frustration about not finding the object of her own quest—Pandora's Box— dissolve just like the phantoms she had been encountering. It started differently than her other unearthly episodes; no moans, no wails, no weeps, just a little boy ghost appearing, teasing Rosella, and trying to get her to chase him. With that, he disappeared into the small bedroom, the one where she had encountered the young widow.

When she had first explored the manor those many hours before, my daughter had noted a trapdoor in that room's ceiling, but no way was visible to reach it. When she followed the boy inside, she found that that situation had changed. The trapdoor was now open and a ladder led up into it. Rosella climbed up into the gloom.

The room must have once been the house's attic; it was cluttered with all sorts of boxes and chests—the trash and treasures of a family home. The boy ghost sat there upon a large and interesting-looking chest. Could this, she thought, be Pandora's Box? There seemed no way to find out, however. The young ghost wouldn't move from the top of the lid. Ghosts may be almost transparent, gauzy and ephemeral, but they can be just as heavy and immobile as they wish. Rosella could not budge it. The boy just sat there smiling and giggling, looking at Rosella as if expecting a treat. She walked to the spot where she had crawled onto the attic floor after climbing up the ladder, and she climbed the ladder back down.

Rosella had no choice but to return to the graveyard; what grave was the boy's? Finally she located it on the eastern side, a largish stone in the northwest corner. It was the same inscription that had overcome her earlier. It marked the grave of a boy named Willy; who had been buried with a toy horse on wheels—without doubt the child's favorite toy. The shovel broke as Rosella finished digging. She hoped it was not a bad omen.

The boy was still sitting on the chest when Rosella returned to the attic, still smiling, still giggling naughtily. She gave the toy to the boy and hoped he would disappear like the others so that she could see what was inside of the chest. This ghost took his time; he looked and grinned merrily at the wooden horse, and finally disappeared with a loud POP! Rosella opened the lid carefully and then peered inside. Pandora's Box? No! All there was inside was some sheet music—old, yellow, and near crumbling to dust. That was all. Carefully, she took the brittle pages.

As Rosella carefully made her way back down the ladder and headed toward the secret staircase past the parlor, she couldn't help grinning at a riddle I had asked her once when she was much younger: What is a ghost's favorite kind of music? All the way up that narrow, treacherous stone stair she kept chuckling and repeating aloud, "Sheet music. Sheet music. Ghosts like sheet music!" The old joke helped release much of her tension and anxiety.

Two flaming torches illuminated the tower room containing the organ, although how they had been lighted is a mystery. Rosella moved directly to the instrument and played the sheet music on the organ. The melody was deep and somber, the tempo a slow march. As Rosella played, a small, secret drawer opened out of the organ's front; in it was a key. "After what I've been through, I'll bet it's a skeleton key," Rosella murmured to herself cynically. She finished playing the music and took the key; she had decided it must be the key to the crypt. After all, she reasoned, it was the only thing in or near the house that was locked.

She survived her final trip down the tower stairs and again thought bad thoughts about the person who invented the long skirt. In the front hall she paused but a moment to see the time. It was almost midnight, time was running out for her father and Genesta. Then she sped out of the house and straight to the crypt in the mountain.

The key fit. Rosella unlocked the door, slowly opened it, and stepped inside to the most elaborate burial chamber she had ever imagined. She found herself on a platform above the tomb's floor; hieroglyphics were scribbled over all of the walls, and a massive coffin stood in one corner. So colorful and exotic was the place that Rosella imagined that it must have been dug into the mountain in the days of ancient Aegypt. On the opposite side of the crypt, resting by itself, alone on the floor, was a small box. Pandora's?

A rope ladder lay piled at Rosella's feet, left there for people to climb up and down between the door and the floor. She took the rope and dropped it down, climbing quickly after it. That's when the ancient coffin opened and a figure lurched out at Rosella. The mummy walked heavily for several steps, arms reaching for my daughter; then it stopped short. Rosella felt the obsidian scarab vibrate more rapidly in her pocket. The undead one returned to its resting place. My daughter sighed with relief; if the scarab had not worked, she would have had no place to flee.

211
The Perils of Rosella

The box was not particularly large; it could be easily fit in one hand. It was made of some unfamiliar, heavy, black metal and decorated with blasphemous shapes. It both looked and felt evil; it was indeed Pandora's Box, hidden away and guarded by the mummy for eons. Rosella took the box and climbed out of the crypt. She turned her back on both the graveyard and the haunted house and walked south, knowing Lolotte's flying monkeys would find her as she started up the mountain path. She almost welcomed their rough embrace.

Lolotte was in a frighteningly light mood when my daughter was brought before her for the last time. The evil one asked Rosella her name and then announced that she was to get her reward, and it would not to be her freedom—oh no! Instead, Lolotte had decided my daughter would marry her deformed son Edgar in the morning. Until that time she was to spend the night in Edgar's room, alone. Then she ordered her goons to strip my girl of all her possessions, leaving but the clothes on her back. Rosella gasped. She faced a fate, she thought, much worse than death!
The black-garbed guards escorted my princess to a room at the top of one of the castle's high towers. They slammed the door shut and stomped down the stairs. Before they left, she heard the click of the door being locked, and no matter how hard she shoved and pushed, she couldn't budge it open. Despondently, Rosella looked around the tower room that she soon would be forced to share with the witch's son.

My daughter had just about given up all hope when she heard a small sound at her door, not at all like the tramping of the guards. Rushing over to the door, she saw something that had not been there before—a red rose, still fresh on its long stem. "Who could have placed it there?" she thought. Bending over, she picked it up and brought it to her nose, her eye catching a golden glint. That's when she discovered the little key that had been concealed in the rose's leaves. She took it. Trying it in the chamber door, Rosella heard, and felt, the blessed click of the lock. She turned the knob and the door quietly opened. Rosella was free! Now she had to find Lolotte and somehow get the Talisman from her.

The stairs down were so dimly lit that she could barely see where to put her feet. Slowly and quietly, as silent as a zombie, Rosella made her escape down the cold steps, each one taking her further from her prison. As she rounded the last curve, she spotted one of the monkeys standing guard at the bottom. It looked as if it were sleeping on duty.

Rosella hugged the wall as tightly as she could, trying to blend with the shadows, thinking quiet zombie thoughts. The guard still did not move. She crept along, keeping as far away from it as possible. Inch by inch, she came closer to the open archway at the bottom of the tower, and then she was through.

She found herself in the castle's cheerless dining room where a large table and benches covered most of the floor. Rosella imagined this was to be the site of her wedding breakfast; it was a meal that she planned never to taste. Another guard was posted here, near two new doorways. It too was nodding in light sleep; the lateness of the hour seemed to be favoring her escape.

Rosella continued hugging walls and their shadows as she passed in front of the guard across the room. The first of the doorways she came to led into Lolotte's throne room, but she continued on to the second, within short reach of the flying monkey. Rosella could hear its soft snoring as she went by, holding her breath and wishing herself as skinny as she could. This door led to the kitchen, which was deserted, cold, and with no other exit. Rosella made a silent search of the place, and in one of the two large cabinets, she discovered her stolen possessions; she took them all. She was overjoyed and spent an extra moment caressing Cupid's bow and its lone arrow. Putting her fingers to her lips, Rosella lightly breathed, "Lolotte! This one's got your

The Perils of Rosella

name on it!" She touched her kissed fingers to the arrow's tip and crept out of the kitchen the way she had entered. The guard still snored.

Two final monkey guardians had to be passed. The first stood by Lolotte's throne, and she just ran past it, sprinting silently by the bottom of the throne's stair. The last guard was beyond the door on the other side of the throne room, at the base of the second tower's stairs—the same tower where she had been taken when she had been imprisoned in the torture chamber. Both of the guards slept; in fact, all she had encountered had been dozing. Could it be that they cared for their mistress so little that they thought nothing of sleeping on duty? She knew not.

Rosella had to keep moving if she were to find Lolotte and recover Genesta's Talisman. Dawn would come shortly, and the fairy queen would die soon after if Rosella were not successful. Up she climbed, terrified of any misstep. Up she climbed, each step, she dreamed, taking her closer to the witch. Halfway up, she saw light from the hallway that led to the torture cell. She saw guards moving about there, definitely not asleep. That meant up again, to the top of the tower.

My daughter suspected that Lolotte kept her private chambers at the top of the stairs, much as Edgar's were at the pinnacle of the other tower. She double-checked the bow and arrow; they were ready for their intended target. Up and up she climbed and arrived at an ornate door, identical with the one in Edgar's room.

Shooting someone, however evil they be, however necessary the act may be, is not a task for the faint or indecisive. Neither is it an act to be performed lightly. Rosella knew that the fate of those she loved—and of our entire world!—was attached to the single arrow she carried, just as firmly as the feathers of the arrow's fletching were glued to its shaft. She readied herself in body and mind, breathing deep to slow her heart and steady her eye and hand. She put all thoughts out of her mind save that of the deed she had to do. She felt neither joy nor fear, just focus and action.

The little gold key fit in the lock, just as she had suspected it would. Softly she opened the door, trying not to waken the evil witch. Rosella found her deep asleep in her huge bed—easily large enough to hold an ogre and his wife comfortably. My brave child wasted no time in idle observation. She drew the bow's string to her ear, aimed at Lolotte's sleeping heart, and shot. The golden arrow of love flew true to its target!
Lolotte sat straight up from her next to final sleep, Cupid's arrow buried deep in her chest. Agony and pain distorted her face. "Aaah," she screamed. "The pain! The pain! I cannot stop the pain!" In her last instant, Lolotte saw Rosella standing there, the bow still held straight in front of her. The evil witch made a last effort to rise, to get to my daughter, but she crumpled over.
"I'll get you, peasant girl. I'll get you!" With that, she fell finally silent. Her body stilled, empty of life.

Edgar entered his mother's chamber with the dawn. He looked at her body silently for a moment and then offered Rosella her freedom and the freedom of the castle. He still wore his puppy eyes and looked at my daughter with longing. Then he left Rosella alone. He never looked back at his mother.

Rosella found the Talisman hanging from a chain around the dead witch's neck. It could only be that because goodness radiated from it, not evil. She took it and walked out of Lolotte's chamber. She had not intended to kill her enemy, merely control her as she had the unicorn, transforming the evil witch with the power of love. Killing the evil one had left Rosella feeling empty and shattered, but it did not totally cover her sense of triumph.
The guards bowed to Rosella as she entered the hall halfway down the stairs. They informed her that they had never loved the witch; she had cast a

spell over them and forced them to do her bidding. Rosella acknowledged their apologies with a smile and short nod of her head. The moment was shattered then by the raucous squawking of a hen from behind the door by which she was standing. She opened it. Inside was the hen that laid the golden egg. In the far corner rested Pandora's Box. Rosella took them both.

It was now time to return the Talisman to Genesta, and to hide to box again in its crypt to prevent someone else from trying to use its evil. Rosella slowly walked back down the stairs and back through the witch's throne room, vowing never to return. She turned her back on Lolotte's throne and walked outside to freedom.

Near the front gate of the castle stood a small stable, and Rosella found the unicorn imprisoned inside of it. She opened the gate that confined the great magic beast, and it bolted to its own freedom, kicking and waving its forelegs and neighing in joy. As the unicorn disappeared down the mountain, Rosella wished she were riding it; she didn't relish her own long walk to the sea.

My daughter was weary. The strains of the past two days had left her mind and body on the verge of exhaustion. She had rested little and eaten nothing since being taken to be sacrificed to the dragon—Oh, how that seemed so far in her past at that moment!—but she pushed on down, taking extra care not to lose her footing on the dirt path. Once down, it was but a short way to the ornate crypt where she returned Pandora's Box to the exact spot from which she had taken it. Then she closed the crypt door and locked it behind her. Rosella kicked the key back under the door so no one would ever possess the evil of Pandora's Box again. Then she walked the last distance to the sea.

The swim to Genesta's island seemed never to end, but my daughter arrived there before her strength gave out. The fairy queen was still in her bed, barely conscious. Praying that she was in time, Rosella gave the

Talisman to Genesta. She watched Genesta's eyes open wide as the healing powers brought life back to the fairy's face.

"You have saved my life, Rosella! Tamir and I owe you a great debt!"

A short while later, Rosella and Genesta stood on the beach, looking at the hen that lays golden eggs. In her fatigue my daughter had carried the remarkable hen all the way over the sea from Lolotte's. It had squawked and screamed the entire time. Genesta was surprised to see the hen; it had once been hers, but had been stolen and never recovered until now. The fairy queen could hardly believe her double good fortune.

The rest goes quickly. Before returning my daughter home to Daventry, Genesta told her that there was another person who had performed a brave deed and was deserving of reward. With a wave of her magic wand, poor, twisted Edgar was on the beach beside them, blinking madly from his unexpected transport and the bright sun.

"Edgar was the one who brought you the key that let you escape. He has a beautiful soul trapped in a horrid body, and I shall make that injustice right." Another wand wave and Edgar was transformed completely. In place of his deformed body, he now stood straight and tall and handsome.

Edgar loved my daughter—he may still love her—and asked Rosella to marry him as soon as he saw that she was there on the beach with him. Rosella looked at him for a few moments and smiled.

"I'm sorry, Edgar. Perhaps we will meet again." She gave him a quick kiss. He blushed.

Another wave of the wand and Rosella's filthy peasant clothes were replaced by her own relatively clean court gown. One last goodbye, one last pass of the magic wand, and Genesta sent Rosella home bearing the magic fruit that would soon heal her father—my dear husband.

My baby was home safe!

We both finally cried.

Iconomancy: A Magic Without Words

by Alexander of Daventry

King's Quest

I find it somewhat ironic, if not humbling, to realize that the more one learns, the more one learns that one has not learned enough. The more a person studies and explores the mysteries and secrets of Magic; the more questions found answered in scrawled worm-munched and mold-infected parchments; and the more foul dungeons and death-cold catacombs wandered in search of new wonders, the more the thaumaturgical tourist becomes baffled. Each new discovery brings a few new facts, but with them come a passel of new perplexities. Like a flea on a dragon's hide, we think that the little we perceive is all there is to the beast. Then we bite, and the dragon scratches. If we survive the encounter, we find ourselves elsewhere on the beast, its smoking snout perhaps, discovering in the process that there is more to the dragon than we could ever have imagined. Magic is like that. As soon as we think we know what it is, how it works, and how to control it, the universe absently raises a hind leg and...off we go again.

Of course it's not fair. On the other hand, the lack of fairness on the part of the multiverse, all of the universes of existence, is one of the few things we do know for sure.

Elsewhere, I have written at much length concerning the proper practice of the magical craft. I have shown how would-be magicians can never be too careful in following all the proper instructions and steps in the casting of spells. If the proper ingredients are not used in proper amounts and in the proper order; if the proper words are not intoned at the proper time; if the magic wand is not properly charged; and if it isn't properly waved at the proper time, then the envisioned magical spell will not work properly—if at all. Also, the would-be wizard will most probably suffer consequences of the direst nature. In cooking, a misread direction might only result in a baked cat instead of a baked pudding. In Magic, a missed or misread direction might easily turn the spellcaster *into* a cat. Or dead.

Or much worse.

Iconomancy: A Magic Without Words

In the past I have written that there are but two kinds of magicians. I have since reconsidered. In truth, there are just three kinds of magicians: Magicians, dead magicians, and those who wish most heartily that they were dead.

Sometimes we are so busy looking at water that we miss seeing the ocean. Some things, and some facts, are so obvious as to be missed. Thus it is with magic. The small and simple household spells, ensorcellments, bindings, petty conjurations, love potions, and enchantments are passed around from mouth to ear, seldom inscribed on parchment. Their simplicity is such that, even when mistakes are made in the casting, the worst that might befall the practitioner is an occasional blood blister, wart, partial baldness, or a week or two of bladder incontinence. Minor annoyances for minor spells, simple maladies for simple magics.

The greater magics and sorceries, because of their very complex natures, must be recorded in some way. Obviously, to learn and use such incantations, the sorcerer must be able to read the words inscribed in the scrolls and books of the Art. To practice the Craft of Magic, it is not enough to be careful, to follow directions perfectly, and to keep your magic wand fully charged. *To be a magician, you must know how to read!* How often we overlook this. How often we have blithely assumed this to be true.

Moreover, many of the most powerful and fearsome of the magical tomes are inscribed in languages and symbols either long dead, unknown to the magician, or from races other than that of the human folk. Some are reputed to have existed since the times before the Lizard Folk crawled out of their swamps to raise their gargantuan cities, and rule the stars for untold millions of years. The Lizard Folk themselves died out, victims of other arcane sorceries from beyond the multiverse itself. Some even claim that those insane and incomprehensible magics which destroyed the lizards—the very sounds of which cannot be conceived nor reproduced by humans—exist still, written into the very shapes of the clouds and patterns of the winds. How can one read the words of such spells? How can a sorcerer utter the proper sounds?

We magicians are smug, I believe, in a certain picture of ourselves surrounded by our paraphernalia, our flasks and retorts and glass tubes and jars of dried esoterica. We wave our wands and invoke all of the powers we can command while those tools and supplies of our Craft look on without comment, silent acolytes at the altar of Magic. We take our time, make our gestures, cast the spell that we will, and then return to our books or our cups. In our peculiar liturgy, we control the time we take, and not the opposite. What then if sorcerers clash in battle, when one might not have the luxury of slowly building a spell to some titanic climax? Or, is it true, as some folk say, that the winner in any such contest of magical mayhem is the one who doesn't die of boredom?

When King Graham of Daventry, my father, fought and defeated the evil sorcerer Mordack in magical combat, he used a type of magic that was unknown to me until that time. King Graham is not a magician and, to the best of my knowledge, has not studied any grimoire or other compendium of the sorcerous arts. Mordack threw spells at my father potent enough to defeat great necromancers with just the wave of his wand. Yet King Graham vanquished the wizard, perhaps the most powerful mage I have ever encountered, after having studied this unique form of magic for only a few moments. True, my father has a good memory and is well trained and able to remember whole pages of manuscript at a glance, but he had not the luxury of lingering over Mordack's syllabus of mystical spelling, *The Objurgation of Souls*, for long.

To be a magician, you must know how to read. Although overlooked, it is nonetheless taken for granted; a truth so obvious as to be paid no mind. It is a conventional wisdom that is never doubted. The trouble with conventional

Iconomancy: A Magic Without Words

wisdoms, however, is that they are conventional. But the multiverse is large, and occasionally the dragon scratches.

All of the rules of spellcasting as I knew them were broken in that conflict which concluded, happily, in my father's favor. Later, like the scratched flea suddenly sitting on the dragon's nose, I began exploring Mordack's book, touring this new land of magical mysteries. In it, I discovered a different type of wizardry, one completely without words, artifice, or artifact. I have named this new form of spell-casting *Iconomancy*—conjuration through pictures.

It is because of its very simplicity that King Graham was able to master it as quickly as he did. I suspect that anyone of normal intelligence, and even average memory, might learn it with little effort and in a modest amount of time. It works thusly.

Sometime in the past, certain potent images—I call them Icons—were crafted, drawn onto the pages of the *Objurgation of Souls* to be studied and used. Whether it was by Mordack or by someone else, I do not know, although I suspect the manuscript is of a great age and protected from decay by magical means. Whoever created the icons, was a very strong sorcerer, able to imbue his or her mystic power into the very pictures which were created. So strong and powerful is the magic drawn into the icons, that all one needs to do to use them is to strongly and accurately recall the mere image of the desired spell. Concentrating with the eye of one's mind, the magician merely clears the intellect of all extraneous thought, forms a clear picture of the spell, and lingers with that image for a moment, much as one would caress the memory of a lover. This takes but a moment or two.

Our language has no word for the ultimate step, activating the magic. For that reason, I have taken the liberty to suggest a word to describe the willing of the spell into reality. The mind *clicks* on the spell in a moment of finality, one which tells the universe that, yes indeed, we perceive the image representing the spell as real and, at once, the spell *is*.

Thus it truly happens. It is much easier done, than described. Like relieving one's bladder, one doesn't know how it's done, one just decides, then does it.

It goes without much saying that the spellcaster must be in possession a of potently charged Wand of Magic during this act. Few magics work properly, if at all, without the stick of sorcery to channel and propel the magical energies through the aether from the caster to its culmination. *Iconomancy* is not one of the exceptions.

Much like I have transcribed portions of *The Sorcery of Old*, I shall now reproduce, as accurately as my modest artistic skills will allow, such excerpts from *The Objurgation of Souls* as I feel safe in bringing to the knowledge of others. Many of the magics contained within those always-new pages can set the stars reeling drunkenly between the realms of night, and others can melt the mind of almost anyone who might gaze on their images.

What is recorded here are a number of *changings*, spells of transformation to and from various mortal forms. Using these spells, the mage will be able to change from the human form into another and, indeed, from any of these forms into still another. These castings are most powerful and aggressive, and seem to have been intended for use in wizardly warring. If you must use or experiment with them, do so wisely.

Much evil and misery has passed through the lands of our world, despite good folk and better intentions. Use these powers of *Iconomancy*—use all the many magical powers—in the cause of good, and for a world filled with peace.

Dragon of Fire

Dragon of Fire is used to turn the spellcaster into that most fearsome of beasts, the fire-breathing dragon. It is a spell of great power, and can be used for both attack and defense. Few can remain in the dragon form for much time, and repeated change into this shape is impossible.

Such monsters come in many sizes, and some even come with many heads. This particular spell will create a dragon large enough to easily crisp a dozen people with one incendiary snort of its single snout. The fire dragon is a most misunderstood creature. Though excessively dangerous, they are known to be shy and reclusive beasts who live in dark, cool caves, especially ones where gold or gems may be found. They are most attracted to sparkly and glittery things, and normally use their bright flames in order to look at the bright reflections caused by their fire illuminating the rich walls of their dens.

    Despite their armored hides, massive size, and terrifying appearance, fire dragons have an enormous weak spot. They are among the dullest, most stupid of creatures. For that reason, a magic user of even modest power can overcome the dragon's weak will and easily bind it to their biding. Oft times sorcerers use the dragons as war beasts, to terrorize and immolate all who might stand against them. Again too, they are frequently employed to stand guard over the treasures of mages or countries, and it was such a dragon that King Graham was forced to overcome as he quested to save Daventry and become its monarch.

    The dragon which I slew in order to rescue my sister, Princess Rosella, was most likely also under some ensorcellment. If it had been marauding on its own, it would have cindered her quickly and moved on to new victims. It is still a mystery to all as to who set that particular dragon of fire to ravage Daventry, as it could neither have been Manannan nor Mordack.

    Fire dragons have extremely poor eyesight. This fact is of scant use to humans and many of the little folk as the beasts can still see things as small as a young child. However, it is almost entirely vague to smaller animals and the tiny fairies. This fact was all but unknown until one aspiring magician promised to rid a small principality of its overpopulation of rabbits. She entranced a fire dragon and directed it to a carrot patch that was a particular favorite of bunnies. With a theatrical wave of her wand, she commanded the beast to use its breath and to, "Fire!". The dragon breathed, but with no effect on the rabbits who bolted back into their holes in fright, even though the flame was not cast in their direction.

    And so it was that the castle lost both its scarecrows, and the poor magician lost her job.

Iconomancy: A Magic Without Words

Rabbit Run

Rabbit Run seems a most incongruous of spells, one of limited use to any but those who prefer their vegetables raw. Nonetheless, this is an excellent spell for both defense, unseen exploration, and getting into and out of tight spots.

Rabbits are among the quickest, nimblest and most agile of creatures. By transforming into one, a mage can easily dodge most humans or large beasts, either with speed, a sudden hop, an impossible seeming change of direction, or a quick bolt into a tiny hole. Rabbits are quite attuned to dangers, and one who transforms into the furry shape attains much of that sensitivity. One can recognize peril much sooner than in human form and scoot from it before it gets too close. Once safely shrunk, the mage then has the freedom to explore where he or she dare not stick an arm or hand. The safety of a bolt hole also allows time to plot new strategies or consider further transformation. It is not considered wise, however, to turn into something much larger whilst sequestered in a small and enclosed space, especially underground.

Many feel that rabbits, because of their quickness to flee or spook, are cowardly creatures. Nothing could be further from the truth. Their hind feet are quite strong and have been known to knock other rabbits, cats, small dogs, or snakes senseless.

Against other opponents their own size, the advantage of being a rabbit shrinks. What good is it to dart into a tight hole if you're fleeing from a hungry weasel or fox? In times like that, a dead-end burrow can become exactly that as the unfortunate spellcaster ends up dead.

Iconomancy: A Magic Without Words

Ring of Fire

Ring of Fire is the least potent of an entire family of fire transformation spells, the rest of which, because of their awesome magnitudes, will be omitted here. Their names, *Walls of Flame, Total Holocaust, Chaos and Conflagration,* and *Eater of Worlds* give some small idea of how powerful these others are. This is not to imply that Ring of Fire is but a candle's flame compared to the solar orb. No. It is deadly and destructive, but its power is contained in a small area, the size of which is easily controlled by the spellcaster.

Because of its ability to be finely controlled, Ring of Fire is unique amongst flame spells. Firstly, it is most often used to contain its victims, surrounding them with flames so as to eliminate any possibility of escape. The wizard can then choose to capture his or her foe alive, or not, as the mood strikes them.

This leads to the spell's second unique property. It effects only living matter; when closed on its victim it only touches that unfortunate being. Thus it can be used indoors with great effect. Without this property, many an unwary spellcaster might find themselves consumed along with their foes in the fierce flames.

As awful as the effects of Ring of Fire are, I am grateful that it only works over a small area. It is most harrowing to envision some evil or mad being able to cast a magic which would immolate all life in a town, city, castle or country, but leave all else untouched. This would imply a value choice of the deepest perversity. It is vile and evil enough that one might choose to destroy individual lives on such a vast scale. How much more evil is it then to choose material and lifeless things—lands, dwellings, possessions, treasures and geegaws—over life itself. I shudder and sweat cold at the thought, the same as the multiverse itself must.

229
Iconomancy: A Magic Without Words

Rainmaker

Rainmaker seems to have originated as an attempt at creating a benign agricultural spell. As is true for most Iconomancic spells, however, the full geographical range of its effect is somewhat limited. In my own experiments with it, I have been unable to use it to bring rain to an area much larger than the palace garden at Castle Daventry. As a drought fighting spell, therefore, it is of limited usefulness. In theory, Rainmaker could be cast as often as necessary to cover a much larger region. But, the toll it would take on the energies of the magician would likely prove fatal long before sufficient rain might be conjured. It is also likely that the spellcaster's Wand of Magic would be consumed into nothingness by attempting to channel so much magical energy. Especially among magic users, it is always good advice to never spread oneself too thin.

On the other hand, Rainmaker is an excellent example of the magical laws of Opposites. There are several such laws that we know of, although I suspect that there are still more to be uncovered. In general, the laws of Opposites allow a wizard to manipulate one form of energy, matter, or *simile* in order to achieve its apparent opposite. An example might be the death of a sacrificial being in the attempt to create life in another. Another might be endless removal of portion upon portion of a single cake in order to feed sweet treats to multitudes; in consuming the cake, more is created.

Another form of the laws of Opposites concerns the idea that for every magical spelling, conjuration, or ensorcellment, there exists a negating incantation or enchanting; an opposite that is used to cancel, or oppose, the first.

Thus it is with Rainmaker. Because it cleanses the air, it can be used to nullify smoke spells or enchantments of psychic befuddlement and depression. It goes without saying that it opposes many of the fire magics most effectively.

Rainmaker can be used indoors, but the mage should be careful that the water has a way of escaping the closed space lest the spellcaster drown in his or her own success.

Snakemaker

Snakemaker turns the spellcaster into one of the most dangerous of vipers, the King Cobra. Such a snake is most fearsome and deadly. In such a form, the wizard can hold at bay, frighten, or attack most mortal creatures quickly and with a most mortal effect. Some beings are impervious to the cobra's venom, and creatures much larger than the human can withstand the effects of the poison longer. But, if the mage recognizes the exceptions, this can be a most lethal of transformations.

Besides the ability to strike with poisonous swiftness, Snakemaker, much like Rabbit Run, allows the shape-changer to venture into places too small or tight for humans. On the other hand, snakes do not have good vision in the dark so this is not a particularly effective transformation for exploring dark places. It is a good form, though, to chase cats in. If I had known the spell whilst being terrorized by Manannan, as his brother Mordack's prisoner, I would surely have used it.

Because snakes tend to make their diet of small critters and vermin, this is an excellent spell to be used in household or barnyard pest control.

Iconomancy: A Magic Without Words

Riki Tiki Tavi

Riki Tiki Tavi is a most unusual name for a spell, as it seems to be nothing more than a somewhat pleasing sequence of sounds. Oft times in magic, though, mere sounds can contain great powers in themselves. The aged and great Grand Wizard Crispinophur practices a magic that relies much on such words of power. "Open Sesame!", "Abracadabra!", "Shazam!", "Etaoin Shrdlu!", and "Iä R'lyea! Cthulhu fhtagn! Iä! Iä!" are some obvious examples of sounds which, of their very nature, have extreme potency. I shall not dwell on this particular topic any further at this point, except to bring your attention to another pair of highly efficacious sounds, "Scat!" and "Git!". To the felines and canines of the world, these are extremely powerful exclamations, and magical in their effect on such creatures.

I suspected Riki Tiki Tavi to be much as explained above. When I had the leisure to study *The Objurgation of Souls* at some length, however, I discovered a short note in the margin of the page which contained this particular spell. Faded so as to be almost invisible, it appeared to be of some antiquity and most likely was already there when Mordack attained possession of the magical tome.

Riki Tiki Tavi transforms its caster into a small rodent-like creature, the mongoose. Mongooses are kept as pets by some because of their docile natures, except when it comes to rats and poisonous snakes. These are the natural prey of the mongoose, and they will attack and kill these creatures whenever they come across them. So it is for this reason that they are kept and treasured in domains much afflicted by the above.

Riki Tiki Tavi, so the marginal note states, is the name of one particular mongoose that once lived in the *Other World*. It is said that his bravery and courage in protecting his keepers from a family of cobras are renowned throughout that universe. Evidently, tales of his exploits were carried along at a time when some folks who knew the tale *withdrew* here. I suspect that the fabricator of the spell was especially taken by the story (which is totally unknown to me, nor recorded anywhere that I can find), and named the spell after the creature. Perhaps Riki Tiki Tavi himself was able to *withdraw* here and was known to the spell's author. Or, mayhaps he became a familiar to the unknown wizard. Whatever; if the short note is accurate, then the unique name is explained.

This spell, of course, has much practical use in vermin and viper control.

Tiger's Claw

Tiger's Claw transforms the spellcaster into one of the the most feared felines in the universe. A thousand pounds of furred fury, stiletto fangs, and diamond-cutter claws, the wild tiger is a flesh-eater that must consume massive amounts of fresh meat each day. It is a fast, quick, strong and bloodthirsty beast whose thick fur helps protect it from many of the stings and arrows of its prey. It is quick enough to swat enemies from out of the air, swift enough to run down almost anything it desires, and strong enough to wrestle the strongest of enemies. Many tigers have been known to have developed a taste for human flesh, having discovered that two-legged prey is easy hunting.

The only other big cats more feared than the jungle tiger are its larger relatives, the were-tiger and the saber- toothed tiger, Growl Tiger the Bravo Cat, and the mysterious Cheshire Cat, who attacks and disappears so fast as to leave only its deadly grin behind, so quick is it gone.

Tiger's Claw is one of the better spells to use if suddenly attacked, and a transformation is needed. Because of the tiger's savagery and versatility, the spell can be used to quickly overcome most foes, unless they are much larger or much stronger. Against tigers, fire is an excellent defense since their claws and teeth can do no damage to flames.

Flying Sting

Flying Sting is one of those spells that appears to be of an age earlier than that of the human folk, or from before the very creation of the multiverse. It is even possible that it originated in a place beyond the stars. If not these explanations, how can one explain how *alien* it looks and the miasma of repulsion it exudes?

Flying Sting turns the wizard insane enough to use it into an apparent fleshless flying monstrosity armed with a curving poison stinger that kills horribly at a touch. No cure is known for its poison, and the death throes and agonies of its victims brand burningly into one's nightmares after merely reading of them. I know; I have read.

And, I have dreamed.

The general appearance of the Sting is that of a large chitinous bug with no soft flesh, just hard armor and tough leathered, featherless wings. It has a long, fluted, transmuted-mantis head, and makes sounds like a creaking coffin lid squeaking like hard chalk across slate. Acid pours from a lipless, jagged, and fanged hard mouth; one that can rip through flesh as a sharp blade slices through old, soft meat. Its long sting curls inward in a spring-like spiral beneath its segmented and plated belly, and between its many crustacean-like shelled legs. The sting uncurls as quick as sudden death, outward to its target spewing its ample poison in deadly drops as it does. Death comes with certainty, though neither easy nor quick. It is not a huge scorpion with wings; it is much worse.

The Sting is a foul creature from beyond our most fevered and feared nightmares. To face one is to face certain death. *The Objurgation of Souls* claims that it is impervious to fire and ice, and that the only possible protections against its strike are a quick reflex, a thick hide, or an armored one.

It also states that the very aroma of the Sting is enough to kill a human if breathed very deeply, or for very long.

10

Absence Makes the Heart Go Yonder

(From the Chronicles of Daventry, Part 5)

240
King's Quest

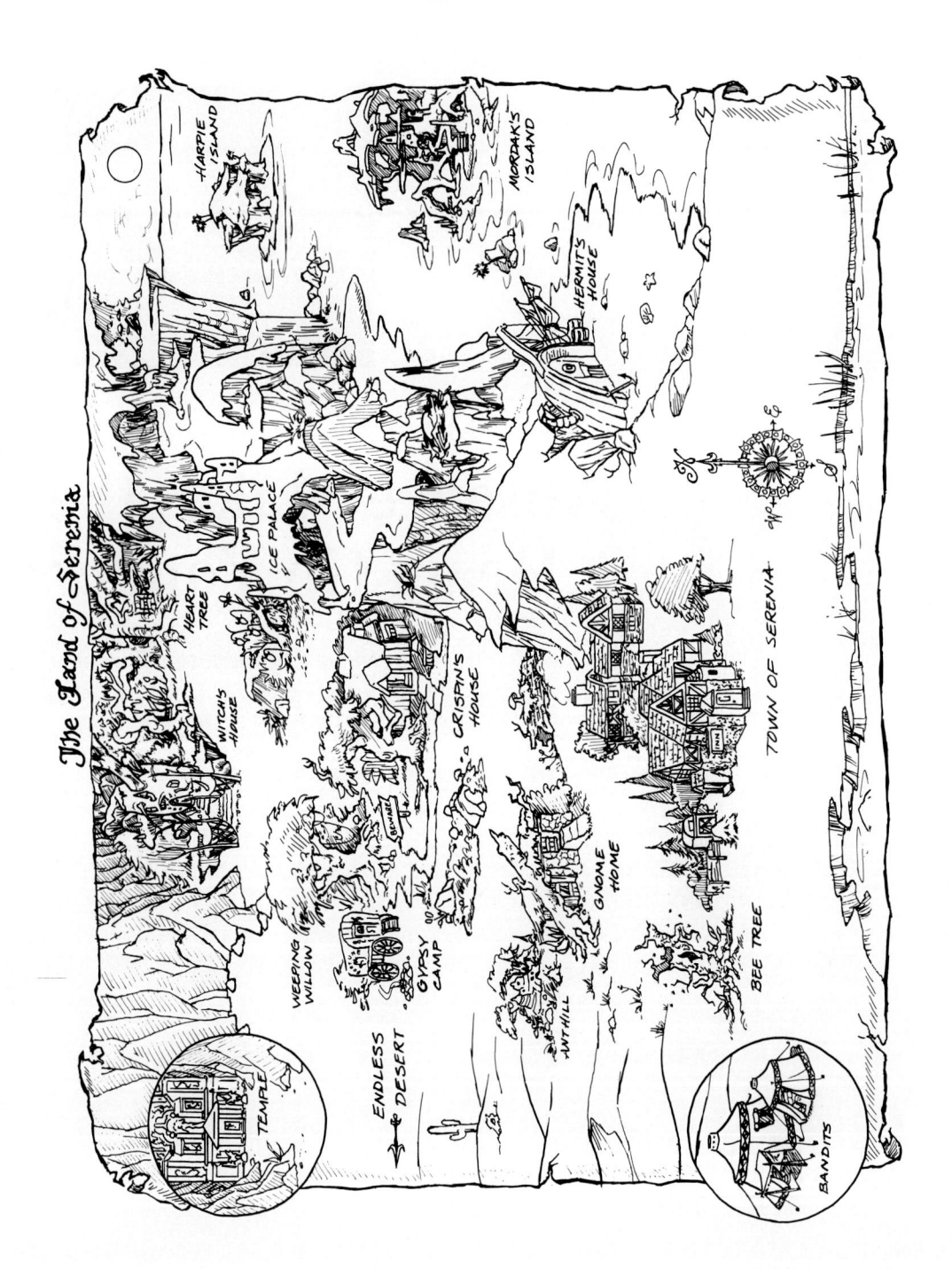

Absence Makes the Heart Go Yonder

A note to readers: The events of the past few moons have been horrifying and harrowing to all the good folks of Daventry. The abduction of the realm's royal family, all of its retainers, and Castle Daventry itself was an evil of such magnitude and monstrosity that it transcends the commonplace wonders of our magical dimension. That our emotions still reel as if drugged, back and forth from ecstatic relief to numbed revulsion, is everyday testimony to the common psychic wound we all suffered. It is a laceration that will be a long time healing even with magical remedies, and which may never heal fully cleanly. That King Graham and his family suffered yet more is beyond the easy comprehension of this editor.

Derek Karlavaegen, a frequent, distinguished, and popular contributor to The Times of Daventry, *is closer to the story of those events than most. A friend of Prince Alexander and a frequent house guest of the royal family, he has a unique perspective on the personal impact of the outrage upon them. Karlavaegen also resides in the former home of the renegade Manannan, and has since soon after the sorcerer was turned into a cat by Prince Alexander. He feels fortunate, if not unduly lucky, that Mordack left him unscathed.*

Derek Karlavaegen was invited by King Graham and his family to spend some time at the refurbished Castle Daventry with them, not long after their ordeals. They asked him to write and record, for all who might read, the quest of the King of Daventry. We print it here in its entirety, unedited, with Karlavaegen's personal observations included.

PRELUDE

The universe is not fair. It never has been fair and never will be. Indeed, the entire multiverse is not fair. It wasn't made that way. It wasn't made to accommodate the folk and creatures and mountains and seas that blemish the worlds and celestial orbs. It is much too large to be conscious of such less than trivial things. The silent universe concerns itself with the greater things, and with the cosmic balances; the symmetry of forces that keep the stars and planets in their paths, the tides and oceans in their places, and the magical pumps and reservoirs primed. And it concerns itself with the fine balance between the Light and the Dark, the eternal war between Good and Evil. The universe could care less about what happens to the players in those battles.

Thus it is, it seems, that King Graham of Daventry and his family are forever charged (although some might say *cursed*) to play a grave and crucial and essential role in the very existence of our universe. For these forces, Good and Evil, are unlike the impersonal ones, which function to keep the sky from falling, and creatures from floating off into the heavens. Good and Evil are only seen through the actions and compulsions of the human and other folk—Good the urge for life and harmony and renewal for all creatures, Evil the urge to chaos, destruction, dissolution, and self above all else. At some times Good predominates; at others, Evil.

These twin forces are not only part of the very fabric of the universe, they cannot exist unless the other does. Without Evil, there is no Good, and if there is Good, it must be balanced with the Dark force. This is, I suspect, the universe's way of preventing stagnation. Conflict causes change, and change keeps time and existence from coming to a dead stop. And change keeps existence interesting. Could the maker or makers of the universes bore easily, and do our life and death struggles amuse them? I would hope for better from them.

In any case, all the natural philosophers and scholars and metaphysicians I have consulted are unanimous in one fact: At this time in the existence of Daventry, the conflict between Good and Evil is represented by the dark wizard Manannan and all his family on the side of Evil, and King Graham and his family for Good. Neither side chose to be what they are nor understand why they were chosen. The final winner will determine the course of our world until the next crisis arrives, and the fight is renewed again with new players.

Graham, of course, disagrees with my theory. He chortles and says I think too much. But he does not laugh deeply as he dismisses my musings, and usually finds a way to quickly change the subject. Perhaps he doesn't want to dwell on the trials that have beset him and his loved ones. You really can't blame him. He may be a king, but he is most definitely a mortal man. And mortal men, even kings, cry.

PART—THE FIRST

As is his habit, King Graham began his day with a stroll through the forest to Lake Maylie where a vigorous swim dissolved the last sticky threads of sleep from his brain, and the morning fuzz from his eyes. He says his dawn exertions keeps his body firm and his thoughts clear.

Graham is no longer the young knight who won the throne of Daventry. More than a score of years have passed since then, and those decades have been spent in rebuilding his ravished kingdom, only to see new troubles and disaster strike when all seemed finally well. Not all of the acts and decisions he has made over the years have been good ones, but he has always done what he felt best for Daventry, even to the sacrifice of his only daughter. Rosella has forgiven him for taking her to the dragon, but Graham says the memory of her tied to the stake, awaiting death with her eyes open and dry, still sometimes disturbs his dreams. That she was rescued and survived only eases the horror a little.

The responsibilities that are placed on a king's head along with his crown are many, and they have put a few deep lines in his face. Valanice, his queen, says they make him look dashing. He says they are "laugh lines" from his joy of living with her.

Graham is no longer the slim knight that scampered up a narrow beanstalk to the Land of the Clouds. The decades have filled him out, but with hard muscle, not soft flesh. His eyes are not quite what they used to be, and he would no longer care to attempt outrunning an ogre, but he is still in splendid physical condition. Although shaven by preference, he nevertheless looks like the monarch he is.

That morning he was wearing his usual attire, the short tunic, pants, and high boots of a Ranger. His head was topped with a long cap, rakishly adorned with one red feather. He calls it his adventurer's cap because it has accompanied him through the adventures that had won him Daventry's throne, and the hand of Valanice. He had a leather travelling bag on his back, something he always carried in case he discovered something interesting to bring home.

I will not recount much detail about how Mordack appeared on a hill overlooking Castle Daventry that day. As the king busied himself picking a few bright flowers as gifts for Valanice and Rosella, the sorcerer invoked magics powerful enough to rip the castle out of its very foundations, shrink and whirl it, and all within, up into the sky and away. Witnesses to the awful event say that when Mordack and Castle Daventry vanished in front of their unbelieving eyes, they did not go "Poof!" They thundered.

Absence Makes the Heart Go Yonder

It was this sound that brought Graham hurrying back. For a moment, he thought he had taken a wrong fork in the path back to his home. His eyes saw the great gash in the ground, and his nose smelled the lingering odor of the explosive energies, but his mind did not register what he was perceiving at that instant. How could he, really? Those who saw it happen had trouble believing. Graham spent a while staring, jaw getting closer to the ground. He is an intelligent man and the evidence of his senses soon stirred his tongue.

"What is going on? Where's my castle?" Considering the circumstances, Graham may be excused talking aloud to himself.

It did bring a result. From above, an unusually deep and hollow voice surprised Graham, coming, it seemed, invisibly out of the air.

"Perhaps I can be of some help." A look around and up finally showed the king the owner of the mysterious voice.

His name, Cedric with no surname. He was short and stout, and clad just in a vest and monocle, that's all. For an owl, that is overdressed. And so it was that king Graham met he who was fated to be his companion during the coming hardships and adventures, and it was an uncommon pairing indeed.

Cedric was, and still is, both familiar, servant and companion to the ancient and powerful high wizard Crispinophur. Crispinophur is said to have been the leader in our first *withdrawal* from the Other World to Daventry. He now lives a quiet and anonymous life in the Sovereignty of Serenia, unnoticed and forgotten by most folk of our world. He tells me he prefers it that way, having had more excitement in his life than he wishes to remember. In his words, "Everybody needs a bit of peace and relaxation every millennium or so!" He prefers to be called Crispin, he says, because it is just too much bother for him to remember his entire name anymore.

Cedric explained to Graham what had happened to Castle Daventry, although he knew not why. He suggested that his master might be able to help; Crispin knew Mordack somewhat and had had dealings with him in the past. The king, with no where else to turn, accepted Cedric's suggestion.

"How far is it to Crispin's?" he asked.

"Too far to walk," was the owl's reply. "Let's fly!"

With that, Cedric flapped his wings, and fell off his perch in an oak tree.

"Oops, clumsy of me," he apologized, and fluttered awkwardly back to his branch. Graham winced in disbelief.

Cedric then conjured a small bag from somewhere and sprinkled a light powder down on Graham's head.

"Fairy dust to give you flight! Just flap your arms with all your might."

"I'm allergic to fairy dust," Graham objected. Then he sneezed loudly. The force of the sneeze lifted him into the air and kept him aloft, and frantically flapping to stay upright. After a few moments, the king just began flapping harder, and followed Cedric higher into the sky. Between sneezes he hoped the dust's magic wouldn't wear off before they got to Serenia.

It didn't, but it didn't quite get him to Crispin's house either. Graham's impromptu flying was a little short, and he ended his aerial journey neck-deep in a small pond which stands next to the cottage. The water washed the dust from Graham and brought relief from the sneezes. The splash brought the old man outside to see what was the matter.

If Crispin's beard were any longer, he would be unable to walk for fear of always tangling it around his ankles. He walks stooped, assisted by a staff, with short slow steps. His eyes, though, are a clear, bright blue, almost iridescent. There is a keenness and sharpness behind them, in strange contrast to his constant forgetfulness. It is as if he is playing the role of old fool.

Crispin invited Graham inside and offered him peppermint tea for warmth and for something to wrap their hands and conversation around. He said he knew that Mordack was "A bad one, with an evil mind," but could give no clue as to why he might kidnap the king's castle and family. Crispin told Graham that he would offer him what little help he could provide.

That help came in three parts. The first was a foul tasting piece of smoked magical whitesnake. As Graham swallowed it (proud that he did not gag it back up), Crispin informed him that its power would allow him to understand, and even speak with, animals, trees, and the entire natural world. The king suspected that would be quite useful.

The second piece of aid was a dull, dusty and nicked magical wand. Crispin said it was an old one of his, with little power left. However, it could be charged and might even take a liking to Graham. It wasn't much, but it was the only one he could give. The king suspected that it would not be very useful, but he took it to be polite.

The last thing he offered Graham was Cedric.

"Whoo, whoo, me?" Cedric hooted.

"Don't do me any favors!" Neither Graham nor Cedric approved of the idea.

"Now both of you get out of here before Mordack does something worse," Crispin commanded. He nearly shoved the two out of the house.

"Thank you, sir, for all your help," were the king's last words to the wizard. He was being polite. He didn't think Cedric would be useful at all.

Cedric sat silent on a branch, pecking lice from between his feathers, pausing often to retrieve the monocle, which would fall from his beak each time he lowered his head. Graham leaned against an odd device that adorned Crispin's front yard, occasionally spinning one of its moving parts. This finally got the owl's attention.

"Be careful, king. That's a Universe Interpreter, and it keeps the stars aligned, or something like that. It's not a plaything!"

Graham grumped, removed his hands, and tugged at an ear.

"Don't call me 'King'. Graham is fine, and I hope you have better advice to give than that."

"Now that you mention it, *Graham*, Serenia towne is not too far south of here. It's a place to begin looking and, at the very least, it is a good place to obtain food and other provisions."

"That's not a bad idea. Lead on, oh brainy bird. And try coming up with some ideas for me to get a few coins to pay for those things."

South through the woods they began, ignoring the steep trail that began a short way from Crispin's doorstep, and which led up into the Great Mountains. Cedric informed Graham that beyond the mountains lay the Northern Sea, and that was where Mordack kept his castle, or so it had been in the past. It was on a strange island in that ocean, and it appeared, at times, to float above the waves. They both realized that they must eventually venture that steep road up, but only after they gathered the necessary supplies to survive a trip through the icy heights.

A viper was sunning itself warily in that trail also, alert to all signs of movement. Its presence made that hard eastward path even less desirable. As they looked on the snake, Graham heard a series of noises coming from within a stand of trees just west of him. It sounded like sobbing. That's what it was.

A young man, a noble by his dress, sat despondently on a log, head in hand and holding back tears. Cedric suggested that it would be a good idea to see what was the matter.

"He looks like he could use a little cheering up, I would say."

Graham walked over to the young man. His name, Graham discovered, was Prince Herbert of Greys, and his story was sad and simple. Herbert told Graham that he and his sweetheart had been strolling hand-in-hand through the woods, looking at little else but each other's eyes. As if from nowhere a particularly ugly witch appeared before them and demanded that Herbert become her love. Revolted at the thought, he rejected the old hag and embraced his blond princess more tightly too him. This did not please the

Absence Makes the Heart Go Yonder

hag at all. The next thing he knew, Herbert was standing in the forest alone, the witch and his Alicia both gone. He had been searching for her for months since, and his desperation was almost too much for him to bear.

Graham and Cedric listened, but could offer no help other than to be alert for the princess as they ventured upon their own quest. This slight hope, though, was enough to swell life back into Herbert, and gave him new resolve to trudge onward.

"Fare thee well, stranger," he waved to them. "A man must do what a man must do, and I must be going on. Thank you for your small kindness, and may both our quests be successful!" He disappeared from sight, but the tune of his travelling song lingered a bit behind him.

From the spot where they first heard Herbert sobbing, it was but a short hike to Serenia towne. The largest collection of human folk for leagues around, it rested lazily at the base of the Great Mountains, dipping its water-wheeled toe into the fast, deep river which flowed rapidly by its walls. Its thatched roofs and smoking chimneys gave invitation to all to pass a little time, and a little coin, within its gates. It was an invitation that Graham accepted. Cedric chose to wait outside.

Few folks were about that day in the towne square, a child or two chasing hoops, a matron or two shopping, and an occasional dog barking at phantoms or doing its business on the cobblestones. By an alleyway, Graham noticed a man attempting to fix the broken wheel of his wagon. He was at the edge of bad temper, and was using his hammer to release frustration.

Graham is among the kindest and most helpful of people. It matters little to him if he is a king; if he spies some folk or creature in need of assistance, he feels it his duty to offer assistance.

"Is there anything I can do to help?" the king asked the man.

"Nah, but thanks anyway," the fellow replied. "I've been trying to fix this for years, but never seem to get anywhere. It's alright, it gives me something to do."

"If you insist. Have a good day!"

This slight conversation had gone nowhere, but during it Graham's nostrils had detected the aroma of fish, and not a very fresh one. A quick glance into a barrel near to where he stood confirmed the smell.

"Yuk!" he murmured.

Let me pause for a moment to say something else about King Graham. He has a set of rules that he follows without exception whenever he goes adventuring.

"I have gone adventuring too often in my life," he told me. "But when I do, I always heed the advice my father gave me when I was a boy. My daddy used to tell me, 'Boy, if I have learned anything in my life, I have learned this: When in doubt, or in trouble, pick up anything that is not nailed down, and if it is, check for loose nails or boards. Check carefully into, under, above, below and behind things. Read everything, you might learn something. Wear clean undergarments, brush after meals and always remember, nothing is as it appears'."

Graham had no doubt that the old fish looked as disgusting as it smelled, but his family was in trouble and the fish wasn't nailed to anything. He took it, glad there were so few about to notice his revulsion. With that done, he hurried back out the gate of Serenia before the scent had him kicked out.

"Smells yummy, Graham old boy. I didn't realize you had such gourmet sensibilities."

Cedric refused to let the king's find go unnoted. Graham repeated his father's maxims to the owl and invited him to leave if he disagreed. Cedric did his best to wrinkle his beak, then pointed his wing toward the west.

Absence Makes the Heart Go Yonder

"There's much better food that way, *king*. After you!"

Indeed, there was. The road west first went past a bakery. The cakes and other sweets must have just left the oven, because the smells of sugar and butter and cinnamon and spice in the air was almost enough to cover that of the fish.

With no coin in his pocket, though, Graham could not go inside, despite the urgings of his sweet tooth. Instead, he continued on the road away from towne. The Swarthy Hog Inn beckoned next with the smells of roasting meats and the clatter of emptying cups. This too was passed with reluctance.

At home in Daventry, the king has a magic chest, which always stays filled with gold. He and his kingdom have no financial concerns because of this, but that very situation made his lack of coin at that moment more acute. He wasn't hungry yet that day, but he was beginning to know what being poor was. Graham wondered what he would do when it was time to eat; he has known little hunger in his life, and did not want to make its acquaintance again. So, with those thoughts in his mind, and the smell of thoroughly putrid fish in his nose, Graham left the more populous parts of Serenia in search of treasure. Cedric followed at a safe distance.

The fish didn't stay with Graham for very long. Not far from the Inn, where the trees of the forest were just beginning to thin into wide brushland, the king spotted a large black bear ripping his claws at a dead tree. Thousands of honey bees zipped furiously around the beast, attempting to save their honey from the belly of the bear.

We have noted before that a creature in need always touches the heart of King Graham. In this case, the bear apparently needed food, and the bees, salvation. Despite the wisdom of his father's advice, Graham had been having serious second thoughts about the dead fish. And, bears like fish almost as much as they like honey. So, with one true toss, Graham was able to come to the assistance of both bee and bruin. He hurled the decaying thing and hit the bear sharply on its side. According to Graham, it squished more than anything else, but it caught the beast's attention, reminding it that a dead fish in the paw is worth more than an angry bee up the nose. The bear happily bounded off, licking the slime from its new meal.

"That should do a lot to clear the air between us." Cedric quipped. But before Graham could tell him that the remark stank, another voice filled the meadow with a soft buzz.

"I thank you, King Graham, for saving my nest." Startled, Graham glanced quickly to the hollow tree. One large bee flew out of a large hole in it and directly up to his face. It hovered there, wearing a crown and carrying a sceptre, making no attempt to attack him.

"I am Queen Beetrice, ruler of all the bees. I know of your quest, and am grateful for your aid. There is little I can do to help you, but please take a honeycomb from our tree. It may be useful to you at some time. Also, I grant you protection from the stings of all my subjects. No more can I do. Go now with our best wishes. Until we meet again!" As one, Queen Beetrice and all the thousands of her subjects turned and buzzed quickly off.

"I'm not going near that hole," said Cedric. "You get the honey." And this is just what Graham did, although he was sure at least one of the insects would stick him while his hand was groping in the tree's hollow. He was wrong.

"That stick's not nailed down, your majesty," Cedric chided at Graham. He was pointing one wing to the ground at the base of the tree. "Aren't you going to obey your dear old dad and pick it up?"

Cedric was starting to annoy the king. Reaching down, Graham grabbed the stick, intending to heave it at the bothersome bird. He held his irritation in check though, and planned instead to pay the owl back in kind. Cedric saw the motion, however, and with a terrified "Squaawkkk!" winged quickly away and dead-smack into the tree trunk. Graham's laughter stung more than any bee, or the thump.

PART—THE SECOND

When Graham's son Alexander defeated the wizard Manannan, he was able to finance his escape from Llewdor by separating a band of bandits from part of their treasure. Graham knew this story well, and it gave him inspiration. He needed treasure in order to journey across the Great Mountains in pursuit of Mordack. Like most folk, he had heard the tales told of the thieves of the Endless Desert, a two-score band of cut-throats who preyed on caravans and travellers there. Here Graham was on the very edge of the Endless Desert, and he needed coin....

"You have got to be crazy," squawked Cedric. "You are going into the desert to search for bandits so you can rob *them*? You're going in without water? Without a map? You're going in without knowing where the oases are? Forget it, I'm staying here where there are worms and water. I'll send flowers to the funeral—if anyone ever finds your body. You cannot be serious."

Graham was quite serious, even though he agreed with Cedric's assessment of his chances. His wife and family were worth most any risk, and while he realized that he could wander through Serenia begging for coin and assistance, it would not be a seemly thing for a king to do. Besides, evening was not far away, and the desert would be cooler then. If all went right, he would have treasure by morning. Then it would be off and after Mordack. As a plan, it seemed reasonable to him.

"It seems insane to me!" Cedric insisted for the last time. His protests went unheeded, though. Graham scratched Cedric's head, and headed out into the desert. He intended to walk directly west from the bee's tree until he found an oasis, or decided to return in failure. He did not intend to wander aimlessly. If that plan didn't work, he would try again from another spot.

Graham chose well. West, west, farther west he plunged, stumbling at last onto a few palm trees surrounding a pond of sweet water. Gratefully he drank his fill, wishing he had something with which to carry water with him as he hiked. As he rested, he thought he could see the outline of high hills or cliffs in the far north. He wasn't sure that he wasn't seeing a mirage, but decided to walk toward that horizon anyway. If he kept his bearings, he should be able to return to the oasis if he were mistaken.

The sameness of the desert sands, and the heat that refuses to go away, are enough to make a person mad. A lapse of attention, or a moment's confusion as to direction, both mean a hard death. But Graham had not seen a mirage, and he kept his wits. He soon met what proved to be cliffs, but they were too steep to climb. Taking note of where he was, he trudged his way farther west, always hugging the cliff base. About the time he felt he must return, or perish, he found a small spring. He also found the desert thieves for whom he had been searching.

At first he thought that thunder had come to the clear dry skies. The heat had slowed his mind some, so it took a few moments for it to register the sound as hoofbeats. It seemed to come from several horses. Graham immediately looked for cover, not knowing if the galloping was good news or bad. He suspected the latter. Some rocks near the spring looked as if they would hide him from sight, provided the riders did not stop to drink. It was a chance he had no choice but to take. Peering from his shelter, he watched as the bandits, which is what they were, careen past him and through an opening in the cliffs.

255
Absence Makes the Heart Go Yonder

It had been there all along, of course. Graham had fixed his focus on the water, and then the bandits. In following their ride, he finally noticed that which he had not seen before. The cliffs were breached for a hundred yards or more, and on the other side of the opening was an enormous temple carved out of the living cliffs themselves. Great stone statues of winged horses and lions stood at the bottom of a wide stone stair, and the carven image of some unknown demon or deity stared down from the temple's portal. The bandits raced their mounts straight to the temple steps and then dismounted. Carrying a heavy bag in one hand, most likely loot, the leader of the small band waved a long staff which he held with the other. He shouted the words, "Open, Sesame!" and the great door to the temple dissolved into the air. The thief rushed inside, and moments later emerged with just the staff. At once, the door solidified again behind the man who then remounted his panting steed and sped back into the desert. The others followed, leaving Graham alone and unharmed.

"Open, Sesame! huh? I think I've found what I've been looking for—where the thieves hide their treasure. And, the magic word! Alright Graham, let's get some gold and get out of here." It is Graham's habit to speak aloud to himself, a habit best indulged in private.

Graham left the shelter of the concealing rocks, and made his way to where the bandit had shouted the words of opening. They didn't work for the king. He tried them accompanied by a wide gesture. No luck. He tried the words both loud and soft. Same lack of results.

"I guess I need the staff," he told himself. "And that means I need to find their camp. So get moving, big ears. And don't forget to get a drink before you leave!" Graham made sure he drank at the spring.

The bandits had ridden both out of and into the southwest. It seemed most logical to Graham, therefore, that southwest from the temple was where they kept their hideout. Thoroughly refreshed by the spring's cool water, he chose to explore westward for two hours, and then south. Another oasis was his reward, and the water there tasted better than the sweetest wine Graham had ever known. Then it was south again as the sun sank mercifully below the horizon. For three more hours he stalked in that direction, until he thought he heard the sound of drums and cymbals drifting from the west. With much care and little concealment except for the growing dark, Graham approached the sound of revelry. He was not to be disappointed. Graham shortly found himself on the periphery of a desert camp. From the look of the man collapsed drunk on the sand, the encampment was that of the desert thieves.

On the far side of the camp, loud voices and music came from one large tent. Through an opening in it, Graham could see the sleek, sweaty bodies of the swaying dancers. Their noise, he decided, would cover the sound of his movements.

By the campfire, he discovered a clay jug full of water. Staying as much in the shadows as he could, hoping to blend in with the bandits, he approached the fire and quickly drank his fill. As he did so, Graham decided to first investigate the small tent that was closest to the fire. Loud snores came from within it, fluttering hard the tent's fabric. He knew that he must be swift and silent or he would be discovered.

Before entering, Graham inhaled deeply and held his air lest the sound of his own breathing betray him. *Swift and silent*, he reminded himself. *Swift and silent.* Then he stepped through the opening.

The bandit sleeping inside was snoring, but his sleep was restless. Knowing that he might awaken at any moment, Graham surveyed the tent's interior, and discovered that he had chanced upon the tent of the staff's owner. He wasted no time marveling at his luck; silently Graham rushed to the back of the tent. Careful not to make a noise, or touch the lightly sleeping man, he snatched the staff firmly and retraced his path to the outdoors. Releasing the breath he had been holding, Graham dashed east into the desert darkness, listening for any sound or alarm or pursuit. There was none.

Absence Makes the Heart Go Yonder

Graham escaped through the desert night, forever eastward. In fleeing with the staff, he had lost his bearings in the dark. Confused and disoriented, he decided to push on in the same direction. After several hours, he at last turned north, certain he could smell water. He must have. The oasis he finally drank at blessed him with a night of liquid dreams.

The morning appears hot and fast in the Endless Desert. Heat steals appetite, so with fresh water in his belly, Graham felt ready to take on the bandits again. Or, at least, their treasure house. He turned his eyes north, hoping to spy the cliffs, but saw only dune and sand.

"No matter," he told the cloudless heavens, "They are out there, and I'll never get to them by standing here."

Graham's trek north that morning took him past a sun-bleached and vulture-picked skeleton. From its size, he assumed the unfortunate person had been a man, although that had become a meaningless fact after years in the sun. Lying next to the bones were the tattered remains of a boot, all that remained of the dead man's possessions. Graham recalls that it was a boot for a left foot, but doesn't know why he remembers such a trifle. Maybe he could envision himself in the same state, discovered by another wanderer, with no identity and just a single left boot to remind the universe that he had once been more than white, dry bones.

Graham took the boot with him as he continued onward to the northern cliffs. He moved more slowly, conserving strength, lost in thoughts of his own mortality, and the mystery of his family's fate. In time, he reached the cliffs and, looking around, realized that he was nearly at the temple. That knowledge gave him strength, and he hardly staggered at all as he walked the short way west to the life-restoring spring. The water still tasted good.

After a while, Graham was ready to conquer the temple. Equipped with the staff, and knowing the magic words, he was sure he could enter with little trouble. What concerned him, he says, was the speed with which the bandits entered the temple and left. It was as if they hurried lest they be trapped inside when the door returned to solid. Graham wasn't sure of his conclusion, and hoped to discover a lever or button or something in the interior to allow him to stay for some time. But he resolved to enter and leave as quickly as he had entered and departed the bandit tent, snatching what he could. He reasoned that he didn't need very much treasure to serve his needs, and the bandits might return unheard, and surprise him if he stayed too long.

Graham climbed to the temple's top step. Holding the staff aloft, he intoned, "Open, Sesame!" At once, something he hadn't expected happened; the staff shattered in his hand. But before Graham could react to that apparently disastrous twist of fate, the great stone door dissolved, inviting him inside. The king wasted no time in remorse or confusion, but hurried the few steps inside and looked quickly around. No buttons. No levers. No pulleys. Lots of jewels and golden chests and bulging leather bags. The ransom of a world, perhaps two, lay a dozen steps away. Nearly at his feet, shone one, lone gold coin, and a golden bottle. Graham wasted no time on decision, and scooped up the coin, grabbed the metal bottle, and sprinted outside. He felt the magical door turn solid behind him, and was sure it pinched off several stray hairs from the back of his head. Graham decided that he *didn't* want to know for sure that he was correct about that.

"That was quick!"

Graham sighed, releasing his tension, and wiped sweat from his brow. He was sure it wasn't all from the heat. After a few slow, deep breaths he tensed, thinking he heard horsemen approaching the temple again, perhaps in pursuit of him. Wasting not even the time it took to examine his treasures, Graham sprinted eastward along the cliffs.

Despite his sudden flight, the king knew that safety lay in that direction. All he had to do was retrace his steps from the temple back to the oasis he had stopped at when he first ventured into the Endless Desert. Of course he had to avoid capture, but in theory it was a fine idea. Anyway, it worked, and he never heard nor saw any further signs of being chased. In fact, he tells me, there may very well never have been any bandits after him at all, just his overwrought nerves imagining pursuit.

At the oasis, he drank deeply, and rapidly pushed east out of the sands to where he hoped Cedric was waiting. As annoying as the owl sometimes became, Graham welcomed the idea of seeing the talking bird. Perhaps Cedric would fall off a branch when he saw Graham; the king needed a laugh.

Cedric didn't tumble, but Graham was happy to see him anyway. And thus it was that king Graham conquered the Endless Desert of Serenia, eluded its bandits, and escaped with some of their treasure.

PART—THE THIRD

Although I have tried, I have never been able to meet and speak with Cedric. For that reason, I have no idea whether he was relieved to see King Graham lurch out of the Endless Desert that day. Graham claims that the bird was still sitting in the bee's tree, calmly munching on a grub and attempting to clean his monocle at the same time. He had to shout to get Cedric's attention

"Oh, there you are. I was beginning to wonder if you were *ever* coming back. At least you no longer smell like old fish. What, pray tell, is that thing in your hand?"

Graham held up the golden bottle and showed it to the owl. "Treasure, Cedric. Treasure! With this we should be able to obtain all the provisions we need to cross the Great Mountains."

"It is, is it?" Cedric flew down beside Graham for a closer look. "It looks like a worthless hunk of brass to me."

Graham looked more closely at the bottle, licked it lightly with his tongue, and discovered that, indeed, his golden dream was tarnished.

"There might be a genie inside, if that's any consolation, king. Want to open it?"

Graham thought about the idea for a few moments. Once, in Kolyma, he had obtained a brass lamp which, when rubbed, produced a genie that presented him with gifts. He rubbed the bottle lightly a few times, but nothing happened. Then he considered removing the lid.

"On second thought," cautioned Cedric. "There might be a daemon or evil spirit inside. Let's take it back to Crispin, just to be safe."

Graham nodded a reluctant approval, then bit into the coin he had also taken from the temple.

"Why not? Anyway, I know this coin is really gold. I'm sure it'll come in handy. Let's move on, I've got a family to find." With that, Graham dusted himself off and turned north. Crispin flew behind, narrowly avoiding the tree.

From ahead, Graham could hear a low ruffing accompanied by the sounds of a creature scratching the earth. As he came into a small clearing, the king could see a large dog, frantically trying to paw its way into a huge anthill. The hill resembled, if nothing else, an earthen castle. In many ways it reminded Graham of Castle Daventry. He could also see millions of black ants fleeing from the destruction the dog was inflicting on *their* home. The analogy was too much for Graham to bear. He quickly reached into his travelling bag and retrieved the stick he had found by the bee's tree.

"Here, boy!" he shouted at the pooch, and deftly threw the stick in front of the dog. It looked up, saw the new toy, and darted to it. A sniff, a pair of licks, and a sudden grab with its jaws; the dog dashed off with its treasure.

As the dog disappeared into the brush, Graham walked nearer the anthill to survey the damage. It wasn't severe; apparently the king had arrived not

Absence Makes the Heart Go Yonder

long after the four-legged flea-bag. As he was examining the anthill, Graham was surprised by the appearance of of an especially large ant who climbed to the very top of the structure. It seemed to be wearing purple robes, which was strange. It was even stranger when it began talking.

"Thank you, noble sir, for saving our home. I am King Antony, monarch of the ants. Who may you be?"

It must be the magic whitesnake. That's why I can understand him, murmured Graham to himself.

"I am King Graham of Daventry," he replied politely.

"Ah, King Graham. I have heard of your quest, and wish you good fortune. Alas, there is nothing I can do at this time to aid you. But, take our best wishes, and if there is anything we can do in the future, be assured that we will do all we are able. Adieu!" The ant king turned away sharply, and followed by his myriad followers, disappeared beneath the earth.

"You sure meet the most unusual folks," commented Cedric. He broke the momentary silence from his new perch on a bush overlooking the anthill. "And speaking of folks, isn't that a gypsy wagon just ahead of us? Gypsies claim to be able to read the future, and see things that happen far away. Maybe they can help discover us what's happening to your family."

"Cedric," exclaimed Graham, "I knew you'd come in handy eventually. That's a good idea; let's go."

The gypsy camp could easily be seen from the anthill, and it was just a short stroll up an wide path to get to it. One wagon, with a large FORTUNE TELLER sign painted in clashing colors on its side, was all that was in the camp. A dark, strong man sat near it on a rocking chair, braiding a leather belt and warily watching for strangers. As Graham approached the wagon, the man got up and challenged him.

"Eet vil cost you a gold coin to see the mystical Madame Mushka." The sullen man held out his had expectantly.

"A *gold* coin?" hooted Cedric. "I thought gypsies wanted their palms crossed with silver?"

"Times are hard," was his curt reply.

Graham listened to the exchange and decided that if Madame Mushka could help unravel the mystery of his family's kidnapping, then it would be well worth the price of his lone piece of gold. He placed it in the gypsy's calloused palm, and the man stepped aside to allow Graham to enter the wagon. Cedric decided to sit in a tree.

I believe that it must be true in all the universes that the interiors of all gypsy wagons are dark, stifling places reeking of too much cheap incense and unwashed feet. It is part of their ambiance. So too are the worn exotic rugs, and the overuse of striped and patterned fabrics.

Madame Mushka looked as if her palm had been crossed with gold often, and most of the profit had gone to food. Each of her fingers wore a ring, sometimes several, and most seemed a size or two too small. They probably had fit correctly in the past. Graham says that her features were difficult to make out behind all the smoke, but her eyes burned through the choking haze and into his skull. By them alone he was sure that the gypsy was no fraud.

"Sit," she commanded. Graham obeyed.

"I can see that you are on a great and dangerous quest, with much danger to you and others....others that you love." Madame Mushka waved and crossed her pudgy hands several times above and around a clear globe sitting on the table in front of her.

"Ake wata. Atu wata. Eesta sa seseway! Look deep into my crystal ball.......King Graham. Yes, you are King Graham of Daventry. Your family has been taken from you. Far away they are. Look!" Ensnared by the enchantment of the crystal, Graham leaned closer and looked deeper. A sudden "Gasp!" escaped him.

Absence Makes the Heart Go Yonder

Inside the globe was his home, shrunken and imprisoned in a glass retort, sitting on a laboratory shelf. In front of Castle Daventry stood his family, imprisoned in the same small bottle. Next, a smoke filled the crystal ball and when it cleared he was looking at his son, Alexander. Alexander was clutched in the clawed hand of a sorcerer who could only be Mordack. He was holding Alexander just out of the diamond claws of a large black cat who was snarling and swiping at him. Ghostly voices filled Madame Mushka's wagon.

"Look at the treat for you, Manannan, my brother. See how it wiggles and squirms." Mordack held the prince closer to the cat, teasing it and pulling Alexander away just before Manannan's claws might tear him apart.

"Look what you have done to my brother, princeling. Look. Only you can transform him back into his real form. Only you!" By now, Mordack was screaming.

The crystal clouded again, and Graham was looking closely at his son's face.

"You've made some kind of mistake, Mordack. I don't know anything about magic, I promise. I just turned Manannan into a cat by accident. Believe me!" Alexander was obviously trying to deceive the wizard, trying to protect his mother and sister.

"I believe you not at all, worm. I will give you one final warning. Return Manannan to his proper form, and soon, or I shall start feeding the cat. Oh, yes; your lovely mother will be the first to become catfood, bit by painful bit. Think on that. Sleep on that. I'll be back for your decision."

The image changed again, back to that of the people and castle in the bottle. Manannan was clawing at it, trying to bite through the glass. The cat's spittle flowed thickly down the outside of the glass. Graham's family looked upon the mad Manannan. Holding hands, they faced their coming deaths with courage. And quite a bit of fear.

The crystal ball clouded for the last time, and when it cleared, no image dwelled within it. Graham could only stare at it. Stunned, angry and horrified, he knew he had just witnessed truth.

"Mordack is an evil one," the gypsy said softly. Your task is much more dangerous than I foresaw. Please take this; it is not much, but it will protect you from all but the most powerful magics."

Bringing her hand from beneath the table, Madame Mushka handed Graham an amulet containing a single softly-glowing stone. "Put this on when you go outside. Good luck, King Graham of Daventry!"

Madame Mushka pulled a curtain between her and Graham, leaving him alone. For several long moments he sat. Then he slowly wiped one eye and left the wagon.

King Graham is not one to dwell too long on the pity of self or the unfairness of fate. By the time Cedric fluttered near him, his normal good humor had returned. Or so he says. I suspect that new lines of determination had impressed themselves to his jaw, and that there was a hardness behind the twinkle in his eye. He looked at Cedric and asked, "How were the bugs?"

"There are better ones near Crispin's house, and it's not far from here, to the east."

"Then, that's the way we're heading. Watch out you don't fly into any more trees."

Graham placed the gypsy amulet around his neck, and looked at the stone's glow for a moment. Leaving the gypsy man and Madame Mushka's wagon behind, the two went on their way.

Absence Makes the Heart Go Yonder

PART—THE FOURTH

The road to Crispin's skirted just north of a small pond. Thinking that he would like a drink, Graham bent and took a handful of water. He spat it out at once because of its saltiness.

"Yuk!" The royal family's favorite word of disgust spat out with the water. As he did so, he looked up and saw that a large weeping willow tree was partially shading the pond. From its branches, which overhung the water, Graham could see small drops of liquid falling, drip, drip, drip, drip....

Not only was the tree's shape like that of a sorrowing woman, its twists and bumps and hollows even had the image of a beautiful girl. In her hand was a harp, and Graham was sure magic was at work there.

"She seems to be playing a sad tune, Graham," said Cedric. "Maybe we should try to cheer her up."

"Cheer up a tree?" Graham was not amused by the owl's suggestion, but it was something to do to take his mind off of his own troubles. He walked closer.

"Do you take requests? Do you know Greensleeves?" To Graham's immense surprise (although why, at this point in his quest, he should have been surprised at anything is beyond me) the willow spoke.

"That was not funny, sir."

"Why, you can talk!"

"Why not? Once I was a human woman."

"What happened?"

"One day my sweetheart and I were walking through the forest when we met an ugly old witch. She was smitten at once by the fairness of my prince's face, and she tried to steal him from me. He refused."

"I think I've heard this story before. Is your name Alicia?" Graham asked.

"Of course. Have you met my dear Herbert? Oh, you must have. Anyway, since she couldn't steal his heart, she put him to sleep and then stole mine. Then she turned me into a tree."

"She stole your heart?"

"She turned it to gold and carried it away with her. Her last words were that if anyone were to return the heart to me, then I would become a human princess again. Until then, I must forever stand here and weep."

"A sad story, indeed," said Graham. "If we see Herbert again, we'll tell him where to find you. If we come across your heart, we shall return it. I can promise you not more."

The weeping willow, Alicia, fell silent except for the drip from her branches. Graham motioned Cedric that they should continue on, and they moved eastward silently.

They had not gone far when they noticed a large sign next to the trail. It simply stated, ENTER AT YOUR OWN RISK! Snaking past it to the north was a much narrower path that seemed to disappear into deep gloom.

"You don't want to go there," sputtered Cedric. "That's the Dark Forest, and it's so easy to get lost in it that no one ever enters it any more. Crispin is always grousing about an old hag who has her home in there. He says she's a particularly nasty witch with a taste for human stew and roast bird."

"A witch? Perhaps she's the one who stole the willow's heart. We did promise Alicia we'd return it if we found it." Graham's kind heart was tugging him northward.

"We? *I* don't recall making any such promise." Cedric was not happy about the direction the conversation was taking.

Absence Makes the Heart Go Yonder

"Well, I did, Cedric, and I'm obligated to take a quick look around. Stay here if you wish. Besides, we still need to find something to pay for our provisions. Who knows what we might find in the Dark Forest?"

"Whoo, whoo! That's what I say. I'm staying here, king. Go if you'd like, but the Dark Forest scares me. I'll wait for you— but not as long as I did while you were in the desert." Huffily, Cedric began preening his feathers for lice as Graham walked into the deep woods.

The Dark Forest is called so not so much because little light enters (which it doesn't), but because of the dark mood that seems to drop on folks while they are there. Decay is everywhere, and all the trees and bushes and flowers and plants are twisted, *wrong* somehow. Toads and fungi find the place delightful.

A few moments of damp walking brought Graham to a fork in the path. The choice between east and west was of little matter to him, both ways were equally unappetizing and rapidly vanished into heavier forest. Graham chose east, and almost at once was swallowed by the undergrowth.

"This may have been a mistake," Graham mumbled to no mushroom in particular. After a few steps up the path, he attempted to retrace his steps, and discovered that he was lost. He could find no trace of the way back out, and all he could do was trek on. Graham did; at times he was sure he was walking in circles, even though he was positive he was merely walking north. The rest of the time he walked in perplexity.

Eventually, the path widened a bit, and turned to wander west for some reason. Graham saw a grotesque tree, near where the trail turned, that was larger and more ominous than the others he had been seeing. From a distance, it appeared to have a small door inset in its trunk, and a slimy critter-trail leading right to it. The tiny path was well-worn and edged with bones, some of them human. When Graham got up to the tree, his observation of a door was confirmed; in fact, the door even had a keyhole, and it was locked tight. After a few hard tugs, the king gave up, shrugged his shoulders, and continued on to see where the main trail was leading him. It led him to the witch's house, and the crone looking to cause trouble.

Let me pause for another brief aside. In his adventures, King Graham has encountered three witches of which I am aware. Dahlia, the mistress of the gingerbread house, he was able to avoid and sneak-up upon, pushing her into her own oven. Dame Hagatha, Manannan and Mordack's repulsive sister, he was able to avoid altogether—much to his relief—although he has since said that he regrets not pushing her into her own stewpot when he had the chance. In retrospect, it might be said that Graham had had the upper hand in his dealings with witches up until then.

This third one (Graham never learned her name) acted as if she had been waiting for Graham. Perhaps she was just defending her home. No sooner had he noticed the odd bridge crossing to the house, than the hag materialized in front of him and cast a spell in his direction. It hit Graham full upon his face, and his body tingled for a moment. As he glanced down, he could see Madam Mushka's amulet glow brighter and *absorb* the malevolent energy. Graham escaped unscathed. Of course, he still had a nasty witch to deal with.

Maybe I can buy her off with something, Graham improvised. *Maybe she'll make the same error I did, and mistake the brass bottle for gold. Maybe I should do something fast!*.

"Good day, madame. I am lost. Would you, by any chance, know the way out of these woods?" Graham tried politeness first.

"These are my woods you are trespassing in, stranger. There is no way out. You are my prisoner, now. Would you care to join me for dinner?"

Graham's options had quickly become extremely limited. Taking the brass bottle he had carried from the desert, he casually sauntered to the hag and handed it to her.

"Perhaps this gift of mine might change your mind," he ventured.

Absence Makes the Heart Go Yonder

The witch greedily snatched the bottle from Graham, and with a phlegmy cackle unhesitatingly opened it. It was (we hope) her ultimate mistake. Cedric had been correct about the possibility of a genie residing in the artifact. However, it wasn't a benign genie, and it wasn't granting any wishes. The instant the genie poped out, he glanced around with a hateful look in his eyes. He saw the witch with the tell-tale lid still in her hand, pointed to her with a long, taloned finger and boomed, "Ha! Free at last. Let's see how you like spending 500 years in a dark bottle!"

A great flash lit the sky, and when Graham could see again, the witch, the genie, and the bottle had all disappeared.

"I'm sure glad I didn't open it!"

King Graham's gift of understatement is legendary.

Graham contends that it is good policy never to let an evil witch's home go unsearched. "You never know what you might find in there, and the stench isn't too bad after a while." Some feel that what you might find in a witch's house might be worse that the witch herself. Of course, it is a monarch's right to make policy. Since Graham is not my monarch I feel free to state that it is not a policy with which I would agree. With that said, let me also report that Graham made the proper decision in entering the hag's house. If he hadn't, he would have lost everything.

Free of deadly distraction, Graham took a moment to look at the witch's misshapen house. It looked like it was made from a hollow rock through which more of the forest's eerie trees were growing, although it may have been the other way around. The house could only be approached via a narrow bridge that had no hand rails, just huge rib bones as sides. In all directions, the Dark Forest smothered the place, giving Graham the impression that to enter there was to enter a grave.

But he did cross the bridge to the witch's home; the bridge spanning a deep crevasse. Graham could see no bottom to the chasm, just the hot, bright glow from the fires of Hades. In contrast, the inside of the place was cold and frigid, like the breath of the dead. Graham shivered, and not just from the cold.

It took the king but a short while to search the odd structure. In an old trunk he found a small spinning wheel with specks of gold dust in its joints. A hanging incense burner, which apparently used dried mugwump for fragrance, hid a tiny brass key. Graham was sure it fit a locked door in a certain nearby tree. Finally, in the drawer of a small pedestal, he discovered a leather bag. Inside were three green emeralds. Treasure, indeed; any one would buy his assault on Mordack. He took them all, and with light steps headed off to test the key in the tree.

The key fit when Graham tried the lock, as he was sure it would. Inside lay a little golden heart on a red satin cushion. That the heart belong to Alicia, the willow, was a certainty. As he picked up the heart, however, he realized that getting our of the Dark Forest was not such a sure thing.

Back the way he had come, of course would not work; he had already tried that and failed. That left onward, beyond the witch's home. He knew he could travel either west or south there, and chose the western route. This took him through even stranger forest, with soft flesh-eating plants and fungi that oozed phosphorescent liquids that most likely killed at the lightest touch. On all sides, Graham was sure he saw pairs of bright eyes watching him, following every movement. He ignored them and continued on. And, on. And, on. Around and around in a large, confusing loop, the path soon brought him back to the tree where he had found the heart. Sure he had missed a small path, Graham tried again. Back he came once more. The third try took the king south from the witch's bridge, and that returned him to the tree even sooner. Desperately, Graham tried to push through the brush and bushes, but could get nowhere. Around and around he went, finding no exit at all from the Dark Forest. All the time he was watched by those bright eyes.

Absence Makes the Heart Go Yonder

Exasperated, Graham finally realized that his only chance to escape the woods lay with the watchers. But no matter how still he waited, though, they would not make an appearance, nor a noise. Just quiet blinks.

At this bleak point, Graham was standing at a place just past the witch's house, where the path turned from west to south. There seemed to be more of the watchers there than anyplace else on the trail, so it was there that he set his bait.

He picked the emeralds for his lure because of their bright sparkles. His plan was to drop one of the gems near him and catch whatever might come to claim it. It wasn't much of a plan, Graham admits, but it was all he could come up with at the time.

The first emerald hit the ground and rolled several feet away from Graham. So swiftly that the king was unable to reach the errant stone, one of the little folk bolted out of the bushes, snatched the emerald, and disappeared again. By its appearance, the king thought it might be a small elf.

"Drat!" Graham exclaimed. "Let's try another one."

The second emerald suffered the same fate as the first, stolen away by an elf almost as soon as it touched the ground. This time Graham had a clearer view of the culprit, so he knew he was dealing with elves. He also knew he had only one gem left, and if he couldn't catch an elf with that one, he'd have no idea what to do next. As he pondered just how to make his scheme work, he recalled that his mother often said that one could always catch more flies with honey than with seawater. He never quite understood what that meant, but it served to remind him of the honeycomb he was carrying. Perhaps honey could catch elves as easily as it caught flies.

Graham took the honeycomb and strongly squeezed it. The nectar that had been stored inside by the bees slowly oozed to the ground, forming a small golden puddle. Graham stuck the remaining beeswax back into his pouch and very carefully placed his final emerald in the sticky stuff. Quick as a blink, an elf darted out and became stuck in the goo. Graham picked the little one up and held him in front of his face.

"Let me go! Let me go!" the elf squealed. "Please don't hurt me!"

"Small sir," Graham spoke, "I'm looking for a way out of this infernal forest...."

"If you let me go, I'll show you the way out," the elf interrupted. "I give you my word."

"Your word is good enough for me," replied the king as he gently placed the elf back on the ground, away from the honey puddle. The small mannikin looked up at Graham briefly and seemed to make a decision. He whistled.

At once, what Graham had thought to be a large, vine-covered rock stood up and moved. The path continued on, past where the strange creature had been.

"Follow me." The elf gestured for Graham to follow, and dashed down the newly revealed road. "Hurry up and stop gawking at Rocky the Jinx," the elf shouted back at him. Graham wasted no more time, and hurried after.

The road quickly dipped below the ground into a tunnel that was obviously made for use by the little folk. Graham was forced to crawl through it on his hands and knees, and once or twice was forced to shimmy on his belly. He never got stuck, though, and soon emerged into a large, high cavern brightly lit by huge fires glowing from deep pits descending into the guts of the earth.

The elf who had led him was waiting when he finally arrived in the cave.

"Sir, we are not so ignoble as to take without giving something in return. In payment for the three emeralds, we give you these fine elven shoes. We trust they will serve you well. The small passage you see across from you leads out of the Dark Forest. We wish you well on your journeys. Adieu!" With a wave, the elf stepped out of sight into the shadows. Graham waved back, knelt down, and began his crawl to sunlight.

Absence Makes the Heart Go Yonder

PART—THE FIFTH

"It's about time you got back. Just look at yourself, all covered with dirt, and I'm sorry I'm downwind of you. You smell like you've been standing in fresh mugwump. Phew!" By the tone of his squawks, Cedric seemed delighted to see Graham again.

The tunnel had delivered on its promise of escape, and had brought Graham out to a secret opening by the forest's warning sign. Cedric's complaints were a joyful noise.

"I must admit you were right, feather-head," Graham conceded. "It was dangerous in there. I'm lucky to get out alive. But I found Alicia's heart, so let's go back and return it to her."

Graham and Cedric did just that, giving the golden heart to the tree when they arrived there. The small heart pulsed once and filled the grove with a white light. The glow condensed, rushing inward, and coalesced into the slight form of a pretty blond woman holding a harp. In the process, the willow tree vanished.

"I'm a princess again!" the girl shrieked. "I'm a girl; I'm a girl; I'm a girl!" Alicia slung the harp away from her in disgust. "I don't ever want to touch that thing again in my life," she exclaimed. "All I want is some new clothes, and to see my Herbert."

"Did I hear my name being mentioned? Alicia!"

"Herbert! Herbert! Oh, Herbert! Where have you been? Where did you just come from?" The answer was lost amidst their hugs and kisses, and hand in hand the disappeared into the bushes. Graham never did find out how the prince happened to show up at that moment.

"Isn't young love grand?" commented Cedric. "They didn't even take the time to thank you."

Graham picked up the discarded harp, examined its workmanship, and strummed a few melancholy chords. By this point, the king had become confused and as moody as the music he was playing. He and Cedric had traipsed east and west and north around Serenia finding much and discovering little. What little they had learned of his family had come from Madame Mushka, and the king was fresh out of ideas. Over Cedric's objections, Graham started walking back to the gypsy camp in hopes that he might learn more from the fortune teller. True, he had no coin to cross her palm with, but perhaps she would take something in its stead.

Graham's disappointment was sharp then, and his mood darkened again, when the two reached the cold gypsy campfire. The wagon with Madame Mushka was gone, and the clearing was deserted. Nothing remained of the former encampment other than the tracks of their wagons. As the king stared at the ground, desperate for inspiration, he noticed a glint among the high grass. A bit of rubbish, uncharacteristically left behind by the travelling folk, he assumed. When Graham went to pick it up, though, he found that what he thought to be trash was really a tambourine. Perhaps it had fallen out of a wagon as it bumped over a stone. Graham took it, if only because his father would approve.

Cedric hooted his annoyance. "Look, king; it's time to stop moping about and to do something constructive. Why don't we head back to Serenia towne and take our chances there. It's better than nothing."

"I suppose you're right," agreed Graham, without much enthusiasm. But let's go there by a way we haven't been. That way we may stumble on something interesting. Who knows, hoot owl, we just might get lucky!"

"Or, dead."

"Thank you for those words of encouragement, Cedric."

"Lead on, great monarch. Time flies when you're standing still!"

The roundabout route which Graham and Cedric chose to take to Serenia towne meandered south to King Antony's castle, and then veered eastwards.

Absence Makes the Heart Go Yonder

This led back into the more settled parts of the country, so it was not surprising that they soon came upon a small house in the woods. It was built of fallen logs, most covered with moss, but looked to be watertight and cozy. In front of the place, a young gnome played merrily with a toy, a finely carved marionette. On a nearby stump, sat a much older gnome smoking a pipe filled with some aromatic herb. The homey sight threatened to bring new tears to Graham's eyes, suggesting to him that if he were not successful in his quest, he might very well never know the joys of being a grandfather.

Graham moved closer to the old gnome. As he did so, he began to notice that the gnome's features looked somewhat familiar. His brain, usually quite clear in such matters, was unable to put a name on the face.

"Good day, sir gnome. My name is Graham. You seem familiar; have we met before?"

"Don't seem to recall, kid. Can't say I do."

"What is you name? Perhaps I'd recognize it."

"It's much too difficult to pronounce."

"That's strange. I'm sure we've met, but my brain seems clouded on the details. Whatever. I've been admiring your son's toy, it is quite beautiful."

"Should be. Made it myself. He's my grandson, not my son." The gnome's replies were short and to the point.

"Well then; would it be possible for me to purchase the toy from you, or perhaps trade for it?" Both the gnome and Cedric, who was sitting on a branch listening to the exchange, looked surprised.

"Not very likely. What would an adventurer like you want with a marionette, anyway?"

"It's for my grandchildren."

Cedric hooted for attention. "You're not a grandfather, Graham. What are you talking about?"

"I want to be."

Graham paused a moment, then took the petite spinning wheel out of his pack and offered it to the gnome.

"Would you take this in trade?" Graham asked. The gnome took a quick step backwards.

"Where did you get that? It's mine."

"From an old hag in the Dark Forest. She has no need for it anymore." The gnome reached out quickly and snatched the spinning wheel out of Graham's hand.

"Give it here! So that's what happened to it. I bet that dumb crone never understood that this wheel can spin straw into gold. Thanks for returning it to me!"

"Sir, even though it is rightfully yours, would you consider *giving* me the marionette in return for it?"

"Sure, kid. You're owed that. I can always make another one quick. Here. Have a good journey. 'Bye!" the old gnome gently took the toy from his grandson, handed it to Graham, and led the boy inside.

"You didn't like that old toy anyway. Wait 'till you see what this spinning wheel can do!" The door to the snug house closed tight behind them, leaving Graham and Cedric alone.

"A toy, king? You call this getting lucky?"

"It's better than getting killed."

You've got a good point there. The main road to town is just a little south of here. Let's be off."

The path from the gnome's home took Graham and Cedric past the back of the Swarthy Hog Inn. The fine smells of cooked food still spiced the afternoon air, reminding Graham that he hadn't eaten yet that day. With no way to pay for a meal, it was a thought best forgotten.

Next to the inn stood a tall haystack, tempting travellers rest a few moments in its cushioned comfort. Graham told Cedric that he was going to laze a bit

Absence Makes the Heart Go Yonder

in the hay before they continued on. Cedric agreed that it was a good idea, and found himself a comfortable perch on the inn's sign post. As he waited, he cleaned and polished his monocle.

The king leaned back against the hay with a contented sigh. He wished he could spend the moment, and a lot more like them, with Valanice. The thought of his wife resting beside him in the hay stiffened his resolve to not just rescue her and their children, but to thoroughly trounce both Mordack and Manannan. He leaned back deeper into the hay in his reverie. A sharp jab to his backside shattered the daydream.

"Ouch! What was that?" he wondered, scratching the slight prick. Kneeling down, he began searching the haystack for whatever stung him. He knew better than to expect to find anything.

"May we be of assistance, King Graham?" From behind him came a small familiar voice. King Antony and an army of his subjects began streaming into the hay pile. A few minutes later, the monarch of the ants reappeared. Looking up at the kneeling Graham, Antony held forth a golden needle which his followers had found the in haystack.

"We promised to help you if we could, King Graham. Please take this golden needle with you as a gift from us. Perhaps it will be of some use on your journey. I'm sure this is what you sat on. Adieu!" Leaving the needle for Graham, the long black line of insects disappeared into a hole in the ground. Graham put the needle in his pack and voiced a "Thank you!" to the ant king. He felt like he was talking to the dirt.

"Just what are you doing talking to the dirt?" Cedric asked, hovering in the air in front of Graham.

Graham look up, smiled at the bird, and said nothing. He began walking toward Serenia towne, knowing that his silence was paying back the owl for two days of jibes. He strolled and whistled while Cedric sputtered.

As the two were passing the bakehouse, still engaging in their friendly spat, Graham heard a loud shrieking from behind him. Turning quickly, lest he were being attacked, Graham saw merely a slim rat being pursued by a snarling, ragged-eared cat. Normally, such an encounter would receive little heed from Graham (or from anyone for that matter), but the king was not feeling particularly sympathetic toward felines just then, especially cats with live suppers in mind.

The first thing that came to hand was the old boot he had found in the desert. Taking quick aim, Graham threw the tattered leather at the cat. It smacked into the road right in front of the cat's face, bounced off of its nose, and rolled into the river. The cat veered off sharply at the sudden attack, and sprinted for safety.

"Git!" Graham shouted after it. "Go pick on something your own size. Git!" As the cat's dust settled, the intended victim snuffled up to the king's feet.

"Thank you for saving my life, kind sir. And that of my babies too, for they would have no one to feed them if that cat had fed on me. Perhaps I can repay you sometime." *Talking bees, talking ants, talking trees, and now a talking rat. That whitesnake is powerful stuff*, Graham thought as the mother rat disappeared down the road.

"Talking to the animals again, king?" Cedric inquired. "Was that what you were doing by the haystack?" Once again Graham just smiled and hummed a tune. He walked into Serenia towne happily leaving the owl's question unanswered.

Despite the fact that Graham had no coin in his possession when he entered the towne that day, by the time he left it he was almost ready to take on the Great Mountains. Only a few shops were still open, and the streets had not many people about them. The broken wagon from the day before remained in the same place blocking an alley, but its owner was nowhere to be seen.

Absence Makes the Heart Go Yonder

Near the broken wheel, not far from the fish barrel in fact, a small silver coin lay lost among the cobblestones. Graham watched it for a bit. It didn't move (which was to be expected), and no one came to claim it (which wasn't).

"One problem solved," muttered Graham as he took the coin. "It's not much, but it should buy us something."

The king looked up and down the streets for some time deciding where to go first. He picked the tailor shop where, between the fabric bolts, silken shirts, and paeans to the quality of the shop's goods, Graham found a warm fur-lined cloak. Such a garment would be a necessity in the high mountains. It fit Graham perfectly, but cost much more than one silver coin.

Taking a cue from his meeting with the gnome, Graham suggested that the tailor might be interested in trading the cloak for the golden needle that had stuck him. The needle had the same effect on the tailor as the spinning wheel had on the old gnome. It belonged to the him, the tailor told Graham, but he had lost it, or had it stolen. In either case, the needle had disappeared in the vicinity of the Inn.

Graham had no choice but to return the golden needle to the tailor. However, the man was so grateful to the king that he gave Graham the cloak he had been seeking. When the king left the shop, both men were satisfied with the outcome.

The next stop was Serenia's shoe shop. There, the king found that the old couple who ran the establishment had nothing at all to sell. Graham had hoped to trade the elven boots, which were much too small for him, for something that might be more useful. Finding nothing, he listened to the poor proprietors' tale of woe, and how they were penniless with nothing to eat.

King Graham's heart is such that he will always attempt to aid those in need, even at his own expense.

"I don't know if these would help, but perhaps you could sell these fine elven shoes for some profit. Take them." The shoemaker and his wife were stunned. "We cannot," they cried. "These boots are so valuable that we can sell them for enough to close this shop and live in comfort for the rest of our lives."

"They are yours," insisted Graham. "I have offered them to you, and they are of no use to me. And, I have no time to spare to try and sell them." He handed the boots to the man, who took and caressed them.

"Look at the workmanship! Look, the buckles are solid gold. Mama, we're rich!" The couple embraced in their happiness. As Graham made to leave, however, the shoemaker handed the king his cobbler's hammer.

"Perhaps this will be of some use to you in your journey, noble sir. Take it with you. Today we stop making shoes, and I'll need it no longer." Graham followed them out the door, hammer in hand.

The only other shop open that day was Serenia's toyshop. While an unlikely place for the king to enter, he had noticed a snow sled hanging on one wall. Such a sled could be very valuable in the mountain snow and ice.

This transaction became both the easiest and the hardest for Graham. The sled, of course, cost more coin that the king had. Graham didn't want to part with the marionette, but it was all he had to offer in payment for the sled. *Anyway*, he said to himself, *if I don't rescue my family, I'll never have grandchildren. The price is steep, but necessary*. That decided, the deal was made, although the toymaker kept insisting that he was getting the better of Graham.

And with that third transaction, King Graham left Serenia towne and went looking for food.

Cedric was waiting for Graham as he left the towne, and listened with little approval to the king's telling of what he had acquired.

"Those things may be well and good for you, king, but I have no use for a cloak, nor a sled, no hands to hold a hammer, and no need for a silver coin to buy my supper. Tree grubs and small rodents are perfectly fine, and free,

Absence Makes the Heart Go Yonder

thank you. But for you, *king*, that coin will buy what is considered the best pie in all of Serenia. You will need food on this trip, you know."

"I know. And my stomach knows even better," Graham agreed. "Wait here; this shouldn't take long."

The reason it didn't take long was twofold: Graham's silver coin was just enough to buy one pie; it was custard (his favorite, although when it comes to pie, all kinds can be considered Graham's favorite), and it was the only kind of pie they had left to sell at that time of day. Secondly, Graham knew if he stayed very long in the bakeshop, he would be tempted to just start eating. He was hungry, true, and custard pie does not travel well, but he wanted the pie for eating in the mountains, preferably as a dessert. If he didn't leave the bakeshop quickly, he would have neither coin nor pie. He would have a very satisfied sweet tooth, however. Graham did not linger at all.

Despite his preference for pies, Graham knew that more substantial food would be needed to sustain him in the mountains. Having had great success with bartering that day, he wandered down the road the Swarthy Hog to attempt trading for some meats and vegetables to carry with him. The tailor had mentioned to the the king that the owner and clientele of the place were much less savoury than their food, but Graham had no qualms about entering the place. After all, it was a public alehouse.

There are alehouses, and there are alehouses. Graham recalls The Swarthy Hog as having an unremarkable decor, and remarkably nasty patrons. He entered the inn, and at once begun inquiring about provisions. That's when he lost consciousness, whacked on the head by some heavy weapon. If he had not been wearing his adventurer's hat, he is sure he might have died from the blow.

When Graham awoke, he was in the cellar of the inn, bound tightly to a chair, and no matter how he struggled, he was unable to free himself. This was his situation for several minutes when he received aid from a quite unexpected source. The scrabbling of sharp claws on the stone floor alerted the king that he was sharing his make-shift prison with some sort of rodent. He was; only it was no common vermin, but the slim rat whom he had saved earlier that day. Graham didn't know this at once, of course; all he knew was that the rat was climbing over him. Then it started chewing through the ropes. When his bonds fell to the floor, Graham looked at his small savior and recognized her at once.

"Sir, I am glad to have been able to help you. Thank you once again for saving my life, and that of my babies. The blackguards who frequent this inn are a bad lot. It is best that you be away from here. Good luck on your journey. And don't forget to take the rope with you. It might come in handy." With that, the rat disappeared into a tiny hole in the cellar wall.

The rat's advice concerning the rope made sense, so Graham picked it up off the floor. A close inspection showed that a goodly length still remained intact despite the rodent's gnawing. A search of the cellar, however, turned up nothing that might be useful in the trek ahead. It also showed that the lone exit from the place was a locked door.

When the ruffians had tossed Graham in the inn's cellar, they had deposited his travelling bag along with him. It is most likely that they had no fear of Graham escaping his bonds, and they intended to return soon to finish their dirty business. This mistake turned out to be their undoing. Graham took the small hammer which the shoemaker had given him, and as quietly as he could, used it to break through the door's latch. Immediately, he pushed through to another room, which turned out to be the inn's small kitchen.

Through the doorway on his right, Graham could hear drunken noises coming from the inn's public room. To his left, the second door led to outside, and escape. Against the far wall was a tall pantry, which the king searched before leaving. To his delight, it held a large joint of mutton, still warm and waiting to be sold.

Scant payment for my most courteous treatment, Graham mused silently, *but it will do*. Silently removing his supper from its shelf, Graham slipped

Absence Makes the Heart Go Yonder

...Graham realized that he was caught between a Roc, and a very hard place.

through the door leading out. Loitering not at all, lest the hooligans note his escape, he silently motioned Cedric, who was sunning himself of a tree branch, to follow. They didn't stop until they arrived at the foot of the trail that led into the Great Mountains. There they rested, sure that they had not been followed.

And thus it was that King Graham and Cedric prepared to leave Serenia, and begin the most perilous parts of their adventure together.

PART—THE SIXTH

The road to Mordack would snake itself into and through the Great Mountains and beyond. At the far end, the great cobra dragons were waiting to blast any who made it as far as the wizard's island. Those stone snakes were unknown to Graham as he and Cedric began moving up out of Serenia. He was, however, most acutely aware of the live serpent that blocked his steps at the start of the road up. The venom dripping from its fangs, and the alert way with which it held its head aloft, informed the king that this was a creature to be avoided. The trouble was, it had coiled itself in a part of the path bordered by high rock formations. Getting around them, and the snake, looked difficult.

"Owls hunt snakes, isn't that true Cedric?" Graham asked of his companion. "Why don't you just fly over there and scare it away."

"Hoo, hoo, me?" protested the bird. "I don't care for snake. You take care of it. Don't you have a flute you can play to charm it?" Graham shook his head in disgust.

"No flute, Cedric. But I do have this harp." Graham began playing for the snake, hoping its music, like that of a flute, might charm the creature. Graham, as always, played beautifully. The snake was not charmed. Graham next tried shaking the gypsy tambourine we was also carrying. Walking closer to the serpent, he began making a loud rattle, shaking and banging it like a mad dancer. Whether it was the king's gyrations, or the noise, it didn't matter. The snake fled, leaving a clear, steep path beyond.

"Thanks for all your help," Graham told Cedric without rancor. "Maybe I can return the favor and rescue *you* some day."

For hours, the two climbed upwards, and the landscape changed from warm, green, fertile forest to snow and ice-covered rocks. Graham's footing became more treacherous by the minute, and the air turned more and more frigid. The cold and exertion both exploded as hunger in his belly, and sent uncontrollable shivers through his body.

"I think it's time to stop for a bit," Graham breathed through chattering teeth, "get that heavy cloak on me, and some of the mutton into me." He did just that. The long, fur-lined cloak cut the chill wind, and began to bring warmth to his cold arms. The high collar gave welcome relief to the back of his neck. The meat reminded him that he had not eaten in almost two days. The king, though, ate but half of the joint, saving the rest for another meal. Cedric didn't eat any of the proffered food, but sat on a snowy rock wiping frost from his monocle and shivering slightly.

Refreshed, they resumed their journey upward, stopping only when they came to a place where the path had been washed away by a waterfall. There seemed no way past the frozen obstacle.

"Any ideas?" Graham prompted Cedric.

"There's the limb of an old tree up above us," the owl replied. "It's easy for me to reach, but you'd need to catch your rope to it and climb." Graham looked to where Cedric was pointing. The idea seemed a good one, and he was sure he had enough rope to reach the limb. He was not sure, though, if the dead branch would support his weight. It would be a long, cold, fatal fall for the king it that happened.

As he was surveying his chances, Graham spotted a long rock jutting out of the cliff a little distance away from the tree.

"That rock looks stronger, Cedric. I think I'll try going up that way. Wish me good fortune." Taking the rope from his bag, Graham made a loop and tried tossing it around his target. After a number of tries, the loop caught. Graham pulled it tight, tugged twice, and began pulling himself up hand over hand. Cedric flapped up ahead of him.

The successful climb brought them to a higher icy path. This one, also, had been washed out by the waterfall, but the break in the trail was not as great as it was on the one below. Nonetheless, it was still too wide for Graham to jump. The frozen cascade, however, flowed around a number of small rocky outcroppings, which looked much like stepping stones across the chasm. Beyond those steps, a fallen log made a bridge across the rest of the way. To venture farther on his quest, he had to go across.

"What do you think," Graham asked the bird. "Will they support my weight?"

"They'd hold me, but I'm an owl," replied Cedric. "Even then, then I'd fly across anyway. The three on top look the most stable, try those. After that, maybe the one nearest the log, and then over. Try not to slip. If you fall, I'll have no one to talk to all the way back to Crispin's." The king shrugged, and carefully began following Cedric's proposed route.

Since before he became King, Graham has been renown for his speed and agility. As it does all folk, the ensuing years have robbed him of some of both, but it has left him enough to make it across the frozen slide that day. Graham tells me that he slipped twice, nearly losing both his footing and balance. By the time he alighted on the small ledge to which the rocks led, the narrow log spanning the remaining gap looked wide and secure enough to pass a blinded army of drunken pachyderms. I suspect Graham exaggerates a bit, but he did traverse that snow-covered bridge without incident. Cedric

Absence Makes the Heart Go Yonder

beat his wings together at the conclusion of that crossing, although Graham never found out if it were for applause, or for warmth.

The reason for this ignorance is simple. After alighting from the slippery log, Graham and Cedric kept moving. Before the king had any opportunity to speak with his companion, the mountain stillness was violated by the sound of the owl's screams. As if from nowhere, as silent as a midnight snow, a pack of dire wolves rushed the two, knocking Graham to the ground, and snatching Cedric from the air. The wolfpack never stopped in their coursing attack, continuing headlong down an icy slope and into the distance. Graham picked himself up and followed as quickly as he could, alternating racing and sliding, as he gave pursuit. He soon had to stop short, as the large paw prints he was tracking disappeared across a narrow, shallow ice bridge. The king knew, just by looking, that the slight span would not hold his weight long enough for him to survive crossing. But it took just a few moments of looking back and forth between where he was, where he had been, and where he wanted to go, for the king to realize that the chase was not over. Graham retraced his steps, and scrambled back up the slope to where they had been ambushed. The toymaker's sled had been abandoned there in the confusion, and it was just what the king was looking for. Running as fast as he could in the hard snow, Graham pointed the sled's nose downhill, jumped on board, and with a strong push propelled himself down the slope, directly at the fragile bridge.

"Cedric, I'm coming!" he screamed, hoping that the bird might hear his shout and take heart from it. Faster, yet faster the little sled sped. By the time Graham reached the chasm, he was hurtling at such a speed that the sled lifted out of the snow and flew across to the other side. The snow on the other side cushioned Graham's hard meeting with the ground, but it wasn't enough to save the sled. That was smashed into a dozen fragments. Dazed only slightly by the impact, Graham hurried on in the direction he had last seen the wolves.

In fewer that a dozen strong strides, the king dashed around a sharp bend in the path to be confronted by the sight of a mighty palace in the distance. Clad in snow and ice, the structure stood on the highest pinnacle in the mountains. The trail he had been following led directly to it, and that was where he must go to rescue Cedric.

Graham stopped a moment to collect both his thoughts and his wind. As he did both, he noticed an eagle perched on a rock at the edge of the trail. Thin and shivering, the bird appeared to be starving.

"I am very hungry, traveller, and have not the strength to fly any longer. Can you spare food for me?" No longer surprised at his conversations with animals, Graham, as is his gentle nature, hesitated not at all. Taking the remainder of the mutton from his bag, he placed it in the poor bird's claws, and watched as it consumed its meal.

"Thank you, traveller," it said after finishing. "Your kindness and compassion are great, and you have saved my life. May you have a safe journey." Reaching out with its great wings, the eagled soared into the distance. The king, now more rested and composed, started towards the ice palace.

He had not gone far before the wolves arrived. They snarled and growled and bared their fangs at him as they raced out of a tunnel that led into the mountain. The saliva from their jaws steamed in the cold air, as they took hold of Graham's cloak and began pulling him back the way they had come. The hatred in their red eyes made it look as if the wolves would rather have had their jaws pulling at the king's throat. Graham ceased struggling, and let himself be led inside.

After a labyrinthine course through the lower tunnels and corridors of the palace, Graham was finally brought in front of the Ice Queen. Icebella is her name, and her realms stretch across the highest peaks of the highest mountains, and encompass all of the world's polar regions. So private a monarch is she, that the tales told of her have, until now, been considered fables and fancifications. Graham had heard of Icebella and her army of wolves, but had not given the stories about her much credence.

The queen's audience chamber was vast and cold, with her throne carved from a single block of clear, blue ice. It sits high above the room's floor, and is reached only by climbing a steep set of thirty steps, they too carved out of the same blue ice. Long, sharp rays of rock grow from the apex of this staircase, framing the queen in a granite star. Next to the stairs was a granite and ice cage, with Cedric imprisoned inside.

"Cedric, you're alive," exclaimed Graham.

"Kneel!" interrupted the imperious queen. Graham did.

"You are invaders, and have entered my realms without permission. You must die. Take them away, my wolves, and kill them!" Growling deeply, the great grey beasts moved toward the king.

"Graham, do something quickly!" screeched the now vocal bird. "Remember your family!"

The king says it took no prodding from Cedric to move him to action. He had no weapons, and knew words would do no good with either the wolves or the queen. He says that he hoped to distract or placate the beasts when he began playing his harp. I, for one, find the action quite illogical—especially given the circumstance—but the kings maintains that it was the only idea he could come up with at the time. "Music has much magic," he said. "Anyway, if it didn't work, I was going to use the instrument as a club."

No sooner had the first surprising notes left the strings, than Icebella called off her wolves.

"Your music softens my heart, somewhat," she announced. "Therefore I will give you and your cowardly bird a chance at life. There is a yeti who lives nearby in a crystal cave that belongs to me. Defeat the beast, and you will be allowed to leave these lands alive. If you fail, the owl will follow you in death. Sir Greywolf will lead you to the cave. Do you accept?"

"Your wish is my command," was Graham's foregone reply.

At the time of year that these events occurred, there is not much darkness at night in the northern reaches of our world. Thus, while the moon was full, and high in the sky, there was much light for Graham to see by as Sir Greywolf led him over the narrow mountain paths that took him to near the yeti's cave.

"I will wait for you here," he warned. "If you try to escape without vanquishing the yeti, I will kill you. If you succeed, I will return you to my mistress. And if you don't start going to the cave now, I'll rip your throat out!"

"Since you put it that way...," Graham replied, and set his steps toward the large opening he could see in the near distance.

Graham still had no idea as to how one went about defeating a yeti. His son Alexander had met one once, but had been able to avoid it through the use of magic. Graham had neither magic nor ideas. As a result, he decided to stop and think further on the matter, and perhaps munch on a bit of pie to help stimulate his thinking. *I might as well meet the beast on a contented stomach*, he reasoned.

Now the yeti is a huge and fearsome creature, human-shaped (but several times larger), covered with coarse and pungent fur, and overly equipped with long claws and fangs. It is said that their intellectual capacity is nil, but no one I have ever heard of has survived initiating a conversation with a yeti. Graham saw no sight of the beast as he neared its cave, so he picked his stopping place close to the entrance so that he could keep watch while he ate. On the trail behind him waited the wolf, and ahead, the path twisted behind a large boulder. A vast precipice plunged down beside the trail to his right, and the cave was to his left.

The custard pie, of course, had not travelled well. It still had its oval shape, but it was greatly dented and smeared. Even to Graham, whose sweet tooth never saw a pie it didn't like, found it unappetizing. It was at this moment, as the king was staring disappointedly at the custard pie, that the snow monster arrived on the scene. It had the courtesy, at least, to announce its arrival with a killer roar, and that is what saved the king's life.

What would you do, dear reader, if confronted that quickly by such a monster whilst stupidly looking at a pie, instead of looking out for danger? What Graham did was totally reflexive; startled, he jumped at the roar and flung what was in his hand in the direction of the attack.

The king's aim is good, it always has been. The custard pie splatted squarely in the yeti's face. The creature, literally, never knew what hit it, and with vision totally obscured by by the gooey filling, it stepped off the cliff's edge. The beast may be falling still. So quickly had it all happened, that it took the king a few moments to realize that he had beaten the monster.

"Did I really do that?" he asked the heavens. Shaking his head in befuddlement, he entered the yeti's lair to make sure there was no other beast about.

The interior of the yeti's cave was a multi-colored crystal fairyland, with nothing else inside but the flashing sparkles of reflected light. One particularly brilliant crystal near the cave's center caught Graham's eye, and he liked it so much that he decided to carry it with him. The little cobbler's hammer made easy work of breaking it loose. The king then turned his steps back outside, and down the trail to the waiting wolf. Together, they returned to the Ice Queen.

PART—THE SEVENTH

Queen Icebella's demeanor was much warmer toward Graham and Cedric after the king informed her of the death of the yeti. Indeed, she revealed to Graham that she knew who he was, and wished him good fortune in his quest.

She too had little love for Mordack. With a slight motion of her hand, Cedric's bars disappeared, and the owl and the king were finally reunited. After another, broader gesture, Sir Greywolf led the two out of the palace, and through the snow to a spot where a trail out of the mountains began. He silently stood watching as Graham began his long trek down to the distant sea. A silent Cedric flew along a little ahead, watchful for danger.

As it happened, Cedric's vigilance wasn't enough. The path did not go smoothly down; at times it rose up steeply before it resumed its course to the lower altitudes. It was at the top of one such climb that the owl's frantic screech of, "Graham, danger!" came too late to help the king. Cedric's words were still in his beak when the loud thumping of enormous wings, and the impact of beaten air cast Graham to the ground. A set of strong, yellow talons grabbed hold of him, and in moments Graham was soaring high in the cloudless sky, staring into the beaks and eyes of a giant Roc.

The suddenness of the attack stunned Graham; one second, he was on his feet, and the next he was dangling so far above the peaks that they seemed no larger than toys. As the king glanced down at the cliffs far below, and his captor's two heads inches above, Graham realized that he was caught between a Roc, and a very hard place. The thought did not amuse him, and he prayed that the Roc would not drop him.

It didn't. In fact, the two-headed monster bird placed Graham most gently down, and then flew off.

"Down" was the Roc's nest, and it had been built on the tip of a tall rock spire which soared up to the very clouds. However, that there was no way down other than to fall, was a fact of little immediate concern to the king. The more urgent problem was that Graham was sharing the nest with a giant egg, the shell of which was beginning to crack from the inside. There was no place to run, no place to hide, and a baby Roc—a *hungry* baby Roc—was about to join the king in the aerie. Graham knew that if he could fly, he could escape; but, of course, he could do neither. Therefore, all he could do was

Absence Makes the Heart Go Yonder

attempt to bury himself beneath the twigs and branches that made up the large nest, and hope the baby, or its mother, wouldn't notice him. He had little hope that it would work.

As Graham tried to conceal himself, a bright glint in the nest caught his attention. He grabbed for it as if reaching for life itself. As his hand closed on the object, and then opened, he had but a moment to notice that it was a delicate golden locket that he had obtained. How it had come to be there was of no import to Graham; birds often pick up bright bits to add to their nests, Graham was more concerned with the shrieking that was approaching the nest, and his quick glance showed that is was coming from a speeding eagle.

Thus, again, King Graham's kindness to a creature in need repaid him beyond measure, for it was the same bird whom he had fed on the icy trail coming to his rescue. Its arrival could not have been more timely; the Roc had finally broken its heads out of the egg and was hungrily pecking at the king. The brave eagle swooped low, and for the second time within moments, Graham was airborne in the clutches of a bird. So close had he come to being bird food, that his cape remained in the baby roc's beaks.

"I was hoping to repay you, traveller," the bird screeched above the wind. "When I saw you taken by the Roc, I knew I must fly fast to your aid. May the rest of your journey be safer than what you just endured. Farewell!" As it spoke, the eagle carried Graham lower and lower toward a sandy beach far below and in the distance. Its farewell was uttered as it dropped the king the final few inches to the ground. Upward it winged, catching an up-wind and soaring inland, dipping a wing once in salute. Graham waved his own farewell in reply.

"You most surely have interesting ways of getting around!" From atop some small rocks, Cedric's husky voice greeted Graham. "What happened? I was afraid the Roc had killed you."

Graham explained what had happened to the incredulous owl.

"If I meet any more birds on this quest," he finished, "I think I may grow feathers of my own!" Cedric hooted in laughter.

Graham found that the beach they were on was not very extensive. A short way to the north, a waterfall tumbled down cliffs to the sea. A small boat was beached near it. Those same cliffs extended south past Graham, and prevented him from climbing back into the mountains. As his eyes followed the cliffs south, the king saw a small hut with a thin stream of smoke wafting out of its chimney.

"We've reached the ocean, Cedric," Graham exclaimed (somewhat needlessly). "If you are correct, then Mordack's island lies across these waves to the east. Let's see if the person in yonder hut knows anything about the island. Perhaps we'll be able to borrow a boat." Setting his steps down the beach, the king started for the hut, stopping only briefly to pick up a rusty iron bar he found laying in the sand.

"Whoo? Hoot?" queried Cedric.

"Daddy's advice," answered Graham.

The hut had been built in the shape of the bow of a ship, and a ship's bell hung next to its door. After clanging the bell loudly many times, the door was finally opened by an old man, an ancient mariner so deaf that his entire vocabulary seemed to comprise of, "What'd you say?" and "Speak louder, I can't hear you!" There was obviously no help to be obtained from him, so Graham and Cedric left. They trudged back up the sand to examine the boat Graham had noticed.

Close examination of the small craft showed why it had been abandoned. The small sail, though serviceable, was quite tattered and would not survive a hard wind. The boat's hull was in need of much scraping and several coats of paint. Graham even found a small hole in the boat's bottom. However, both Graham and Cedric could see the faint outlines of small islands to the

Absence Makes the Heart Go Yonder

north and east, and any one of them might be Mordack's. After travelling so far, Graham was not about to be stopped with his goal within sight.

The king had been carrying with him the wax from which he had squeezed honey in the Dark Forest. It had occurred to Graham that he could use the substance to firmly plug the hole in the boat. True, the patch would not last long, but it should be enough to sail to the islands and back. Rocking the craft so as to get access to the hole, Graham pushed the wax into place and made a tight seal.

"That should do for a while," he told Cedric. "If it doesn't, you can always fly back to shore."

"Aye, aye, captain," saluted Cedric. "When did you ever learn to sail?"

"Whoo, whoo, me?" the king replied. With a great heave, he pushed the boat into the ocean and hopped aboard. Cedric followed after.

King Graham decided that his best course across the ocean was one which could bring them back easily, as opposed to one that might get them lost. Therefore he first maneuvered just a bit south and dead center of the strip of beach. He then pointed his craft east, and leaned back to enjoy the ride.

"Leave due east, return due west," Graham told Cedric. "Even a bird like you would have a tough time getting lost this way."

And so they sailed for several hours, staying away from the occasional shoals and rocks they spotted. Graham planned to explore the first island they came to, and if Mordack wasn't there, go on to another. Eventually, they were sure to stumble on the wizard's island.

Things did not quite work out that way. The first island they came to looked tall and green and lush in the distance. A small sheltered beach gave the impression that it would provide a safe harbor.

"Land, hoo, hoo!" shouted Cedric, and Graham sailed for shore. Just as the boat grounded itself, horrible screaming cries pierced out of the sky.

"Not again!" despaired the king. Diving out of the sun came three hideous winged forms, part woman, part flying daemon. The harpies screamed right down on Graham and Cedric, snatching them out of the boat and into the sky. Then they separated, bearing the king and Cedric in different directions. Graham fought to escape the pair that were bearing him, but their clutches were too strong. The harpies finally dropped the king with a hard thud in the center of a high clearing near the island's top. When Graham recovered, Cedric was nowhere to be found, and he was surrounded by a score of the monsters. They were fighting over their dinner, and that meal was going to be the King of Daventry.

It is said that to compare the voices of harpies to chalk scratching slate, is unfair to the chalk. Graham concurs. He told me that their shrieking contracted the muscles of his back, and shivered his spine. It was so bad, that he began playing his harp, the same as he had done for Queen Icebella and her wolves, if only to cover up their voices.

"They are named 'Harpies', after all," he told me.

At once, the hideous hags stopped fighting over Graham, and began fighting over Graham's harp. One particularly large harpy suddenly flashed down and snatched the instrument from his hands, and then flew away. This so outraged the others that they began screaming as one, and began to give chase to the monster with the harp. All disappeared, flying into the north, screaming to scare the dead as they went.

As soon as Graham's knees stopped shaking, and his ears ceased being outraged, he began searching to discover what had happened to his companion. As he picked himself off of the ground, he jabbed his palm on something sharp. When he looked to see what it was, he discovered an old fishhook. It was rusty, but its bite had not gone deep, nor drawn blood. He put it in a pocket, and started walking downhill on a broad path. He at last found Cedric. The owl lay crumpled in the sand by the path, barely breathing. When

Absence Makes the Heart Go Yonder

Graham tried to speak with him, all Cedric could do was moan weakly. Without aid soon, the bird would quickly die.

Graham picked Cedric up, praying that his effort would do no further damage to his friend, and hurried the rest of the way to the beach. The boat was still safely there, the waves lapping at it gently. A large seashell stuck out of the sand by its side.

"A conch shell!" The discovery brightened the king much. Oft times folk use such shells to help the partially deaf hear. Graham could take Cedric back to the mainland, and perhaps the old man might be able to help him. It was the owl's only chance. Graham took the conch, put Cedric into the boat, pushed off, and sailed back the way he had come. His scheme of taking the straight and direct route had born its fruit, and the boat sailed directly up to the beach in front of the old man's hut.

Graham rang the bell again, and eventually the ancient mariner responded.

"Eh? I can'ts hears ya. Speak up, sonny!"

Graham handed the shell to the man, who looked at it and smiled. Holding it to his ear, he waited for Graham to speak again.

"Can you help us? My friend Cedric, an owl, has been seriously wounded by some harpies. He needs healing."

"Harpies? Why didn't you say so sooner? Come on in; I'll help anyone who's been hurt by those foul beasts."

Inside, Graham laid Cedric on the mariner's bed. The old man boiled some water and placed some poultices on the injured bird. Next he fed him him some herb tea.

"That should fix 'em," the man said finally. "Make him good as new; maybe better." On the bed, Cedric was already showing encouraging signs of vigor and alertness.

"Sir, my name is Graham, and the wizard Mordack has kidnapped my family. Cedric and I were trying to reach his island when we were attacked. Do you know where it is, and can you help us?"

"Well, sonny, I wouldn't want ta' deal with that mad Mordack myself, but I can't stand in your way from trying to help your loved ones. Tell ya' what I'll do—yer friend there should be ready to travel in a few minutes. In the meantime, I'll whistle up a friend of mine. She'll be able to take you to Mordack's island, but no further. Whatta' say?"

"Is, Thank you, enough?"

"That'll be fine, sonny. That'll be just fine."

The old man's friend was a mermaid named Pearl. Mermaids are not the most talkative of folk, and this one was even less so. She quietly listened as the man asked her to show Graham and Cedric the way to Mordack's. She nodded her assent, and waved for Graham and Cedric to get into the boat and follow her lead. In the brief time that it took Pearl to arrive, Cedric's strength and good humor had returned. Graham held the bird, gently scratching its head, while the old man had asked the mermaid for her help.

"Thank you, sir. I don't know how Cedric and I can ever repay you." The king and Cedric got into the boat and waved farewell to the ancient mariner.

"May your quest be successful, King Graham. May you and your family survive this adventure safely. If you do, that'll be reward enough for me. Fare ye well!"

Graham pushed the small boat into the waves for the last time, and sailed off following the mermaid. His eyes glued themselves to the far horizon, searching for Mordack and hoping he was not to late to save Valanice, Alexander, and Rosella.

PART—THE LAST

Mordack's island loomed like a dark storm cloud on the edge of existence. No natural storm, though, this was thoroughly black and *evil*. The island appeared as if it had been melted into creation, with black and purple and inorganic green drippings giving the landscape a soft and repulsive appearance. Mordack's island may actually have been floating above the waves; most surely the bulk of it hung suspended above the ocean. Graham thinks that the chances are good that those parts that did seem to touch the water were illusion. The only exception was one tiny, rocky beach that was guarded by a pair of ominous stone pillars, and sea creatures of the more repulsive (and dangerous) kind.

Pearl waved goodbye to Graham and Cedric while the island was still a fair distance away. Her face had turned grey, and her eyes had filled with fright. It was quite apparent to Graham that she had used all of her courage in order to take them as close as she did. He begrudged her nothing as she sped away, and prayed that she had not brought them too far before she fled.

The sea guardians did not get to Graham and Cedric's craft; the rocks and surf did. Twenty feet or so from shore, the boat was capsized and crushed. Graham, Cedric, and the pieces washed up on the small beach. All lay still for several minutes until Graham was able to stagger to his feet and cough the seawater from his lungs. As he did, he heard Cedric call for help, and was able to pull him from beneath the wreckage of their former craft. They were now on Mordack's island, and had no way off. If they failed, they wouldn't need one.

Graham took stock in their surroundings. A crude set of rock stairs had been carved out of the island's weird stone, and dared the two to follow them up.

"Graham, I don't like this place at all," whispered Cedric.

"Neither do I, Cedric, but my family's here. I must go on."

Graham looked around some more. Stuck between two rocks was a dead fish. In many ways, Graham's adventure had started with the smelly fish he had found in Serenia, and it had proven useful. This was was much fresher. Graham took it anyway—both as omen, and for good luck.

"Not another dead fish?" Cedric complained.

"Just keep looking out for Rocs," was the king's rejoinder. They faced the stairs, and Graham began climbing. Cedric followed at a safe distance.

The Cobra Dragons were waiting for them at the top of the stairs. Massive carven stone statues they were, with great gems for eyes. As Graham and Cedric approached them, the eyes began to glow with an incandescent light that seemed to follow the king's every step. They flanked both sides of the narrow path that passed between them, and led to a lightless, lifeless castle beyond. The castle had the same burned, melted look as the island itself.

Graham knew that they must pass the stone guardians in order to reach Mordack's castle. Cedric had no ideas as to what approach to take, except to point out a series of scorched gashes in the ground at the point where the Cobra Dragons looked at the path.

"There is danger here, Graham," the owl observed. "I don't like the look of those statues." The king could not agree with Cedric more, and inched closer to the watchers to get a better look. The eyes grew yet hotter and brighter, and they gave the king an idea.

Absence Makes the Heart Go Yonder

As a student at the Royal University, Graham had often experimented with crystals. He had learned of crystal's curious property of not just breaking up and defracting light, but the less-known one of redirecting rays. "Making light bend and turn cartwheels back on itself," is the way one of his learned teachers had described the natural phenomenon. Graham remembered his lessons well, and had a crystal with which to duplicate those old experiments.

"If I'm wrong," he told Cedric, "remind me not to try this again." Holding the crystal that he had taken from the yeti's cave high above his head, he walked still closer to the statues. The eyes now pulsed with even greater light and energy, and together, with dual flashes, both guardians shot bolts of flaming lightning at the king. They struck the crystal at the same time, as if attracted to it. The crystal seemed to absorb the deadly energies, glowed momentarily with an energy of its own, and shot the rays back at the statues. The cobras' eyes exploded and died. The crystal shattered, destroyed also by the act. The smoke thinned, and Graham and Cedric were free to approach Mordack's castle.

The path to Mordack's soon turned from dirt to solid stone blocks. Those blocks then changed to air, abruptly ending at a chasm, which protected the great, carved main door from intruders. A small stone stairway, though, led down away from the walkway, and meandered into the distance around the lower side of the keep. Since it was the only way forward, Graham took it.

The second stone path took Graham around the side of the very base of the keep. It ended on a great stone platform which also dropped off into a deep crevasse. Beyond this point, there was no going forward.

In the platform, though, was embedded an iron grate. Graham knelt and attempted to peer down into its depths, but could see nothing but darkness. He tried lifting it, pulling and tugging with all of his strength, but was rusted tight. The king was unable to budge it.

"Time to go back," announced Cedric. "There's nothing left to do here."

"I'll think of something," responded the king. He took the iron bar from out of his travelling bag and began using it for leverage as he began to pry at the grate.

"I'm sure I can get into the castle through here," he said. Finally, his efforts were rewarded, and the heavy iron bars began to move a little, and then lift. Once the rust had been broken, the king was able to lift the grate enough to use his iron bar as a prop. The way into Mordack's castle was open.

"I'm going in," announced Graham. "Are you coming?"

"Owls are outdoor birds," Cedric replied. "We don't like it indoors. Anyway, I think it's too dangerous. I'm staying out here—to keep watch."

"That's a good idea, Cedric. But I'm going down anyway. Wish me luck."

"May good fortune go with you, King Graham. You're going to need it." The king climbed down through the narrow opening and into the bowels of the wizard's castle.

There was some light, to the king's relief. It came mostly from a greyish glow given off my the walls, but some faint illumination did seem to slant down from above through slight cracks in the ceiling. The place looked like a dungeon, and it had passages twisting and turning in every direction. *This might as well be a maze*, Graham mused. *A person can very easily get lost in here.* Looking up, he could see the opening through which he had entered the castle. It was too high to jump and reach, but it would provide a bearing if he became lost.

"Pick a direction; any direction," he commanded himself. He chose south—behind him—and began exploring.

Graham says that he wandered that maze for hours before he discovered the door out. Most every way he went looked the same as the one before. A dozen times, if once, he returned to where he had started, and in none of those instances was the return intentional. Graham started feeling that he was alone in the universe down there, with the hollow sound of his footsteps the only music in creation.

Eventually, however, he thought he could make out another sound. It did not appear to be the drip of water on stone, or even that of another's breathing. Instead it sounded like the deep steady rumble of a rock chanting, "Dink. Dink. Dink."

In a far corner of that maze, Graham finally encountered the source of that sound. It was not a rock, but a very large creature, the likes of which the king had never seen, heard of, nor read about before. Slightly taller, but broader and more massive than a human, it seemed made up from the parts of a number of beasts, especially those with massive limbs and large teeth. The most bizarre thing about Dink (which is what the king later learned it was called—because of the sound it always makes) was the fact that his hair, or mane, was tied into a topknot on his head, and held in place with a pin. So comical was its appearance that Graham forgot for the moment that the creature was most likely deadly. Combined with its incessant patter of "Dink. Dink. Dink," it was enough to make the king begin to giggle.

Graham says that it was the rhythm of Dink's chanting that moved him to begin playing the tambourine. He says that the beast's cadence was like the beat of a gypsy dance. But, Dink did not respond when Graham banged and shaked. His eyes lit, but he just hulked there doing nothing.

"Here, you try," said Graham. When he handed the instrument to Dink, the beast jumped alive with pleasure. Imitating what the king had done, Dink banged and smashed a cacophonous rhythm, punctuated by happy leaps and clumsy attempts at dance. Graham says he was lucky he was not stomped in joy.

Still shaking and booming, Dink moved away from where Graham had found him and began dancing away down a corridor and out of sight. All that was left of his presence was a lone hairpin which had fallen as result of the revelry. Graham picked it up for reasons which have been discussed earlier.

Other than the meeting with Dink, Graham encountered no others as he wandered Mordack's maze, and at last turned one final corner and found a door in (he thinks) the northern wall. As you might guess, the door was locked.

"After all I have been through, no mere door is going to keep me from my family!" Graham announced to the dungeon. He began pushing and pulling and tugging, but to no effect. The door was too thick for him to make any impression on with his shoulder. Finally, he examined the lock again. It was not large, and the key that would open would have to be small.

With no other alternative, Graham took out Dink's hairpin and began to fiddle and pry at the mechanism. To the king's astonishment, his attempt at picking the lock worked. The small "Click!" was one of the most satisfying sounds he had ever heard in his life. So smoothly did the attempt go, that Graham suspects that the pin may very well have been the lock's key. With a gentle push, the door opened. Graham went through the open door and emerged in the castle's pantry.

A wide set of steps led up from the dungeon into the storage room. Rough-hewn wood shelves lined two walls, but the king could see nothing on any of them which might help him. The pantry contained one large, closed cupboard. The only item inside of it that was portable was a sack of dried peas. He took it.

Why not, Graham thought, *at this point, anything could come in handy. Perhaps I'll have the opportunity to push Mordack into a pot of pea soup.* As the king was thinking, he heard a series of scrapping noises from the next room, which he suspected was the castle's kitchen.

Graham carefully peeked a look through the archway into the kitchen, staying as tight to the shadows as he could to avoid detection. The kitchen was filthy and in disarray, and it had one large iron pot boiling over the cooking fire. It seemed that witch's stew was on the menu that night.

The room appeared at first to be empty, but a second look revealed a young dark-haired girl with bleeding knees in one corner scrubbing the floor. Although she was filthy, and her clothes rags, she projected an aura of dignity and nobility. Graham was sure that she was no ordinary scullery maid, and was most likely a slave or prisoner to Mordack. Rather than try to slip past her unnoticed, Graham walked boldly out of the shadows to catch her attention. He risked raising an alarum from the girl, but suspected she might hate her master enough to help him.

As Graham approached, she looked up, stifled a scream, and shrank back from the king in fear.

"Leave me alone!" she cried.

"Please, be quiet. I won't hurt you."

"You're one of Mordack's evil men. Stay away." The girl was terrified of Graham, and with constant, quick, fearful glances up at him, went back to her work. Graham could see that he must take another approach to overcome her fear.

The king had never inspected the small gold locket he had grabbed in the Roc's nest; events had carried him along to quickly for that. Nonetheless, he removed it from his bag and glanced at it briefly to make sure that it was gold. Gold it was, crafted in the shape of a small heart closed shut by a tiny clasp. It was attached to a dainty golden chain. *Perhaps a gift will calm her*, he thought.

"Here, take this. I won't hurt you. Please. I'm just trying to rescue my family." Reaching out to the scared girl, Graham offered her the locket, trying to convince her of his good intentions. As she saw it, her eyes widened with surprise and delight.

"Why, this is mine. Where did you get it? I thought I had lost it when Mordack kidnapped me." She opened the locket and showed Graham the two portraits that it contained.

"These are the likenesses of my parents, the rulers of the Green Isles. My name is Princess Cassima, and Mordack kidnapped me when I refused his offer of marriage. He transported me here and set me to work scrubbing floors and cleaning chamber pots until I accept his hand. It is something I will never do, so much do I hate him!"

Graham told Cassima the tale of his family, and the girl said that the bottle containing them, and Castle Daventry, was in Mordack's laboratory on the second floor of Mordack's home. She told the king that she would help him any way she could, and he promised to free her if he defeated Mordack. Cassima also warned Graham to beware of Mordack's monstrous blue henchman; a creature who always prowled the halls of the castle, never sleeping.

"And most especially, King Graham, do not let the cat see you— not even a glance. For the cat is Mordack's brother Manannan, and I fear that you will be doomed to horrible death if he catches any sight of you." Cassima pointed to the wide stone passageway that led beyond the kitchen.

"Mordack's living quarters begin through there. May good fortune go with you, kind sir."

"My family and I shall return for you, princess," the king promised. "I must go now. Farewell!"

The corridor beyond was quite different from the utilitarian decor of the kitchen and pantry. Decorated with massive statues of daemonic beings, and stone gargoyles whose faces turned to follow him as he walked, it also contained a huge and bizarrely carved pipe organ. So hideous was it that Graham is sure that it played music only for the denizens of the deepest hells.

He was careful not to even brush it as he passed through, touching his boots to the stone floor as noiselessly as he could.

The corridor brought Graham to the castle's long dining hall, although the king winced at the thought of just who, or what, Mordack might invite to entertain in it. From behind, the king heard the sound of Mordack's henchman approaching. He quickly dashed through the hall, and emerged in the castle's main entry. Immense statues of winged women loomed above him here; the images of either beautiful vampyres or succubi, he was sure. A set of stairs led up beyond this point, through a stone arch loomed over by a feathered snake-daemon. Mordack's sense of fine art was beginning to overwhelm Graham with horror, but he was sure he had discovered the way up to Mordack's laboratory, and his family.

Graham's slight pause to cringe at Mordack's statues, was his undoing. From out of the dining hall burst a beast which was both part ram and part praying mantis. Its red eyes locked on the king, and in a quick bound had the king in its tight grip. Graham could not pull free, as much as he fought. Then, a magical door appeared in the air next to both of them. Inexorably, Mordack's guard moved to that aperture, carrying Graham despite all the king's struggles. It stepped through.

King Graham picked himself out of a foul puddle in the dirty cell where Mordack's henchman had cast him. Soiled straw scantly littered the floor, and the bone remains of former victims hung from the damp walls, still bound in their chains. Vermin scampered all about, as if anticipating new food. Once the magic entry had disappeared, there were no doors at all. Graham was trapped, and doomed.

The sight of a rat vanishing through a tiny hole in a wall, reminded the king of the one who had rescued him from imprisonment in Serenia. He was sure there was no chance of that happening to him again, but he nevertheless stretched out on the floor to peer after where the rodent had gone.

Like the rest of Mordack's dungeon, the stones themselves gave off a slight illumination, and because of this light, the king was able to look within the rat's hole. The creature was not to be seen, but its cheese supper was. The sight made Graham hungry, but his reach was just the slightest bit too short to reach the morsel.

I bet I can spear it with something like a fishhook, the king reasoned. *And that is something which I happen to have!* Taking the large hook from his pocket, Graham tried again, and got his prize.

"Yuk! It's moldy," he exclaimed once he saw what he had taken. Graham would have thrown the cheese away on the spot, except for what happened at that moment.

The squealing of a huge stone block moving on poorly oiled rollers drew his attention to the far wall. There, a portion of the prison wall was moving inward creating a passage leading out. Through it came Cassima.

"Cassima! Where did you come from. How did you get here?"

"Through the maze of course, King Graham. I have spent much time down here with Dink, my only friend. I discovered this secret way into the cell, and when I heard Mordack's henchman capture you, I rushed down here to let you out. Hurry, follow me." Crawling out behind Cassima, Graham found himself once again in Mordack's maze. The girl sped ahead of him so quickly that the king was sore put to keep her in sight. By the time he reached the kitchen, she was already back at work as if she had never left.

"Good luck, again, King Graham," she uttered. "Please try and stay away from that blue meanie because I'm sure I'll be noticed if I try to rescue you again."

Graham knew that her words were wise, and realized that he had to deal with the guard in some way to avoid being captured a second time. He moved back into the castle's corridors with more vigilance, and headed for the stairs going up.

Absence Makes the Heart Go Yonder

Graham met the guard almost at once. It was just entering the hallway with the hideous organ as the king arrived. Again the henchman's hooves dashed over the stone floor. This time, Graham's planning executed perfectly. The king had taken the bag of peas and was holding it at the ready. As soon as the creature started racing at him, Graham tossed the dried pellets on the floor in front of it. With its footing turned to rolling peas, the guard lost all traction and crashed its head to the stones with a hard thump. It lay there unconscious, but Graham knew that would not be the situation for very long. He dashed off, hoping to make it up the stairs before the creature awoke.

Manannan was waiting for him in the dining hall. Princess Cassima, if you recall, had warned the king about the cat. Here he was now, the same evil one who had kidnapped his son, and was now threatening to eat his family. Here he was, looking at Graham with hateful blue eyes. If Graham could not silence the cat some way, his mission was doomed.

"So, you want to eat my family, Manannan," Graham whispered. The king took the fish he had found on the beach and tossed it across the room. Manannan might be a wizard in feline form, but he was still a cat. Unable to resist fish, the cat rushed to it and began sniffing. At once, Graham ran over to it and, using the bag that instants before had held peas, scooped Manannan up into it. The wizard yowled and thrashed within, but the burlap muffled its cries, and Graham was able to tie the bag securely closed. He tossed it into a corner knowing that Manannan would be no further bother for quite a long while.

Let me digress briefly. King Graham, in bagging Manannan and leaving him in Mordack's dining room, intended to return later and secure his captive. As events turned out, he and his family returned to Daventry before that could be accomplished. What became of Manannan? Did he perish there, unable to claw out of his burlap prison? Or is he at large again, freely plotting new and more terrible revenge on the royal family of Daventry? As I write this long narrative, we do not know. We hope the cat came to a final end on the castle floor, but until I or some other travels there to determine the final truth, we shall remain in ignorance. We pray that our ignorance does not return to bite us.

The way to Mordack was now clear. Graham rapidly moved through the dining hall to the stairway, and most quietly and carefully ascended. No one was about at the top, and no noise came from either of the doors which Graham could see. He found that he was on a small landing, loomed over by a huge clawed skull carved of stone. The king chose the far doorway, paused to peer around its edge before entering. No one was within.

Graham found himself in Mordack's bedroom. More of Mordack's obscene statues cluttered the room, all of them staring at the sorcerer's bed with lecherous leers. The king's stomach briefly turned, unwilling to imagine the acts which might take place near where he stood.

At the far end of the room, a smaller portal led beyond to Mordack's library. Graham went to it, and on a large table, discovered an open book of magic. At the top of each page was inscribed the legend, THE OBJURGATION OF SOULS. The pages were so smooth that they may been made of the smoothest, thinnest ivory. Few words were inscribed there; mostly there were ornate drawings with the names of what could only be spells next to them. The remainder of the text was in symbols that Graham could not decipher. The king says that he felt what he describes as a *ripple* vibrate through him as he gazed on those pictures. It was as if an energy entered and passed through him, and the drawings branded themselves into his brain. At the time, Graham attributed the feeling to fright.

There was good reason for Graham to be frightened at the moment. No sooner had he taken his eyes from the grimoire, then he heard a POOF! explode in the bedroom. Sure he had been discovered, Graham looked back and saw that Mordack had materialized in the other room. However, the

Absence Makes the Heart Go Yonder

wizard seemed not to notice the king, and lay down in his obscene bed. In moments, he had commenced to snore softly.

I guess I must pass close past the very jaws of the wizard now, Graham thought grimly to himself. *He's between me and my family—so be it!* With silent steps, Graham tiptoed into the bedroom again, through a door framed by the tusks and skull of some ancient monstrosity.

Graham took a moment to look on his unchosen enemy. He affected a small black mustache, and a beard shaped like a spade. His hair came to a point from beneath his skullcap into a widow's peak. His complexion, while not exactly black, was of a duskiness much like feet left unwashed too long. Mordack was dressed in a long cloak with a tall collar. Next to his limp hand, on a small bed table, lay his wand of magic.

Without the wand, he is powerless, thought Graham incorrectly. This made up the king's mind. On the way out of the room, he snatched it from its place near Mordack's unknowing grasp. The king moved out of the room and into the hallway with Mordack's wand in his possession.

The second doorway led into the wizard's laboratory, a large room of two levels filled to bursting with the apparatus of magic. An iron spiral staircase wound its way up to a balcony, where more arcane equipment awaited its master. As Graham scanned the room, his eyes found a familiar glass beaker sitting on a long table. The king could not restrain himself and rushed headlong to it. He had finally found his family and Castle Daventry!

Graham says his tears flowed most freely when he at last saw Valanice and his children imprisoned there in Mordack's laboratory. They looked up and saw him, then waved and hugged and cried themselves. No sound, however, escaped from the bottle. The king reached to take the beaker and race away before Mordack returned to his workplace, but he could not move it at all. Graham's heart which had been soaring in joy, crashed to his feet in hopeless frustration.

All the king could do was to search Mordack's laboratory in hope of finding some way to either free his family or escape with them. The lower level proved fruitless, so Graham sprinted up the stairs to the balcony. This place too offered the king little inspiration, except for one large contraption—a machine—which was burping away at the far end. Graham rushed to the thing in order to inspect it more closely.

The machine had the smell of technology about it; metal gears, and levers, and cogs, and spokes waited to be set in motion. It was an unclean thing, bearing two narrow platters, one on either side, and metal rods which ran between them. At its center, near the bottom, was a pool of burbling liquid, simmering expectantly. Graham had no idea what the metallic monster's purpose might be.

The platters, however, suggested to Graham that they might hold something. Two somethings, actually, with dimensions like those of a stick, or a wand.

"Magic wands!" Graham exclaimed loudly. "The platters are the perfect size for holding magic wands."

Maybe it was the fact that he still had Mordack's brightly glowing wand of magic in his hand which gave him the inspiration. Whatever its source, the king knew that he possessed two of the items, and the other was dead and powerless. *Could it be that this is how Mordack charges and recharges the power of his wand? If so, I can steal its power and put it in Crispin's wand. With it, perhaps I can restore my family to normal size and escape this evil place.*

I think that the king did not think that thought in such detail. He had not the time. Graham placed Crispin's wand on one side of the contraption, and then put Mordack's on the other. He waited, but nothing happened.

"Drat!" he spurted. "How do I make this thing work?"

When Cassima had rescued Graham from the dungeon cell, he had absently put the piece of old cheese into his pocket, along with the fishhook.

Absence Makes the Heart Go Yonder

Now he recalled it, his memory jolted by the aroma of the machine's liquid heart.

"Maybe odorous old cheese is what powers it?" he mumbled. "It most certainly smells that way, and stranger things have happened in this adventure of mine." Graham placed the moldy morsel into the bubbling brew and stepped back. Nothing happened again.

"Drat!" "I was hoping I was right." He was.

Mordack's machine finally started to do something. Evidently it took some time to begin operating (a sure sign that technology was at work), but the thing slowly started to glow, and unknown powers began building, then running over and through the myriad parts. The powers then concentrated themselves on Crispin's wand, which glowed with new power. Brighter and brighter it shone, and at the same time Mordack's wand dulled. The entire process was accompanied with crackles and hisses and sharp booming crashes. When it all finished, in sudden silence, Mordack's wand had blackened, and a tiny wisp of pale smoke drifted away from it. Graham paid it little heed, but went and retrieved the wand Crispin had given him. It was vibrating with fresh power.

Graham was granted no time to admire the thing. From the main floor of the laboratory below, he heard the unmistakable sound of a wizard's magical arrival. It was Mordack.

"What has happened here?" he intoned malevolently. Looking up, he saw Graham standing beside the strange machine.

"So, it's you, King Graham. Consider yourself dead!"

Mordack made a wide, sweeping, melodramatic gesture in the direction of the balcony. His wand, no longer smoking, flew off from the machine and down into the wizard's hand. He never looked at it, but used it to cast a spell in Graham's direction. The king saw his ending coming.

Nobody, however, saw Cedric coming. Cedric, you might ask, Cedric? Yes, indeed. Because Mordack's wand had been drained to near powerlessness in the machine, the spell it cast at Graham did not act instantaneously. Rather, it flew at the king. Cedric, who had been keeping watch on the outside of the castle, took this moment to arrive in Mordack's laboratory.

"Graham, good news. Crispin's coming to...." Before his words were finished, the owl dropped to the ground lifelessly. Unaware of what was happening, he had flown between the king and the wizard's spell.

"Curses!" screamed Mordack. "You have nearly destroyed my wand. You shall pay for this—now!"

With or without a wand of magic, Mordack was among the most powerful of sorcerers. With another magical gesture, he immediately transformed himself into a perverted mockery of a giant, flying scorpion; although no being like it had ever existed in our world before that moment. Mordack rose into the air and flew at Graham.

The king, seeing the transformation happen to his opponent, immediately recalled the pictures he had seen in *THE OBJURGATION OF SOULS*. He somehow knew with certainty that they were spells of transformation. He recalled the tiger, and wished he could become one himself so as to battle Mordack.

Thus it was, and thus it became—unknowingly, the king had memorized spells from an ancient and obscure school of magic that uses the picturing of images to cast its spells. When he wished clearly to become a tiger, he did. It was not what Mordack expected. The wizard stopped his attack in midflight so as to avoid Graham's tiger claws, and then fled away when the king leaped at him.

And so it went, the magical battle; back and forth between the great wizard who wielded an almost useless wand, and the great king who defended himself with a powerful one.

Next, Mordack became a dragon, a great firedrake. As that, he breathed death flames at the king. Graham wished himself into the small, quick, and darting form of a brush bunny, and eluded them all.

Absence Makes the Heart Go Yonder

A cobra will easily slay a rabbit, and Mordack tried this next. Graham became a mongoose and brought the fear of physical death to the magician's hooded eyes.

"You cannot slay me, puny vermin," Mordack hissed. "I shall burn my revenge into your flesh!" Mordack's roar filled the room as he transformed himself for the last time. He had become a fiery ring, and surrounded Graham completely. The wizard closed the circle on the king, and prepared for his kill.

Valanice, Rosella, and Alexander all witnessed the titanic struggle between Graham and Mordack that day. All three knew that the king had no chance against the sorcerer, and waited in horror for Graham to be annihilated. They could do nothing to help, and realized that their end would come soon after the king's. That Graham had lasted so long against Mordack gave them a little hope, but the end, they were sure, was inevitable.

From Graham's point of view, Mordack's appearance as fire was a big mistake on the part of the wizard. There was one more spell which he had seen in the magic book, and Graham pictured it with glee. It did its work in two stages: first, Graham was returned to his own form; second, he brought rain down on his head, and down upon the flames that were Mordack. In a sooty puddle, the great and evil wizard Mordack was destroyed. King Graham and Daventry were avenged.

Graham spent no time strutting over his victory. He went at once to the bottle where his loved ones were. He knew no spell to restore them, but pictured them clearly in his mind as standing next to him, again wearing their full forms. The magic didn't work. In despair, Graham threw Crispin's wand to the floor and wept.

The patter of bare feet brought Graham out of his remorse for the moment. It was Cassima. She had watched the final battle from the shadows, and had come to see if Mordack were really dead. Graham assured her that he was, but was weeping because he had no way to help his family.

It is sometimes said that when all is darkness, the faintest light will shine the brightest. It was then, when all Graham could see was despair and failure, that Crispin appeared. While the king and Cedric had battled their way to Mordack's, Crispin had learned what had happened to Graham's family. He had then embarked to set things right, and battle the evil Mordack himself. He was too late for that task, but not too late for King Graham and his family.

With one easy magical gesture, the king and his family were together once more, all hugging and kissing and embracing and crying and rejoicing. When they finally calmed, Graham introduced all to Cassima, who had saved his life in the dungeon. They thanked her with new hugs and kisses. Alexander was especially grateful for the pretty maiden's aid in setting them free. To the surprise of all, he begged leave to visit her on the Green Isles. She blushed, then accepted. Hugging Valanice closer, Graham had new visions of grandchildren.

With another wave, Crispin magically sent Cassima on her way home.

With another wave, Castle Daventry disappeared, sent back to its appointed place in Daventry.

With another wave, poor forgotten Cedric was returned to health. He had not died; the spell cast at Graham had turned him to stone. A new tear came to the king's eye, so happy was he to see the owl who had become his friend.

With a last wave, Graham, Valanice, Alexander and Rosella found themselves on a hill in Daventry. Below, they could see the castle and hear the cheers of their people welcoming their return. Arm in arm, they went home.

11

The Easy Way Out

Notes on Winning the Games

Welcome back to our world. Welcome back to the universe that sees Daventry only as a place of fun and games—a world that only exists inside computer games.

This is an honorable point of view; try as I might, I don't suspect I'll be able to produce hard, bite-into-it-and-see-if-it's-real proof of Daventry's physical existence. No amber stones of teleportation, no chests of gold that never empty, and no golden-egg-laying hens are in my possession, items that would be indisputable proof of the words that Derek has been sending me. Heck, if I had any of those things I probably wouldn't show them anyway. Nothing personal, mind you; if I had some of that stuff, I'd just live in luxury somewhere and pass Derek's words off as fiction—if at all.

What follows is a step-by-step guide for playing the King's Quest computer games. It's the most direct route through the adventures, with strategies and specific tips on surviving your own personal encounters with the games. These routes are not always the same ones Graham, Alexander-Gwydion, or Rosella took. They live in their real world, we live in ours, and we still cannot duplicate real life inside of a computer. I leave it to you to decide which roads you may wish to follow; they all end at the same place. I encourage you to discover your own individual ways through the stories—ways that might even be more fun.

Each adventure is looked at by itself. You'll see the best path through each game and get specific solutions to the toughest problems. In some cases, there is more than one way to get through a problem. I'll explain those also; they can affect your score for both good and bad. Used along with the maps and scorecards at the back of the book, you should have little trouble successfully completing any, or all, of the King's Quest games.

Of course, you don't have to read this chapter at all. You can solve the adventures just by following the earlier narratives from Daventry. However, some specific game problems, especially in King's Quest 3: To Heir Is

The Easy Way Out

Human and King's Quest 4: The Perils of Rosella, come directly from the fact that the adventures have been translated onto a computer. These problems must be solved in the context of interacting with your computer; they don't totally exist in the context of the King's Quest universe. This chapter also helps you through those sticky spots.

I've titled this chapter "The Easy Way Out," and it is. If you're stumped, this is definitely one place to go. But consider the spirit of adventure, the pleasures of figuring out something for yourself, the joy of discovery, and those gratifying, light-bulb-going-on-over-your-head moments of triumph you may be missing. I will restate my point:

The journey is the reward!
Getting there is half the fun!
It's not whether you win or lose, it's how
you play the game!

Enough, already! You have been given your last chance to mend your evil ways. No more platitudes, just answers.

Doesn't that make you feel a whole lot better?

SPEAR'S 12 RULES FOR PLAYING COMPUTER GAMES

(Version 1.0)

Save the game

Save often, save early. Save as soon as you've accomplished something difficult, after you've discovered some goodie, and before you do anything at all dangerous. When in doubt, save. The more saved games you have, the better. Sometimes you'll find you've saved a game after you've done something stupid, although you didn't realize it at the time. Going back is usually preferable to starting over.

Know where you are at all times

Make maps; these not only show you where you are, but where you've been. They also give you some idea of where you haven't been—you may have missed exploring some key place. Write down on the map who and what you find in the various places. Know where north, south, east, and west are. In King's Quest, north is to the top of the screen, south to the bottom, east to the right, and west to the left. If you need to, indicate up and down. Most importantly, be sure you can understand what you draw and write.

Look at everything

Every time you get to a new place, LOOK at it, then LOOK at everything in it. LOOK at the ground, the walls, the trees, the stumps, the tables, the chairs—you get the idea. LOOK on top of, on, under, around, into, through, and behind.

The Easy Way Out

Open everything

Doors, chests, cabinets, drawers, bottles, whatever—things are kept in them, and you'll never know unless you open them up and look inside.

Take everything

Moss, worms, stones on the shore—if the game program lets you take something, do it. It will probably score you some points or be useful later.

Think creatively and accept nothing at face value

Just because it's a bucket of water doesn't mean you can't use it to defeat a dragon. Kiss frogs, kiss witches, throw bridles at snakes, and always look for secret doors. Often it's the illogical response or act that's the right one. Sometimes it isn't, but everything is worth a try.

Do the obvious

Pet dogs, give dogs bones, pet cats, wear things, feed hungry wizards, plant beans, read notes, and don't kiss evil witches. You'd be surprised what you miss just because it's so obvious.

Save the game again

Just in case you've forgotten already, SAVE! Especially before you do creative or obvious things.

Remember everything

Take notes; hints are everywhere. Jot down whatever other characters say to you, you may need it later.

Walk away from problems

Often you will meet puzzles and problems that you can't seem to solve. Sometimes this is because you still haven't done, met, discovered, or found something yet, but other times it's because you're just plain tired or stumped. Letting the problem slush around in your mind for a while—not concentrating on it—helps. How can you tell the difference between them? Often, you can't. That's what this book is for.

Don't play too long

Computer games can easily become compelling and addictive. You can find yourself playing for hours upon long hours, not knowing where the time went. Worse, if you play too long at a stretch, there is always the possibility of eye strain, a stiff neck, and headaches. Give your body and mind a break. Take it easy. The game, no matter how good, doesn't have to be solved in a day. Play wisely, play well, play healthy.

Always remember—it's only a game!

It's supposed to be fun. It's not brain surgery.

King Graham's Rules for Adventuring

If I have learned anything in my life, I have learned this:
- Pick up anything that is not nailed down.
- If it is nailed down, look for loose nails or boards.
- Check carefully into, under, above, below, and behind things.
- Read everything; you might learn something.
- Wear clean undergarments.
- Brush after meals.
- Always remember: Nothing is as it appears. Nothing.

King's Quest 1: Quest for the Crown

Object of the Game:

You're Graham, a young knight of Daventry. Your quest is to discover the three great—but now lost—treasures of the kingdom, and return them to King Edward. The three treasures are

A magic mirror

A magic chest

A magic shield

If you complete the quest successfully, you will become King of Daventry.

Things to Come:

As you wander through Daventry, you will notice that if you go straight and far enough in any direction, you'll end up back where you started, provided there is no roadblock like a mountain, chasm, or unfordable stream. When this happens, the game world and map are said to "wrap around." This is very useful for shortcuts—like walking south to get north and things like that, and is something Graham, I'm sure, would have found extremely useful.

There are five creatures you must avoid during your initial wanderings:

- The **wolf** will kill you. The wolf lives in just one place—the area immediately east of the well and west of the big oak tree with the golden egg.

The Easy Way Out

- The **ogre** will kill you. The ogre lives also in just one place in the classic KQ1—it's the area immediately south of the rock where you find the dagger, east of the back of the woodcutter's house, west of the river bank where you can see only the mushroom. In the *SCI Version*, the orge lives in the two screens south of the rock. He also can be found in the main Sorcerer screen, which is the one just west of the walnut tree.

- The **Sorcerer** will paralyze Graham. In the classic KQ1, he only lives west of the walnut tree, and nothing happens to Graham while he is under the sorcerer's spell. In the *SCI Version*, however, there is a good chance that the dwarf will come by and steal things from Graham, or the orge to kill him—both are sure ways to lose the game. He can also be found in the dwarf and orge screens.

- The **dwarf** will not kill you, but he will steal your possessions, and you can never get them back. If you're carrying the magic mirror and he steals it from you, you lose the game. Period. You can't win! Beware! The dwarf wanders in the area surrounded by the ogre to the north, the walnut tree to the south, the rock with the small hole to the west, and the river bank to the east. In the *SCI Version*, he also shows up in the orge and sorcerer screens. In all versions, the dwarf can be found on the stairs (or suspended walkway) going up into the mountain, if you use that route up to the Land of the Clouds.

- The **witch** flies around immediately north of the well, south of the gingerbread house, and east of the big cave. She'll capture you if she sees you and will put you in a cell you can't get out of, ever. In the *SCI Version*, Graham does not languish long in the cell. The witch will soon make a Graham Cracker lawn ornament out of him. However, you will have to deal with the witch eventually, inside the gingerbread house. She won't be there if you are protected, so only go there when you are vulnerable.

The best way to handle these critters is by not encountering them at all and simply avoiding the screens where they live. However, the elf's ring will make you invisible to them for a while, the goat following you will scare them off, the fairy godmother's spell will protect you for a short while, and the magic shield will protect you from them permanently. If you have none of the above and insist on visiting these folks' stomping grounds when they're around, use the *old edge-of-the-screen trick*. What you do is enter the area in question, and move around on the very edge of computer's screen. The instant the creature appears, step back out of the screen. Next, return to the dangerous screen and try again. You can walk around this way, as long as you are on the screen's very edge.

In the *SCI Version,* the old *edge-of-the-screen trick* still works, but the monster screens have been changed somewhat to make the trick harder to use. While the monsters still will not follow you off the screen, bushes and rocks and trees have been placed on many of the screen edges in order to prevent Graham from walking right through without stopping. Also, the monsters usually do not appear—if they are there at all—until Graham has moved farther into the screen. In the classic version, they are usually there when the screen appears. In this new system, Graham can enter a screen, stand there for five minutes, and not encounter a monster. Then, when he moves to cross the screen, the monster in question might still appear. The "trigger" for the monster's appearance is not on the edge of the screen, but in its interior. And since Graham cannot skirt through on the screen's edge, the probability of a nasty encounter increases dramatically.

If you're playing the *SCI Version,* I suggest—if you really must enter these screens—save the game before entering. If you're caught, restore and try again.

However, here's an *edge-of-the-screen* solution. Enter the monster screen from a safe screen. Stop at once. Follow the screen edge until you hit an obstruction. Exit the screen there back to the safe screen. In the safe screen,

The Easy Way Out

continue in the direction you wish to travel for several steps and the return to the monster screen. There, if you're not past the obstacle, try again. If you are past the rock or bush, continue safely on the edge of the screen until Graham is through. Remember, for the old *edge-of-the-screen trick* to work, you must use the north or south edges to travel in the east/west direction, and the east and west edges to go north/south. This is true in both game versions.

Finally, if you must visit the monster screen, try taking the goat along. In the classic game, the monsters will flee when they see the goat. In the *SCI Version,* they will not appear at all. The disadvantage of this though is that the goat will not go back to his pen, down the well, or into the witch's house. Nor will the condor pick Graham up if the goat is with him. The goat runs away forever in most of these instances, and the goat cannot be locked back into the pen for safekeeping. If you decide to use the goat, do it just prior to dealing with the troll.

In the classic KQ1, the magic ring would always protect Graham from all of the above nasty types, and was effective in getting past them (albeit for a short time). This too has been changed in the *SCI Version*. If Graham is invisible before he enters a monster screen, he won't be noticed—indeed, the monsters won't appear. If he becomes visible, the monsters might appear. And, if he becomes invisible after seeing a monster that's visible on screen: the sorcerer will see through the spell and paralyze him, the ogre will sense and kill him if he gets too close, and the wolf will smell him and kill. But the witch will not see him, and the dwarf will get spooked and disappear.

While the monsters are usually found in their appointed areas, sometimes they are not home at all. That is good. You will find that if you do encounter them, use the old edge-of-the-screen trick, and then immediately step back, they might not be there at all when you return. This is one of the best tricks around and can be used successfully in all of the games. Remember it; it's called the *old edge-of- the-screen trick*—it will save you a lot of lives.

It is also useful when you need to find somebody or something that isn't there when you go to visit—the elf with the gold ring, for instance. Just step out of the area and return at once. Repeat as necessary until successful.

How to Do It:

Cross the bridge over the moat with care; this is the beginning of the game, and you're too young to die! Go to the castle and bow to King Edward. He'll tell you about the treasures and the reward and then send you on your way. After you leave the castle, you won't be able to get back inside until you have all three of the treasures in your possession.

Note: In the IBM-compatible versions of this game *from October 1990 onward,* there is an animated opening sequence that details the moves we just covered. In this version—the *SCI Version*—the player-controlled action begins here with Graham standing outside of the castle and after having had his audience with good King Edward. Also, Castle Daventry is three screens wide in this version, not two. Nonetheless, this has no effect on the game play, and Graham still will be unable to return inside until after all his quests are completed.

As soon as you leave the castle, cross the bridge to the west. Look at the rock. Stand to the north side of the rock, then push or move the rock. Look in the hole, then take the dagger. Don't stand to the south of the rock when you move it or else it will roll on top of you with terminal consequences.

Go north to the next screen. Look at the tree. Climb the tree and be careful where you step in the branches. You will discover a bird's nest. Look at the nest. Take the egg—it's gold— and climb back down. On the ground again, walk east one screen. You are at the garden behind the castle. Look at the garden, then take a carrot. Walk north. The next screen is the home of the elf; talk to him and you get the magic ring that makes you invisible when you rub it. The screen north of the elf contains the ceramic bowl, you'll need it in the woodcutter's cottage. Look at the bowl. Look into the bowl. The screen north of this has a river bank where you will find pebbles—ammunition for the slingshot in the Land of the Clouds. In the *SCI Version,* the pebbles are *not* here, but we'll get to them soon enough.

At this point, retrace your steps south to where you picked up the bowl and move one screen west. There are walnuts on the ground under the tree. Pick one up and open it; there should be gold inside. If not, keep picking them up and opening them until you do find the treasure. After you get the gold, go south. You'll come to a mountain with a door in it, which is the way back from the Land of the Clouds. You don't have the key to get you up there, so continue south two screens to where you found the dagger.

Walk one screen west. Graham is on the eastern edge of a lake. This is where the pebbles are if you're playing the *SCI Version.* Look at the ground by the lake's shore. Take the pebbles—they are not here in the other versions, but we'll wait for you anyway. Good. Swim west across the lake; the screen after the lake's west shore has a log and stump. Look inside the stump and take the pouch of diamonds. Go back to the western lake shore and turn south.

The house you find here belongs to the woodcutter and his wife. Forget about the ax and pump you see in front, they don't do anything, and you can't take them. Walk inside, put the bowl on the table, and say the word that's written in the bowl. The people are so grateful that they tell you to take their fiddle. It's on the floor in the corner, but make sure you don't step in the hole in the floor getting it—it's another way to die. Play the fiddle before leaving.

Note: In the *SCI Version,* this scene is slightly different. Once inside, the woodcutter will talk to Graham. Say the word in the bowl, then give the bowl to the man. Take the fiddle, play the fiddle, then leave. There is no hole in the floor to worry about.

Leave the house and travel south past the lake. The gingerbread house, the witch's home, is in the screen south of the lake. Go to the front door and open it. If the wicked one is at home, use the old edge-of-the-screen trick and get out at once, continue out of the screen the house is in, and then return to the house. Repeat until she isn't there. Once you are safely inside, go to her bedroom, pick up the note next to her bed, and read it. It's the clue for solving the gnome's name riddle, and it scores points. The jail cell you see in the house is where the witch puts you if she captures you.

Wait in the bedroom until the witch comes home and starts cooking. Walk quickly up behind the witch and push her. Be careful that the witch doesn't see you do this. In the *SCI Version,* she'll turn our hero into a Graham cracker if he's noticed! You score points by killing her. Open the cupboard and get the swiss cheese—you'll need it for the rat in the land of the leprechauns.

There is an alternate solution for getting the cheese that does not include killing the witch. Wear the ring and rub it outside the front door. When you go into her house while invisible, she is not there, nor does she return while you're in that state. You'll have plenty of time to read the note, get the cheese, and leave. You won't score as many points this way, but it's a more elegant, nonviolent way to solve the problem. Don't forget to eat the house after you go back outside; it is gingerbread and chocolate and you get points for lunching on the place.

From the gingerbread house, scoot straight west three screens until you meet the troll on the troll bridge. Ignore him and walk one screen south where there is a patch of clover. Pick the clover because you need it to get by the leprechaun guards. You now have the majority—but not all!—of what you need to get the major treasures and win the game. You'll pick up the other necessary stuff as you go along.

This is decision time for you, dear player. Which treasure do you wish to go for first, the mirror or the chest? In the *SCI Version,* the shield cannot be obtained until after the mirror and the chest are in your inventory. The condor

The Easy Way Out

that flies Graham to that part of Daventry will not appear if Graham doesn't have these items. We will follow the *SCI Version* constraint, although in other versions it doesn't matter in which order the three treasures are found. We'll walk through each quest individually.

Getting the Magic Mirror:

From the clover patch (that's where I left you, remember?) go south one screen. This is the fairy's godmother's patch of turf. If you meet her, she'll sprinkle you with fairy dust for protection. You won't need it where you're going, but what the heck, you know how to avoid the monsters now anyway. You are going to a well, which is three screens east past the fairy godmother. As you walk, notice the goat in the pen. You and he will become companions later in the game.

When you reach the well, cut the rope with the dagger and take the bucket. (If all you see is the rope, then the bucket is lowered into the well. In that case, raise the bucket with the crank, cut the rope, and take the bucket.) Now lower the rope into the well with the crank, and climb down the rope. You fall in the water when you reach the end of the rope. Swim. Dive. Underwater, you will see an opening on the left side of the screen; swim into it. In the *SCI Version,* jump when you reach the end of your rope (so to speak), dive, swim west and then up to the pool at the top left of the screen. Type, "climb out". Fill the bucket, because in this version it doesn't do so automatically; it does so in the other. You are now in the dragon's lair, and the dragon is guarding the magic mirror. Save the game. There are two ways to get by the dragon, and both require that you get just close enough to the monster that he can't fry you. Watch his flaming breath and see where it stops; you want to go almost to that point. In the *SCI Version,* the dragon doesn't breath at Graham. Walk only to the edge of the dragon's tail and not beyond it. It's cinder time if you do. If you throw the dagger at the dragon, you kill it. You either lose

2 points or score 2 fewer points for solving the problem this way. You earn points if you throw the bucket of water at the dragon. The dragon will leave, and give you an exit out on the west side of his lair. With the dragon out of the way, take the mirror. Look into it for a glimpse of your future.

There are two ways out of the dragon's lair. Depending on which version of the game you have, one is preferable to the other. You can follow the beast west. In the *SCI Version,* you will enter another part of the cave. The exit is in the upper left of the screen. This scores points, and you will come out of a cave just north of the goat pen. This is where you hitch a ride on a condor later, so remember this place. The second way out of the draggon's lair is the way you entered. It scores you points in the "classic" version. Go back out through the opening you came in, and then swim to the surface. From there you can grab the rope and climb it back out of the well. Please do this slowly, you don't want to fall back in.

Congratulations! You have now completed one part of your quest for the crown.

Getting the Magic Chest:

Go back to the goat pen and open the gate on its eastern half. Close the gate, or the goat might escape. Walk up to the goat and show the goat the carrot. He then follows you almost anywhere, but not inside the gingerbread house!

Caution: Do not give the carrot to the goat or he'll eat it and not follow you.

With the goat tagging along, leave the pen and walk two screens east to the fairy godmother screen. From there go north two more screens and

The Easy Way Out

encounter the troll. There are two ways past the big fella. If the goat is with you, it will attack the troll, butting it off the bridge and scoring you points. The goat then disappears from your life forever. If old Billy G. is not with you, the troll will accept a treasure—the gold egg, gold walnut, pouch of diamonds, or the leprechaun king's scepter. You lose points, however, solving the problem this way.

Cross the bridge and talk to the gnome. He will give you three tries to guess his name. If you fail, he gives you the key that fits the door into the mountain. The door is west of where you met the elf, south of the walnut tree, and north of the oak tree with the golden egg. If you guess correctly, he gives you magic beans. His name, Rumplestiltskin, is a wrong answer. The answer is IFNKOVHGROGHPRM, which is Rumplestiltskin spelled in a backwards alphabet (you substitute the letter "z" for "a", "y" for "b", and so on for the entire alphabet).

Note: For years this has been the King's Quest question that Sierra On-Line has received the most requests for hints about. The problem was twofold: the player realizing that he/she must start with the the name RUMPLESTILT-SKIN, and deducing that the key to the problem is a backwards alphabet—not a backwards spelling. Many thought the puzzle was too tough, if not unfair. In the *SCI Version,* players have been given two breaks. First, a spinning wheel and a pile of gold appear in the screen along with the gnome. This is a broad hint and reminder of the Rumplestiltskin story.

The second break might bring tears to many an experienced King's Quest player's eyes. The backwards alphabet answer—IFNKOVHGROGHPRM—still works. However, the backwards spelling answer—NIKSTLITSELP-MUR—is also correct. Gasp! This bit of information, of course, is of little comfort to those millions of players who have struggled with the problem in the past, or those without the *SCI Version*. Nor is it of any solace to Graham who had to come up with IFNKOVHGROGHPRM in real life.

When Graham guesses the name correctly in this version, the magic beans are put directly into his inventory. This is not the case in the classic version.

One last note on the name matter: although the backwards alphabet answer is supposed to work, at least one early *SCI Version* did not allow it. The backwards spelling solution, of course, worked as advertised. If you have one of those, I guess you have some sort of a collector's item.

Guessing the name and getting the beans gives you the most points. In the classic version, whichever way you solve the problem, don't forget to pick up the gnome's gift from the ground.

If you have the key, walk to the door, unlock and open it, walk carefully up to the Land of the Clouds and wait for me there. The rest of us are taking the beanstalk. If you go this way and are not carrying the shield, be cautious going up. You could be robbed by the dwarf. If you are robbed by the dwarf, you cannot get your treasures back. If you lose the mirror to the dwarf, you lose the game. Save the game at the bottom and use the *edge-of-the-screen trick*. Keep trying. Obviously, if you have the shield at this point you are not playing the *SCI Version*.

If you took the beans walk east from the gnome's hut across that bridge. You want to go to the flower patch two screens east of the gnome. Plant the beans and watch the stalk grow. Save the game. Repeat: SAVE THE GAME! It's time to climb.

Climbing the beanstalk and walking through the clouds after you get to the top is a matter of trial and error and patience. Use the keyboard to move Graham. Change the game's speed to its slowest setting and put aside the joystick or mouse you may be using; you'll have more control of Graham. Climb. After you've gone up a few steps, save the game. That's it; climb, save, climb, save. It's not as easy as it reads. When you get to the top, save again, then move directly east, staying in the center of the screen as you walk.

The Easy Way Out

You will see solid ground when you reach the next screen; keep moving due east in the center of the screen until you reach it. Save the game.

Walk one more screen east, then one screen south. From here go two more screens east, being careful to stay out of the clouds and on solid ground. You don't want to fall to your death now, do you? There's a tree with a hole at its base; look into the hole and then take the slingshot you find. It can be used, along with the pebbles, to kill the giant. Finding it scores points. Walk one screen north. You are at the mouth of a cave—this is where you arrive if you walked up through the mountain. Hi! The giant and the magic chest are one screen west of you. Go there. Notice the giant is carrying a chest, it's the one you have to get.

Rub the ring and become invisible; if you have the shield, don't worry. In either case, the giant will leave you alone and not kill you. If you have no magical protection, run away from the giant but don't use the old edge-of-the-screen trick. It is possible to elude the giant long enough for him to get tired and fall asleep. To get the chest from the giant, you can just kill him using the slingshot and pebbles, but the nonviolent solution scores more points. Since you're protected by being invisible, just hang around there for a while. Wait for the giant to fall asleep, then go up and simply take the chest. You can also wait out the giant by hiding behind a tree. In the *SCI Version*, leave the screen containing the cave at the bottom left corner. You will enter the giant's screen near a tree in that screen's bottom right corner. Walk Graham north right up to the trunk as far as he can go—rub his nose on the bark. If the giant is in the north or center of the screen, he will probably not see Graham, and will eventually fall asleep. If you see him moving west to east in Graham's direction, exit the screen at once and try again. Rubbing the magic ring and staying as far away from the giant as possible, however, is still the safest solution. After that, walk east to the cave, and go to the bottom of the stairs. As on the beanstalk, use the slowest speed. Be careful on the stairs; you can fall to your death!

In the *SCI Version,*, the stone stairs have been changed to a rickety suspended walkway. However, just take your time and be careful. At the bottom, the door will magically disappear as Graham approaches it. When he's outside, it will rematerialize. You are now at the bottom of the the mountain outside of the door. Congratulations! You have completed the second of your three quests.

Getting the Shield:

From the door in the mountain, go south one screen, then east five screens to the goat pen. At the gate, walk north one screen. You will reach a cave, the same one from which you can exit the dragon's lair.

What you want to do here is wait for the condor to appear. If it doesn't, use the old edge-of-the-screen trick until it does.

Caution: Be very careful if you use the east side of the screen for the trick. If you haven't killed her, the witch could be flying about over there.

When the bird does show up, you must jump and let it grab you in its claws. Go to the middle of the screen and wait for the bird to swoop; then jump so that you are at the top of your leap when the condor is at the bottom of the swoop. This will take a number of tries, but be patient. When the bird finally gets you, it will drop you near a hole in the earth. You are now in an area three screens in extent. You cannot leave by foot, by swimming, or by bird. You must go down the hole.

But first, walk one screen west of where you get dropped—be careful you don't fall in the hole yet. Pick the mushroom you find there—don't eat it!—and return to the hole. Step into it—just fall in. Whee! At the bottom you find you can't climb out. Follow the cave south and then east. The moment you see the rat, stop. Save the game. Deal with the rat much as you

The Easy Way Out

handled the dragon. Watch where it walks, and see how far it roams. It does not come all the way east across the cave. Walk up almost to that point and give the cheese to the rat; this may take a try or two. The rat then disappears. In the *SCI Version,* the rat just sits there and does not move. Move Graham to near the center of the screen and give the cheese to the rat. He'll say to come closer. Move Graham one step at a time closer, and offer the cheese after each step. Eventually, the rat will take the cheese. If Graham gets too close and doesn't offer the cheese, he'll get caught and die. You can also get past the rat by offering it a treasure—the gold egg, gold walnut, or bag of diamonds. If you do, though, you lose points. With the rat gone, you can now open the door.

I hope you didn't forget the clover; the guards will attack you if you don't have it. Play the fiddle, and the guards will dance off. In the *SCI Version,* play the fiddle the instant you're asked "What are you going to do?" Do not hesitate. Otherwise the guards will leave too quickly for you to score the fiddle-playing points. Walk south and you are in the leprechaun king's throne room just in time to see him leaving. Take his scepter, it's in front of the throne. Next to the throne is the magic shield. Go ahead, take it, it won't bite. Got it!

Leave the room by going west, and climb the stairs. Be careful you don't fall! There is a small opening at the top, but it's too tiny to crawl through. Eat the mushroom and you shrink. Exit through the hole at once. You are now one screen north and one screen east of the gingerbread house.

You now have all of the lost treasures of Daventry! Walk north two screens, and then east to the castle. All that remains to be done is to take the three treasures back to King Edward. The doors will now open for Graham when he gets there. Open the door.

Depending on which version of KQ1 you have, the game will end slightly differently. In the classic version, walk to the throne room. Don't forget to bow when you see the king again—this will score you points. In the *SCI*

Version, the game will go on auto-pilot and you don't have anything else to do.

Congratulations! You have now completed King's Quest 1: The Quest for the Crown.

The Easy Way Out

King'Quest 1:
Quest for the Crown (Daventry)

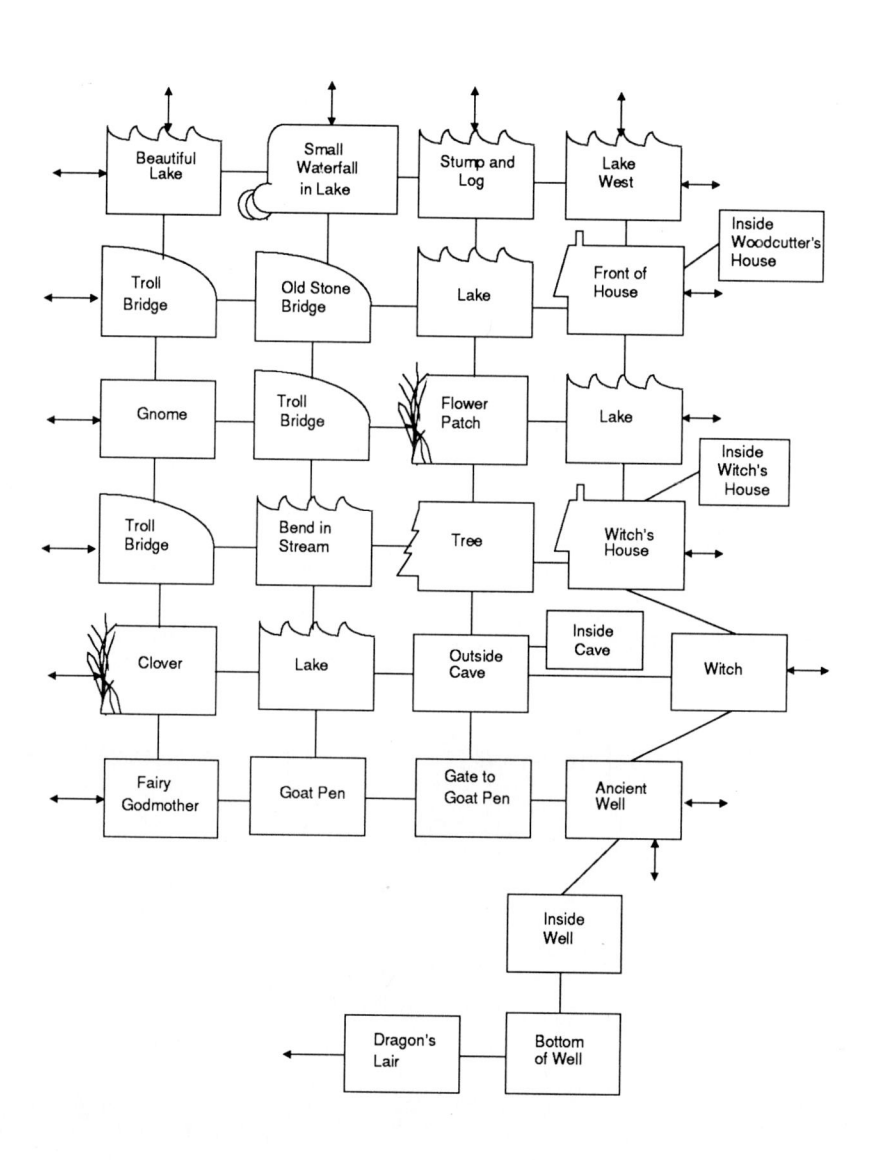

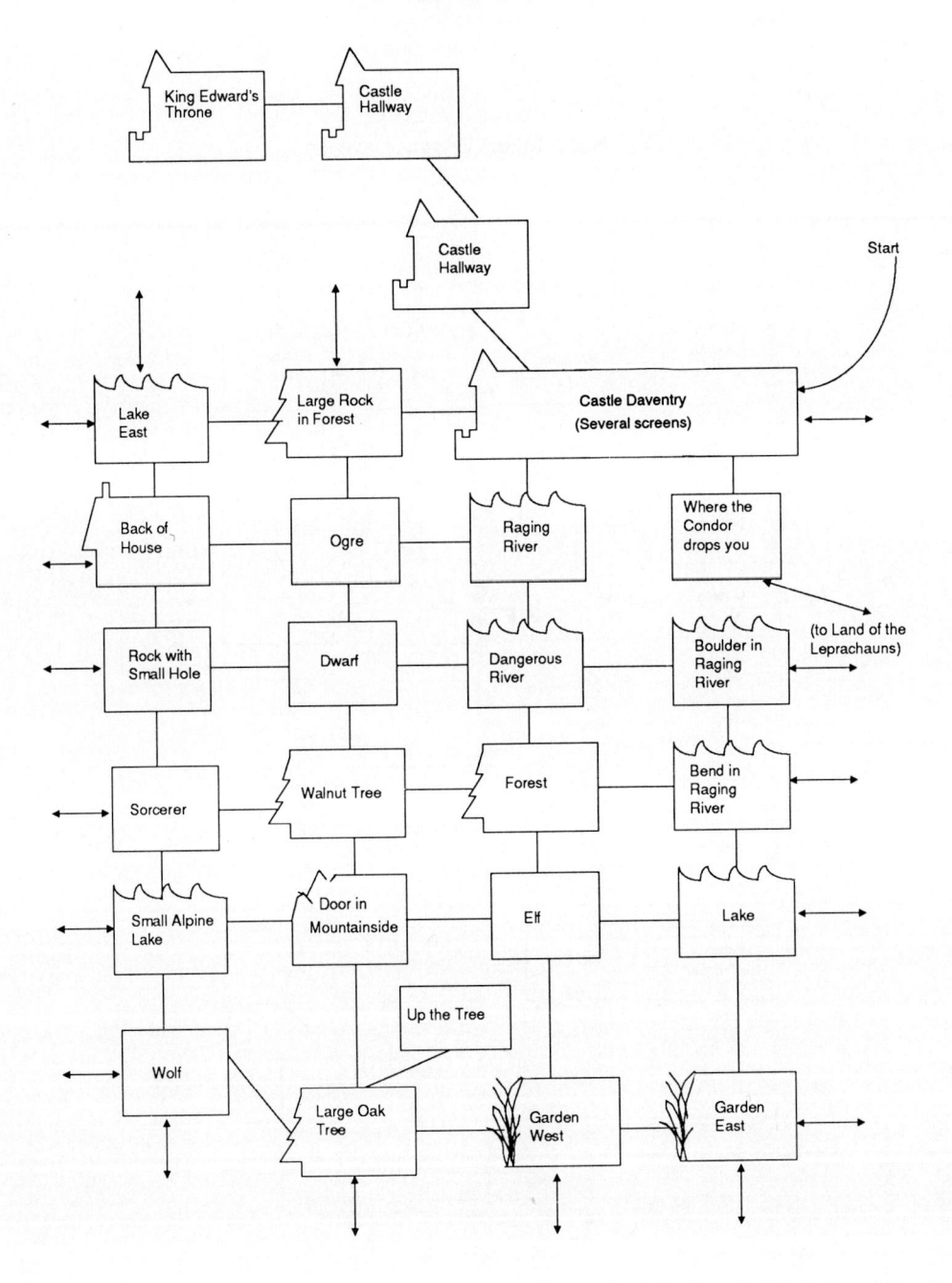

King's Quest

The Easy Way Out

King's Quest 1:
Quest for the Crown (Land of the Leprachauns)

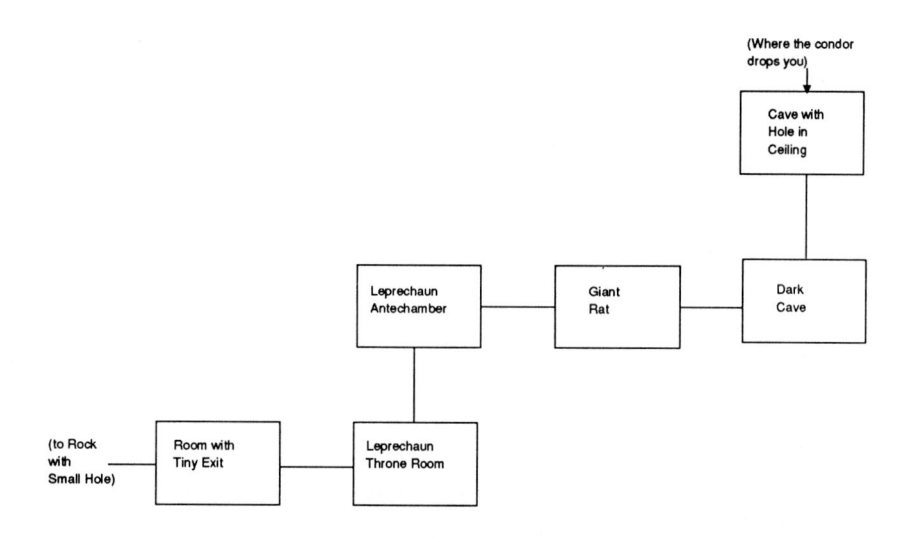

```
                                              (Where the condor
                                               drops you)
                                              ┌─────────┐
                                              │ Cave with│
                                              │ Hole in  │
                                              │ Ceiling  │
                                              └────┬────┘
                                                   │
         ┌──────────┐      ┌──────┐       ┌──────┐
         │Leprechaun│──────│Giant │───────│ Dark │
         │Antechamber│     │ Rat  │       │ Cave │
         └─────┬────┘      └──────┘       └──────┘
               │
(to Rock  ┌─────────┐     ┌──────────┐
with   ───│Room with│─────│Leprechaun│
Small Hole)│Tiny Exit│     │Throne Room│
          └─────────┘     └──────────┘
```

King's Quest 1:
Quest for the Crown (Land of the Clouds)

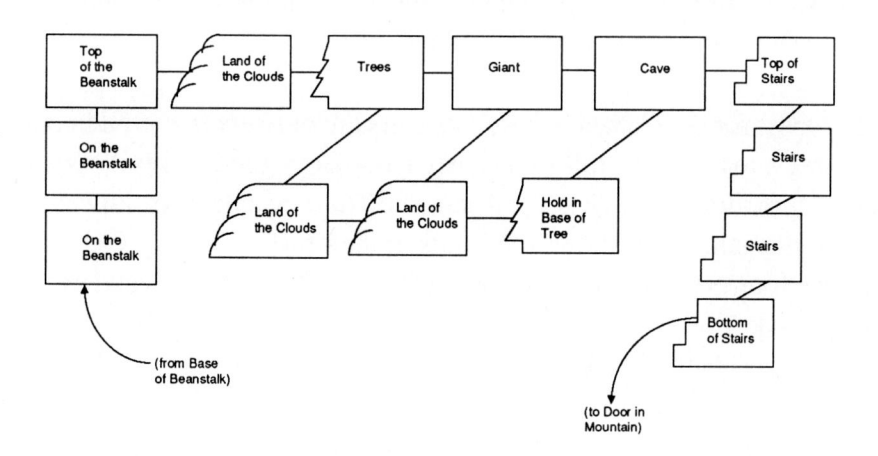

```
┌────────┐   ╱Land of╲    ╱Trees╲   ┌──────┐   ┌──────┐   ┌──────┐
│  Top   │──│  the    │──│      │──│Giant │───│ Cave │───│Top of│
│ of the │   ╲Clouds ╱    ╲     ╱   └──────┘   └──────┘   │Stairs│
│Beanstalk│                                               └──┬───┘
└───┬────┘                                                   │
    │                                                    ┌───┴──┐
┌───┴────┐                                               │Stairs│
│ On the │                                               └───┬──┘
│Beanstalk│   ╱Land of╲   ╱Land of╲   ┌──────┐               │
└───┬────┘  │  the    │──│  the    │──│Hold in│          ┌───┴──┐
    │        ╲Clouds ╱    ╲Clouds ╱   │Base of│          │Stairs│
┌───┴────┐                            │ Tree  │          └───┬──┘
│ On the │                            └───────┘              │
│Beanstalk│                                              ┌───┴───┐
└────────┘                                               │Bottom │
     ↑                                                   │of Stairs│
  (from Base                                             └───────┘
  of Beanstalk)
                                    (to Door in
                                     Mountain)
```

King's Quest 2: Romancing the Throne

Object of the Game:

You are now King Graham, and you are searching for a beautiful maiden to become your wife. The woman you're looking for is named Valanice of Kolyma. She has been kidnapped by the witch Hagatha and imprisoned in a Crystal Tower on some enchanted island. She is said to be guarded by a wild beast. You must journey to Kolyma and find three keys to unlock three magic doors that lead to Valanice.

Things to Come:

While adventuring through Kolyma, you will notice that if you walk far enough north and south, you end up back where you started. Kolyma "wraps around" in these directions both in the game and in reality. Mountains and chasm block the eastern edge of the country, and the ocean borders the west. There is nothing you can swim to in the western direction; if you swim too far, you drown. When it's time to visit Neptune's home beneath the western waves, transportation will be available. After you finally walk through the magic doorway, movement is very limited, and wrapping ceases to be a consideration.

Unlike Quest for the Crown, where monsters are only encountered in one specific screen, many of the folks you meet here—both good and evil—wander around at random through several screens. These wanderings, however, are limited; the game map shows the limits of their turf.

There are four creatures you would prefer to avoid in your wanderings around Kolyma:

The Easy Way Out

- **Hagatha** will capture and kill you, but you must enter her cave at some point in order to win the game. Her area covers a total of six screens in southwest Kolyma, to the north and west of her cave.

- The **enchanter** will turn you into a frog permanently, thereby ending the game. His area covers six screens in west Kolyma, to the east, west, and south of the antique store.

- The **dwarf** will beat and rob you of treasure. In this game, though, there is a way to get it back by robbing the dwarf's house—a place you'll probably want to go anyway. The dwarf's area covers five screens in south Kolyma, north and west of the bridge.

- The **wolf** will eat you. He is only encountered in Grandma's house, two screens east of where you start the game. He can only be avoided by going there when he isn't.

As always, the best way to handle these critters is by avoiding them altogether. When you do run across them, use the old *edge-of-the-screen trick*—leave the screen at once, and then return. Repeat as often as necessary until the monster is gone.

There is another way to avoid these monsters. If for some reason you are not near the edge of the screen when they arrive, hide behind something and be patient. As long as no part of Graham is visible on the screen, the monsters leave you alone. When they get far enough away, you can run away—if there is enough distance between you and them. Just make sure you run off the screen.

There are three folks that you might want to encounter early in your travels:

- The **monk** will be found praying inside the monastery in northeast Kolyma, immediately south of the bridge. He has a cross for you to wear.

- The **good fairy** has an area that covers six screens to the east, west, and south of the monastery. She will sprinkle a magic protection spell on you, fairy dust that lasts for a reasonable amount of time—usually a minimum of twenty minutes of time as you and I experience it.

- **Little Red Riding Hood** has an area that covers a total of seven screens, to the east, west, and south of Grandma's house. When you return her basket of goodies, she will give you flowers.

There are a few other folks you will have to deal with as the game progresses, and treasures to be discovered. We'll look at them when we get there, so let's get going.

How to Do It:

As the game opens, you find Graham standing on the beach. Go east one screen and you are in Riding Hood's area. If you don't encounter her at once, continue one more screen east to Grandma's house. Open the mailbox by the front gate. Look inside, then take out the basket of goodies. Continue east if you still haven't met Hood. If you still haven't run across her by the time you reach the west end of the monastery, go back and pull the old edge-of-the-screen trick until she appears. In this case, enter one of her screens, wander around for a time; if she doesn't appear, leave and immediately return. Repeat until you meet. Talk to the girl, then give her the basket. Take the flowers she offers. You will give these to the mermaid later.

The Easy Way Out

If you would like to take this opportunity to visit Grandma, be my guest. Open the door to her house. If the wolf is in bed, leave at once. The game randomly puts either the wolf or Granny in the house. Return and leave until the old gal is there. She's not feeling well and can do nothing for you now. It was a nice visit, though.

Walk directly east until you come to the door of the monastery. You are in the good fairy's area now. You don't really want her protection spell yet, so if she appears, move off the screen, and return, etc. Open the door to the monastery and enter. Walk to the altar and pray. The monk will ask you your name. Say, "Graham." He will give you a silver cross. Leave wearing the cross. If the fairy's around, avoid her again.

One screen north of the monastery is a rickety bridge. You'll be going there a few times, so remember this: when you walk north to the bridge from here, do it from the left center of the top of the screen; otherwise you might fall to your cybernetic death. Always take your time going between screens around the bridge and on the other side of it. There are several long drops for those in a hurry.

Being careful not to fall into the chasm, cross the bridge. Note this very well: *you can only cross this bridge seven times, and you must cross it seven times to complete the game.* No extra trips across are allowed. You have been warned! Now walk one screen east and one north. Look at the door; read the door: "... make a splash," huh? Cross back over the bridge. We've now been across twice.

Opening the First Door:

Walk south one screen to the monastery, then trek due west all the way to the beach—just where the game started. Turn north and walk two screens.

You will see something lying on the ground. Take it and examine it—it's Neptune's trident. Move north from there another two screens. Look at the sand; the white thing in the sand at the center of your screen is a clamshell. Pick it up and you find a bracelet. Take the bracelet. Neat, isn't it? Now walk one screen east into the woods. There is something lying against the tree in the center of the screen. It's a tent stake. Take it; there may be vampires around. Now turn back west to the beach and go one screen north. A mermaid is around, and you're about to meet her.

Note: The mermaid does not appear until after you read the first door.

Walk into the ocean and swim to the rock—you can't climb on it, so don't try. Give the flowers you got from Riding Hood—you did get the flowers, didn't you?—to the mermaid. She will summon a seahorse and then disappear into the waves. You may also give her one of your treasures—the bracelet, for example. This will also gain you the seahorse, but lose you game points.

Swim over to the seahorse, and then ride it. It takes you on a journey to King Neptune. Enjoy the ride, there is nothing you can do till you get there. When the seahorse stops, move in front of Neptune and give him the trident. He will give you a bottle with a cloth in it. Next, go over to the open clam. There is a key sitting in it. Take the key; it fits the first door. Go east, and as soon as you leave the screen with Neptune, relax and watch the animation. When you pop out of the water, swim to shore. Get the cloth that's in the bottle. It's just a rag, but you will need it later in Hagatha's cave.

Before that, though, we're going back to the floating door. Since we've been avoiding the fairy's spell, we'll take the safe way back—north two screens to where the game started and then east to the monastery. Avoid the fairy if she shows up. Go north from the monastery door screen to the bridge, cross it, and go to the door. Unlock the door with the key. Read the second door: "... set your sights high," huh? Go back to the bridge and cross it again. We have now been across four times.

Opening the Second Door:

Move one screen south, back to monastery. This time we want the fairy's spell—we're going treasure hunting. If she's not around, go south, east, or west one screen till you find her and she zaps you with some fairy dust. Then go one screen south of the monastery door. There is a lake and a big rock with an opening. Look into the opening and take the brooch. Swim south across the lake; you are now in the enchanter's area, but you are protected. Notice the building—an antique store—and read the sign in the window. It doesn't open until we've read the inscription on the second door. If we go inside now and give two treasures to the woman, she'll give us the oil lamp at the lower center of the screen. We need the lamp to get the second key, but we lose points doing it this way. Let us, therefore, pass up the shopping spree for a moment; we'll come back after visiting Hagatha.

Turn west from the antique store and go one screen to the shore of the lake. It's poison so don't drink or swim in it. From here walk south three screens; we'll pass the lake and enter some forest. In the center of the screen, there is a large tree with some rocks at its base. Stand next to the tree, behind the rocks. Look at the tree, then look into the hole you can't see on the screen. You'll find a mallet; take it. Walk west one screen, then south one screen. That tree with the chimney is the home of the dwarf. We're going inside.

Normally, the dwarf is not at home, but occasionally he is. The old edge-of-the-screen trick works if this happens, and fairy dust also protects you. If the dwarf walks in on you while you're stealing his things, only the fairy's spell or a saved game, can get you out of the jam! However, he is very, very seldom home.

Open the door and walk inside; then climb down the ladder with care. Move east into the dwarf's room. Go to the trunk on the east side of the room. Open it. Look inside. Take the earrings. If you have been robbed by the dwarf, this is also where he stashes your treasure. Take that also. Or don't if you wish; you're the one playing the game. Now walk to the fireplace and look at it. Take the chicken soup, Grandma needs her medicine. Now leave the way you came in.

Once back outside, go one screen west. You are now in Hagatha's territory, but the fairy dust should still be working. Hagatha's cave is one screen east of here, but we're not going there yet. Instead, walk one screen north. You should be on the shore of a small lake, with a big log at the bottom of the screen. Look at the log. Look into the log. Take the necklace; it's a treasure fit for a queen. Now again walk west one screen and then south one screen. The place with the skulls on the posts is Hagatha's cave. Walk inside. If Hagatha is home cooking, your spell protects you for the moment. Anyway, she's paying attention to her cooking and shouldn't notice you until something makes a sound. If you are unprotected and she's home, use the old edge-of-the-screen trick. Take a moment, nonetheless, to enjoy the sights and smells of the cave. OK. Back to adventuring.

There's a birdcage containing a nightingale inside the cave. Go over to it. Put the cloth over the cage—it scores points, and if Hagatha is there, it muffles the sound that the bird makes. If she hears the bird, you're the turkey dinner. Take the cage and leave the cave. Save the game as soon as you get outside the cave and are sure Hagatha is not there. Evidently Hagatha's cave is also the entrance to someone else's cave, but don't go looking for it, because it can't be found. However, every once in a while you will be followed out of the cave—not by Hagatha, but by *something else that shall remain nameless*. If you want a surprise, just keep going in and out of Hagatha's cave for a while. You'll know it when you see it. Use your saved game if Hagatha gets you; the chuckle is worth the wait.

349
The Easy Way Out

Go south one screen, then east a screen. You are in front of Grandma's house. I hope you haven't forgotten that she's not feeling well. Open the door. If the wolf's there... well, we've been over that part before. Give the chicken soup to Grandma. Yummy! Look under the bed. Take the ruby ring and black cloak. Wear the ring. Wear the cloak. Remember "... the children of the night." Leave the house. Go east to the monastery door, then south two screens to the antique store. It's been tough so far and, as the saying goes, "when the going gets tough, the tough get going—shopping!"

Go inside the store. Give the cage to the woman. She will give you the oil lamp and kick you out of the store. Go north one screen to the lake; it's safer there and you don't want the enchanter to get you. Rub the lamp and get the magic carpet. Rub the lamp a second time and get the sword. Rub the lamp a third time and get the bridle. The lamp will disappear—easy come, easy go. Ride the carpet.

You are now on top of the cliffs. Walk east one screen. When you see the snake, save the game. Walk up near it, but not so near that it can bite and kill you. There are two solutions to this problem. Did you notice the snake carved in the handle of the sword? You mean you haven't been looking at everything? One solution is to kill the snake with the sword. You can then get by. The second solution is a nonviolent one. Throw the bridle on the snake, and it turns into a winged horse. Talk to the horse, and it gives you a sugar cube. The cube makes getting to Dracula's Castle later a lot easier. A *whole* lot easier.

In either case, after the snake has been dealt with, continue going east and enter the cave you come to; nothing else can harm you here. Inside the cave, take the key. It opens the second door. Walk outside and ride the carpet; it will take you back to the antique store. Go north, across the little lake, past the monastery, and to the bridge. Go to the door and unlock it. Read the third door: "... a stout heart," huh?

Cross back over the bridge. The count is up to six. Only one more trip across is possible. I wonder how we are going to get back after that?

Opening the Third Door:

Other than a brief glimpse, we've stayed away from the poisoned lake in the middle of Kolyma. Now get a good grip on yourself and your black cloak and go two screens north, through the dwarf's turf, to a small lake. From there walk west two screens. You are on the south shore of the lake with a castle in the distance. There is a death-like boatman here who will row you across. (He does not appear in the game until the inscription on the third door is read.) If you give the boatman a treasure, he takes you to the castle, but it costs you points. If you are wearing the cloak and ruby ring, he takes you across for free, and you score points. Such a deal!

Enter the boat. When you're across, leave the boat and don't move. Eat the sugar cube the winged horse gave you; there are brambles around the path and they will kill you if they scratch you. If you killed the snake, you don't have the cube and must walk to the front gate. This is possible, but very, very difficult. If that's the case, save the game every time you gain a step or two. Good luck!

Walk up the path; the door will open. You will encounter two ghosts. If you're wearing the cloak and ring, they will be fooled into thinking you're the count himself. If you're not wearing the costume, the silver cross the monk gave you will protect you from them. If you're wearing none of the above, you're history. Open the second door. Welcome to Dracula's Castle.

Go through the left doorway and up the circular stairs. In the room at the top, open the drawer in the dresser, and then take the candle. Start back down the stairs—please don't fall! On the way down, light the candle on the torch. Once you're down, walk through the doorway that was on your right when you entered. Take the ham from the table in the dining room, and then go

The Easy Way Out

through the doorway on the far right. These are the stairs down into the crypt; without the lit candle, you will fall. At the bottom on the stairs, on the left-hand side of the screen, is where Drac's coffin is hidden.

There are two things that can happen here, depending on whether the coffin is open or closed. If the coffin is open, the count is flying around somewhere else. Look in the coffin and take the satin pillow. You now see a gold key. It opens the third door, and you can complete the game. However, you must kill Dracula to get the treasure in the castle's second tower. If the coffin's empty and you want the other treasure, keep leaving and returning—you remember the old edge-of-the-screen trick!—until you find the coffin closed. If you find the coffin closed, open it. You must now kill the vampire. If you take too long doing this, he wakes up and tries to bite you. If you're wearing the silver cross, he will get scared, turn into a bat, and fly away—at least you met the guy! If you got to the castle by wearing the ring and cloak, but not the cross—I hope you had a saved game nearby!

Kill Dracula. Look into the coffin. Take the silver key. Look into the coffin again. Take the satin pillow. Take the gold key. Leave the crypt and walk up the stairs to the dining room.

If you got the gold key without killing Drac, you can leave now; we'll meet you outside. If you hang around, though, you might spot him flying around looking for a spare neck to bite.

From the dining room, walk through the doorway at the top of the screen. Walk up the stairs. You might have difficulty walking as you get higher up. If you do, use the keyboard and walk into a wall, and then go up or down one step, walk into the wall, and repeat until you reach the top. This works well on most stairways in all the games, especially in the Perils of Rosella. When you reach the top, go to the chest. Unlock and open the chest with the silver key and take the tiara. We're now done in the castle, so walk back out to the boatman. He's waiting.

Enter the boat and leave it when you're across. Go east two screens, and then south two. Watch out for the dwarf. Cross the bridge. If you try to cross back now, for any reason, you plunge to your death. Go to the door and unlock it. We're going to rescue Valanice.

Rescuing Valanice:

If you're playing the game on a color monitor, don't worry about it, the colors really are as weird as they look—pink sky and all. As soon as you get adjusted to the local color, walk one screen north. Pick up the net and walk to the edge of the cliff—please, don't fall in. Throw the net; in a try or three you will catch a large, golden fish. Look at the fish. Pick up the fish. Walk to where you threw the net, and then throw the fish in the ocean. When the fish offers you a ride, step off the edge. It will carry you across the waves to the enchanted isle.

The enchanted island is small; only three screens by three screens, with no way off. From where you come ashore, go one screen east. Look on the ground and take the amulet. It's your ticket home. Look at the amulet. Remember what's written there. Walk one screen south—a tower! Look at the tower; a woman's hand is waving. Walk to the door and open it. Yes, another twisty stairway. At the top you will find a very hungry lion guarding the door to the tower room. You can kill the lion with the sword; you'll score points. If you remembered to take the ham from Dracula's table, however, you can give the ham to the lion. It puts the beast to sleep and scores more points than killing does. The King's Quest games tend to greater rewards for nonviolent solutions than easy kills. Except for the major evil types, always solve a problem without killing.

Open the door. It's her, it really is. Kiss Valanice; it doesn't score points, but it's the way these stories are supposed to end. Now it's time to leave.

353
The Easy Way Out

Remember the word on the amulet? Say "Home," and watch the closing movie.

    Congratulations! You have now completed King's Quest 2: Romancing the Throne.

King's Quest 2:
Romancing the Throne (Top of the Cliffs)

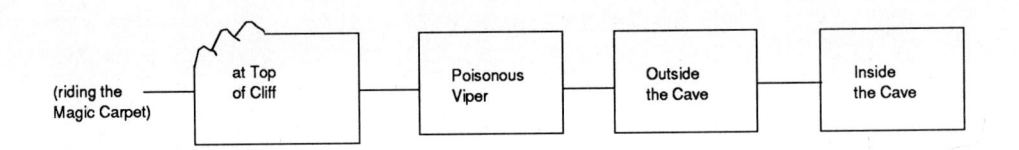

(riding the Magic Carpet) — at Top of Cliff — Poisonous Viper — Outside the Cave — Inside the Cave

King's Quest 2:
Romancing the Throne (Neptune's Kingdom)

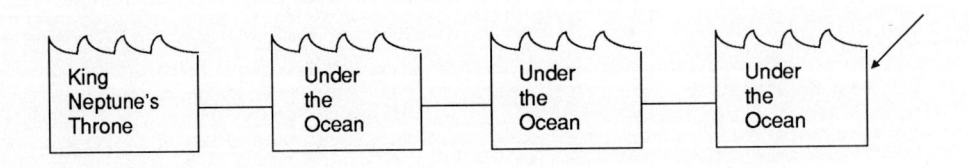

King Neptune's Throne — Under the Ocean — Under the Ocean — Under the Ocean

The Easy Way Out

King's Quest 2:
Romancing the Throne (Kolyma)

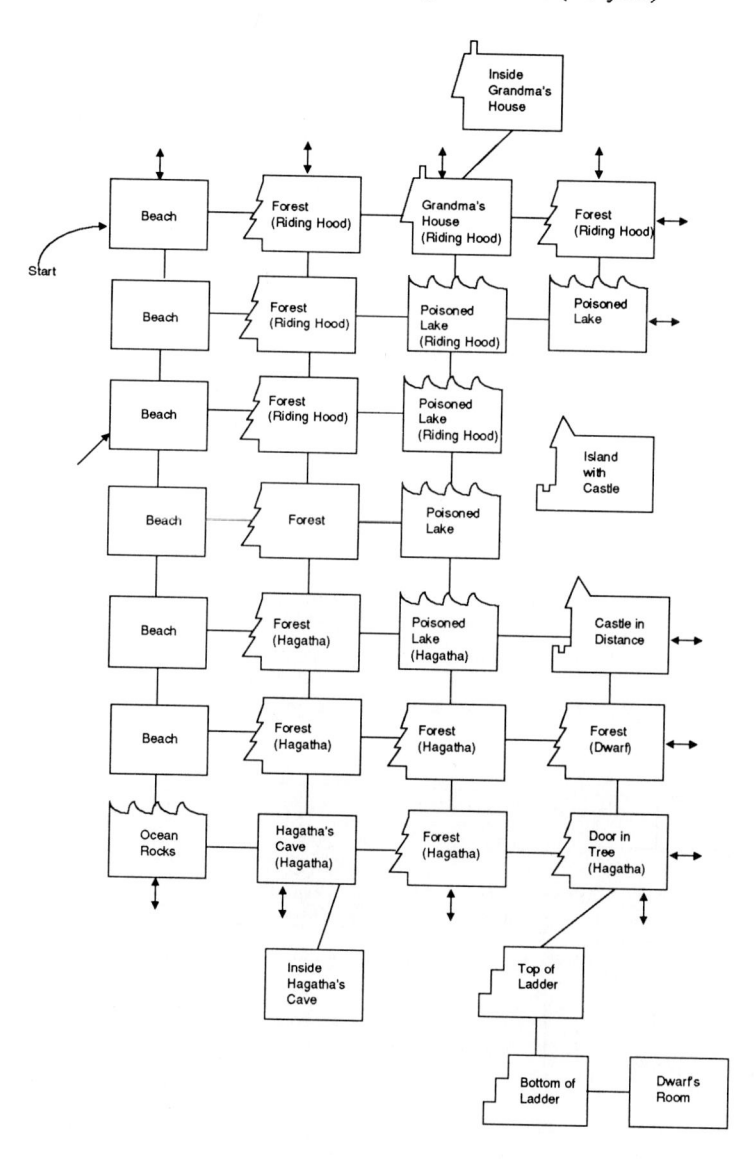

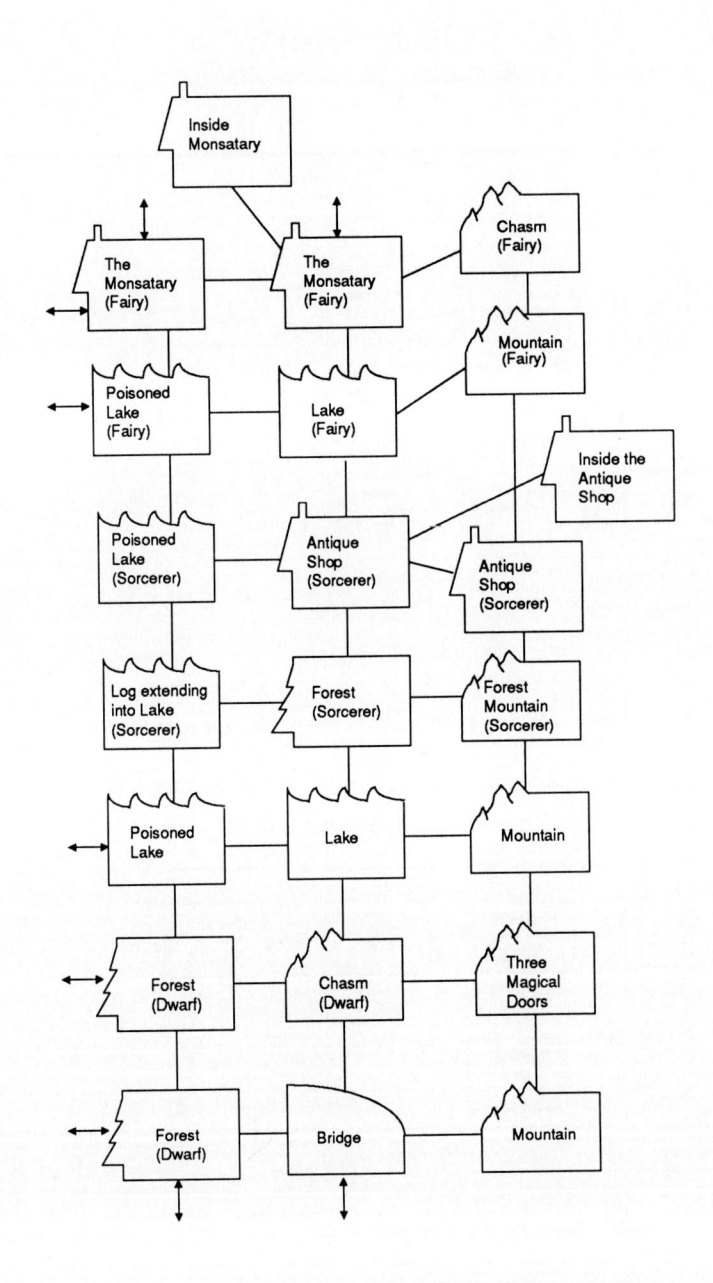

King's Quest

```
                    ┌──────────┐
                    │  Inside  │
                    │ Monsatary│
                    └────┬─────┘
      ↕              ↕   │
┌──────────┐    ┌──────────┐    ┌──────────┐
│   The    │    │   The    │────│  Chasm   │
│ Monsatary│────│ Monsatary│    │ (Fairy)  │
│ (Fairy)  │    │ (Fairy)  │    └────┬─────┘
↔└────┬─────┘    └────┬─────┘         │
      │               │          ┌──────────┐
      │               │          │ Mountain │
      │               │          │ (Fairy)  │
┌──────────┐    ┌──────────┐    └────┬─────┘
│ Poisoned │    │   Lake   │─────────┤
↔│   Lake   │────│ (Fairy)  │
│ (Fairy)  │    │          │        ┌──────────┐
└────┬─────┘    └────┬─────┘        │Inside the│
     │               │              │ Antique  │
     │               │              │   Shop   │
┌──────────┐    ┌──────────┐    ┌──────────┐
│ Poisoned │    │ Antique  │    │ Antique  │
│   Lake   │────│   Shop   │────│   Shop   │
│(Sorcerer)│    │(Sorcerer)│    │(Sorcerer)│
└────┬─────┘    └────┬─────┘    └────┬─────┘
     │               │               │
┌──────────┐    ┌──────────┐    ┌──────────┐
│   Log    │    │  Forest  │    │  Forest  │
│ extending│────│(Sorcerer)│────│ Mountain │
│ into Lake│    │          │    │(Sorcerer)│
│(Sorcerer)│    │          │    │          │
└────┬─────┘    └────┬─────┘    └──────────┘
     │               │
┌──────────┐    ┌──────────┐    ┌──────────┐
│ Poisoned │    │   Lake   │    │ Mountain │
↔│   Lake   │────│          │────│          │
└────┬─────┘    └────┬─────┘    └────┬─────┘
     │               │               │
┌──────────┐    ┌──────────┐    ┌──────────┐
│  Forest  │    │  Chasm   │    │  Three   │
↔│  (Dwarf) │────│ (Dwarf)  │────│ Magical  │
│          │    │          │    │  Doors   │
└────┬─────┘    └────┬─────┘    └────┬─────┘
     │               │               │
┌──────────┐    ┌──────────┐    ┌──────────┐
│  Forest  │    │          │    │ Mountain │
↔│  (Dwarf) │────│  Bridge  │────│          │
└────┬─────┘    └────┬─────┘    └──────────┘
     ↕               ↕
```

357
The Easy Way Out

King's Quest 2:
Romancing the Throne (Dracula's Castle)

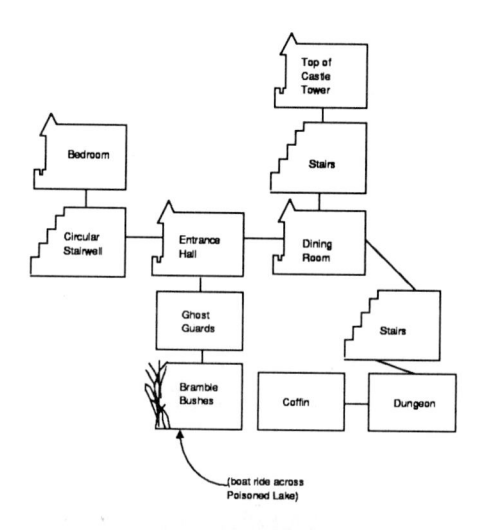

King's Quest 2:
Romancing the Throne (Enchanted Island)

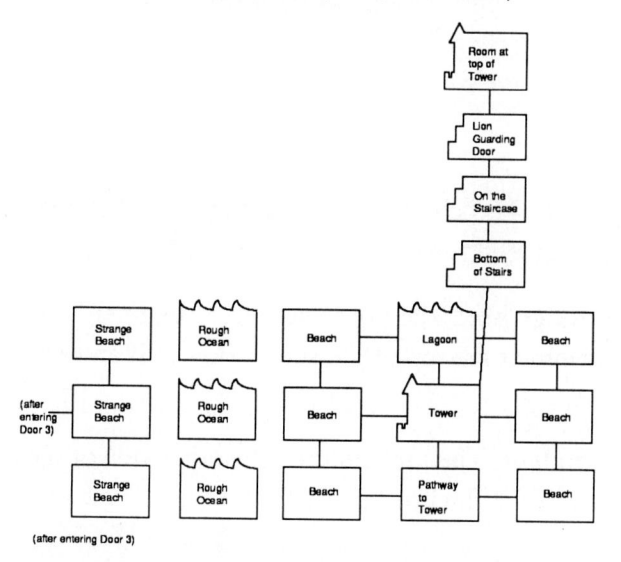

King's Quest 3: To Heir Is Human

Object of the Game:

You are Gwydion, a 17-year-old boy who is the slave of the evil wizard Manannan in the land of Llewdor. Your master will kill you when you turn 18—something that will happen very soon. You must escape the wizard, discover your true identity, find out who your true parents are, return home, and rescue your twin sister from a three-headed, fire-breathing dragon.

Things to Come:

The first part of this game—the bulk of the game—is a series of races against time.

When Manannan is home, he will demand you perform some chore: empty his chamber pot, feed the chickens, feed him a meal, clean the kitchen, or clean his chambers. These chores must be done within three minutes or you will be punished. The punishments are amusing to us—although they weren't to Gwydion—but the sixth punishment is always death. Manannan will wander around for five minutes of game-playing time, plus the time it takes to complete the particular chore. Here's how to get the chores done:

- **Feed chickens:** The chickens are outside. Get the feed from the shed behind the coop, enter the yard, and feed the chickens.

- **Empty chamber pot:** The pot is next to Manannan's bed on the second floor—the room at the top of the screen. Go to it and empty the chamber pot.

- **Clean the kitchen:** The kitchen is on the other side of the dining room on the first floor. Take the broom you find there and clean.

The Easy Way Out

- **Dust the wizard's office:** The study is on the first floor, at the top of the screen. In the study there is a cabinet against the wall in the left-bottom of the screen. The feather duster is on top of the cabinet. Take the duster and then dust.

- **Feed Manannan:** The food is in the kitchen, on the table at the right side of the screen. Three meals are there: mutton chops, fruit, bread. Any one of these is enough to satisfy his demand. A fourth meal can be obtained—must be obtained—at the Three Bears' house in Llewdor. After that, nothing else will feed him.

After doing your chore, you're free to wander the house and yard a bit. Manannan has forbidden you to enter his chambers and study, however, so stay out while he's around. After the five or so minutes are up, Manannan will leave—he will either disappear on some journey or go to sleep. The first time in the game, he leaves the house. In either case, the wizard will be gone for 25 minutes of game time. This is when you are able to explore, discover his secret laboratory, search the house, gather items you need for spells, and hide things under your bed so he cannot find them. Use this time efficiently—note the time he leaves on the clock in the screen, and be aware of when he'll return.

Note: This clock does not appear in Apple 2E/2C versions of the game.

If Manannan catches you away from the house, anywhere in the world, he will kill you. Until you have disposed of him, he will always catch you. If he catches you with any items that are marked with *STAR* on your inventory list, he will also kill you. The rule is to hide everything under your bed. The only exception is the magic wand, which must be replaced and locked up before Manannan returns. He will kill you for these transgressions, and for leaving the door to the secret laboratory open, or for not moving books back to where they were when he left.

When you get down the mountain, you will find that Llewdor "wraps around" from north to south. If you go far enough in those directions, barring obstacles, you return to where you started.

There are three monsters you must avoid as you initially explore Llewdor:

- **Medusa** lives in the desert; she will turn you to stone if you look on her face. The desert begins two screens west of where the mountain path starts and ends, and extends north and south forever. Do not go any farther west into the desert than its first full screen; you will end up lost, and although it is possible to walk out, the odds are very slim that you will do so. Until Medusa is conquered, the moment you enter a desert screen, turn north or south at once. That way, if Medusa sees you, you won't see her.

- The **giant spider** lurks above the cave that is one screen east and two screens north of the path. It will eat you.

- The **bandits** roam throughout western Llewdor. They will beat you, and then rob you of your possessions. When you find their hideout, you can get your stuff back.

The best way to avoid these folks is to not encounter them until you are ready. If you stumble upon them earlier, use the *old edge-of-the-screen trick*—stay on the edge of the screen, step immediately out at the first sign of trouble, and then return. Repeat as often as necessary.

To escape Manannan you must find his secret laboratory, read his spell book, collect the proper ingredients, cast the spells properly, and eliminate the wizard as a threat early. It's best to do this in as few trips down the mountain as possible. While it is theoretically possible to do it all in one trip, you'd have to be real fast and efficient. I don't recommend this approach; besides, it would take a lot of the fun out of the game.

How to Do It:

The game opens in Manannan's house. The wizard appears and orders you to do some chore. Do it at once. Then go into the dining room. There is a cup on the table. Take it. Now walk up the stairs to the second floor, and walk off the screen to the right. Straight ahead is your room. You are safe from Manannan in there; he never enters your room. Put the cup under the bed. This is where you can put everything you collect—except the magic wand—to keep them safe. Wait for Manannan to appear and tell you he is taking a journey. Note the time—write it down; you now have 25 minutes until the wizard returns.

Note: This clock does not appear in the Apple 2E/2C version of the game because of memory limitations. If you're playing on one of those computers, keep a clock or watch handy, and keep track of the time with it. The wizard will be gone for 25 minutes, but the time is suspended while you're checking your inventory or pausing the game in any way. In other words, as long as Gwydion is moving or doing something, time passes; time stops while the game is paused, you're checking your inventory, or typing commands. The 25 minutes of game time is usually much longer than 25 minutes of real time.

Enter Manannan's bedroom. At the foot of the bed is a vanity. Open the drawer and get the hand mirror; you will need this for Medusa. Go to the dresser against the right wall. Open the drawer and get the rose petal essence. Go to the tall closet—it's a wardrobe—and open the door. Look inside and then look behind the clothes and get the parchment. This is a magic map that teleports you to any screen in the game that you have already visited; take it with you whenever and wherever you travel. Look at the map; it's blank now. Close the closet door. While you stand in front of the wardrobe—anywhere from smack-dab against it to two or three steps away—examine the top of the closet. You now have the key that gets you the magic wand.

Let us pause for a moment and consider Manannan's cat. You have most assuredly noticed it by now. It is always getting under foot. Feel free to kick it out of the way if you wish, but we do deplore needless cruelty. This cat will trip you on the stairs that go to and from the wizard's secret laboratory. This can result in death. You have been warned! Also, at some point you must take some of the cat's hair; you need it to get rid of the wizard. Walk up to the cat and get the cat. This may take several tries, so keep trying. Take the cat hair.

Let's pause yet another moment. Look at your inventory. See the stars next to the hair, rose petal essence, map, key, and mirror? The stars mean that Manannan will kill you if he catches you carrying them. They must be hidden before he returns. But, not now—now we're going to the tower.

Climb up the stairs next to the wizard's bedroom. In the tower look through the telescope if you like. Look on the floor. Get the fly. Now walk back downstairs to the wizard's study.

In the study walk to the cabinet in the lower-left corner. Unlock the door and get the magic wand; you need this to cast spells. Walk over to the bookcase in the upper-right corner. Doesn't that look like a computer screen? I think this is Derek's "Eye Between the Worlds." Move the books and you will discover a lever. Pull the lever and watch the trapdoor open. Save the game. Walk down the stairs. Watch out for the cat, and don't try to pass it on the stairs. Wait for it to move, and then pass it. At the bottom is Manannan's laboratory.

Go to the shelves, and look at the ones in the center of the screen. Here are many of the magical ingredients you will be needing. Right now, get the saffron—we'll make the spell for "Flying Like An Eagle Or A Fly."

363
The Easy Way Out

Note: If you have not yet read the chapter on magic, do it now. It contains the spell ingredients and how to make the spells. Follow the directions to the letter, comma, and period.

Now, go to Manannan's worktable and look at it. Look at the book. Open the book. Save the game. Open the book to page IV. Perform the spell; checking your spelling and punctuation as you go. You'll know if you make a mistake, that's why you saved the game before you began. You now have magic rose essence in your inventory.

Walk back up to the wizard's study. Pull the lever and move the books back. If you don't do this, Manannan will know where you were and kill you. Go to the cabinet, unlock it, and put the magic wand back—for the same reason. Now go to the kitchen. There are shelves against the left wall. Look at them and take the bowl you find. Go to the wall to the left of the fireplace. Look at the rack. Take the knife and then take the spoon. Great! Walk outside; it's time to go down the mountain.

First, let's pause and feed the chickens. The feed's in back, outside the fence. Go there—don't fall off the mountain—and feed the chickens. While they're eating, open the gate and go inside. Catch a chicken; take a feather. Leave. Save the game. Start walking down the mountain path.

The mountain path is tough. Slow the game speed down if you must, and take your time. Save the game every couple of steps. There is a place in the middle of the screen where the path goes behind a big rock and appears to be continuing east to west on the other side of the rock. Wrong! As soon as Gwydion is behind the rock—remember, you can't see the path—walk south as far as you can go. Turn and walk east. Now stay on the path to the bottom. Whew!

I see by the old clock on the screen that I've used half of the 25 minutes; it's time to get crackin'. First, keep your eyes open for an eagle flying around; it appears from time to time around northern Llewdor, near the path and around the stream. Sometimes it drops a tail feather as it goes by. When it does, go and take the feather, we'll need it later. Even as I wrote that, the eagle flew by and dropped one. Go to the feather and then take it.

Note: Get yours when you can—I've got mine. You can also wait at the bottom of the path a few moments for the bird. If it doesn't show up, step out of the screen and then back. Wait. Repeat until successful.

From the bottom of the path, go one screen east and then one south. You are now in town. Go to the tavern door and save the game. Open the door. Talk to the men; they'll brush you off. Dip the fly wings into the essence. As a fly, listen. You score points as the bandits talk about where their hideout is hidden in the forest.

Note: If they don't talk about it within ten seconds, go back to your saved game, outside the door. If they are not inside at all, step out and then back. Try again. As soon as you have heard what they have to say, exit the tavern.

Fly west two screens. You are near the large oak tree the bandits were talking about. There is a hole in its base. Fly into the hole, this scores you points. There is a rope ladder in the hollow tree. Fly out of the hole, and recite, "Fly, begone. Myself, return!"

Look on the ground. Take an acorn—you're looking for dried ones. Keep trying if you don't find one at once. Look into the hole. Reach into the hole, and the ladder will descend. Climb the ladder with care—a fall will kill. At the top of the ladder is the bandit hideout. Go inside. If the bandit sees you, step back out, he won't follow. Do this until the lookout is asleep when you enter. Look on the table and take the purse. On the far side of the place there is a bin. If you have been robbed, that's where your stuff is. Open the bin and look inside. Take all of what's there. Now get out before the guard wakes up and "offs you"—so to speak.

Once you're back on the ground, you're fair game for mugging again by the bandits. You now want to get back to the mountain path as quickly as possible—it's one screen north and one screen east of you. Look at the magic map and you will notice some of the squares have been filled in. Point to the square with Manannan's House. Select Teleport, and you're at the bottom of the mountain path. Sorry, you can't teleport directly to the house; you must walk back up.

If you prefer, you can walk back to the path. As soon as you are down from the tree, move to the right edge of the screen—the closest edge. Enter into the next screen east, then move north—staying on the left edge of that screen. If the bandits show up, use the old edge-of-the-screen trick.

Look at your time. I've been gone 20 minutes—there are 5 minutes left till Manannan gets back and the walk's tough. Let's do it. Take care, take your time, save often, and don't shave the time too close. Always start back up with at least 5 minutes to go, just to be safe.

When you get back to the house, go to your room and put all you have under your bed. Now stop and think: is the wand put away and are the books moved back in place? Check if you're not sure. Now wait for Manannan to return. He will be hungry when he gets back. Feed him as soon as he demands, and wait. There is nothing you can do now until he goes to sleep. When that happens, you're going back down the mountain to collect all the other magic ingredients you need—with one exception. We'll get to that one later.

It's sure hard to wait, isn't it? If you need something to do to pass the time, take a look behind the tapestry hanging on the wall outside of Gwydion's room.

As soon as Manannan goes to his room, go Gwydion's. Notice the time. Take all the objects from under the bed. Look at the map, move the pointer to the square with the town, and press Teleport. Whee! A shortcut down the hill. Once you enter a square, it is activated on the map. You might have been able to use this trick when you were down the hill the first time, but you were too busy exploring and ducking bandits.

You are now back in town. Go to the store and open the door. Talk to the man and look at the shelves. You are going to use the coins we took from the bandits. Buy a leather pouch, salt, fish oil, and lard. When you're finished, go to the dog that's lying on the floor. His name is Kenny. Pet the dog. You now have the dog fur you need for one of the spells. Leave the store.

Walk south one screen. There is an oak tree in the center of the picture. Look at it, then take the mistletoe—another necessary ingredient. Go one screen south from there. There's a cave here; we'll visit it later. For the time being, go east one screen to the ocean. Walk into it a short way—go on, get your feet wet. Take some sea water with the cup. Good. Turn around. Walk two screens west to a stream and a nice waterfall. Go to the bank of the stream where it zigzags, and get some mud with the spoon. Go west one more screen. You are now on the edge of the desert, but you're not in it.

Walk west into the desert. The instant the screen changes, turn south. Do not hesitate. Walk south, and walk until Medusa appears. Stop. You can't see Medusa because she always approaches from the west, and you're looking south. Wait until the monster gets closer to you, then show the mirror to Medusa. Don't let her get so close as to touch you; that too will turn you to stone. When Medusa sees herself, she turns to stone, and you won't have to worry about her any more.

Go back to where you entered the desert. You will see something lying on the ground in the middle of the screen. Look on the ground. Get the snakeskin. Walk two screens south. There is a large rock to the left of the screen. Look at the rock and you'll see a small cactus. Get the cactus. Gee, we're really moving now, aren't we?

The Easy Way Out

Walk one more screen south, then one east. We are back in bandit territory, so stay near the edge of the screen. One more screen east takes us to a cottage—the Three Bears' house. Knock on the door. If there is no answer, no one is home. If there is an answer, step off the screen and come back. Do the same if any of the bears are visible outside the house. Don't go inside until there are no bears and no answer at the door. Open the door. Look on the table. If there are no bowls of porridge there, leave and come back. Take the smallest bowl of porridge. Go upstairs. There is a dresser in the corner of the bears' bedroom. Open the drawer and then look inside the drawer. Take the silver thimble. Go downstairs and leave the house. If the bears come back while you're inside, they'll kick you out. If that happens, come back and try again.

There is a flower patch outside of the house; look at the flowers. Get the dew with the thimble. Congratulations! It's time to head back to Manannan's. Look at the magic map. Point to the square with the wizard's house. Teleport. Oops! You're at the bottom of the path. Right, you've got to walk up. I know it's unfair; just save the game and do it.

As soon as you're back, check the time left. I've got about ten minutes left till Manannan gets home. Make sure you have at least seven or eight minutes. You'll need it to make the cat cookie safely. Go to the study, unlock the cabinet to get the magic wand, move the books, pull the lever, and walk down to the laboratory. Watch out for the cat.

Go to Manannan's ingredient shelf and get the mandrake root powder. Go to the workbench and open the book to page XXV. Following the directions perfectly, make the cat cookie. Yummy! Yummy! Look at the cookie, then crumble the cookie into the porridge. Look at your inventory. The porridge is now poisoned and has no star next to it. You can carry it safely in the wizard's presence.

Note: If there is enough time left, feel free to make as many spells as you wish while you're here. Just keep track of the time. You have the ingredients for eveything except "Teleportation at random." That spell needs a stone, which you won't get until after you're finished with Manannan. You might want to make the magic dough that lets you understand the language of creatures. You can then go outside and hang around the chickens; maybe you'll hear something interesting. Anyhow, it's a way to pass the time.

Leave the laboratory. Pull the lever, move the books back, and unlock the cabinet to put the magic wand away. Don't forget to lock the cabinet again. Now go back to Gwydion's room and hide everything but the porridge under the bed. It's hurry-up-and-wait for Manannan to awaken. He's sure to be hungry.

Well, he's awake and demanding food. Go to the dining room and feed him his last human meal. Give the porridge to Manannan. It sure is a relief to get rid of him.

Go back to Gwydion's room and get all the stuff that's under the bed. Go back to laboratory. Make all the other spells, except for teleportation. Be careful, please. When you're done, look at the magic map. Point to the square containing the cave. Teleport. There's the cave again. Don't get too close; there is a giant spider waiting to get you.

Dip the eagle feather into the essence—you haven't forgotten to get the eagle feather, have you? Get it now if you didn't get it before. After you turn into an eagle, you will grab the spider that was hidden above the cave. When you return from disposing of it, enter the cave. Relax, and watch what happens.

Now you have some information about yourself. If you would like more, here's how to do it. You should have the magic dough in your ears by now. Just walk around Llewdor listening to the animals talk. Watch out for the bandits, though. In the desert, you'll overhear the lizards tell you some stuff,

The Easy Way Out

and birds and squirrels will have more on who you are. The chickens at the house just complain.

You might consider doing this listening before you get the stone from the oracle, and for the same reason we got the stone last. It seems that your escape from Llewdor will be on a ship, and the ship doesn't dock until you've obtained the amber stone. Then it's only there for 30 minutes of playing time. You should have plenty of time to listen around after you get the stone, return to the house, make the last spell, and then teleport back to town to get passage on the ship. But if you want to play it safe, teleport or walk around some, and then get the stone.

With that said, walk back up the path for the last time. Go to the laboratory, and make the teleportation spell. Great! It's time to go home. Don't bother to close up the laboratory or the house because Derek Karlavaegen will be around eventually to move in. I wonder where he found the wine cellar?

Teleport to town and then go to the tavern. Open the door and go inside. Talk to the sailors drinking there. Give the remaining gold to the captain, and they'll all leave. Exit the tavern and go east along the pier. There is a boarding plank in the second screen. Walk onto the ship and become the prisoner of bloodthirsty pirates.

You wake up in the hold of the ship. There's a ladder above you, but you can't reach it. Walk east. Two things are here: a small crate, which you take, and some rats. The rats will talk about some buried treasure. If you don't hear them, leave and come back until you do. They have a lot to say, and you may have to come back a few times. Next, go back to where you woke up and drop the small crate by the bigger one. Jump on the crate. Jump on the other crate. You can now reach the ladder. Jump; then climb the ladder. Please don't fall; it's fatal in many cases.

The ladder takes you to the second deck. Before you get off of it, look to see if the captain is in his cabin on the left of the screen. If he is, go down and come back until he's gone. Fine. Go to the captain's cabin. There is a trunk at the foot of the bed. Open the trunk and then look inside. You now have your possessions back. Leave and walk one screen east of the ladder. There is a lifeboat here with a shovel next to it. Get the shovel. Go back to the ladder and climb down. You're safe.

Let's pause a moment and consider the pirate ship. You can avoid the captain and crew below deck by using the old edge-of-the- screen trick. If they do catch you, they take your things again and return you to the hold. You can also climb the ladder to the top deck. If you're caught there, though, you'll walk the plank. Anyway, there's nothing for you topside until you escape.

There are several ways to escape the pirate ship. You can climb up to the top deck and dive overboard at once, but it will probably be a longer swim than you can survive, especially with sharks in the water. However, if you make it to shore, you'll have to deal with the pirate that will appear there.

You can rub the magic stone and teleport at random, but there is no way of predicting where you'll end up—you might even be returned to Manannan's. He's no problem, but the last boat to Daventry has left port. On the other hand, you can just keep rubbing the stone until you're on land someplace you've never been before. On the assumption that you have visited all of Llewdor and you're not in the desert, you should end up in Daventry. Of course you won't score points for putting the pirates to sleep, and you might not get the buried treasure. It's a fun way to travel and explore, however. At the worst, you can keep rubbing the stone until you're back in the ship's hold.

The best way to escape is to wait patiently until the lookout shouts that he's spotted land. This takes some time. If you're interested in how close you are to Daventry, look at the magic map; it also charts the ship's progress. If you try to teleport using it, you just end up swimming in the middle of the

The Easy Way Out

ocean. Just wait. When you hear "Land, ho!," cast the "Causing a deep sleep" spell (the hold is a dank, dark place). This puts the crew to sleep.

If you haven't gotten your stuff or the shovel yet, this is your last chance. Climb up on deck, go to the front of the ship, save the game, and then dive overboard. If you can avoid the shark, you'll make it to shore. The sleeping pirates won't follow you.

Swim due east on the bottom edge of the screen. Try not to change screens. If the shark gets between you and land, keep swimming straight. You should make it to a second screen with land. If you don't, go back to your saved game.

You're now on land. Go to the palm tree. Walk east five very slow paces. Dig. Treasure! OK. Go one screen north, then one screen east. There is a path here. Follow it a short distance up and to the west. In the next screen you will see a large rock next to the path. Crawl up the rock—up, a little to the left, and then the rest of the way to the right. Whew! Continue following the path to the east. In two more screens, you will come across a small stream dropping from above. Climb up the stream.

The next screen finds you climbing into the snow. You have now reached Abominable Snowman country. Leave the screen at once if you see it. Otherwise, climb till you get onto the path through the snow. Follow the path east to the next screen.

You must get past the snowman to finish the game. There are two ways past it: fly past as an eagle or a fly, or rub the stone and teleport past. If you fly, continue to go east past the snowman's cave. The teleport should take you to the screen east of the cave. You will get a message congratulating you for getting past the monster. However you do it, the only way past the screen east of the cave is down. The trail goes over the bottom edge of the screen in two places, one wide and to the right, and the other narrow and on the left side of the screen. Take the narrow path. When the scene changes, you are crawling down the vertical face of a cliff. Go straight down to the ledge and save the game.

Look around you, there are six cave openings; three high and three low. The only way past this screen is to go through the caves in the proper order—you can't teleport. OK. Enter the cave on your ledge.

Caution: Once you're in a cave, don't touch the keyboard, mouse, or joystick until you're out the other side. You are, though, permitted to press ENTER or RETURN to clear the message about the cave being dark.

You come out of the cave in the upper-right of the screen; but as soon as you appear, stop before you fall. Save the game. From here you must crawl down to the cave in the center on the bottom. Looks hard, and it is! From the left edge of the ledge, go up a hair, left, straight down until you're even with the snow, left, and straight down. This may take several tries. As soon as you reach the ledge, stop and save the game. Go into the cave walking west, and come out of the lowest cave on the left of the screen. Save the game. Now you must climb to the cave in the center of the screen—the middle one that you haven't been in. Go up a little, left a little, and up. As you get almost level with the ledge, move left away from it a bit, up and a bit above it, and then right to safety. Save, and breathe a sigh of relief. Enter the cave and emerge at the lower right. As before, stop, at once, and then go to the bottom of the screen. Exit the screen at the right-hand corner, traveling east.

Follow the narrow path, and make sure you don't fall off. The path continues down the mountain in the next screen and exits to the south. Follow it. Oops! There's no way to avoid that fall. Dust off and welcome yourself to the kingdom of Daventry. There is a chasm near your feet, watch out for it. Walk west one screen to the stone wall, and then north one screen. Talk to the gnome; he'll explain who you are and what you still have to do. When

The Easy Way Out

this is finished, retrace your steps to where you stumbled into the country. There are stairs going up into the mountain; follow them.

Follow the long staircase up, and don't fall. In three screens you will reach the mouth of the cave. Leave the cave and save the game. If you walk into the next screen west now, you're a fried adventurer. Go to near the left edge of the screen. Rub the invisibility ointment on your body. Now walk west as an invisible man.

You'll be greeted by a dragon, ready to roast Rosella. Cast the "Brewing a storm" spell, and watch the fireworks. Walk around the carcass to the north—if you go south, you fall through the clouds. Untie Rosella. Look at Rosella, then give her a brotherly kiss. Walk back down the mountain—carefully. Don't worry about Rosella, she'll follow you.

When you're down the mountain, walk to the gnome's shack. You'll be hailed as a savior. Follow the gnome north. Enter the castle and meet your folks.

You have completed King's Quest 3: To Heir Is Human.

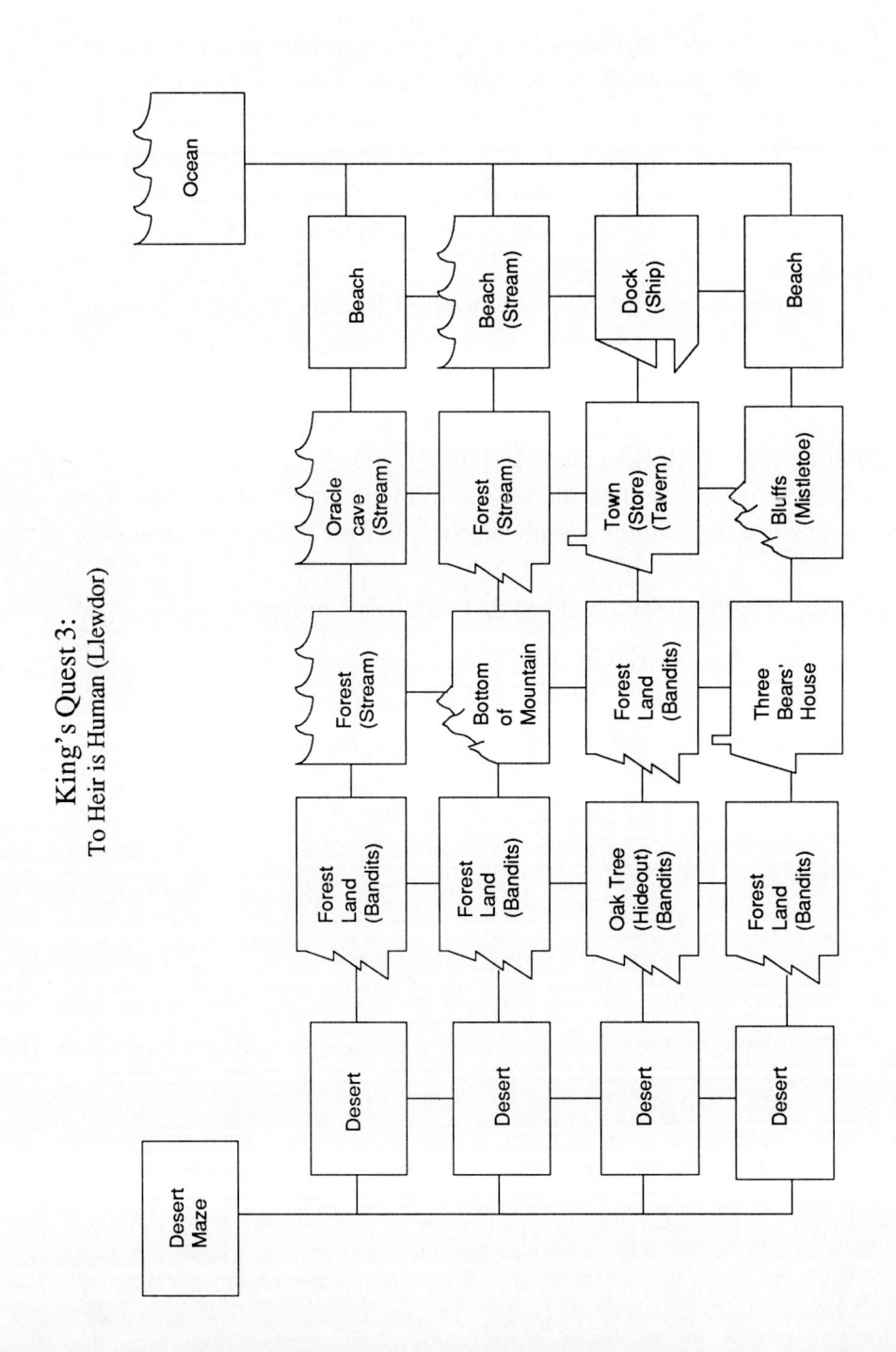

King's Quest 3:
To Heir is Human (Llewdor)

The Easy Way Out

King's Quest 3:
To Heir is Human (Daventry)

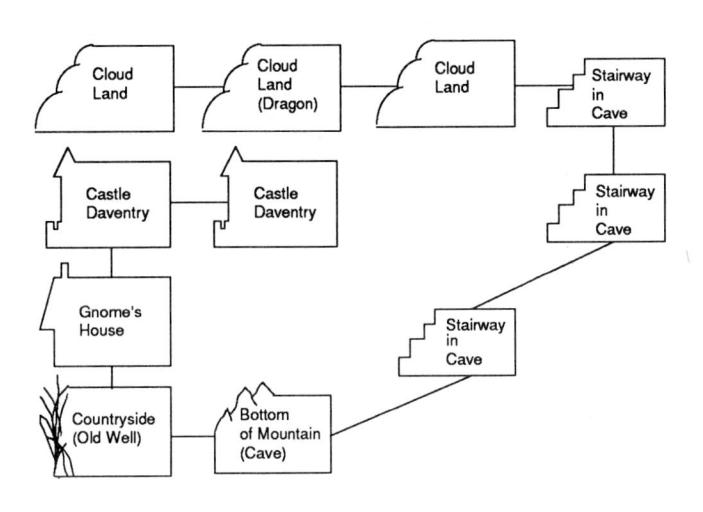

King's Quest 3:
To Heir is Human (Pirate's Ship)

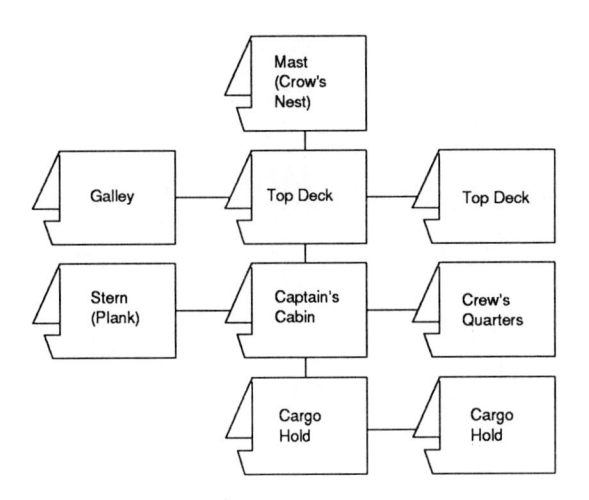

King's Quest 3:
To Heir is Human (Manannan's House)

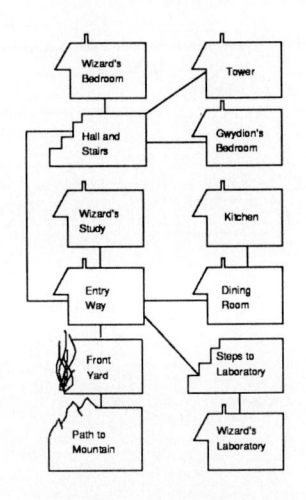

King's Quest 3:
To Heir is Human (Beach and Mountains)

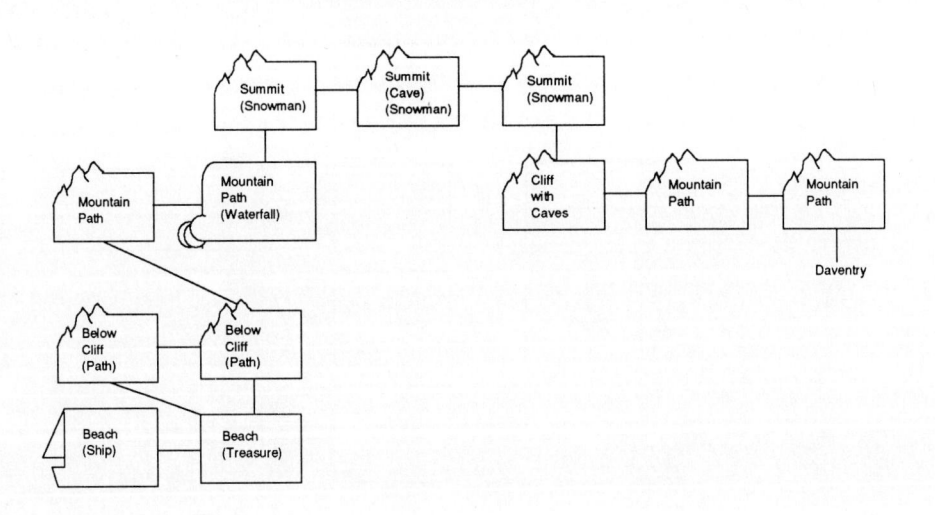

The Easy Way Out

King's Quest 4: The Perils of Rosella

Object of the Game:

You are Princess Rosella, daughter of King Graham and Queen Valanice of Daventry, and twin sister of Prince Alexander (formerly known as Gwydion). While celebrating your rescue from being sacrificed to a three-headed, fire-breathing dragon, and Alexander's return from a lifetime of captivity, your father collapses to the floor, clutching his chest. He will die if you do not find a magic fruit that exists somewhere in the distant land of Tamir. The good fairy Genesta magically transports you there, but reveals that it is impossible to send you home with the fruit unless you also recover Genesta's magic Talisman, which was stolen from her by the wicked witch Lolotte. If you do not return the Talisman within 24 hours, both Genesta and your father will die.

Things to Come:

There are five separate quests that must be completed in the 24-hour time span. There is a clock in the haunted mansion; if you want to check the time, go there, look at the clock, and type **TIME**. The game day begins at dawn—6 AM—and you must recover the Talisman from Lolotte before the following dawn. Certain things, however, can only be done at night, and others only during the day. While you can get the magic fruit at any time, it is best to get it first, and then go to Lolotte's.

The five quests are (in the order they should be done):

Obtaining the magic fruit

Capturing the unicorn

Capturing the hen that lays golden eggs

Obtaining Pandora's Box

Recovering the Talisman

In your initial wanderings about Tamir, there are five areas you should avoid:

- The **ogre's house** is south of the diamond mine, east of the Roman Pool, and two screens north of the western half of the cemetery. The ogre also can be found one screen south of his house, one screen north of the cemetery. The ogre will kill you if he catches you, however you must go inside his house in order to win the game.

- The **scary woods** are north of the eastern cemetery and haunted house and east of the two ogre screens. The scary woods surround the witches' cave. Without an ax, the trees will kill you.

- The **path up into the mountains** will take you to Lolotte's castle. It begins two screens east of the diamond mine and one screen south of the waterfall. Her goons will capture you after you've started up it. Avoid this until you've gotten the magic fruit, then go there at once.

- There is a **cave** on the other side of the waterfall. There's a troll in it that will kill you, especially if you don't have a lantern.

- The **cemetery** is not dangerous at all during the day. After dark though, zombies crawl from the ground to kill you. Don't go there at night until you've obtained the scarab.

The Easy Way Out

Except along the mountains, the land of Tamir "wraps around" from north to south. If you walk south from the unicorn meadow, for instance, you eventually come back to it from the north. Mountains form the eastern border, and the ocean is on the west. Genesta's island is in the ocean, and it can only be reached by swimming.

How to Do It:

Obtaining the Magic Fruit:

The game starts with a long movie that sets up the plot. When it is finished, you are standing on a beach. Walk east one screen and you are in the unicorn meadow. If the unicorn is not there, walk off the screen and back again until you see it. It's a pity you're going to have to shoot it later. Walk up to the unicorn; it's afraid of you and will remain that way until you use Cupid's bow and arrow. Go one screen east; the unicorn can also be found here.

Walk north one screen; there is a stone bridge over the pretty stream. Look under the bridge and get the golden ball. Walk north again one screen. There is a frog in the pond. Go to the northeast shore of the pond and drop the ball; the frog will recover it. Pick up the frog. It's wearing a little gold crown. There are two ways to get the crown; simply taking it is one way, the other is to kiss the frog. You'll score more points, and meet someone who gives princes a bad name, if you do kiss it. Pucker up! You now have the gold crown.

From the pond walk east one screen to the first part of the cemetery. If you want to start reading tombstones now, do it; you're going to have to find specific graves later in the game. Go east two screens and don't worry about the house for the moment. You're now in the eastern half of the cemetery. There is a locked crypt built into the mountain; you'll be in there later. Look at these tombstones for further reference, and take notes. (By the way, if you haven't noticed, many, if not all, of the inscriptions appear in the article from the *Bruce Banner* that is reprinted in Chapter 7.) Now walk west one screen to the house and go to the door. Open the door.

You are in the entry to the house. There is a clock in front of you. Look at it and type **TIME**. Go west through the open doorway to the parlor. There is a large painting over the fireplace. **Look** at the picture; if you don't do this, you will never be able to find the hidden latch to the secret door. OK., go to where the left wall and bookcase meet. Look at the left wall; you now notice a latch. Flip the latch and walk through the secret door. You are in the secret tower. Look; then take the shovel you find against the wall. Carefully climb the stairs to the top of the tower. Go ahead, sit down and play the organ, but we'll be back for more music later. Now walk back downstairs.

Go back to the parlor, and walk to the bookcase on the right side of the picture. Look at the books. Take the book of Shakespeare. You're now done with the house till after dark. If you want to explore it, go ahead, by my guest; otherwise, walk back outside. From the front of the house, walk three screens west to a meadow with a stump in the middle of it.

There should be somebody sitting on the stump playing a lute, badly. If the minstrel is not there, leave the screen and come back as often as necessary until he does appear. Talk to the man and listen. Then give the book to the man. You now have a lute.

Walk north one screen, and you'll see the back part of a shack. In this screen, or the ones immediately to the north and east of it, you will see Pan playing on a flute. Walk back and forth between these screens until you find him. When you do, play the lute, and then give the lute to Pan. Pan will now give you his flute; you'll need it to charm a snake later.

Go to the stone bridge where you found the gold ball, and walk one screen east. This is the house of Seven Dwarfs. Open the door and go in. The place is a mess. Type **CLEAN** to clean the house. The dwarfs will come home

The Easy Way Out

when you have finished. They will ask you to eat with them. Talk to them several times during the meal. After they leave, look at the table. Take the pouch and look inside. Diamonds! Leave the house and walk one screen south to the diamond mine. Enter the mine. Carefully follow the path that goes down and deeper into the mine. Walk one screen east, and go to the dwarf at the far right—the one with some stuff at his feet. Talk to him. Give the diamonds to the dwarf. He will refuse and give you a lantern. Leave the mine.

Note: If you enter the mine before you have the diamonds, the dwarfs will be unfriendly and kick you out. Cleaning the house is what makes the dwarfs dig you, so to speak.

From the front of the mine, go one screen east, then one screen north. You are by the river. Look for a bird pecking the ground and pulling up worms. Go there and take the worm. If the bird is not there, leave the screen and come back until it is. The worm can also be found sometimes in the screen immediately east of the dwarfs' house. Wherever you get it, get it now. On the assumption that you are at the river bank, walk one screen east. You are at the waterfall, the eastern part of the cemetery is just north of you, and the mountain path is the next screen south.

Go into the water and walk to near the falls. Wear the crown, and turn into a frog. You will return to your own form in a small clearing behind the waterfall. Look, and take the board you see next to the cave. Light the lantern. Save the game.

Note: Do not enter the cave without the lantern, board, and flute.

Enter the cave and stop. If you see the word "GRRRR!" on the screen, it's the troll. He'll kill you, so leave the screen at once, return, and repeat until he's not there. As soon as you enter, look for a pile of bones by the entrance. Take a bone. Now, let's start walking.

There are two ways to get to the same place—one screen east, then one south, or one screen south and one east. If you call the screen just inside the cave screen 1, then you want to go to the bottom right corner of screen 3. The troll is still wandering around in there, so save the game when you change screens, and good luck.

What I do is continue straight east across screen 1; if there is no troll when I enter screen 2, I save the game. If the troll is there, I back out to screen 1 and return. In the second screen, I continue walking due east until I'm just past the center of the screen. Then I turn south, and continue all the way until I leave the screen. In the third screen, I look for the troll, etc., and then continue south as far as I can go. Then it's a short jog east, turn south to the bottom of the screen, and then east until the exit. If you have made it this far, save the game again before you exit into the fourth screen. If the troll is there, it is waiting for you—without warning—when you come in. You'll be very lucky to escape—very lucky.

Slow your game speed to its slowest setting. Walk straight east until you're not quite at the center of the picture. Look. If you do not fall into the chasm, save the game. Type, **PUT THE BOARD OVER THE CHASM**. This bit can be frustrating, but keep trying. Trial and error is all you can do.

Once the board is over the crevice, save the game and walk straight east. When you're over, you will get a message. Make sure you have the board with you. Turn north and exit at the tiny blue light. There is one more cave screen; exit via the blue light you see there. You're out! Great! Save the game.

Go to the edge of the swamp nearest the string of grass tufts. Jump 11 times, you will be on the last tuft just in front of the island with the cobra. Lay the board down and you have a bridge. Cross over the board but do not set foot on the island; if you do the snake will kill you. Play the flute. The snake does not remain hypnotized very long, so walk quickly over to the east side of the tree and take the fruit, and at once walk back to the last tuft of grass. You now have the magic fruit. Resist the temptation to taste it; King Graham cannot be cured if you do.

Note: It is very easy to step off the island and get killed here. Do be careful.

Once back on the tuft, pick up the board, and jump your way back to the cave. Save the game. Now all you have to do is walk back through the cave the same way you came in. The troll's still there. The chasm's still there. I'll meet you when you come out.

Welcome back I don't like the troll's cave at all! Now that you're out, step into the water and walk to the falls. You will be swept safely out to the other side. When you get there, shake yourself off and go one screen south. It's time to visit Lolotte. Walk up the path heading east, being careful you don't fall off. When you get to the next screen, stop and wait. The witch's goons will come to fly you up. Relax and watch the movie.

Capturing the Unicorn:

Well, we're back at the foot of the mountain. Walk west five screens until you reach the beach. (If you didn't get the worm before, make sure you get it now; we're going to need it!) From the beach, go two screens south to the fisherman's shack. Knock and see if he's home; he probably isn't. Walk west out to the end of the pier where he's fishing. Talk to the man, but he won't be very responsive. Follow him back to his house. Knock on the door; open the door. Go to the man and talk to him. Give the diamonds to the man. You now have the fishing pole; let's go fishing.

Walk back to the end of the pier. Put the worm on the hook. Fish. Repeat until you catch a fat one. Got it? Walk off the end of the pier and swim due west. Remember the old edge-of-the-screen trick? As you swim west, stay at the very bottom of the screen. That way if a whale or shark tries to eat you, you can escape—leave the screen—and immediately return. Keep swimming, Genesta's island isn't far.

Genesta's castle is dab-smack in the middle of the island. The first thing you should do is walk around the beaches; you're looking for a peacock feather lying on the sand somewhere. If you see a peacock, follow it. Keep at it until you get the feather. Fine. We can leave now.

Note: There is nothing else you can do there now. However, go to the front door of the castle, open it, and go through the doorway to your left. Climb up to Genesta's bedroom and see how she is. We'll wait for you.

Enter the ocean from where you came ashore, and swim due east. Again, stay at the bottom of the screen. If the shark appears, get out. On the other hand, you do want to be swallowed by the whale this time; it's the only way to win the game. When the whale appears, you will be pulled under.

Inside the whale, you're swimming in a pool of stomach acid that you want to get out of. Climb onto the whale on either the far left side or far right of the screen. You must now climb up and over the whale's flesh until you can stand directly under the black thing you can see dangling there.

Note: There is a bottle floating around in the whale's belly. If you get the bottle, get the note and read it; you might be amused. Then again, you might not. Some people find "plugs" amusing.

The Easy Way Out

Save the game, and put it on its slowest speed. You must now move in a series of over-and-up scrambles. It's mostly trial and error, so save the game when you've made some progress. Follow the curve of the flesh as much as you can. Eventually, you stand up. Save the game, and walk towards the teeth. Tickle the whale with the feather—just another great escape!

You are now in the middle of the ocean. Swim north to the island you see. It's deserted. Go into the wreck there. Look at the ground and get the golden bridle. There should be a pelican on the island; if there isn't, wait, it'll come. Throw the fish (remember, you caught a fish earlier) to the bird, and it will drop something. Go to it, and look on the ground. Get the whistle. Whistle. A dolphin will appear; ride the dolphin.

Note: You cannot spend very much time on the desert island. If you don't finish your tasks quickly enough, you will die from lack of water.

You return to land one screen north of the fisherman's shack. Go east two screens, you will come to a Roman pool. Cupid likes to visit here, and you need to see him. Wait; if he doesn't show up soon, step off the screen and try again. When Cupid appears, he will put down his bow and arrows and begin bathing in the pool. Walk into the pool, directly at Cupid. You will startle him, and he will fly away. Go to the bow and arrows he has forgotten. Get the bow and arrows. Now for the unicorn.

Walk north one screen; this is one of the two unicorn screens. If the unicorn is not here, go west one screen to the other unicorn area. Go back and forth between these two screens until you encounter the beast. Shoot the unicorn. If the unicorn runs away before you can type the command, type it early and press ENTER or RETURN as soon as you see him. The unicorn is no longer afraid of you.

Go up and put the bridle on the unicorn. You can now take it to Lolotte. Ride the unicorn. You will automatically be taken straight west until you come to the path. Go up the path, and Lolotte's monkeys will capture you. You have finished Lolotte's first task, and the ungrateful witch will give you another.

Capturing the Hen That Lays Golden Eggs:

You're back at the bottom on the path. Walk two screens west to the diamond mine. Go one screen south; you are looking at the ogre's house. If the ogre is walking about outside, leave the screen and return. Repeat as necessary. Go to the door and open it. Type **THROW BONE TO DOG**. Walk inside; as soon as you see the dog, it sees you. Press RETURN or ENTER to throw the bone to the dog. In some versions, but not in all, as soon as you begin typing the command, you stop the dog's attack. Use whatever method works for you.

Go upstairs to the ogre's bedroom. Go to the east wall. Look, then take the ax you see. Return downstairs. You will see a doorway lead off to the right and a closed door next to it. Do not go through the open door, the ogre's wife is there, and she will kill you. Open the door to the closet. Go inside the closet and wait. When you hear the ogre come home, look through the keyhole. Keep looking. As soon as the ogre falls asleep, open the door and leave the closet.

Go to the table and take the hen. Save the game. Type **OPEN DOOR**. Leave the house by walking west to the door. Make sure you are on the rug as you pass the dog. The ogre will wake up just before you get to the door because the chicken squawks. Press ENTER or RETURN as soon as this happens, before you get to the door; it has to be open when you get there for you to escape. Keep going, don't touch the keyboard, and hope you make it.

The Easy Way Out

That's why you saved the game. Repeat until you're out and then run straight west or north. The ogre won't follow you there.

Close call! If you fled west, you are at the pool. Walk north one screen. If you escaped by running north, ignore this move. Turn east and walk until you're at the path. Start up, and meet the goons and their mistress again. You have completed Lolotte's second task. There is a third.

Obtaining Pandora's Box:

Our first stop is the scary forest. From the path, walk one screen west all the way to its center. Go one screen south and stop at once. Look. Swing the ax. You're now safe from the trees.

Note: You can also get to the trees by walking three screens north from the path; however, if it's night, the zombies will get you as you go through the graveyard.

Assuming you are now where I took you—at the back of the ogre's house—walk one screen east. You should be outside of a cave that looks like a skull. Three witches are inside.

Note: The witches don't get there until you've taken the hen to Lolotte.

Save the game, and enter the cave. Stop at once and look. The witch on the left will come after you. The trick here is to get her to come past the left side of the cauldron while you scoot by on the right side; then you can run to the spot between the two other witches and take their one eye from them. Ready? Let's try it. Move around, back and forth, on the left side of the cauldron. Let the witch come closer and closer. As soon as she has passed the cauldron, move directly to the right side, and cut up past it. The witch should be chasing you. Get right up between the other two—make sure you don't touch them—and take the eye. As long as you have it, you're safe.

Leave the cave and then return. They will throw something to you; if they don't, leave and return until they do. Take the scarab. Walk to the bottom of the screen. Just before you leave, throw the eye to the witches. It scores extra points. Don't wait around or they'll kill you, get out as soon as you throw it. You now have the scarab that protects you from the undead. Do not enter the cemetery or crypt after dark without it.

If it's not night yet, it should be soon, darkness falls at 9:00 PM. Go to the haunted house and wait; there's nothing else you can do until after dark. The house is two screens south and one screen west of the outside of the cave.

I can see by the old clock in the hall that it's 9:00, and there's a baby howling. If you didn't get the shovel the first time you were in the house, get it now, it's past the parlor, on the other side of the secret door.

Note: The shovel can only be used five times—one dig for each of the ghosts that you must appease. If you dig in the wrong spot with it, you cannot win the game.

When you hear the baby cry, go to the west graveyard. Look for a tombstone in the upper-left part, partially obscured by the big tree limb. It reads "HIRAM BENNET." To see it, read the tombstone. Dig. You now have the rattle. Ignore the zombies and go back to the house. Walk upstairs and enter the door on the top left. Walk through the bedroom to the door on the top left of that screen. You are in the nursery. Put the rattle in the crib.

You hear a second noise. Walk downstairs. You should see a ghost in chains; if not, look around. Look at the ghost, and leave the house. Go back

The Easy Way Out

to the west graveyard and look for the MISER's grave. It's in front near the left of the screen. Dig. Take the bag of coins to the house and look for the ghost downstairs. Give the coins to the ghost.

You hear new crying from upstairs. Go into the right doorway at the top of the stairs. Look at the ghost. Leave the house and walk to the east graveyard. Look in front for the tomb of BETTY COWDEN. Read the tombstone. Dig. You now have the locket. Take it back to the house, and give it to the ghost upstairs in the rocking chair.

You hear wailing downstairs. Go down and find the ghost. Look at the ghost, and then walk to the west graveyard. Find the tombstone of LORD CONINGSBY near the right front. Dig. Take the medal of honor back to the house, and give it to the ghost downstairs.

A boy ghost appears. Follow it upstairs to the bedroom on the right. Climb the ladder with care. To get up and down, type **CLIMB LADDER**. Look. Look at the ghost. Climb down the ladder, and leave the house. Go to the east graveyard. In the back, on the left, find WILLY's tomb. Read the gravestone. Dig. You now have a toy horse, and a broken shovel! Take the toy back to the attic and give it to the ghost. Soon it disappears. Open the trunk. Look inside the trunk. You now have sheet music, and it's time for another trip up to the top of the secret tower.

Go downstairs, through the parlor and through the secret door that we have never closed. Save the game here, and set the speed to its slowest setting. It's still a tough climb—good luck. Save again as you go along. When you get to the tower room, walk up between the organ and the bench. Sit. Play the sheet music. When the drawer opens, look in the drawer. Take the key; it opens the locked crypt. Stand, then take care going down the steps. Leave the house, and walk to the east graveyard. The crypt is in the mountain, and it's in the center of the right edge of the screen. Go to the crypt door; it's partially obscured. Unlock door with the skeleton key. Open the door and enter the crypt.

Stop when you enter. Look. Take the ladder, and then climb the ladder. Laugh at the mummy if you want, but you get no points. Pandora's Box is on the floor. Go up, and take Pandora's Box. Go back and climb the ladder again. Leave the crypt and walk two screens south to the path. Go up the path and wait for your ride.

Lolotte now has imprisoned you in Edgar's tower bedroom. Wait until you hear a noise. Go to the locked door. You will find a rose; look at it. Take the little gold key, and then unlock the door with the gold key. Open the door and leave the room. Save the game. More stairs are ahead, and these have blind spots. Trial and error and hugging the walls is the way down; take your time, and save a lot. At the bottom is a sleeping guard. The way to pass without waking him is to stay as far away as possible, following the curve of the wall, and go out the doorway.

The next screen has another sleeping guard and two doorways. We want the door closest to the guard. Hug the very bottom of the screen and then the right wall. It may take a couple of tries; save the game and take it easy. Inside the doorway is the kitchen; there are two cabinets there. Go to the one in the upper-right portion of the screen, and open the cabinet. You now have your possessions back, especially the bow and arrow. Take everything, and go back out past the guard. Exit the dining room through the door at the bottom right; this leads to the throne room.

The way through the throne room is different. Just walk straight through to the other side. Do not move to the bottom of the screen; just go straight without stopping. You're safe on the rug, however, if you care to stop there a moment. But why?

The Easy Way Out

You are now in the other tower. Hug the bottom wall here to pass the guard and begin climbing the steps. More blind spots are ahead. There is a landing in the second stair screen, with a door leading off it. Don't go in there. The guards will catch you and lock you back in the tower with no key. You lose. Continue up the stairs past the small landing. At the top of the next screen is Lolotte's room.

When you get outside Lolotte's door, unlock the door with the gold key. Open the door. Shoot Lolotte at once with the bow and arrow. You got her. Watch what happens.

Dawn breaks and Edgar arrives. After Edgar leaves, walk to the bed and take the Talisman. Leave the room and walk down to the landing on the next screen. As soon as you leave Lolotte's bedroom screen, save the game; the stairs are still tricky. Go into the doorway at the landing. You will enter a hall, and the guards will bow to you. There is a door at the top of the screen as you get here. Go to the door and open it. Go inside. Get the hen. Get Pandora's Box. Now return to the stairs and walk to the bottom and through to the throne room. Leave the throne room at the bottom of the screen. You are outside.

There is a small stable outside of the castle's front door. Go inside. The unicorn is there. Stand in the middle, and open the gate. The unicorn will leave. Follow the unicorn out of the stable, and save the game because you still have to walk down the mountain! The path down is south from the castle gate. When the screen changes, stop. Now walk with care, please, one slow step at a time.

You're down. The first thing to do is go to the crypt and return Pandora's Box to the spot where you found it. When you've done this, leave the crypt and close the door. Lock the door. You've just scored some extra points.

Now walk straight west, back to the ocean. You can swim to Genesta's from here. Do it; just swim straight west.

When you arrive at the island, open the door to the castle and climb up to Genesta's bedroom. Go to the bed and give the Talisman to Genesta. Watch the end of the game.

You have completed King's Quest 4: The Perils of Rosella.

393
The Easy Way Out

King's Quest 4:
The Perils of Rosella (Ogre's House)

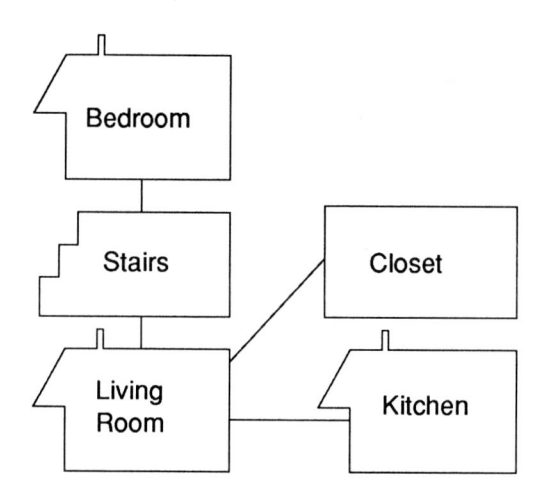

```
        Bedroom
           |
         Stairs ——— Closet
           |      /
       Living ——— Kitchen
        Room
```

King's Quest 4:
The Perils of Rosella (Genesta's Island)

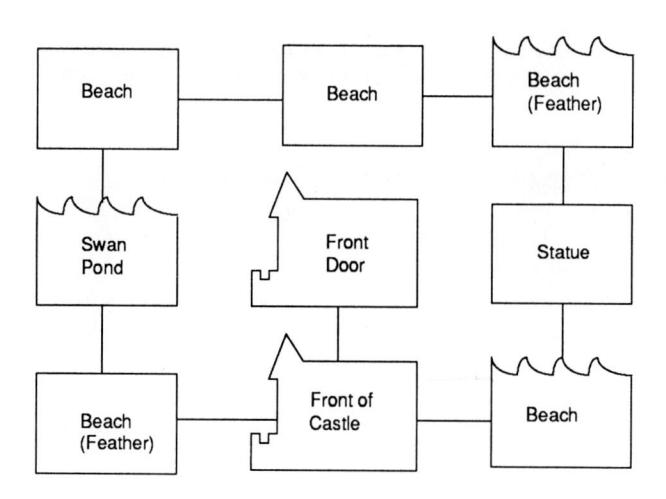

```
Beach ——— Beach ——— Beach (Feather)
  |                      |
Swan      Front         Statue
Pond      Door            |
  |                      
Beach ——— Front of ——— Beach
(Feather)  Castle
```

King's Quest 4:
The Perils of Rosella (Lolotte's Castle)

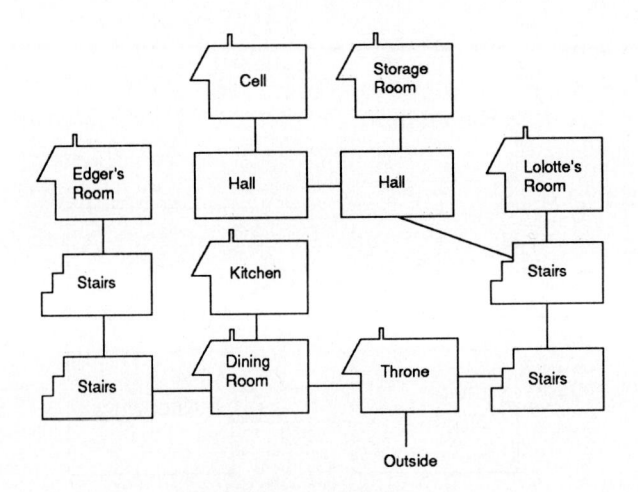

King's Quest 4:
The Perils of Rosella (Haunted House)

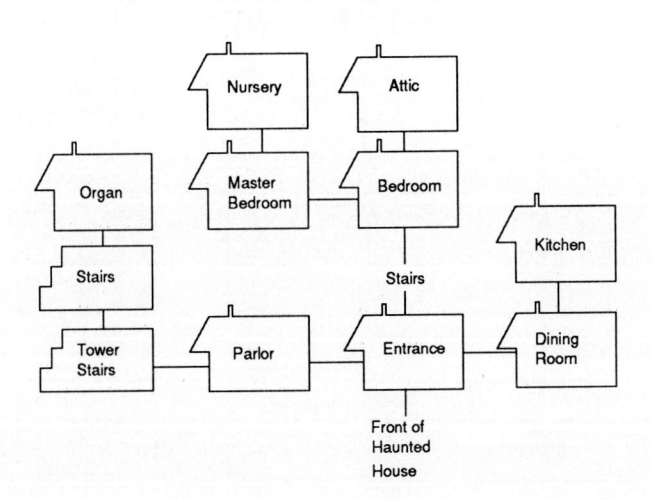

The Easy Way Out

KING'S QUEST 5: ABSENCE MAKES THE HEART GO YONDER

Object of the Game:

You are King Graham of Daventry. You arrive home from a stroll one morning to discover that your home—Castle Daventry—has disappeared, and your family with it. The only eyewitness to the disappearance is an owl named Cedric who informs you that an evil wizard by the name of Mordack did the deed, but for what reason is a mystery. You accompany Cedric to the land of Serenia and meet his employer, another wizard (although a good one) named Chrispinophur—Crispin for short. Crispin also has no knowledge of why Mordack would do such a deed, but does do three things for you to aid you in your quest:

- He feeds you magic whitesnake so you can communicate with animals you might meet on your journey.

- He gives you an old magic wand that doesn't work right now, but just might after it gets to know you.

- He sends Cedric along to help show you the way way around Serenia.

Your quest is to find and rescue your family. You are equipped with only your wits, Crispin's wand, and the clothes on your back. Good luck—you're going to need it.

Things to Come:

You begin your adventures outside of Crispin's house in Serenia. In your initial wanderings, there are several places where you must be careful:

- The **WARNING! Sign** in the woods just west of Crispin's house. There is a witch living beyond there to the north, and she'll turn you into a toad if you're not ready for her. Also, once you enter the Dark Forest, you cannot leave unless you've dealt with the witch and possess specific items. The area with the sign is safe, but do not go north from there into the Dark Forest until you collect the necessary stuff. I'll let you know just what that stuff is in a bit.

- The **River**. If you try to drink, walk, or swim in the river, you will die.

- The **Bee Tree**. The bees will kill you unless you make friends with them, and you can't make friends with them unless you have the right item. On the other hand, even if you do have it, the bear can kill you.

- The **Inn** west of the bakehouse. You can easily get mugged there and lose the game. Later in the game you must experience the mugging, but the beginning is not the time.

- The **Desert**. You will die of thirst unless you find the oases, the temple, or the bandits' camp. In the latter two places, the bandits will kill you if they notice you. Of course, you must go there in order to win the game.

There are a number of important differences between King's Quest 5: Absence Makes The Heart Go Yonder, and the other games in the King's Quest series.

King's Quest 5 is designed to be played entirely by using either a mouse or joystick. Using one of them, players choose from one of a short series of icons—small pictures—that are across the top of their screen. When an icon is selected, the screen pointer—the cursor—changes to show which icon is being used. These icons allow King Graham to:

The Easy Way Out

Look (Eye)

Walk (Person walking) Player must maneuver Graham around all obstacles. This will get Graham to spots he won't be able to using the following icon....

Travel (Person walking quickly) When this is used, Graham can walk long distances while he is avoiding obstacles. This is the movement icon you will probably use most often. Great for walking him completely through a screen, and getting most places Not so great in getting him to some certain specific spots, or places where fine control of Graham is needed.

Talk (Graham's head)

Take, Do or **Use** (Hand)

Bag or **Pouch** (Where Graham keeps his stuff)

Ready The player opens the Bag icon (by clicking on it with the mouse, etc.), and then selects, or clicks, again on one of the treasures inside the Bag. The treasure is then ready for immediate use and appears inside the small window icon.

Using the icons is simple. For example, to move Graham somewhere:

1. Select the **Walk** or **Travel** picture
2. See! The cursor changes to the appropriate icon!
3. Place the cursor where you want Graham to go
4. Click the left mouse button (or its equivalent)

5. See! Graham walks!

To have Graham talk to someone:

1. Select the **Talk** icon

2. See the cursor change

3. Place cursor over with whomever (or whatever) you wish Graham to speak

4. Click the left mouse button (or it's equivalent)

5. Graham speaks

You get the idea. To take something, just select the **Hand** icon, place the cursor over whatever you want Graham to get, then click. Click on the **Bag** if you want to make sure it's there.

To look at something, click the **Eye** on it.

To open a door, click the **Hand** on the door.

To use something, click on the **Bag**, click on what you want to use, close the Bag by selecting **OK**, place the cursor on where you want to use the object, then click. If you want Graham, for instance, to eat a sandwich or drink a potion, click it on Graham. If you want Graham to give those things to someone, click on the person. If you want to throw the sandwich, click on what or where you want it to hit.

If an item can't be used in a certain way, or if the player tries to get the game to do something it doesn't understand, then a large X appears on the screen. At times, the program will take control of the game away from the player. When that happens, an *hourglass* appears. When it disappears, the player will have control again.

The Easy Way Out

The only other icons are

Computer disk to save or restore the game.

Stop to pause, quit or restart the game.

Slide control for increasing or decreasing the sound level, the game's speed, or the level of animation detail.

? (Question mark) lets people get to the help screen, and identify the version number of the game.

(For people who have neither a mouse nor a joystick—or don't want to use them—King's Quest 5 has what are known as *keyboard equivalents* for them. Yes, you do indeed use the keyboard, but you still won't type in commands in order to play. The keyboard equivalents just activate the appropriate icons the same way the mouse or joystick would.)

That's it. The icon system takes almost no time to learn, is very self-evident and intuitive, and after a few minutes it becomes effortless to use and understand. It's so easy that I've even composed a little poem in it's honor:

Behold!
Not once do my fingers
Type a command!
Behold!
Not once do my fingers
Leave my hand!

OK. So I'm not a poet.

The second major change also has to do with the physical game-playing experience. King's Quest 5 is also available to be played in a CD (compact disk) version. CD-ROM is what it's called in computer-speak, and it's a special CD player that a computer can hook up to the same as it would to a standard disk drive. These CD-ROM drives can even play your music disks. In playing the CD-ROM version of Absence Makes The Heart Go Yonder, a person hears King Graham, Cedric, Mordack and the other characters of the game speaking, and listens to an extensive movie-style sound track. Also, the CD-ROM version can contain more scenes and animation than the standard floppy disk based game. In the CD-ROM version, playing King's Quest is even more like taking part in an animated film—but one which you can control. It can be pretty neat.

The game's other differences with the first four King's Quest titles are in the way that the adventure is constructed.

With few exceptions, the *old edge-of-the-screen trick* does not work as often in this game. You can't just step off the screen and return to find the bees or bandits or yeti gone. Most encounters and events are planned to happen at specific times or places, whether you want them there, or not. We'll take care of the exceptions when we get to them.

There is no clock ticking in the background in this game, as in KQ3 and KQ4. However, there are times when certain things must be done in a short period of time or you will either die or not be able to complete the game.

There are also no easily recognized sub-quests to give the game structure as in KQ1, 2, and 4. Instead, Absence Makes The Heart Go Yonder is comprised of segments—episodes—which must be completed before the next one begins. It is more movie-like than the prior games, with one sequence of actions leading into the next, and the next again.

Unlike the first four King's Quest games, the game world of KQ 5 does not "wrap around"—turn back on itself. Except for the desert in the west and the ocean in the east, there are definite north and south borders that will stop your progress in those directions. The desert and ocean are, for all rational

The Easy Way Out

purposes, *endless* in extent and if you didn't get killed (which you will if you try) you could stay lost in them until your computer itself dies.

At times during the game, the player will be asked to cast some specific spell that appears in the game's documentation—the instructions and stuff that comes packed with the disks. These act as the game's "copy protection"—if you don't have the documentation, you can't play the game through. Remember: it is illegal to make a copy of someone else's software for your own use.

Finally, King Graham is not alone in his adventures. He is accompanied by Cedric who will give an occasional bit of advice. Usually, the advice is worth heeding

How To Do It:

Serenia—the first time:

If you haven't done so, watch the opening cartoon. After it's completed, you find yourself in front of Crispin's house along with Cedric—he will be your sidekick throughout the entire adventure. Take this opportunity to experiment a little with the game icons. Look at the contraption in front of Crispin's. Try to take it. Talk to Cedric. OK. Let's walk south along the path. Forward, ho!

In the screen immediately south of Crispin's, if you try to walk east to the next screen, the snake will kill you. We will have to go there later, however.

From the same screen just south of Crispin's, follow the path west. Look at the prince, then talk to him and listen to his story. When you're done, return east to the screen below Crispin's. Walk south one screen. You are now outside the town of Serenia. Enter the town—just walk Graham right up the path into it.

You are in the town of Serenia. Look around. There's a man fixing the wheel on his cart. Talk to him. Behind the man, across the alley is a barrel. Look at the barrel. Reach into the barrel (place the **Hand** icon on it and activate it). Take the fish, and leave town the same way you entered it.

From the outside of town, follow the path west. Under no conditions, enter the river, attempt to drink from it, or get too close. If you'd like to try, save the game now and do it. Death awaits. The house in this screen is the bakehouse; we'll be back. Continue west one screen. There is an Inn here with a haystack outside. Do not enter the Inn now or you will lose the game. If you wish, you can search the haystack, but you will find nothing at this time.

Walk west one more screen and stop as soon as you get there. You will see a bear pawing at a tree. If you get too near the bear, it'll kill you. Throw the fish at the bear (just click on the fish in the inventory Bag, click on the **OK** box, place the new icon over the bear, and click again). When the bear leaves, and you've heard from Queen Beetrice, walk up to the tree. Look on the ground on the east side of the tree. Take the stick. Walk smack up to the tree beneath the hole. Reach into the hole and get the honeycomb by clicking the **Hand** icon on the hole.

The desert:

Walk west one screen. You are now in brushland. To the west is an endless desert that you must explore. However, unless you find either the hidden temple, the bandits' camp, or one of the 4 oases, Graham will die of thirst and excessive sun. The trick to surviving the desert is in knowing that, once inside it, Graham can only walk 7 screens without perishing. The 8th screen is fatal. The safe spots are located so that you can reach everything you need to, and still survive. If you don't drink while at an oasis, Graham will die. Outside of the temple, there is a spring by the rocks in the cliff opening; at

The Easy Way Out

the bandits' camp, there is a clay jar with water in it by the campfire. Remember—Graham needs to drink at the temple or in the bandits' camp!

The obvious strategy is to find a safe spot, save the game, and explore from there using trial-and-error. If you'd like to explore the desert on your own, save the game now and go. Good luck. By the way, there are deadly scorpions living along the desert's southeastern border. They mean death.

For those heading out with me, save the game. Walk west 4 screens from the bee tree. Oasis. Drink. Save the game. Walk north 2 screens to the cliffs, then west 3 screens to the hole in the cliffs, with the temple visible in the distance. There are rocks to the east side of the opening in the cliffs. Stand behind them—you should now be hidden. Wait for the bandits to gallop up; if you're hidden, your safe, if you're not, you're dead. Watch what happens. When the bandits leave, drink at the spring, then go north to the temple door. Try and enter. Return to the opening-in-the-cliff screen. Drink. Save the game.

Walk west 2 screens, then south 3 screens to the next oasis. Drink. Save the game. From the oasis, walk west one more screen, then south until you find yourself in the bandits' camp.

There are two tents here, a large one on the left where you can see reveling going on inside, and a smaller one to the right. There is also a campfire with a clay jar near it. Go the the jar and click the **Hand** icon on it. Graham will drink. Don't try to enter the big tent. If you do, or get too close to it, the bandits will discover and kill Graham. Go to the smaller tent, and save the game. Enter the smaller tent.

Inside, there is a sleeping bandit who will wake up and kill Graham if Graham touches him, or tries to talk to him. This encounter is timed—Graham only has a short amount of time to find the magic staff, get it, and safely escape before the bandit awakens. If the bandit wakes he will discover Graham, and our hero will be captured and killed. This is why we saved before we went into the tent. If this happens, restore the game and try again. Repeat as often as necessary.

Look around. You need to get the staff that's at the back of the tent. Walk straight back on the right (east) side of the tent pole. If you go on the left side, you will surely wake up the desperado. Carefully go and look around in back without touching the sleeping bandit. Take the staff. Again without touching the sleeping bandit, leave the tent. Save the game.

From the bandits' camp, walk east 4 screens, then north 1 to the oasis. Drink. Save the game. From the oasis, go north 2 screens, where you will find a skeleton in the desert. Look at it, then look around. Nearby the skeleton, in the sand, is an object. Look at it. Take the boot. Walk north 1 screen, then east 2 more. Oasis. Drink. Save the game. You are now back at the first oasis you visited, and it's time to return to the temple.

As before, go north 2 screens to the cliffs, then west 3. Walk north to the temple.Drink, then save the game. Walk up to the temple door and click the staff on it. Once the door opens and you enter the temple you'll have a short—a very short—time to loot the place. And, you have only one try at it. In front of Graham, you'll see a small glitter on the ground. Take the gold coin. Next to it is a large brass bottle. Take the brass bottle. Leave at once, don't try to get anything else. If you didn't get out in time, restore your saved game and try again. Practice makes perfect. *This will probably take you several tries—do not dispair.* If getting the coin first doesn't work, try getting the bottle first. Keep trying.

Once safely outside, go to the spring and drink. Save the game again. You have now accomplished all you need to do in the desert and it's time to get out.

From the opening in the cliffs, east 3 then south 2. Oasis. Drink. From the oasis it's just 5 screens east to the bee tree. Save the game. Whew! (From here on, I'll stop nagging you so much about saving the game. I'll assume

The Easy Way Out

you are doing so. I will remind you though just before certain critical points, just to help you be safe.)

Before we go on, a quick note about the brass bottle. Do not experiment with it; if you open it you will be trapped and, incidently, lose the game.

On the way to the Dark Forest:

You are at the bee tree again. Walk north one screen. Look around. Throw the stick you've been carrying at the dog. After the ants promise you their help, continue north one screen to the gypsy camp. Look around, then walk towards the man you see. Give him the gold coin. Enter the wagon to meet Madame Mushka who will fill you in on more details about what's happened to Graham's family. She'll give you a magic amulet.

When the animated cartoon is finished, click the amulet icon on Graham—he is now wearing the amulet. The amulet will not protect Graham if he is not wearing it. Walk east from the gypsy camp. Look around. Look at the Weeping Willow. Talk to the Weeping Willow and listen to her story. Look at the harp, then try and take it. Walk east one more screen. Look at the warning sign. Hmm! Once we go north from here we can't return until we've dealt with the witch and the elves. You must be carrying the amulet, the brass bottle, and the honeycomb. Got'em?

The Dark Forest:

Walk north one screen past the warning sign. Look around. You are at a fork in the path and can choose to go either east or west. Leave this screen using the path to the east and north. You will find yourself deep in the Dark Forest. An unfriendly witch lives in these parts. If you meet her, the amulet will protect Graham from being turned into a toad. If you do meet her, look at her, talk to her, then give the witch the brass bottle. After the witch becomes trapped in the bottle, she'll neither bother Graham nor anyone else for a long time.

Anyway, the only place you are certain to meet the witch is in front of her house, and we're not there yet. Continue north through the forest. In the next screen you will see a tree with a small door in it. Look around, then look at the tree. Go up to the tree and attempt to open the door. Nice try. Now walk west one screen.

You are now in front of the witch's house. If she's there, look at her. Talk to the witch. Give the witch the brass bottle. Look around a bit, then enter the witch's house. Look around. Look at the trunk, then open it. Inside is a small spinning wheel. Take it. Look at the incense burner hanging in the room. Take the small key that is inside it. Look at the tree trunk table, there is a drawer in it. Open the drawer, then take the bag. Once the bag is in your inventory, click on it with the Hand to open it. You now have three emeralds.

Leave the witch's house. Return one screen east to the tree with a door in it. Click the key on the door, then take the heart you find inside the tree. Walk south one screen, then turn west and go two more screens in that direction. as you walk, look around—you are being watched by elves. Walk north one screen and arrive at a small clearing. Look around. You are now in a six screen loop (actually you have been since you left the screen with the fork in the path). You will wander forever in this loop unless you can find a way out.

Drop one emerald on the ground—an elf will scoot out the the brush and take it. Drop a second emerald. Same effect. Squeeze the honeycomb. A puddle of honey will be created on the ground. Drop the last emerald near the honey. The elf that comes for it will get stuck, and Graham will capture him. Look at the elf. Talk to the elf. Graham will let the elf go, and an opening will be created on the west side of the screen by a strange creature. (This critter is a Jinx, but is never identified as such in the game.) Walk west one screen and you will see the elf entering a tunnel farther to the west. Follow the elf into the tunnel.

You are now in the elves' cavern. Look around. During the animated cartoon sequence, the shoemaker elf will give Graham a fine pair of shoes, and Graham will be shown the way out of the forest. When the cartoon is finished, Graham will be in a tunnel which finally ends in the screen with the warning sign. You are now finished with the Dark Forest.

(You can, if you wish, have Graham return to the elves' cavern, although there is nothing to be gained there. You can look around some and admire the sights, but everybody will be gone. Graham can also fall in the chasm there and die. So, if you want to go back, have a nice time. From the warning sign you can even go north back into the Dark Forest, get back in the elves' cavern, etc, over and over again. I wouldn't.)

Serenia—the second time:

You are at the warning sign just south of the Dark Forest. Walk west one screen to the Weeping Willow. Give the heart to the tree. Observe the result and the reunion. Look at the harp, then take the harp.

Walk west one screen. You are now at where the gypsy wagon used to be. It isn't there now. Look around. Take the tambourine they've left behind. (If you had tried the *old-edge-of-the-screen* trick and returned to this screen right after leaving Madame Mushka, the wagon would have still been there. The gypsies don't leave until Graham gives the brass bottle to the witch.)

Walk east one screen back to where you returned the heart to the Weeping Willow. Walk south one screen. Look around; you are in front of a gnome's house. This is one of the places where the *old edge-of-the-screen trick* works in this game. If the gnome and his grandson are not there, leave the screen and return. Repeat until successful. Look at the gnome. Look at his grandson. Talk to the gnome, then give the spinning wheel to the gnome—Oh! It's that gnome! Anyway, the gnome will give Graham a marionette in return for the spinning wheel.

Walk south one screen; you are at the Inn with the haystack. Search the haystack. Since Graham helped the ants earlier, they will help him now and give Graham the needle (what else?) in the haystack.

The next sequence happens quickly, so go to Graham's **Inventory** screen and select the old shoe—not the nice ones which the elf gave him. Have it ready. Switch to the **Walk** icon, and follow the path east to the bakehouse. At some point in this screen, you will see a rat being chased down the path by a cat. Immediatly—as soon as you see it happening—switch to the **Ready** icon and throw the old boot at the cat.

(Actually, the rat/cat sequence will happen the first time you enter this screen *after* you have left the desert with the boot. So, if you wish, you can have this encounter any time after you have the boot. But, you only get one chance at doing it properly. If you waste it, you can't complete the game. This is why we saved the game prior to this scene.)

Now it's time to return to town; it's two screens east. I'll meet you inside.

Welcome again to fabulous downtown Serenia. If you remember from the last time we were here, there had been a man repairing his cart here. He's gone now, but there's something barely glinting in the street near where he had been. Look at it. Take the silver coin. (By the way, if we had immediately returned to town after we had left the first time, the coin would have been there then. It appears in the game the second time Graham enters the town.)

Most towns contain shops, and there are three in town that we must visit, and you may do so in any order. Look at the various buildings.

The shop nearest to where the man was fixing his cart is the Tailor shop. Enter the shop. Look around at the various people and things. Look at the cloak on the tailor's form. Talk to the tailor. Give the golden needle to the tailor, and get the cloak. Leave the Tailor shop.

The Easy Way Out

East of the tailor is the Toyshop. Enter the Toyshop. Look around at the people and things. Look at the sled on the wall. Talk to the toymaker. Give the marionette to the toymaker, and get the sled. Leave the shop.

There is a small Shoeshop at the far eastern part of town. Go inside the Shoeshop. Look around. Pet the dog. Talk to the shoemaker. Give the shoes—not the boot!—to the shoemaker, and get the cobbler's hammer. Leave the shop. Leave the town. We are now finished with the town of Serenia. Save the game.

After leaving Serenia, walk west one screen to the bakehouse. Enter the bakehouse. Look around at the people and pies. Talk to the baker. Give the silver coin to the baker, and get a custard pie. Leave the bakehouse.

Walk west one screen to the Inn. Save the game. Enter the Inn. Look around at the people, etc., in the bar. If Graham walks up to them, or talks to them, they will beat him, tie him up, and imprison him in the Inn's cellar. If he tries to walk through the bar, they will beat him up. Sorry, things are tough all over—talk to the men and suffer the consquences.

Graham recovers and finds himself tied up securely, with no way to escape. If Graham's saved the rat from the cat, it will arrive and free him. Look around. Take the rope. Walk up the stairs to the door. Look at the door; it's locked. Hit the door with the hammer, it will break the latch. Leave the cellar.

You are back in the Inn's kitchen. The Inn's bar is to the east. You don't want to go in there. Look around. Go to the cupboard at the top of the screen. Look at the cupboard. Open the cupboard and look inside. Take the leg of lamb. Exit the Inn through the door on the west side of the screen. (If Graham returns east to the bar, the Innkeeper and his toughs will become quite annoyed that he has escaped the cellar. Graham will be killed this time. This is not something you would like Graham to do.)

From the Inn, walk east to outside of town; then north another screen. We are in the area one screen south of Crispin's house. We are now finished in Serenia.

The mountains:

You are in the screen immediately south of Crispin's house. There is a path going east. Look around; there is a snake on the path. Look at the snake. Shake the tambourine. Walk east.

You are on a mountain trail. Wear the cloak—without it Graham will soon die from the cold. Walk east. Look around. You are on a path in the mountains, and a frozen waterfall has washed out the trail.

If Graham in not wearing the cloak, do so now. Graham will also start becoming hungry here. He can eat either the custard pie or the leg of lamb. Eat the lamb. (If Graham eats the pie, the game cannot be finished. When he eats the lamb, he will only munch on half of it, leaving the rest for later.)

Look around above Graham. There are both a tree branch and a rock overhang. Click the rope on the overhang—it's the one away from the branch. Graham will throw the rope up, and it will catch.

Walk to the rope and climb it to the upper ledge. (The rope will also catch on the tree branch, but the branch will break as Graham nears the top of his climb. Death follows.)

You are now on a higher path through the mountains. Look around. Another frozen waterfall has washed out the trail which heads east. Look at the waterfall, the log, and the rock "steps". Save the game.

The only way across is to jump from rock to rock (by clicking the **Hand** icon on the desired landing place), and then crossing the log. However, certain of the rock "steps" can, or will, collapse under Graham's weight and kill him. The rocks closest to the top of the screen are all stable. The three rocks closest to the bottom of the screen work as follows:

The farthest left (west)—collapses 50% of the time

The middle—always collapses

411
The Easy Way Out

The farthest right (east)—never collapses if Cedric is with Graham. It always collapses if Cedric has been captured by the wolves, and Graham tries to cross back over the rocks.

That's it. Jump Graham across on the upper rocks, then to the rock farthest east on the bottom row, and then to solid ground by the log.

Once again on solid ground, save the game. Set the game to a slower speed and carefully walk Graham across the log. Save the game, and continue east. You are now nearing the end of the level path. It ends abruptly, and you can see it sloping down near the center of the screen.

When Graham and Cedric first enter this area, they will be ambushed by a wolf. Cedric will be carried off, leaving Graham by himself. Walk to near where the path starts down. Don't try and walk down the path or Graham will tumble down. Look around.

And now for an important message...
Once Graham starts the coming sled ride, he cannot return back to retrace his steps. Since this is a one-way trip, make sure you have the following items: Crispin's wand, the tambourine, the remaining lamb, the custard pie, the beeswax that was left-over from the honeycomb, the cobbler's hammer, and the harp. You will need them all to finish the game. From here on, there is no turning back.

We now return you back to King's Quest 5: Absence Makes the Heart Go Yonder....

Click the sled on Graham or on the ground near the slope. Graham will then embark on a wild ride down the path. It will end with a crashed sled, but a live Graham.

If Graham tumbled down the slope, he will find himself on the north side of a thin ice bridge crossing a crevasse. If Graham attempts to cross the bridge on foot, it will crack, and he will fall to his death. It is too wide to jump. All Graham can do at this point is climb back up to the beginning of the sled run and use the sled.

You are at the end of the sled run. Look around. Do not attempt to cross the ice bridge. Walk east.

You are on a narrow path through the mountains. In the distance to the north you can see the outlines of a castle. Look around. Look at the eagle. Talk to the eagle. Give the remaining lamb to the eagle. (The eagle will also take the pie, but that will prevent you from finishing the game. The same fate will befall you if you do not feed the poor bird). Save the game. Follow the path north, and watch Graham get captured by wolves.

Now begins an animated sequence in which Graham is brought before Queen Icebella. As soon as the Queen tells her wolves to take Graham and Cedric away to be executed, game control will be briefly returned to you. Play the harp at once. This will mollify queenie somewhat. After more plot and animation, you will find Graham back on a narrow path in the mountains. Look around, there is a cave in the distance. Look at the wolf. Talk to the wolf. He will prevent Graham from going anywhere except toward the cave. Follow the path northeast towards the cave. Save the game, and leave the screen.

You are now at the entrance to the Yeti's cave. This is another place where the *old edge of the screen trick* doesn't work. A Yeti will come after Graham as he moves nearer the cave entrance. It will come from the right side of the screen—the east. If you attempt to escape Yeti by running away back down the path, Graham will be followed until he is caught. Yeti will catch him if he tries to escape north into the cave. There are no other ways out of the screen. Oh—never, ever, try to hold a conversation with an Abominable Snowman or woman. If the Yeti catches him, Graham will be killed.

Click the custard pie on the monster, and Graham will throw the pie in its face. You and Graham are now rid of the Yeti.

Look around. Enter the cave to the north. Look around—nice crystals. Look at the various clumps of crystals, especially the clump near the center of the screen. Click the hammer on the clump with the "particularly brilliant crystal" that catches Graham's attention—it's about in the center of the screen, so keep looking. He'll take it. Exit the screen to the south, and continue on the path until you return to the waiting wolf.

An animated sequence follows: Graham is returned to the Ice Queen, and reunited with Cedric. When the sequence is over, Graham and Cedric will find themselves on the mountain path with instructions to journey south. Save the game. Walk south.

South leads to a screen with a narrow path which climbs upwards. It is confusing at first, and slippery. Look around. Climb Graham slowly and carefully up the slope toward the east—Graham can easily fall and die here. As Graham nears the end of the path, a great bird—a Roc—will swoop in and carry him off in his claws.

Graham is deposited in the Roc's nest. Look around, you will notice the egg beginning to crack. Soon, a baby Roc will hatch. This sequence, like the sequence inside the desert temple, is timed. Once Graham is in the nest, he needs to find the locket before the eagle rescues him. Look at the nest. Search the nest. Take the locket. Look around some more until the Roc begins hatching. If Graham fed the lamb to the eagle, the grateful bird will now arrive and save him from being the baby's first meal. If not, end of game.

The eagle flys Graham far away—to a trail that leads down to a beach. Look around. Follow the path to the beach. Look some more at the bottom of the path; you will notice an object. Look at it. Take the iron bar.

Note: Not surprisingly, there is an ocean by this beach and the beaches to the north and south of it. Graham can walk into the ocean, but if he tries to swim, he'll die.

Walk south. Look around. Look at the house. Look at the bell. Ring the bell. When the hermit comes out, look at the man. Talk to him. Walk north two screens.

Graham is in a beach area with a waterfall and a boat. Look around. Look at the boat. Stand Graham right next to the boat and look again—look into the boat, as it were. Click the beeswax into the boat to plug the hole—if you don't the boat will sink after you get a short way into the ocean. After Graham plugs the hole, click the **Hand** icon on the boat. Graham will push the boat into the ocean and then jump aboard. It's time to go sailing.

The main part of the ocean is a 4 screen by 4 screen square. It's dotted with rocky islets. These islets should be avoided. Harpies Island is in this section of ocean, and we're trying to get there. However, this part of the ocean is surrounded by an endless expanse of open seas inhabited by sea serpents. It is not advisable to sail there. With that in mind, let's continue.

From the screen where the boat leaves the beach, sail one screen east, then one screen south. You are now due east of the area where the path reaches the beach—the middle beach screen. From here, sail due east. Harpies Island will be sighted in three screens. Look at the island. Sail right up to the bay. As Graham lands the boat, he and Cedric will be attacked by harpies and carried off.

An animated sequence commences, and soon you will see close-up shots of the harpies arguing over who will eat Graham. When the perspective changes to a wider view of the clearing, the game's control is return for short time to the player. Play the harp. If you care to listen to the conversation for a bit, fine. But, when the harpies begin to say, "I am not!" "You are too!", make sure Graham plays the harp at once. They'll say this twice in succession. Then they eat Graham.

After the harp is played, the harpies will take it and leave. Graham is now free to explore the island. Be careful that Graham doesn't fall to his death. Look around the clearing, and take the fishhook you find in the grass. Walk west one screen.

You are on a path on the island. Look around. Look at Cedric. Talk to Cedric. Pick up Cedric. Walk west one screen.

You are at the beach on Harpies Island. Look around. Look at the beach. Look at the conch shell, then take it. Put Cedric into the boat. Click on the boat in order to have Graham push it off the beach and leave. We are now done with Harpies Island. (If for some reason you forgot the fishhook and must return to the island, there's a very good chance the harpies will be waiting for Graham. If he meets them then, he's dead meat—literally. However, the harpies will never appear in the middle screen—the one where Graham found Cedric—so there is safety there).

Sail due west from the island, until you return to the beach. Walk to the hermit's house. Ring the bell. When the hermit comes out, click the conch shell on him. He can now hear Graham, and an animated sequence will begin. When it's over, Graham and Cedric will be shipwrecked on Mordack's Island.

The Wizard's Island:

You are on the beach on Wizard's Island. Look around at the various sights. Take the dead fish. Follow the steps to the next screen. Stop at once after the screen changes.

You are on the path to Mordack's castle. Look around. Look at the castle. Look at the cobra-dragon statues. Save the game. Walk Graham closer to the statues, but not up to or between them. The statues will fry Graham if he gets too close. Click the crystal on Graham or the cobras, and he will hold it up. Beams will zap from the snakes eyes and reflect back at them from the crystal. Continue to follow the path straight toward the castle. Make sure Graham does not fall off the path. When the scene changes, look around.

Graham is now near the front gate of the castle. Look at the door, the castle, the chasm, and the small stairway on the left. Follow the stairs and path around the west side of the castle. Don't fall.

The scene changes to an area next to the castle. Look around. Look at the grate. Click the iron bar on the grate, and Graham will be able to move it. Click the **Hand** icon on the grate and Graham will be able to enter. If Graham has gone this far and does not have the iron bar in his possession, Mordack's henchman will appear and imprison him in a dungeon cell. Graham will die there, ending the game.

The Wizard's maze:

Graham is now in the wizard's maze. Here are some things you should know before you start:

- Somewhere in the maze Graham will meet a creature, Dink. In fact, Graham must encounter Dink in order to leave the maze at all. There are four places where Dink can appear. *If the exit door is reached before the Dink encounter, you'll have to go back until you find him.* When Graham does run across Dink, play the tambourine, or suffer the consequences. When Dink leaves, look around. Take the hairpin.

- There are four places in the maze where Dink can appear. He will only be in one of these, however. When Graham enters the maze, the game program will determine which square of the maze that will be. It is up to the player to discover which one it is.

*417
The Easy Way Out*

- The maze is 8 screens by 8 screens in extent, with solid walls bordering it, and passages throughout. This totals 64 different possible locations. There are several dead ends and a dungeon cell, although you will never see the cell when you enter the maze from the outside world. There is only one exit.

- The maze is seen from Graham's perspective. If he, for example, is facing north and exits the screen to the left (west), the next screen will have him one screen west (as you would expect). However: *the top of the screen in the maze is Graham's view of straight ahead—it is not necessarily north.* It can be any direction in the maze. In this hypothetical case, it's west—the way he hypothetically exited the first screen. Since we are accustomed to the top of the screen always being north, this change of perspective is confusing at first. You do get used to it after a bit of futzing around. Save the game in the maze's first screen, and be assured you can always restore to there if you get lost. *When Graham arrives in the maze, north is at the top of the screen. But do not assume the top of the screen is always north in the maze—it's not!*

- There is a complete map of the maze at the end of this chapter.

How to Map the Maze:

Good maps are essential for navigation through any maze. If you want to make your own, and try the maze without any more help, here's a suggestion to get you started.

Think of the maze as a big square made up of a lot of smaller squares. Draw a 8 by 8 grid on a piece of paper, or get some graphing paper and mark off an 8 by 8 area. Make the top of the grid north, the bottom south and the sides, east and west. From the bottom left corner of the map, write the numbers 0 through 7 next to the squares going north, and the squares going east—one number next to each square in sequence. Now each square has a numbered location—the bottom left corner square is location 0-north by 0-east (0,0 for short). The top right corner square is 7-north by 7-east (7,7). The lower right corner square is 0-north by 7-east (0,7). The top left corner is 7-north by 0-east (7,0), and all the other squares can be numbered and identified in the same manner.

Each time you move to another screen, mark it somehow. If there is a wall blocking Graham, fill in that square to indicate that it's solid. If it's just dungeon floor, put a light dot in the squre to indicate that you've already been there—just in case you get lost. In this manner, you should always know exactly where Graham is. Keep exploring and filling in your map until Graham escapes.

Graham enters the maze at 3-north and 2-east (3,2). Mark it on your map. There is solid wall to the east, and Graham is facing north. Good luck, and remember to pay attention to which direction Graham is walking.

IF YOU WOULD PREFER TO MAP THE MAZE YOURSELF: The rest is up to you. Skip the next few paragraphs, and we'll join you later.

FOR THOSE OF US WHO ARE USING MY MAPS: The maze is a straightforward proposition. Turn to the maze maps at the end of this chapter.

IF YOU JUST WANT A HINT AS TO WHERE THE EXIT IS: It is in the maze's north wall.

Inside Mordack's Castle:

FOR THOSE OF YOU WHO HAVE BEEN MAZE-CRAWLING ON YOUR OWN, WELCOME BACK!

419
The Easy Way Out

Graham is facing a door in the maze wall. Look at the door. Click the hairpin on the door, and Graham will pick the lock. Open the door and walk through to the next screen.

Graham is now in the castle's pantry and supply room. Look around. Look at the cupboard on the left side of the screen. Open the cupboard. Take the bag of peas. Exit the room at the top of the screen.

Another note: from here on out, when Graham enters a room in the castle, there is a chance that he will see a cat. This is Manannan. If Graham sees the cat, the cat sees him. If Manannan sees Graham, Mordack will arrive shortly and kill our hero—no matter where Graham is at the time. Graham cannot escape if he encounters Manannan. Therefore it is a good idea—no, a *great* idea—to save the game just before you leave each room hereafter. Have two different save positions and alternate them, just in case you do something dumb and then save. The *old-edge-of-the-screen trick* does not work with Manannan. In every case but one, we must avoid the cat. Later, we will catch him.

Graham is now in the kitchen. Look around. Look at the woman. Go to her. Talk to the woman. Give the locket to the woman. This starts another animated bit. When it's finished, talk to Cassima again. When she goes back to her work, save the game and leave the room through the door to the east. *Don't forget to save*—in case of cat, and the next obstacle.

Things are now about to get a little more sticky. Graham is in the downstairs area of the castle. Mordack's henchman roams randomly through the rooms downstairs, and will follow and capture Graham. This is something we want to have happen—one time only. Nonetheless, we'd like to explore a little more. So, besides watching out for Manannan, look out for this guy, and restore your game back to the last room if he shows up. Keep trying until he isn't there.

We are now in a hallway. Look around. Look at the organ. Do not play the organ. Save the game before you leave the room. Continue east to the next screen.

This is the dining room. Look around. Save. Exit to the south—more dining room. Look around. Save. Walk west to the next room.

Graham is now in the catle's main entry. Look around at things—you are going to have to make your way back here later. There are stairs leading up. Look at them. Do not climb them at this time. Look around; Mordack sure has interesting ideas about interior decoration. Avoiding the cat, sightsee through the downstairs until the henchman arrives and Graham is captured. He will be taken through a magic door.

Graham finds himself imprisoned in a small cell. Look around. Look in the mouse hole. Click the fishhook on the mouse hole, and Graham will be able to take the piece of cheese hidden in the hole. Graham should get the cheese as quickly as possible. Wait a few moments for Princess Cassima to arrive to free you from the cell; she will not save you if you haven't given her the locket. If this is the case, you can't finish the game.

Quickly follow Cassima out of the cell by clicking the **Hand** icon on the hole. Once outside the cell, Graham is in the maze again, on the bottom level. Cassima will lead him out of the maze—thank you, Sierra, for small favors! Of course, if you don't follow her outside, or return to the cell, she'll leave without Graham. In that case, you and Graham will have to solve the wizard's maze a second time.

Out of the maze, using the cautions we've advised, avoid Manannan, and get Graham back to the main entry. When the henchman appears, click the bag of peas on him, and Graham will throw the peas. The hanchman will slip on them and knock himself out. You now have an empty pea bag, and the henchman will soon awaken.

Now we can deal with that darn cat. Once the henchman is taken care of, we want Manannan to show up. Keep walking and saving around until he does. When the cat shows up, click the dead fish on Manannan. Click the empty pea bag on the cat. You have now bagged Manannan. Continue on until you reach the stairs in the entry. Save the game. Climb the stairs.

(You can win the game without catching Manannan, but you won't score all of the points. In the unlikely event that the henchman doesn't discover Graham by the time he's climbed the stairs, forget him. He's no longer a factor in the game, and the henchman will never appear upstairs. If the henchman doesn't appear until Graham is in the room at the bottom of the stairs, Graham can escape him by going upstairs. Of course you won't score the points for tripping him—or bagging Manannan for that matter. And, if this is the case, you've got to keep watching out for the cat. It is much better to take care of Manannan and the henchman before heading up.)

Upstairs at Mordack's:

If you haven't bagged Manannan, you are still avoiding him in every room.

Graham is now in the upstairs hallway. Look around. Mordack's laboratory is through the doorway to the east. His bedroom is to the west. Save the game. Walk through the western doorway.

This is Mordack's bedroom. If he is there, awake or asleep, use the *old-edge-of-the-screen trick* and attempt to avoid him. If not, restore and try again.

Once Graham enters Mordack's bedroom—while Mordack or Manannan isn't there—he has only a brief period of time to do what he must. Look around. Quickly walk south and exit the screen to the south.

Graham is now in Mordack's library. Look around. Go to the table with the large book. Look at the book. Open the book, and Graham will begin to read it—these are the spells he will need in the coming magical battle. Don't spend too long reading the book. Look through the doorway to Mordack's bedroom. If he isn't sleeping in the bed, wait. Shortly, you will see him enter his bedroom and go to sleep. He will not see Graham if Graham is in the library. Save the game.

Enter Mordack's bedroom. Go to the table by the bed and take Mordack's wand. Leave the bedroom and walk east directly to Mordack's laboratory.

Graham has about 2 minutes from the time Mordack goes to sleep until the time Mordack discovers him in his lab. Use the time efficiently.

Inside the lab, look around. Look at the bottle with the castle inside it. Walk upstairs and go the strange machine on the right side of the balcony. This is a Power-Transfer Machine. Look at the machine. Click Mordack's wand on the left side of the machine, and it will be put on a platter there. Click Crispin's wand on the right side of the machine, and it will be put on the other platter (you did know that it would be needed eventually, didn't you?). Nothing happens. Now that both wands have been placed on the machine, click the cheese on the machine's fuel pot in the lower part of the contraption. Graham has now activated the Power-Transfer Machine.

A message will appear saying that Crispin's wand is now energized. Take Crispin's wand—the glowing one near Graham—at once. Within seconds, Mordack will appear and attack Graham. The final battle has begun.

There is a short animated sequence where Cedric saves Graham. Of course, if Graham had never carried Cedric back from Harpies Island for the hermit to heal, Graham would lose very quickly at this point. The game is returned to player control when Mordack flies up to attack Graham.

Mordack has now transformed himself magically, and Graham must counter with the spells he read in Mordack's library.

First, Mordack transforms himself into a flying "Sting"—a sort of monstrous insect. As soon as this happens, quickly select Crispin's wand in your inventory bag. You will now see the list of icons from Mordack's book of

The Easy Way Out

magic. Use Crispin's wand to select the TIGER spell. This turns Graham into a tiger.

Next, Mordack will transform into a Fire Dragon. Select the wand again and use it to choose the RABBIT spell for Graham.

Mordack's third spell turns him into a cobra. Graham must counter by selecting the MONGOOSE transformation.

Finally, Mordack becomes a ring of fire. Graham should conjure RAIN.

The Rain spell extinguishes the fire, and Mordack is destroyed. Graham has triumphed. The rest of the game runs on automatic pilot.

Congratulations! You have completed King's Quest 5: Absence Makes the Heart Go Yonder.

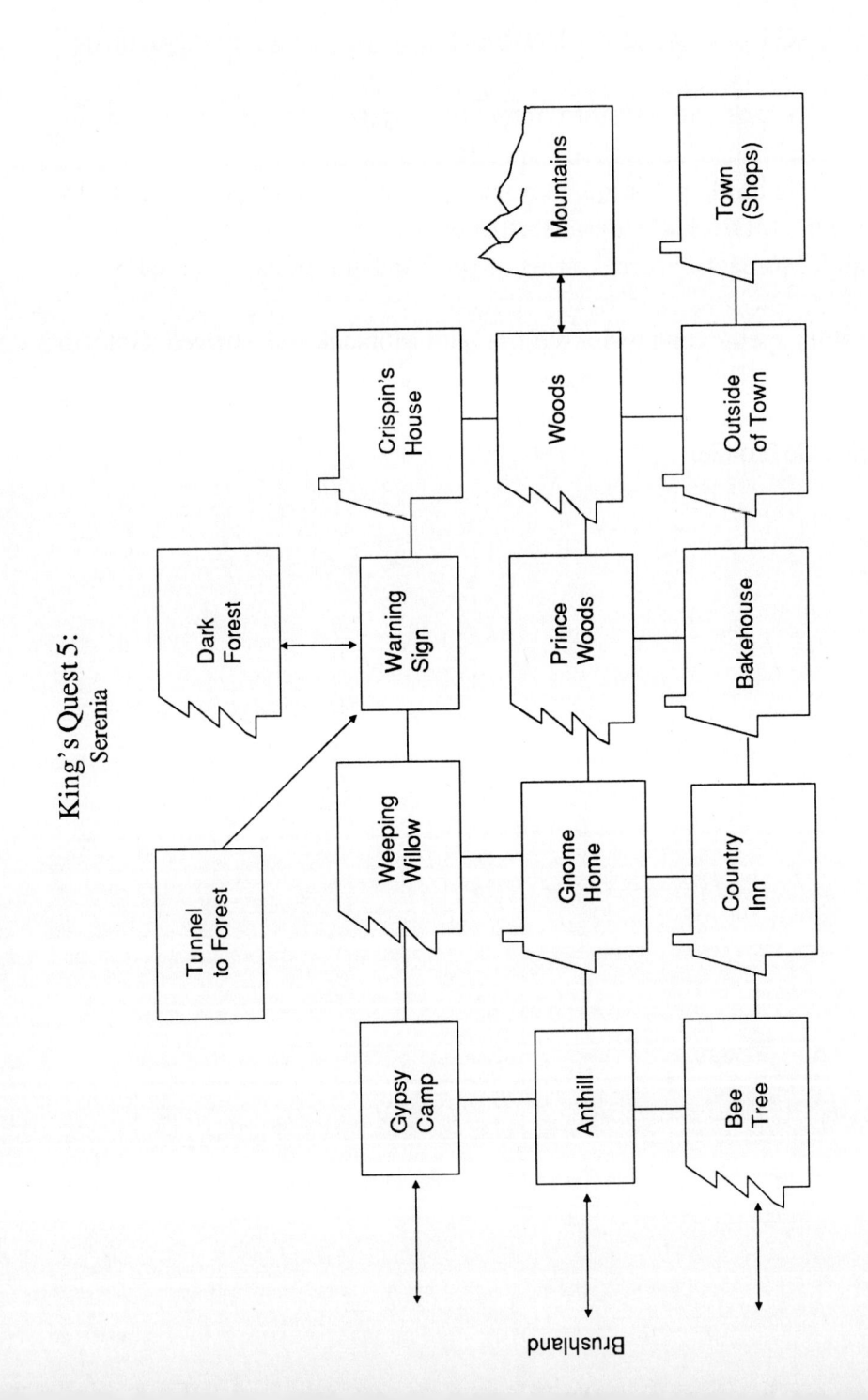

424
King's Quest

King's Quest 5:
Serenia

[Map diagram showing locations in Serenia: Mountains, Town (Shops), Crispin's House, Woods, Outside of Town, Dark Forest, Warning Sign, Prince Woods, Bakehouse, Tunnel to Forest, Weeping Willow, Gnome Home, Country Inn, Gypsy Camp, Anthill, Bee Tree, Brushland]

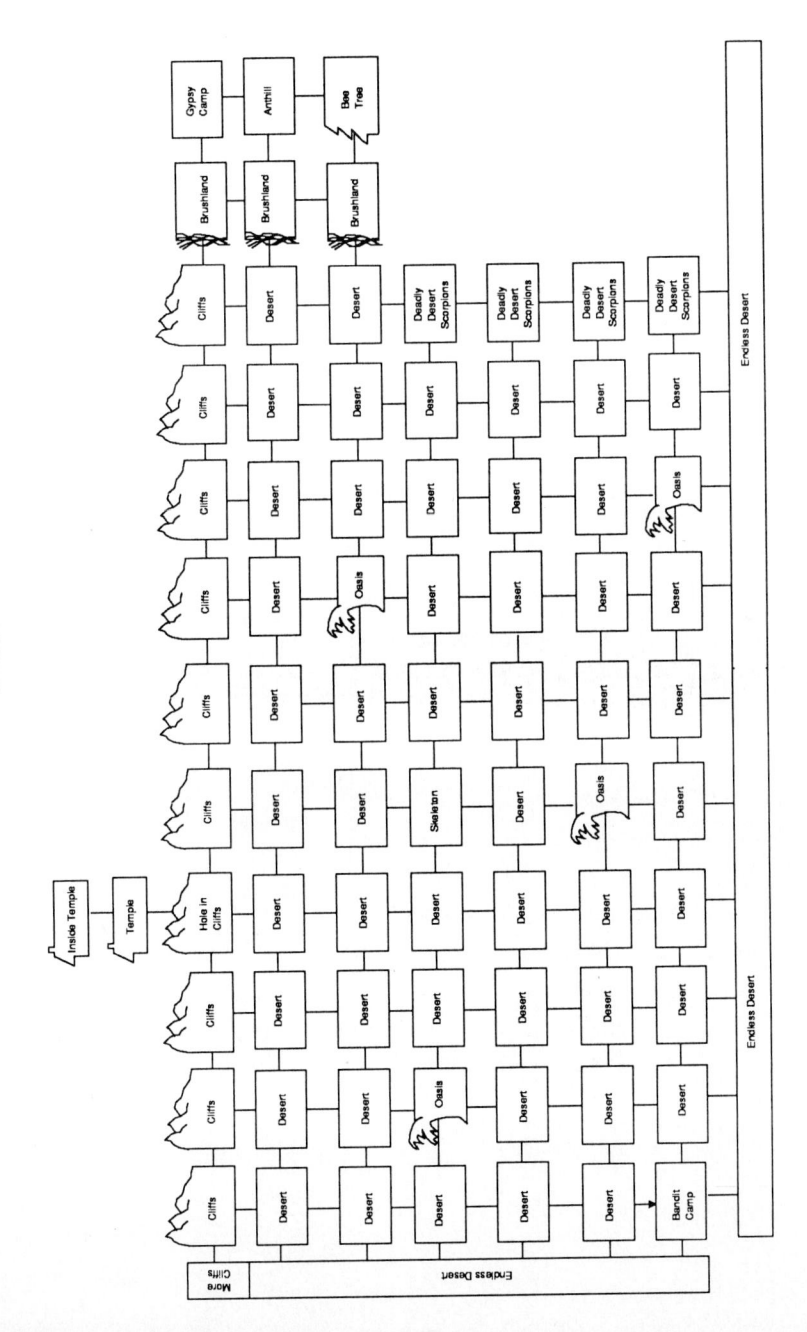

The Easy Way Out

King's Quest 5: Desert

426
King's Quest

King's Quest 5:
Dark Forest

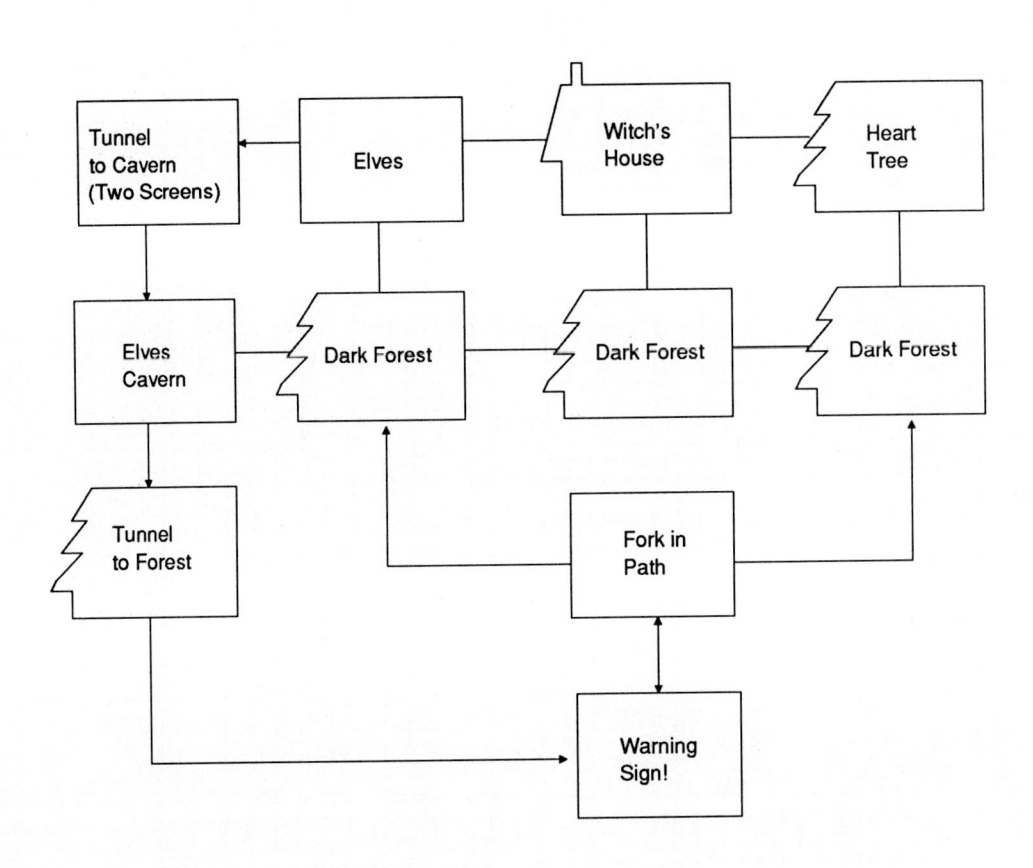

```
[Tunnel to Cavern    [Elves]  ←  [Witch's House]  →  [Heart Tree]
 (Two Screens)]  ←
        ↓              |              |                  |
[Elves Cavern] — [Dark Forest] — [Dark Forest] — [Dark Forest]
        ↓                ↑                              ↑
[Tunnel to Forest]       |         [Fork in Path] ──────┘
        |                └─────────────┤
        |                              ↕
        └──────────────────→  [Warning Sign!]
```

427
The Easy Way Out

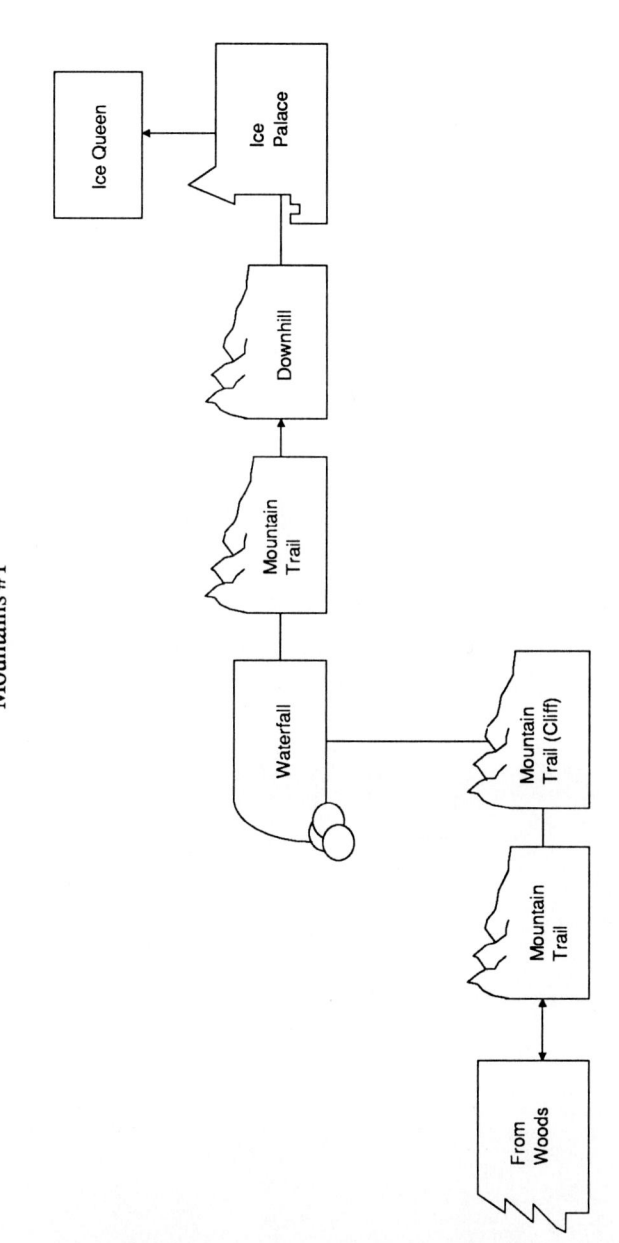

King's Quest 5:
Mountains #1

428
King's Quest

King's Quest 5:
Mountains #2

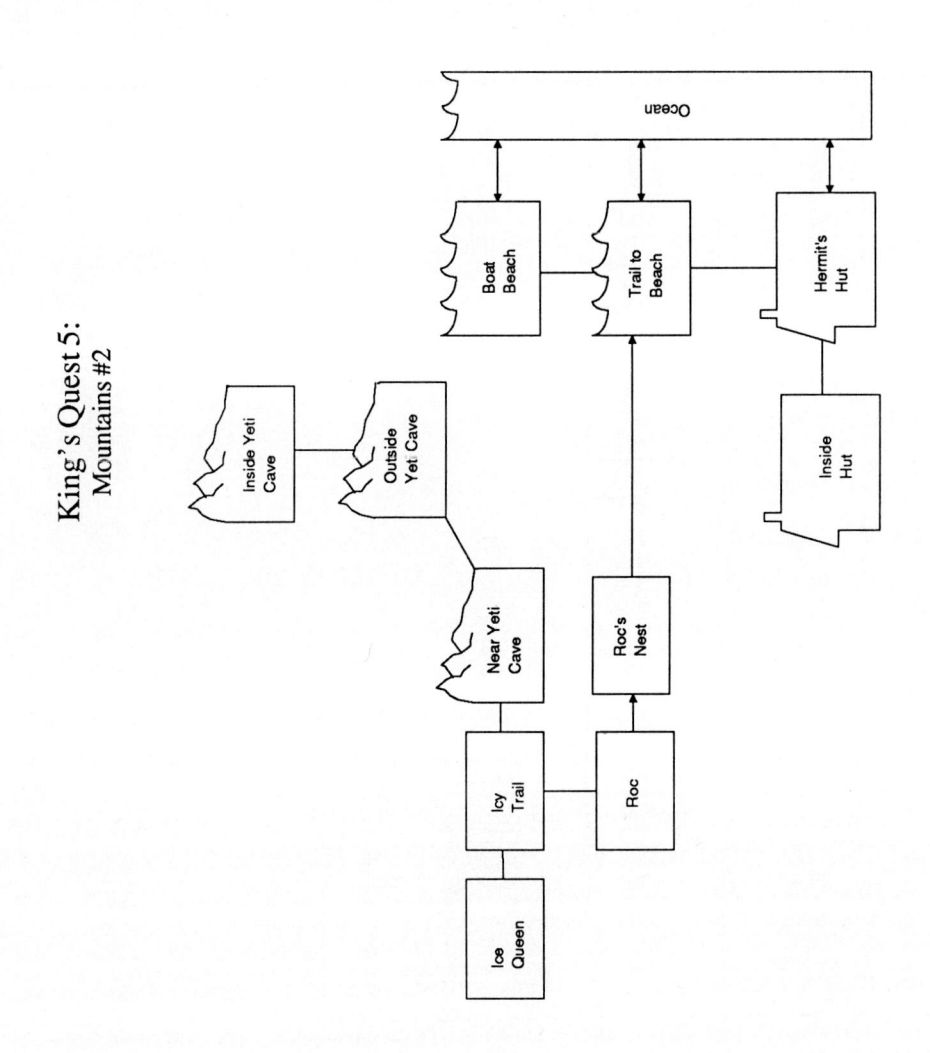

The Easy Way Out

King's Quest 5: Ocean

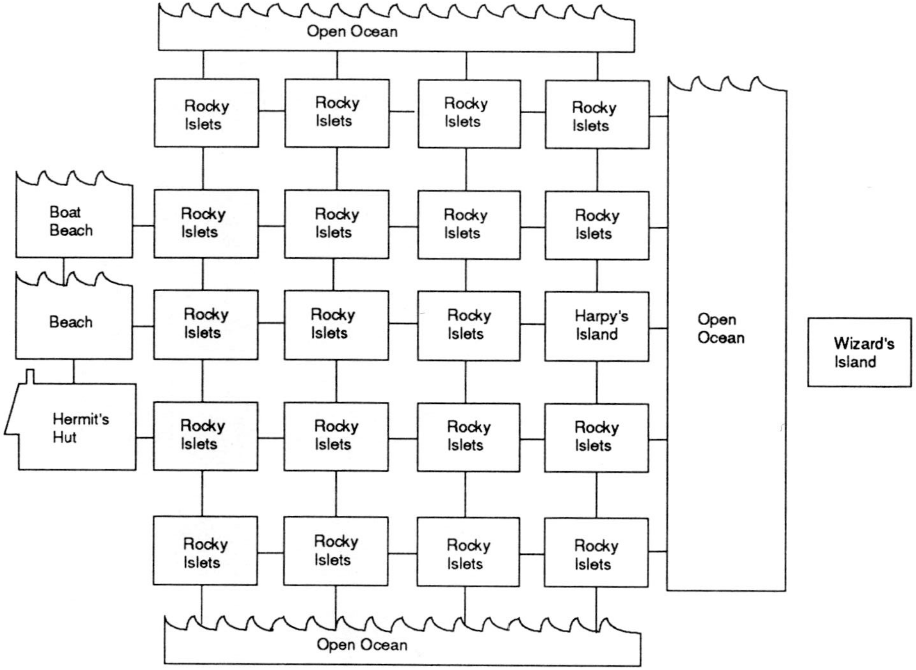

King's Quest 5:
Harpy's Island

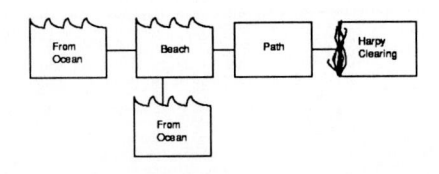

[From Ocean] — [Beach] — [Path] — [Harpy Clearing]

[From Ocean] (below Beach)

King's Quest 5:
Wizard's Island

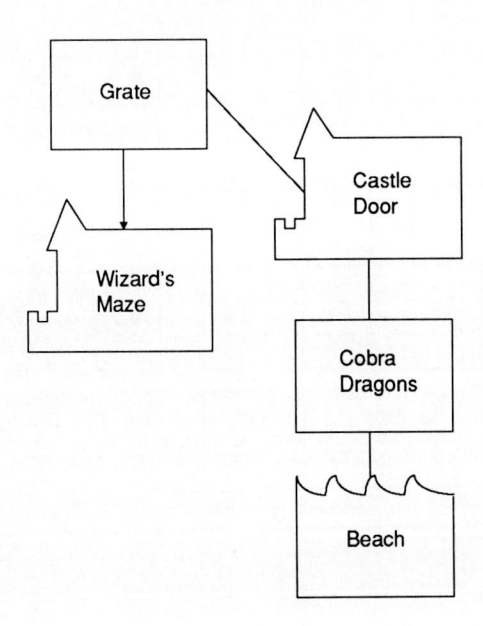

[Grate] → [Wizard's Maze]

[Grate] — [Castle Door] — [Cobra Dragons] — [Beach]

431
The Easy Way Out

King's Quest 5:
Wizard's Maze

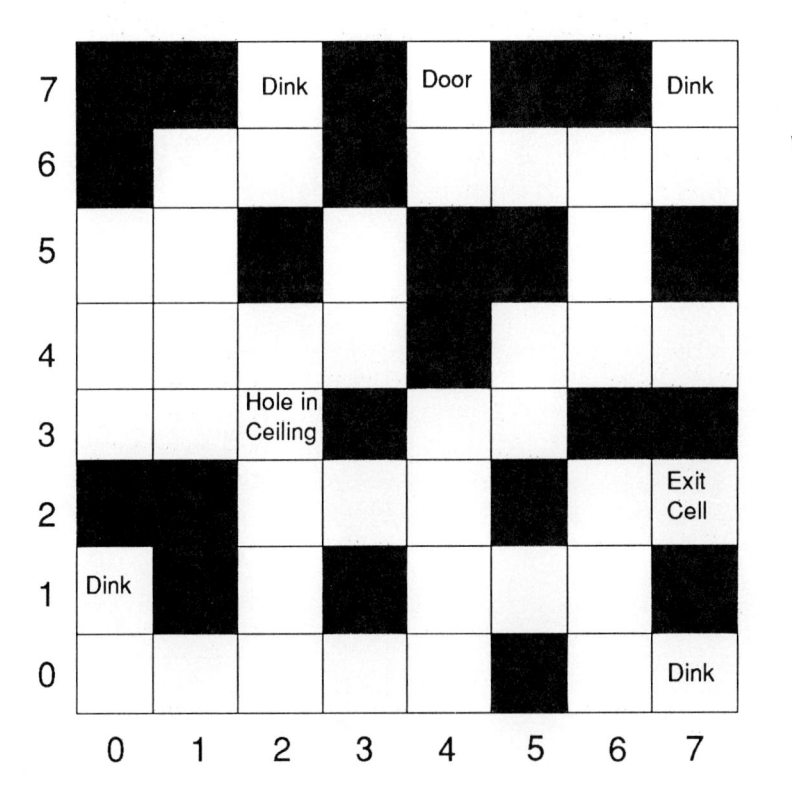

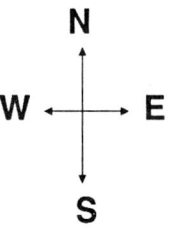

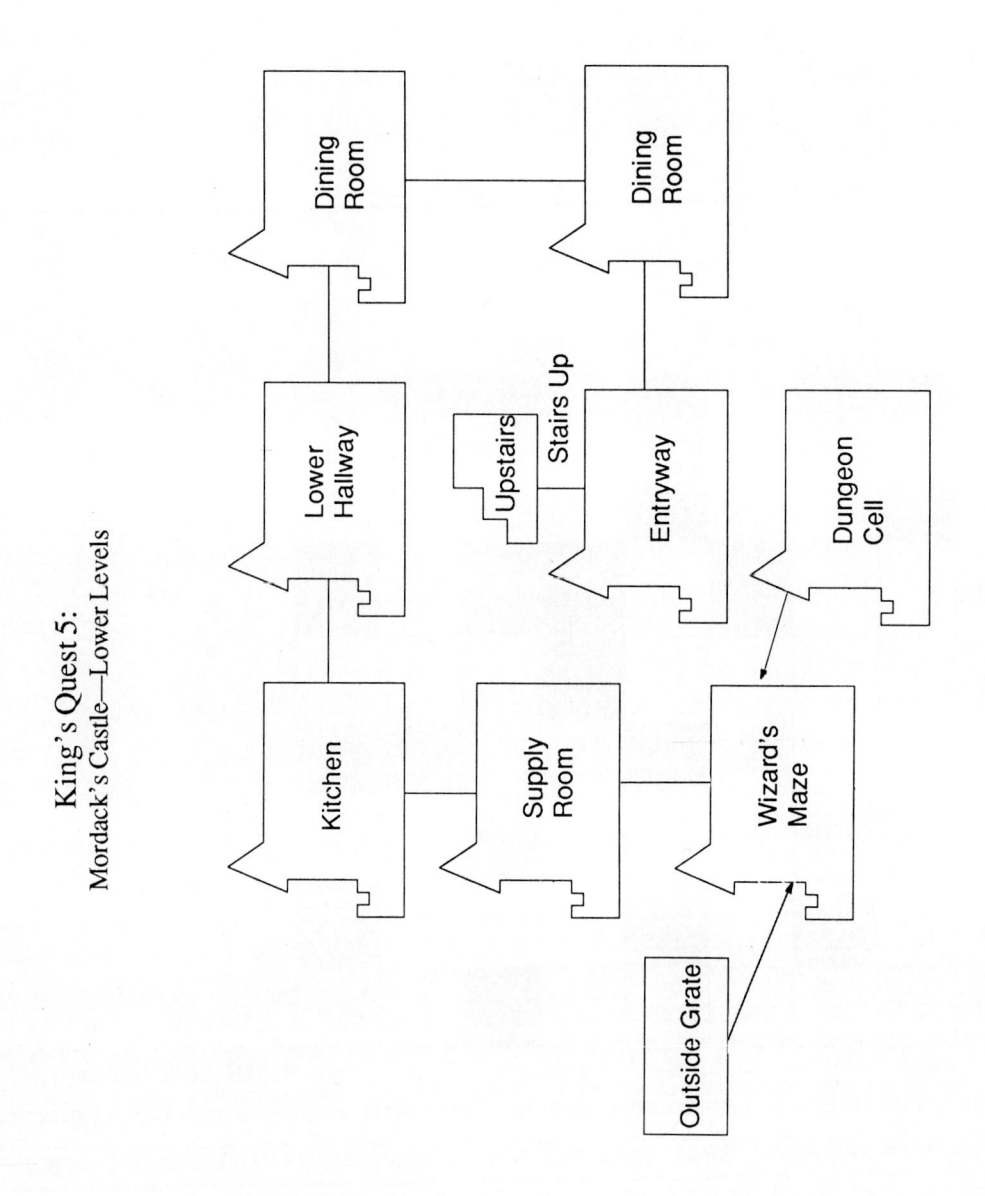

King's Quest 5:
Mordack's Castle—Lower Levels

433
The Easy Way Out

King's Quest 5:
Mordack's Castle—Upstairs

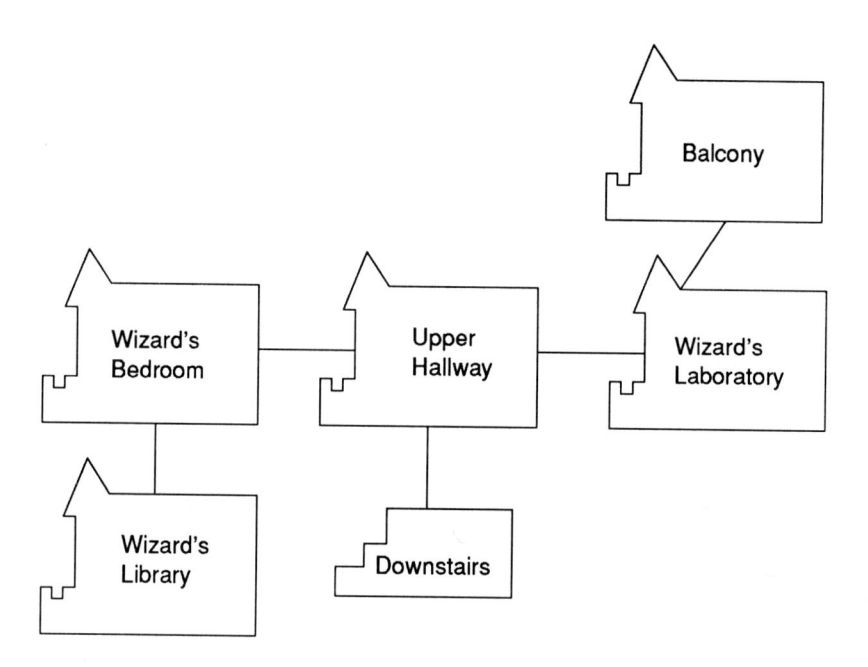

- Balcony
- Wizard's Bedroom
- Upper Hallway
- Wizard's Laboratory
- Wizard's Library
- Downstairs

12

An Encyclopedia Of Daventry

(Abridged)

There are, of course, many close and startling similarities between what is related in the King's Quest computer games and what has been passed down in our universe as folk tales, myth, fiction, and fairy stories. What follows has been compiled from many different sources, and is not by any means the last word on the subject. I leave that task to the scientists and scholars who, I hope, will explore the truth of the universe of Daventry and its inhabitants further.

Included here also is more information culled from the many communications sent to me by Derek Karlavaegen. From them I have taken mostly bits of biography to provide a little background on many of the people, both good and evil, who have crossed paths with King Graham and his family. All together, what follows in this chapter provides many unique insights into the universe of Daventry and its denizens.

I have not, however, reprinted everything that has been sent from Daventry by Derek. Some of what he relates bears no direct relationship to the Daventry we know of in the King's Quest games. Some does though, and I am as curious as anyone to see if any of those tales turn up in other adventures. If it does, then it would be final proof to me that what I have been receiving on my computer screen really is true—it would be my final proof that Derek and Daventry are real.

I'd sure like to see that happen.

An Encyclopedia of Daventry

Abominable Snowman (KQ3, KQ5) Also known as Yeti, this is a tall, hair-covered, human-like creature that is said to inhabit remote parts of the high Himalaya mountains. Long thought to be legend, some scientists feel that it might possibly exist. Many footprints allegedly made by the creature have been found and photographed, and some fuzzy photos of the beast itself are said to exist. A creature similar to Yeti is also said to exist in parts of Siberia, and Bigfoot is yet another similar creature. Many say Bigfoot roams the forests of North America, but it lives at a lower altitude, and in a much more temperate climate.

Derek writes that Yetis are not at all uncommon in the higher elevations of the great mountains of Daventry. The fact that there are records of Graham and Alexander encountering these creatures in their journeys would tend to support this assertion. Yetis are said to live solitary lives until they mate, at which time the the male and female of the species stay together until death. They make their Daventry homes in deep caves that they ferociously guard from all intruders.

Alexander (KQ3, KQ4, KQ5) Prince of Daventry. Alexander is the son of King Graham and Queen Valanice, and the twin brother of Princess Rosella. As an infant he was kidnapped out of his cradle by the wizard Manannan. His parents had taken the babies and some friends on a summer outing on Lake Maylie. Manannan evidently put some kind of a brief spell on the assemblage; one moment Alexander was there, the next he was gone, though the cradle still rocked.

Manannan kept Alexander as a slave, intending to kill him on his eighteenth birthday. He did teach the prince to read and write, but he never revealed Alexander's true identity. The prince only knew himself as Gwydion, until he escaped and returned home to Daventry. To this day he still thinks of himself as Gwydion, although he does acknowledge and use Alexander. Sometimes he signs himself "Alexander-Gwydion."

Prince Alexander was able to escape by learning magic and turning his captor into a cat. He has since studied the theory and practice of that craft, and is considered one of Daventry's leading scholars and practitioners of magic.

However, in an effort to protect Daventry from the ravages of two evil sorcerers, Alexander "played dumb" (as we might say) when Mordack demanded he magically return Manannan to his human form. Mordack knew better than to believe Alexander whose continuing magical accomplishments had made him quite well-known by that time.

Amber (KQ3) While thought of by many people as a stone, amber is really fossilized resin—tree sap—of stone-like appearance and texture. Its color is yellow to yellowish-brown, and pieces of amber can date back as much as 60 million years. Sometimes drops of water or perfectly preserved insects or bits of plants are found encased in the bits of amber. Amber is used to make jewelry and other ornamental objects. It is considered by some to have various magical properties—perhaps because, if rubbed, amber creates and holds an electrical charge. Because of this, some think that the word "electricity" originally stems from the Greek word describing the effect of rubbing amber.

Amulet (KQ2, KQ5) Amulets are charms that are usually hung on one's neck. They can contain special stones, herbs, or inscriptions and are most often used to protect the wearer against things such as sickness, bad luck, or witchcraft. This was obviously the purpose of the amulet given to King Graham by the gypsy. It protected him from "bad magic", as Madame Mushka called it. This is why he came to no harm when he encountered the nasty witch who lived in the Dark Forest of Serenia. On the other hand, I'm sure it was of no use in protecting him from Mordack's much more powerful magic.

The amulet that Graham found on the enchanted isle evidently protected its wearer against being irrevocably lost. Its properties appear quite similar to the Ruby Slippers, with which you click your heels together and say, "There's no place like home! There's no place like home!"

Antony (KQ5) King of the ants in Daventry.

We think little of the lowly ant, other than to curse its presence at picnics and bemoan its ability to stream into our kitchens during rainy weather. Ants are highly organized and social insects who live in various types of nests and hills that they construct themselves. In our world we sometimes compare the high degree of organization in ant colonies to that of rigid totalitarian governments. In Daventry, however, benevolent monarchy seems more the rule.

Antique store (KQ2) An article in *Daventry People* describes Milvia's Olde Antique Shoppe as "The only establishment of its kind in the known world. In it, the proprietress has collected and collated curiosities and conversation pieces from all the crannies and corners of creation." Milvia was married very young to a very old and very rich merchant. When he died, she was left with warehouses full of what she called "junk and other old stuff." She took the gold her husband had left her and spent her life traveling the world in search of rare birds, rare stories, cheap thrills, and unique objects of the more magical persuasion. When she decided to stop traveling, she opened her store, stocking it from her late husband's long-abandoned storerooms and the effluvia of her journeys. It was from here that Manannan obtained the moose head that he later hung on his dining room wall.

Bakehouse (KQ5) The bakery in the town of Serenia is quite renowned for the quality of its baked goods and the background of its owners. *Daventry People* featured a long story about the establishment. It seems that the shop was opened by a pair of brothers, Jym and Tam, whose last name actually was Baker. They had been born into a family of travelling minstrels and spent their early years perfecting the musical and comedic arts, wandering from place to place. Eventually their parents retired and the boys continued on their own, singing and playing in inns and taverns, a night here and a night there.

Their big break came when their wagon-wheel broke near Serenia. The weather was foul and their mood was no sunnier. Tired of endless years on the road, they took their act to the Country Inn in Serenia and persuaded the owner to let them perform there nightly. They soon found fame—and a steady, but modest, income—singing old favorites like "Greensleeves," and also telling funny and off-color stories. Performing in the same place nightly was revolutionary in Daventry, and it might be said that the Fantabulous Baker Boys invented the idea of show business there. They packed 'em in for years, but never were able to please the critics. This lack of critical appreciation finally became too much, and they quit show biz.

Taking all the gold they had saved, they bought the bakery down the road, and turned a hobby into a new livelihood. Using the experience of years on stage, they began by baking what they knew best—custard pies. Often they had thrown them at each other on stage. They had learned early that pies-in-the-face were easier to take if they tasted good. They had also learned that craft well, and soon became known as expert bakers.

Once again they were a commercial success, but this time with a difference. Within weeks the food mavens were praising their culinary work as the entertainment critics never had their act. Commenting on this irony, Jym and Tam were quoted as saying, "The gods work in mysterious ways. That's show business!"

Every once in a while, though, one of the two brothers will be seen in town trying to repair their still-broken wagon. Maybe they miss the applause.

Backwards alphabet   (KQ1)   Also known as a "retrograde alphabet," it is a relatively simple cipher that is used for encoding messages. The letter "A" becomes "Z", "Y" turns into "B," "X" is "C," and so on. The number "0" becomes "9," "1" turns into "8," etc. Because of its very simplicity, the backwards alphabet can occasionally be quite effective in situations where a complex code is expected.

Bandits   (KQ3, KQ5)   In one of his messages, Derek notes that he has to be wary of the thugs and desperados that infect the forest of Llewdor. They still, he supposes, hide in the treehouse, from which they prey on travelers. Because the members of the band are so young, he refers to them as the "Brat Catpack" with "no morals and even less intelligence!"

The bandits of Senenia's fabled Endless Desert are another matter altogether. They are quite reminiscent of the Forty Thieves encountered by Ali Baba. Those desperados also concealed their treasure behind a portal that could only be opened by the sound of a magical phrase. An article in "Daventry Today" describes the Serenian bandits' main strengths as utter ruthlessness and extreme intelligence. The leaders of these brigands had once been students of natural order, magic, and philosophy. They soon differed with their teachers, however, over just what constitutes good and evil. Their studies led them down the dark path that equates might with right and gold with good. Eventually, surrounded by others of the same unsavoury leanings, they left their university for the gold and blood-filled life of preying on desert caravans and travellers. When they left, they took the contents of the school's treasury with them.

Unlike the bandits of Llewdor, they have have a strict moral code—although one, in my opinion, of a truly black and perverse type. From their perspective, their actions are quite moral. They are apparently still at large.

Beanstalk (KQ1) In our world, we have the story of "Jack and the Beanstalk." It tells of Jack and his mother, whose only possession is a cow that has stopped giving milk. On the way to market to sell the cow, Jack trades it to a man who offers him five magic beans—beans that will grow to the sky overnight. The man even offered Jack a cow-back guarantee if they didn't work. Jack's mom was skeptical and upset, to say the least. She threw the beans away and sent Jack to his room without his supper. The beans did grow, however, and Jack climbed to the top the next morning. There he met an ogre's wife who fed Jack breakfast and hid him in her oven so that her ogre husband wouldn't catch and eat him. When he arrived home, the ogre sniffed around and recited:

> Fee, fi, fo, fum,
> I smell the blood of an Englishman!
> Be he live, or be he dead,
> I'll grind his bones to make my bread!

Actually, the ogre wanted Jack roasted or broiled, but he couldn't come up with the proper rhyme. Finding no one about, the ogre ate a few calves, counted a few bags of his gold, and then fell asleep. Jack stole the gold and escaped home. When the gold was all spent, Jack went up a second time and stole the hen that laid the golden eggs from the sleeping ogre. Again he escaped. This wasn't enough for his greedy mother, who sent Jack back a third time. On his last trip, Jack stole a golden harp that kept screaming "Master! Master!" as it was carried away. This time the ogre followed Jack down the beanstalk, but Jack was able to cut the stalk through with an ax in time to plunge the ogre to his death. He and his mother lived happily ever after.

"Jack the Giant-Killer" is another story altogether. In this tale, Jack is a farmer's son who dashes around the country killing various giants in order to get their treasures. In the course of his adventures, he rescues fair maidens, saves the life of King Arthur's son, and gets the "Fee, fi, fo, fum" treatment from one of his eventual victims. In the end, Jack is made a knight of the Round Table, given a great castle to call his own, and marries the beautiful daughter of one of King Arthur's dukes. They live happily ever after.

Bears (KQ5) Bears are massive, furry, short-limbed mammals that have existed for millions of years. Some species can get to be over 10 feet tall and weigh many hundreds of pounds. They also have sharp teeth and sharp claws. Because of their size and power, bears have been feared, and sometimes worshipped, since before humans began to draw on cave walls. Indeed, many of those ancient caves must have once been home to the creatures, and many lives must have been lost wresting them away from the bears. Bear clans still exist in more primitive parts of our world, and it is telling that not one, but two, of the major constellations in the northern sky are named after them—*Ursa Major* and *Ursa Minor*—the big bear and the little bear. This can be said of no other creature.

Despite this primal fear and awe, people have trained bears to dance and perform in circuses. Others have captured them in order to chain and torture the beasts. Bear-baiting was a very popular amusement, especially in England, for hundreds of years.

As Pooh Bear might say, it is a well-known fact that bears love honey. Some bears make almost their entire diet of the sweet stuff, a fact not lost upon the bees. Bears however are also carnivorous and, with their large, sharp claws, insulating fur, and quick reflexes, easily catch their other favorite food—fish.

Bees (KQ5)   It is often assumed that all bees live in hives and make honey. This is not true. The majority of bees are solitary insects who make nests for their broods in holes, wood, shells, brambles, or masonry. The honey bee is the kind we usually think of when we do consider them. They are social creatures comprised of workers and drones and fertile females known as queens. Bees make large hives out of wax they create. This beeswax is a yellowish solid that does not dissolve in water, and it has many uses from polish, to candle-making to sealing holes and cracks.

Bees eat honey, which they make from the nectar of flowers. It's stored in honeycombs, which are also made out of beeswax. People and bears are also fond of honey as a food, and beekeeping is one of humanity's earliest industries. Besides being a food, honey is an excellent antiseptic and has been used to treat wounds for centuries. Honey is very sticky, and because of that property it is sometimes used to catch insects and small vermin. "It's easier to catch flies with honey, than with vinegar," is an old saying.

In Daventry, the bees seem to be somewhat more organized than they are in our world. Their Queen's name is Beetrice.

Boatman (KQ2)   In Greek mythology, there is a personage named Charon whose job it is to ferry the souls of the dead across the river Styx to Hades. He was thought of as a silent, shrouded old man. In time, the image became synonymous with death itself.

Bowl (KQ1)   Found by Graham on his journey through Daventry, it had the word "Fill" inscribed in it. There is an American folktale about a fellow name Jack who went out to find a wife. An old man told him he could marry one of his daughters if he could catch a rabbit, put it in a ring, and make it stay there for 30 minutes. If he failed in this task, though, he would be killed. When Jack brought the rabbit to the appointed spot, he stuck a magic drill in the center of the wide ring, and all the rabbit could do was run around it and around it. When the old man saw what was happening, he made Jack another proposition: if he could keep the rabbit running around and around for the 30 minutes, Jack would be free to kill the old man.

The old man went back into his house and, one by one, sent his wife and daughters out to Jack to try and get him to sell the drill before the time was up. Each one offered Jack more and more, but he refused them all. When the 30 minutes were up, the old man picked up a bowl and went outside to meet his death. First, he asked Jack to sing the bowl full of lies before he did the deed. This Jack did by reciting the false promises the man's wife and daughter had whispered to him, and following it with a hearty, "Fill, bowl! Fill!"

Brass Bottle (KQ5) The use of bottles and lamps to imprison imps, demons, spirits, and genies goes back as far as those creatures have existed. Brass, however, seems to be used more often than most. The bottle that Graham found in the desert temple must have had a high percentage of copper in the alloy since it looked almost like gold. Graham has no need of gold since Daventry possesses a magic chest always filled with the stuff.

I suspect that brass is popular for containing trapped beings because it tarnishes. Often the binding spell gives the imprisoned an out—if the container is rubbed, they might be freed, or partially freed, in some manner. People naturally try to shine brass by rubbing the tarnish, so eternal containment is seldom the fate of the unfortunate inhabitants of brass containers. It is, I suspect, one of the cosmic balances we find throughout the universe.

On the other hand, the bottle Graham found evidently did not have such an escape clause in its binding spell. Rather, it had a top that could be opened, and a spell that would imprison whoever freed its genie for 500 years. It proved once again that opening magical containers is a risky proposition.

See also Pandora's Box.

Brass Lamp (KQ2) In the *Daventry People* magazine story, Milvia, the owner of the Kolyma antique store, says she discovered the lamp under a pile of silk rugs in one of her husband's warehouses. She never tried to clean it because she felt it would fetch her a better price if it looked ancient and tarnished.

It is said in our world that Aladdin, the son of a poor tailor, once possessed a magic oil lamp such as the one Graham used. Aladdin was sent into an underground garden by an evil magician in order to recover the lamp, but he refused to hand it over immediately. In a rage, the magician locked Aladdin away in the underworld, intending to leave him there until he died. Aladdin escaped, however, and was able to return home to his mother. Needing money for food, and not knowing the lamp was magic, they decided to sell it. It was Aladdin's mother who rubbed the lamp with a cloth in order to clean it, hoping it would then bring a higher price. At once a djinn—a genie—appeared, hideous in appearance. Aladdin's mother fainted, but he grabbed the lamp and demanded the genie bring them food.

That was the beginning of a beautiful relationship. There seems to have been no limit placed on the number of times Aladdin could call upon the genie, and in time he and his mother became rich enough to ask the sultan to give Aladdin his daughter's hand in marriage. Eventually the evil mage came back and stole the lamp and bride from Aladdin, and Aladdin was forced to overcome him. Later still, the magician's brother appeared to make mischief and attempt revenge. In the end, Aladdin and his princess triumphed. He became sultan himself eventually, and they lived happily ever after.

Bridles (KQ2, KQ4) There is a belief, not so common any more, that a wicked witch can throw a magic bridle over someone's head and turn the person into a horse. The witch then rides the unhappy person a long distance to some witches' gathering, and rides back in the morning. The victim soon becomes ill and weary from lack of sleep and dies. A number of folktales exist that tell how some victims were able to escape this fate.

The Greeks and Romans said that the great winged horse Pegasus could only be tamed if it were wearing a certain magic bridle.

Bruce (KQ3) A town in Llewdor, although Alexander-Gwydion refers to it as a hamlet. There are a few references to it in the communications I have received from Daventry—Graham's friend, Sir David, is from there; the god Thor fought a great battle with a monster outside its walls; and it has what we would call a newspaper, *The Bruce Banner,* named after the famous flag. Derek Karlavaegen mentions the names of just two towns in all of the messages he has sent, Daventry and Bruce, so I suspect it is of some importance. It is situated in southeastern Llewdor, so it might be the same place as the seaport from where Alexander- Gwydion set sail with the pirates. That, however, is pure speculation on my part.

Cassima (KQ5) Princess of the Kingdom of Green Isles, she was kidnapped by Mordack and enslaved in his castle as a scullery maid. This experience is quite similar to what befell Alexander- Gwydion, and probably explains the instant bond that formed between the two when they met. Was it love at first sight? It is possible. No one seems to know, or if they do, they're not talking. Not even Derek Karlavaegen, who has become a friend to the Prince of Daventry, can shed any light on the mystery.

Derek is unusually empty of facts about Cassima and the Green Isles. Normally one has to hack through much extraneous verbiage when he sends information about something to our world. He does place the Green Isles on a map he has devised of his world, but says nothing about it or its peoples.

He also mentions that Alexander and Cassima have communicated since their meeting, but doesn't say how, or where, or when.

Nothing is as it appears, and we know too little.

In the story of Ali Baba and the Forty Thieves, Ali Baba's brother is named Cassim.

Castle Daventry (KQ1, KQ2, KQ3, KQ4, KQ5) The home of King Graham and his family, and the administrative center of the Kingdom of Daventry. Overlooking the town of Daventry, it was built by King Edward the Benevolent as a gift to his bride, Queen Maylie. It is protected from potential conquerors by thick stone walls and is surrounded by a moat infested by alligators with a taste for human flesh. It is said that secret tunnels worm their ways beneath the castle in a labyrinth of passages not totally mapped. Some even say that there are magical windows at the ends of some of those passageways that allow one to be teleported immediately to other parts of the world.

Castle Dracula (KQ2) This spooky place sits on a small, rocky island in the middle of a poison lake in the central part of western Kolyma. Its only approach is by a boat poled across the polluted waters by a grim boatman that some claim is death itself. Poisonous thorns and brambles make walking there a quick stroll to death, and its gates are guarded by ghosts. It is not known whether Dracula brought the castle with him when he *withdrew* to Daventry.

Cedric (KQ5) An educated owl; guide, counsel, and friend to King Graham as he attempted to rescue his family from Mordack. Although Cedric described himself as being in the employ of Crispinophur, it is more likely that he was a friend and *aide-de-camp* to the great wizard, much like Dr. Watson was to Sherlock Holmes.

In the Merlin legends it is said that the great wizard had an owl as a familiar. Merlin's owl was named Archimedes. It is possible that Crispin and Cedric are Merlin and Archimedes living in Serenia under assumed identities. But we have no evidence at all to suport this supposition.

In the Greek myths, the owl is a symbol of the goddess Athena who was the goddess of wise counsel. She was also a protectress. Because Athena was considered wise, and the owl her symbol, the owl became looked upon as a wise bird. Cedric is this, if nothing else.

In one version of the Perseus myth, Athena is told to give her owl to Perseus to help him in his quest for Medusa. Instead, Athena has a wise clockwork owl crafted, and it aids the hero, almost perishing in the process. This is quite similar to the relationship that developed between Graham and Cedric.

Chest of Gold (KQ1) One of the three great treasures of Daventry; no matter how much gold was taken from it, it never emptied. The chest was stolen from Edward by the witch who called herself Dahlia and was given to a giant for safekeeping in the Land of the Clouds. King Graham won it back as part of his quest for the Crown of Daventry.

Chicken Soup (KQ2) The universal cure for many minor to moderate maladies, its near-magical properties are known and revered by almost all of the folk of both our universes. Brewed from chickens—whole or in parts—onions, carrots, celery, garlic, herbs, some salt, pepper, and perhaps a potato, turnip, or rutabaga, it gains much of its magic from long, slow simmering. My mother says the secret ingredient in her magic soup is a couple of whole cloves.

Cobra Dragon Gates (KQ5)   Mordack's first line of defense at his castle on Wizard's Island. The only way way Graham could get near the castle was by passing between the two huge stone guardians without their gaze touching him.

In our world, there is the story of Atreyu. In the land of Fantastica he had to pass through a similar gate made of two stone sphinx. If they had gazed upon him, he would have been frozen forever. We also have the story of Sam and Frodo at the tower of Cirith Ungol in Mordor. Guarded by the black Watchers, Sam and Frodo were able to pass when Sam held up the elven-glass of Galadriel to them. The glass counteracted the deadly force of their glittering eyes, and the great gate, and the Watchers, were destroyed.

Coignice and Cedric   The parents of Valanice, Queen of Daventry. They appear to be from eastern Kolyma, an area about which we know nothing. Coignice is said to be the daughter of a miller, much the same as the girl in the tale about Rumplestiltskin, and Cedric is supposedly a prince of his land. That's all we know about them. It is apparent, though, that they allowed Valanice to be educated, but at this time there is no way of knowing if that is unusual or not.

Conch Shell (KQ5)   The conch is a sea mollusk with a long shell shaped like a spiral cone. It is considered good eating in many places. In the Greek myths, the conch shell was used as a horn by Triton, the son of the sea god Poseidon. Aphrodite, the Greek love goddess, is sometime depicted holding the conch shell as a reminder that she was born from the sea.

The conch shell has long been associated with hearing. As a horn, it amplifies both the sound breathed into it and the sound entering from the outside. If we hold the conch shell to our ears, we imagine we hear the sea contained within it. Finally, the largest hollow in our external ear is known as a *concha* because of its resemblance to the conch shell.

Condor (KQ1) In order to reach the entrance to the land of the leprechauns, Graham had to get onto an island in the River Fools. A condor swooped around him, beckoning, and when Graham jumped into the air, the bird grabbed him in its claws and flew him to the place. In our world, the condor is a large, vulturelike bird distinct from the eagle. Nonetheless, many people confuse the creatures.

King Graham has said in Daventry that he is quite clear on the difference between the two birds. It was an eagle that saved his life in Serenia by rescuing him from the nest of a giant Roc. Other than that, he's a little hazy on detail.

Country Inn (KQ5) A low-life dive in Serenia; a hangout for thieves, cutthroats, and their less savory kin. Once upon a time, the Country Inn was renown throughout all Serenia for its food, hospitality, and entertainment. That was when the Fantabulous Baker Boys were appearing nightly. After the Bakers quit performing, and started baking custard pies for eating, and not throwing, business in the place fell off markedly. The owners sold it, and the new proprietor began catering to a less respectable crowd, not caring where nor how they obtained their coins—as long as they spent them freely on the dubious beer and questionable women. It was renamed "The Swarthy Hog," but most folks still refer to it by its original name.

The quality of the food has remained adequate, and the portions large. Leg of lamb is the speciality of the house, and it's quite fit to be consumed by man or beast. The only problem is that you must enter the place in order to purchase it.

Crispin (KQ5) A great and ancient wizard. His full name is Crispinophur, but prefers to be called Crispin because it's easier for him to remember that way, and his memory isn't what it used to be. His only companion is Cedric, an owl who helps him keep his house and thoughts in order. The house is always magically locked so as to discourage "...travelling peddlers and meddlers, as well as sellers of washing utensils and encyclopedic parchments."

Crispinophur is a mysterious personage. Some say that he was already an old man when time began. There is also a tale told in Daventry that Crispin was the main instigator of the first *withdrawal* of folk from our world to there, and that the place of their arrival was in front of Crispin's house. It is said that the house was already there when the first folk arrived, and is the nucleus around which the universe was created. In the front yard, there is a strange device of pulleys and levers and whirleygigs, which Crispin calls his "Universe Interpreter". Often he says that he forgets what it's there for, but it might have something to do with keeping the multiverse intact.

Derek Karlavaegen, who has met Crispin, writes that he suspects Crispin is not as old as he looks, as feeble as he appears, nor as forgetful as he claims. Derek says that Crispin is the most powerful magician he has even encountered—his mind keen and deep, and his body an illusion to put all off their guards. He also feels that Crispin is *much, much older* than his appearance.

Crystals (KQ5) Crystals are valued both in our world and Daventry for their beauty, usefulness, magical, and other properties. Both table salt and sugar are crystalline substances, for example. Lasers make use of crystals in order to help focus and concentrate their beams of coherent light, and jewelry makes use of its crystals in order to focus and attract romantic energy. And, we all know what a "girl's best friend" is.

Many in our world attribute healthful, curative, and protective properties to crystals, although conventional scientific thought is quite skeptical about such claims. Nonetheless, people in Daventry are quite skeptical about the laws of science, and what they refer to as "...dread technology." They make daily use of crystal's magical properties in all of its forms—amulets, stones of power, skrying stones, magic crystals, and powders of various powers. Crystals are also used to protect against magic, and physical danger or attack. Held or manipulated properly, certain crystals reflect attacks back at their casters causing them to suffer the effects of their own aggression. These powerful crystals, however, are not common, and are most often found clustered in caves, both in the high mountains and underground. In Daventry, this means there is a dragon or yeti or other monster around, and this helps account for their scarcity.

Crystal Tower (KQ2) The place where Valanice was kept prisoner after she was kidnapped by Hagatha. Rose quartz in color, it reminds us of the tower where Rapunzel was held captive after she was kidnapped by the witch named Dame Gothel. Rapunzel was stolen from her parents as payment for some vegetables in the witch's garden that her mother craved. There were no stairs in Rapunzel's tower nor any door, and the only way that even the witch could enter was by climbing the girl's long, braided, golden hair. One night, a prince, attracted by the sound of the girl's singing, overheard the witch chanting,

> Rapunzel, Rapunzel, let down your hair,
> That I may climb your golden stair!

On a night when the witch was not around, the prince called out the words, and the beautiful Rapunzel met a man for the first time in her life. It was love at first sight for both of them. He visited her often, and they plotted her escape. However, it was not to be. The witch found out about the plot, cut off the maiden's golden tresses and stranded her in the middle of the desert. When the prince arrived at the tower, the evil hag was waiting. She attacked him and he fell into some brambles, which scratched his eyes and blinded him.

The prince wandered the world blind for many years, always searching for the voice of his beloved. Finally he groped his way through the desert in the hope that she was there. She was—of course—living with her twin children in the barren wasteland. They were reunited, and so strong was their love that her tears of joy restored the prince's sight. They returned in happiness to his kingdom and lived happily ever after.

Cupid (KQ4) To the Greeks and Romans, he was the god of love. Cupid took various names and forms, but the one we most recognize is that of a chubby, winged infant. Nonetheless, he was more than that. His mother was the goddess Venus who became jealous once of a mortal girl by the name of Psyche. It was said that Psyche's beauty was so great it rivaled that of Venus. For that reason, the goddess demanded that her son shoot Psyche with his arrow of love. Cupid's love-arrows bring great joy or great sorrow to whomever they touch, and the goddess planned that the girl would fall in love with some ugly, stupid oaf and be miserable for the rest of her life. This was not to be; Cupid accidentally scratched himself with an arrow when he saw Psyche and fell in love with her himself, but left her alone. Eventually Psyche was exiled to a mountaintop, a place where, it was predicted, she would marry a monster. There, the West Wind befriended her and took her to a lovely valley where she found a palace with a wide, tiled pool. She finally met her husband there but was never allowed to see him. They only met at night, and he said that it was for the best that she did not know what he looked like.

Unable to bear not seeing her lover, Psyche crept to his bed one night with an oil lamp. As she discovered that her husband really was the god Cupid, a drop of oil dripped on his shoulder. He awoke startled and angry and flew away, abandoning Psyche. Venus, however, kept harassing the girl out of blind jealousy, and gave her a number of impossible tasks to perform. Cupid finally interceded for his wife with Zeus, who decided that Psyche should become immortal. She was given a cup of ambrosia to drink and thus it was. This made Venus feel much better, since no longer would a mere mortal be said to be as beautiful as the goddess.

Dahlia (KQ1) The name of the witch who stole the Chest of Gold from King Edward. Dahlia had disguised herself as a beautiful maiden. Edward found her hidden in a tree, surrounded by wolves. He rescued her, fell in love, and asked her to be his bride. On the night before their wedding, she stole the keys to the treasure vault and then stole the magic chest. The theft drove the kingdom into poverty, and the king into a despair from which he never recovered. Graham killed Dahlia by shoving her into her own oven.

Dark Forest (KQ5) A twisty and mysterious wood situated in the northern part of Serenia. It is said that no one who enters there can ever leave without making friends of the elves, shy and elusive little people who live both among the misshapen trees and grotesque fungi, and below the forest floor. It is reported that few who enter there ever return, alive or otherwise.

An evil and jealous witch once kept her house there until she attempted to get the better of King Graham. Like a lyric from a country song, her home now is in a bottle and she's waiting for someone to set her free. The twisted house presumably still remains, but no one in the region seems to have volunteered to enter the woods to find out for certain.

Daventry (KQ1, KQ2, KQ3, KQ4, KQ5) The name of the kingdom that is ruled over by King Graham. It is also the name of the continent of which the kingdom is part, and it is sometimes used as a generic name for the universe that contains that kingdom. Daventry came into existence after many of the more magical and mythical elements of our own world got together and *withdrew,* creating a world less bound to logic and science and more attuned to the irrational and fabulous. There are a number of Daventrys in our world, the oldest of which is a town about 75 miles northwest of London. Locally, the name of the town is sometimes pronounced "Dane-tree," and even Shakespeare used this pronunciation in Henry VI, Part III, Act V. It is said that the town was built by Danes.

Derek Karlavaegen The name of the person who is sending messages and documents from the universe of Daventry. Very little is known about Derek—he is a traveler, a writer, a journalist, and a part-time sorcerer. Derek now resides in the former house of the wizard Manannan in the land of Llewdor. He found a device there that he calls "The Eye Between the Worlds," and it is by way of this that he is able to communicate with us. From the tone of several of Derek's messages, it seems that he is content to stick with this endeavor until he has exhausted Manannan's extensive magical library, or his wine cellar.

Deserts (KQ3, KQ5) Deserts are dry, barren regions, usually sparsely inhabited. It is a misconception that all deserts are hot. The Arctic, for instance, is considered a desert by some scientists—the air is dry with little or no precipitation. Few live there, the conditions are so harsh. On the other hand, in our world we often build cities in deserts, piping in water and conditioning the air in order to make the places inhabitable. Many call this progress. Others call it Phoenix, Tuscon, Las Vegas, Barstow, or LA.

In Daventry there are many deserts, usually hot and dry, and usually endless. I suspect this is a property of the universe itself: always inventing itself, the edges of the world must blur and seem to go on forever. Alexander survived the desert in Llewdor by skirting its edges and avoiding the medusas that hunt there. Derek says that that desert is bounded by swamp and the Impossible Mountains on its west, and that a timeless city exists in its center.

The endless desert of Serenia begins on the western border of the Sovereignty of Serenia. The only life in it is the bandits who live in an encampment far from its edge. Only they know the whereabouts of the few meager oases, and they guard the secret with blooded blades. Parts of this desert were once inhabited by a people who worshipped an unknown god, and who attempted the practice of technology. Something went wrong and the land was burnt barren. All was destroyed except the stone temple to the god, and the scorpions. All the other people, cities, plants, birds and animals vanished in a flash of fire. It is said in Serenia that they are not missed.

Dink (KQ5) It is unknown just what kind of a creature the Dink really is. Dink looks to be a cross between an ogre, a lion, a witch and a wardrobe, and gets its name from the sound it always likes to make, "Dink! Dink! Dink!". Princess Cassima called it Dink to King Graham, but she might as well have called it Sam. She claims that Dink has a brother by that name, and we can only assume that the creature goes around making the sound "Sam! Sam! Sam!"

Dink is a simple-minded creature with keen hearing. Cassima told Alexander that it enjoys the sounds and rhythms of music. She also claimed that it spends many hours taking care if its hair, always forming and re-forming it into different kinds of braids, pony tails and top-knots. Dink, she said, could always be found by following a trail of hairpins and clasps.

Djinn (KQ2, KQ5) Sometimes also spelled jinn or jinni, this is another, more accurate name for genies. They are spirits found in Arabian mythology who sometimes take the form of men. The djinn are said to be the children of fire and make their homes on the mountain Kaf. Some, however, say the djinn are demons. There are both good and evil djinn, and they can change their form or become invisible at will. One of the kings of the djinn is even claimed to have built the pyramids of Egypt. It was a djinn imprisoned in a brass lamp that aided Aladdin, and it was, perhaps, the same one who helped King Graham. Nothing at all is known about the one imprisoned in the brass bottle Graham found in the desert temple. Good or evil, one can assume that it was happy to escape. Curiously enough, the singular form of the word is djinni and the plural is djinn.

Dolphin (KQ4) These are large, aquatic mammals who live in the seas and large rivers. Highly intelligent and with their own language, they are not fish. Dolphins have always appeared playful in the presence of humans, and there are records going back thousands of years of them playing alongside sailing ships. Many of these stories speak about the dolphins sometimes aiding and rescuing people who have found themselves lost at sea, and there are also many stories of people riding them. In ancient Greece, the dolphin was sacred to the Oracle at Delphi and even gave the sacred place its name.

Dracula (KQ4) A vampire—a supernatural being of great strength, and immortal as long as it is able to drink the blood of humans at regular intervals. Dracula first appeared in an 1897 novel of the same name by Bram Stoker, and the count has been reborn often in plays and films. Some say that Dracula was based on a madman by the name of Vlad the Impaler who murdered thousands in terrible ways and drank the blood of some of his victims.

Derek Karlavaegen has written that he thinks Dracula is not supernatural at all, but that he was one of the last survivors —if not the final survivor—of the lizard folk who ruled the earth for millions of years before humanity. According to Derek, both the chameleon and the bat are degenerate descendents of that particular line of beings, and this accounts for Dracula's apparent ability to change shape and to fly.

Like bats, vampires avoid sunlight and sleep during the day. The vampire preys on us much as we prey on cows and carrots, drinking blood mostly, but sometimes devouring flesh when in the form of a wolf. The vampire's constitution is such that silver is a most deadly poison to it, as is garlic, but it is also so robust and regenerative that a vampire's lifespan is measured in the hundreds, if not thousands, of years. Of course, they can be killed by a stake driven through the heart, but, then, so would any of us in the same situation.

According to Derek, Dracula fled from the sight of Graham's silver cross for the very reason that it was silver and its touch could kill him.

Dragons (KQ1, KQ3) One of the most widespread creatures of human myth, dragons are usually—but not always—thought of as huge, fire-breathing lizards or snakes. Dragons have been feared and worshipped since the beginning of recorded history, and the belief was ancient even then. While many cultures think of the dragon as evil, the Greeks, Romans, and Chinese sometimes thought of them as wise and powerful dwellers of the inner earth and used the image of the dragon on some of their standards. In more recent times, fantasists have more and more attributed benign qualities to the creatures. It is not known what the origin of the dragon myths is. It cannot be a memory of the dinosaurs because humanity and dinosaurs never existed at the same time.

Dungeon Cell (KQ5) The place in Mordack's castle where prisoners were taken before they were killed or experimented on. The cell was situated next to Mordack's dungeon maze, and the only ways out of it were into the maze, or into a mousehole. Few humans, however, are built to make that particular squeeze. The cell was entered through a magic door that had to be conjured out of the air by either Mordack or his henchman. The cell is small, infested with mice, lice, and rats. The sanitary facilities are non-existent. On the other hand, few of Mordack's guests ever lived long enough to complain about the conditions.

Dwarfs (KQ1, KQ2, KQ4) One of the races of little people. Dwarfs are closely related to the dark elves and gnomes, and the three races are often confused. Some theories even say that they are all the same race, but they do seem to be distinct in Daventry. They stand around four feet or so in height, but weigh well over one hundred pounds—most of it muscle. The majority of dwarfs live underground, but many live in the rockier hills and mountains. There are even some dwarfs that live in the deeper parts of some forests, but they are rare. Dwarfs are renowned for their surly dispositions, short tempers, and mistrust of humans.

Eagle (KQ5) A large meat-eating bird of prey with sharp eyes and powerful wings. Graham saved an eagle's life in the icy mountains above Serenia, and the grateful bird returned the favor.

The eagle was the military standard for the Roman armies, and the bald eagle is the emblem of the United States. Benjamin Franklin thought that this was not a good idea and proposed, instead, that the turkey was a better choice. Franklin considered the eagle a carrion-eater and opportunist. He thought the turkey, which is native to North America, to be cleaner, smarter, more useful, and possessing better habits—all in all, a better choice to represent a nation.

See also Condor.

An Encyclopedia of Daventry

Edgar (KQ4)   The son of the wicked witch, Lolotte. He aided Rosella in her escape from her prison room. Rosella then apparently killed Lolotte, an act for which Edgar showed little remorse. Nobody knows who Edgar's father was—he could have been anybody from a drugged slave to a malevolent sorcerer. He was born deformed—short, stooped, and ugly. The fairy Genesta gave him a more pleasing appearance as a reward for aiding Rosella and thus saving Genesta's life. Edgar lives alone now in his mother's castle on a crag in the Impossible Mountains. His love for Rosella is said to burn as strong as ever.

Elves (KQ1, KQ5)   One of the races of the little folk, elves can be divided into two broad groups, black elves and white elves. The white elves are considered good and are thought to live in the open air of the forest. Generally they appear as fair and lovely children. The black elves are extremely ugly and evil, live underground, and are descended from maggots. They love to inflict injury and sickness on people. While these divisions are generally true, there has been much inter-marriage among the elves of Daventry. As a result, many elves live both above and below the ground, and cannot be fitted into easy categories. In fact, in the Dark Forest of Serenia there is a large settlement of "Gray Elves". Descendents of both the black and the white groups, they are very mischievous. Neither truly bad nor truly good, elves *per se*, like the Leader of the Pack, are, "good-bad, but...not evil". Elves are generally of human form, pale in color, of slim build with pointed ears. While considered "little people," some elves can be as tall as humans, and they have even been known to marry with us. Most, though, are short, ranging in height from two and a half feet to four feet tall. Elves have their own kings, laws, and customs, but do not live together in towns and cities. Some of the rare and tall sylvan elves are known to have built large houses where they live and practice magic.

In general, elves are friendly but do prefer to stay out of the sight of humans. Because of their low visibility, they are considered to be more mischievous than they really are—the thought being something like "if they don't have something to hide, why don't they show themselves more?"

Eye Between the Worlds   When Derek Karlavaegen moved into the wizard Manannan's house, he discovered a device, and it is with this "Eye Between the Worlds," as he calls it, that he is able to communicate with our world. From his description of it, we can only conclude that the wizard was in possession of some sort of computer. How can this be? Daventry may be a land of wonders, but it is not a land of technology.

In our world, a man by the name of Gerbert reigned as Pope of the Roman Catholic Church from 999 to 1003. He is known as Pope Sylvester the Second and is still considered one of the great scholars of his age. His contemporaries, though, thought of him as one of the great magicians of the age. Sylvester attempted to collect manuscripts on all that was known during his time—magic, mathematics, natural history, geography, philosophy, whatever he could obtain. He is known to have constructed many devices for accurately tracking the movements of the planets, stars, and celestial spheres. He is also known to have built calculating machines to solve mathematical and geometrical problems, and he built wonderous clocks and other machines. He traded many of his devices and inventions for rare manuscripts of obscure knowledge.

What gave Pope Sylvester his reputation as a magician-pope, however, was his building of what is described as either a talking statue or a talking head constructed of brass. This head was capable of solving problems that were put to it, and some say it could predict the future. So great was the impact of this machine that stories began to circulate that the Pope had made a pact with Satan. Because of this, many scholars think that Sylvester is the basis for the story of the magician named Faust—a man who made his own pact with the devil. When Sylvester died, his magical head disappeared into the depths of the Vatican.

Had Pope Sylvester constructed some eleventh century equivalent to our computer? Has Manannan? Arthur C. Clarke writes that "any technology, sufficiently advanced, is indistinguishable from magic." If technology can emulate magic, why can't magic emulate technology?

Fairies (KQ1, KQ2, KQ4) A race of graceful and delicate beings with magical powers, fairies are said to live hundreds of years, but must spend one day of each week in the form of some animal—a bird or dolphin, for instance. Most cultures have a tradition of fairies. The English version—the one we are most familiar with—holds that they come from, and dwell in, the Land of Faerie, where they are ruled by a queen. Fairies are said to be interested in human affairs and often aid and protect people. In fact, so many tales have been told about good fairies, that they have given us the term "fairy tale."

Fairies can be tall or tiny in form, but they are almost always winged and good. In the story of Cinderella, Cinderella's godmother was a fairy who carried a magic wand that had the power to transform things—the girl's ugly clothes into a beautiful gown, is a case in point. Some fairies, like Tinkerbell, possess a magic powder—fairy dust—that helps them cast their enchantments. Graham is slightly allergic to fairy dust—it makes him sneeze.

Valanice writes that Genesta is the Queen of the Fairies in Daventry.

Fish (KQ4, KQ5) Creatures that live in water and breathe by extracting oxygen from it by way of their gills. Bears, and sea birds and humans find their flesh to be quite tasty, despite whatever objections the fish themselves might have,

W.C. Fields purportedly said that he never drank water, because "Fish...(perform their bodily functions)... in it!" Or something to that effect.

Fisherman and his wife (KQ4) There is the story of a poor fisherman and his wife who lived in a shanty by the sea. One day the man caught a fish that talked. The fish said it was an enchanted prince and begged the fisherman to set him free, which the man did. The fisherman's wife was furious, and commanded him to go back and demand the fish grant him a wish. The man went back to the end of his pier and shouted:

> Flounder, flounder, in the sea,
> Harken thee now unto me!

The fish now owed the man, so it granted his wife's wish for a lovely cottage to replace their shack. This did not satisfy the wife for long, and she sent her husband back to demand a castle from the fish. She got it.

Thus it went; next she wanted to be King, then Emperor, and then Pope. All of these the flounder granted her. At last she demanded to be Lord of the Universe, with the power to command the rising and setting of the sun. The enchanted fish heard this request and, for her greed, returned the fisherman and his wife to the hovel where they had first lived.

I suspect these are the same people to whom Rosella gave the bag of diamonds.

Fishhook (KQ4, KQ5) It is not true that the purpose of fishhooks is to jab people in various parts of their anatomy. Sometime they are used to catch fish. Bait is attached to the hook, a weight to the hook, the hook to the line, the line to the fishing pole, and the fishing pole to a person's hands. Often, a fishing guide is needed to tell where the fish are. Seen in that light, fishing is much more simple if you are a bear or bird.

When people think of bait, they often think of worms. In this world, worms are only one form of bait or lure. Thousands upon thousands of different tied-flies, mechanical lures, and alchemical concoctions are used the catch the mythical "Big One". In Daventry, however, people stick to the basic four baits— worms, fish eggs, bread dough, and cheese. Those seem to work fine there.

Fly (KQ3) Alexander-Gwydion wonders why someone would want to change into a fly. He had done just this in order to overhear the bandits of Llewdor reveal their secret hideout to him, but it seems apparent that he is not eager to repeat the experience. After seeing the several films made in our world on the same subject, I tend to join the prince in his puzzlement.

Four-leaf clover (KQ1) This type of clover is supposed to bring good luck to its wearer. It is not, however, the same as a shamrock. The shamrock—the symbol of Ireland and the favorite of leprechauns—is a three-leaf clover, and not the same plant at all. This confusion between the two different plants is so widespread that, evidently, even the leprechauns of Daventry themselves get confused.

Frog Prince (KQ4) There are some interesting differences between Rosella's encounter with her Frog Prince and the tale that is told in this world. It seems that the beautiful daughter of a king was sitting under a cool tree, passing time and playing a game of catch with herself using a little golden ball. As these things happen, the ball this day traveled too far; it dropped past her hands and down into a deep well, too far down for her to retrieve it. As she wept for her lost ball, a frog's head came out of the water and the creature offered to dive and bring the ball back to her. There were conditions, however; in return for the ball, the princess must accept the ugly frog as her companion and playmate, and it must be allowed to eat from her plate with her at the dinner table, drink from her cup, and sleep with her in her bed. The pretty princess accepted the frog's bargain, but as soon as she held the golden ball again in her hands, she ran away and deserted the frog.

The next day, as the princess ate with her family and their entire court, a small voice came to the door and demanded the princess let him in. It was the frog, of course. Her father, the king, asked her what the frog wanted, and she was forced to tell him of her promise to the little green one. The king informed the girl that she must fulfill all that she had promised the frog, and he bade it join them for supper. The princess was reluctant and unwilling, but the king pushed her plate and cup closer to the frog so that it could enjoy the meal. When the meal was finished, the frog announced that he was tired, and asked the princess to join him in going to sleep. The princess didn't want any dirty old frog in her clean bed, but her father demanded that she honor her promise.

The princess carried the frog to her room, but when it was time to get into bed, she picked it up and threw it against one of the walls of her chamber as hard as she could. All at once, instead of dying, the ugly frog transformed into a handsome young prince who informed her that he had been captive of a wicked witch's spell. Instead of being upset at the girl for what she had done, he asked her to marry him, which she did. They lived happily ever after.

Most people, I suspect, recall a version of the tale where the princess kisses the frog to transform him. The first version of the tale, however, is the authentic one.

Genesta (KQ4) The Queen of the Fairies in Daventry. Rosella had to recover Genesta's stolen Talisman within 24 hours in order to save the fairy from death.

In our world, there is a story about how the fairy Genesta took a young boy from his parents, a foolish king and queen. Genesta promised to return the boy someday, but said they would not see him again until he was all covered with fur. The boy grew up handsome and intelligent, and because of his small size was called "Mannikin." Mannikin roamed the world and had all sorts of adventures, many times being aided by the good fairy Genesta. Finally he heard of a princess by the name of Sabella whose heart had been stolen by an evil fairy and hidden away in the center of an ice mountain. With no heart, the girl knew nothing of love. Mannikin fell in love with the princess. He vowed to overcome her other suitors and recover the girl's heart, thereby winning her hand. This he was finally able to do, and when he returned from the North Pole with the girl's heart encased in a diamond, she handed it back to him saying that her heart truly belonged to him.

Just then, Genesta arrived in a chariot drawn by eagles, bearing with her Mannikin's parents, the foolish king and queen. When they saw him he still wore the fur coat that had protected him during his icy adventure. Thus Genesta's promise was fulfilled. The coat had been given to him by Sabella, and in gratitude and love for her, he named the animal whose fur he wore after his bride-to-be. That is why today we have animals that are called sables.

Genesta, by the way, lives on a small island in Daventry off the west coast of Tamir. She is the only being I know of who actually does live in an ivory tower.

Gerwain (KQ2) Prime minister to King Graham, and the author of the court chronicle detailing Graham's quest to win his queen. Gerwain also was prime minister to Good King Edward and served him for over 20 years until Edward's sudden death. An article I received from Derek Karlavaegen details Gerwain's retirement from King Graham's service. In the article Gerwain speaks of the King needing and desiring younger advisors, ones lest apt to recommend the sacrifice of maidens to dragons. He says that their parting was amicable, and that he planned on moving to a small cottage in the forest and raising snails.

Ghosts (KQ2, KQ4)   Ghosts are the restless spirits of the dead. It is said that they can only be exorcised or expunged by returning to them that which they desire in their afterlife. Usually this is some favorite possession that was connected somehow with their death. Some spirits become ghosts, however, because of being dominated by a stronger spirit soon after their passing to the other side, and yet others have it thrust upon them as penance for misdeeds committed. In most cases ghosts cannot harm mortals directly, but they can frighten us into doing things that are both stupid and fatal.

The restless ghosts that Rosella had to pacify all needed something from their past life; the baby wanted its rattle, the weeping widow her locket, the miser his bag of gold, the lord his medal of honor, and the boy his toy horse. When they received these, they were able to rest quietly forever—we hope. (For more details, see Chapter 7, Grave Matters.)

Giants (KQ1)   Giants are very large and very strong humans, although there are reports of giants that are merely humanoid, resembling humans. Jack the Giant-Killer, for instance, fought giants with two and three heads—hardly what one would think normal for humans. In London, effigies have been constructed to the giants Gog and Magog. The Bible speaks of giants walking the earth in the distant past. In fact, the most famous giant in western culture is Goliath, who fought for the Philistines against King Saul of Israel.

No warrior dared fight the giant in single combat except for the boy David. David killed Goliath by striking him on the head with a stone shot from his sling. David kept Goliath's sword and used it later when he fought Saul.

Giants are massive beings, the smallest of whom are over ten feet tall, and the largest big enough to have their heads touch the clouds.

Gingerbread house   (KQ1)   The home of the witch Dahlia. This house has been made famous by the story of Hansel and Gretel, the children of a poor woodcutter. The man's wife had died, and he married a woman who did not like children. She told him that they could not afford to feed the children, and convinced him to abandon them in the forest. Hansel and Gretel overheard their plans, however. As they were led deep into the woods, they dropped pebbles to mark their way home. Their stepmother was not at all amused when they returned the next day.

Some time later the wicked woman convinced the man again to abandon the children so that there would be enough food for the two adults to eat. Again the children overheard, so they dropped crumbs behind as they were led even deeper into the dark depths of the forest. This time though, a bird ate the crumbs, and the Hansel and Gretel discovered they were lost. On the third day, the hungry children followed another bird and came to a small house made all of gingerbread, with windows of sugar and windowsills of cake. The house was the home of a wicked witch. She imprisoned Hansel and began to fatten the boy in order to eat him. She enslaved Gretel and made the poor girl do her bidding, intending also to eat the girl.

One day the witch asked Gretel to climb into her large oven to check how the bread was baking. Gretel was clever enough to know that the witch intended to push her in and bake her, so Gretel acted stupid and asked the witch to show her exactly how to climb in. The moment the witch did so, Gretel pushed her in and slammed the door behind. She freed her brother.

They took all the gold and jewels they could find from the house, and eventually found their way home. Their happy father greeted them warmly when he saw them—his nasty wife had died while they were gone and he asked them to forgive him. They lived happily ever after.

Gnome (KQ1, KQ5)   Another of the races of little people. Gnomes are close cousins of both the dwarfs and the dark elves and are associated with the spirits of both the earth and the mountains. Most, but not all, live underground and are said to guard veins of precious metals and stones, as well as vast, ancient treasures that have been buried there. Gnomes were given their name and differentiated from dwarfs by the physician Paracelsus in the early fifteenth century.

See also Rumplestiltskin.

Goats (KQ1)   Goats are well known for their total dislike of trolls. There is a tale of three billy goats on their way to pasture. They had to cross a bridge to get there, and a nasty troll lived under it. Now some trolls like to eat the flesh of humans, but all of them delight in devouring goats. As the first goat went across, the troll went for it; but the clever beast convinced the troll to wait for his bigger brother, as he would make a larger meal. The troll waited and rushed the second goat, who too convinced the troll that there was a yet larger goat still to come. When the largest of the billy goats arrived, he rushed the troll, butted it off the bridge, and killed it.

It is said that goats will eat almost anything; show one a carrot and it follows you anywhere. It has even been said in this world that if you show a goat an old shoe or a tin can it follows you anywhere.

Golden Eggs (KQ1, KQ4)   Graham climbed a large tree in Daventry and found a nest containing a golden egg, but we do not know what bird laid this treasure. There is a story of a goose that laid golden eggs until the person who discovered the goose got greedy and cut it open looking for more.

Rosella was forced by Lolotte to find the hen that laid golden eggs. This bird was guarded by an ogre and his wife.

See also Beanstalk.

Golden Fish (KQ4)   After King Graham opened the third magic door, he was transported to a strange land. There he found a net, which he cast into the sea and caught a large golden fish. Graham returned the fish to the ocean, and, in gratitude, it transported him to the enchanted isle where he found Valanice imprisoned.

There are many tales in our world of fish who do favors in return for being put back. In one, a poor fisherman catches a golden fish who grants him and his wife a castle on the condition that he not tell the woman how it came to be. In time, though, he broke his silence and his new riches disappeared. He became a fisherman again, and again caught the fish. Same deal. Same result. Same story. The third time he caught the fish, it told him to take it home and cut it into six pieces—two to eat, two to plant, and two to feed to his horse. Eventually there grew two golden lilies, the horse had two golden foals, and the fisherman and his wife had two golden sons.

Graham (KQ1, KQ2, KQ3, KQ4, KQ5)   King of Daventry. We know much about Graham's adventures, but very little about his background. What we do know about his life before his quest for the three treasures is contained in Part 1 of the Chronicles.

It does seem strange, though, that the man we come to admire so much during his early adventures could be the same person who sent innocent girls off to be sacrificed to the fire-breathing dragon. Perhaps his good judgment and wisdom hadn't recovered from the shock of Alexander's kidnapping, or perhaps it was just poor advice on the part of his prime minister.

Graham greatly admired his father. Derek Karlavaegen mentions once, in passing, that Graham's father was a nobleman and a close friend of Good King Edward. He wanted his son to be a scholar as well as a fighter. Derek also mentions that Graham's father died defending Daventry in one of the border wars, but never once does he mention the man's name.

Grandma (KQ2) Grandma lives in a neat little cottage in the woods of Kolyma. When King Graham first met her, she was sick in bed and unable to talk. Later Graham brought her a pot of chicken soup that, of course, cured her of her ills. Grandma told Graham to reach under her bed and take the black cloak and ruby ring he would find there; he did, and then he put them on. Thus Graham was mistaken for Count Dracula and was able to obtain easy passage to his castle, and past the ghosts guarding it.

How the woman came by Dracula's cape and ring is a mystery, but it is often said that the Vampire Prince takes living women as lovers. Perhaps they had had a romantic liaison in the past, but if grandma kissed, she sure ain't telling.

See also Riding Hood.

Green Isles (KQ5) The home of Princess Cassima. It is said that they are a warm and sunny place, with women so beautiful as to make jewels weep. Little else is known of the place, but Derek Karlavaegen does include them in his map of Daventry.

Greensleeves The court anthem of the Kingdom of Daventry. The tune is well known in our world.

Gypsies (KQ5) No one knows where the gypsies come from, or where their first home was. The gypsies first appeared in Europe around the 14th century (if not sooner) and spread a tale that they came from a place named Little Egypt. To this day, no one knows for sure where Little Egypt was, but the people soon were called Gypsies, the name is a corruption of the word Egyptian. They call themselves the Rom. Many scholars link them and their language to northern India.

Gypsies are a wandering folk, always moving from place to place, staying a while, and them moving on. We tend to think of them as moving in wagons drawn by horses, but today automobiles and campers are closer to the truth. Another romantic image is that of the gypsy woman dancing around a fire to wild, exotic music, slapping the time on her tambourine, while dark, handsome gypsy men watch with burning eyes and rising passions—I guess that's why it's called a romantic image.

Gypsies also have a reputation as fortune tellers, either gazing through a crystal ball or by the reading of Tarot cards. It is often said that one must cross a gypsy's palm with silver—or, preferably, gold—in order for them to perform that service for you. It makes sense; no one likes to work for free. This is what Graham did, and Madame Mushka then showed him the true nature of the trouble which had befallen Daventry. Later, when he returned to their camp, he found that the gypsies, as is their lifestyle, had moved on to someplace else.

Gwydion (KQ3, KQ4, KQ5) The name Manannan gave to Prince Alexander— Graham and Valanice's son—while he was captive in Llewdor.

In the Welsh legends, there are many tales told of Gwydion, a great magician and maker of illusions. He is said to have had a way with words, and the name Gwydion even means "to speak poetry". Many of the tales of

Gwydion are of his youth as a magician and warrior. Unlike the Gwydion of Daventry, the Welsh youth Gwydion was head-strong. He became embroiled in a number of dubious, if not evil, incidents. In one, he and his brother stole a pair of animals from King Arawn of the underworld. In the ensuing battle of Cad Goddeu, Gwydion transformed a forest into an army of sentient trees. At another time, Gwydion casts his illusions to start a war in order that his brother might obtain a woman he desired. That act led to massacre, murder, madness and worse. The punishment Gwydion and his brother suffered for their acts was to be turned each year into beasts that must mate with each other. Their offspring were to be their reminders of how they had offended nature.

In later life, Gwydion redeemed himself and became known as a giver and restorer of life, working with the natural world for good purposes.

See also Alexander.

Hagatha (KQ2) The witch who kidnapped Valanice and imprisoned her in the Crystal Tower. Graham's rescue of Valanice set off a series of events that have shaped the destiny of Daventry. A *Daventry People* excerpt that Derek sent to us (written soon after Alexander's escape) speaks of Hagatha as sister to Manannan, and claims that Manannan kidnapped Graham and Valanice's son in revenge for Graham deed against Hagatha. It also says that Dame Hagatha disappeared from Kolyma soon after the incident. Of course, Mordack's kidnap of Castle Daventry and everyone in it was a direct, if unforseen, consequence of Alexander's triumph over Manannan.

In his later recounting of Graham's rescue of his family and the castle, Derek postulates that Hagatha's evil family is the cosmic balance to Graham's. He says that nothing has been heard of either Hagatha or

Manannan since Graham destroyed their brother Mordack. He thinks that is a bad sign.

Harp (KQ5)   An ancient stringed instrument which is still used in the late 20th century. Somewhat triangular in shape, it is often confused with its smaller, and equally ancient, cousin known as the lyre. Harps (and harp-like instruments) have been traced as far back as ancient Egypt and Assyria, and many different cultures developed their own versions of it. The smaller harps were easily carried by travelling poets and musicians, and among Gaelic peoples especially, harps and harpists were particularly venerated. It is said that the children of Israel hung their harps on the branches of willow trees as they wept by the rivers of Babylon during their captivity. The harp that Graham found was also in the possession of a willow, this one a weeping willow.

Harpies (KQ5)   The harpies were originally wind-spirits in Greek mythology, and even Homer treats them as winds in the *Odessy*. Later, in the Jason and the Argonaut stories, they became horribly ugly, shrieking birds with the faces of women. These harpies were considered particularly foul, loathsome, disgusting and merciless. In the *Aeneid*, Virgil gives the name of the Harpy chieftess as Celaeno. The name *Harpies* does not come from the word harp, and there are no stories of harpies actually liking harp music, or even having any musical talent. On the other hand, music doth hath charms to sooth the savage breast.

There is a large colony of these beasts residing on a small island off the east coast of the continent of Serenia. This island is well-known to mariners and certain merchants. In the winters, when the harpies have migrated to somewhat warmer regions, the island is mined for its abundant deposits of guano. It is said to be extremely strong stuff, but makes the best fertilizer in world.

Haunted house (KQ4) A large house in central Tamir surrounded by a graveyard on two sides. It's known to some as Whateley Manor, and it is said to have been transported to Daventry when its inhabitants and others—strange others—*withdrew* from our world. Rosella had to pacify five ghosts who haunted the mansion, including the spirit of a former lord of the manor from before the days of old, dark Wilbur Whateley. The house also contains a hidden tower, the door to which can only be discovered by looking at a portrait above the fireplace in the parlor.

See also Ghosts.

Herbert (KQ5) Herbert is the name of the prince that King Graham met at the beginning of his journeys in Serenia. Sitting on a branch that had fallen from an ash tree, weary and alone, he seemed somewhat despondent at the time. Herbert told Graham that he was sad because a witch had caused his beloved to disappear. He was searching for her, although fruitlessly.

It would have been quite easy for Prince Herbert to continue wallowing in his hurt, becoming more and more paralyzed with inaction and self-pity. Instead, he picked up his motivation and determination, got off of his ash, and got on with his search.

Hermit (KQ5) An ancient mariner that Graham met on the coast of Serenia. Although quite old, feeble and almost deaf, age had not taken away his skill with medicinal herbs and natural medicines. He was able to effect a quick cure to the wounds Cedric had suffered at the talons of the harpies. Derek speculates that the hermit might be the same man who once was cursed to wear an albatross around his neck as penance for killing one such harmless bird. That poor soul is said to walk the worlds forever telling his tale, and its moral:

> He prayeth well, who loveth well
> Both man and bird and beast.
> He prayeth best, who loveth best
> All things both great and small;
> For the dear God who loveth us,
> He made and loveth all.

(This is a moral that King Graham seems to embody in his encounters with all that he meets. It is why, I feel, he gets so much aid and comfort from others.)

Perhaps the hermit finally found peace to join his forgiveness in a small hut by the ocean. If so, perhaps that is why he heals wounded birds so easily.

Iconomancy (KQ5) A form of magic that uses no words in its casting. It was used by Graham and Mordack in their final magical battle.
See also Chapter 9.

King Edward the Benevolent (KQ1) The monarch preceding Graham, Edward evidently consolidated the present kingdom of Daventry, increasing its size severalfold. He built the great Castle Daventry—both as a gift for his bride, Maylie, and as the defensive and administrative center of the realm. Edward is well known for losing the three great treasures of Daventry, Merlin's Mirror, the Shield of Achille, and the Chest of Gold. It is said that his love for Maylie is what drove him to perform the great and heroic deeds that created the kingdom. It is also said that it was her death that drove him to the mistakes that almost destroyed it.

Lake Maylie (KQ1, KQ3) A lake northeast of the town of Daventry. It was given its name by the people of the kingdom in honor of King Edward's wife. It was Edward and Maylie's favorite spot, and they could be seen on or by its waters almost every balmy night. After Maylie's death and the misfortunes that befell the kingdom, people began to shun the lake. King Graham and Queen Valanice, however, took to spending much of their time there, and it soon returned to favor among the general population.

Ironically, it was on the shore of Lake Maylie that Prince Alexander was stolen from his cradle by the wizard Manannan. After the incident, many people refused to go anywhere near it, saying it was a haunted and unlucky place.

Land of the Clouds (KQ1, KQ3) A land high above Daventry; the home of giants and dragons. It is accessible by climbing a beanstalk or through a stairway that travels up through the mountains. This place is dangerous not just because of the denizens who inhabit it, but due to the fact that there is very little solid ground. Much of the footing is made up of clouds, meaning there is no footing at all in these spots—not for a long way down!

Leprechauns (KQ1) Another of the races of little people; in our world leprechauns are found only in Ireland. They are shoemakers by trade and are very shy. Although some prefer to dwell underground, leprechauns like to inhabit green, secluded places; unless they want you to see them, they can only be discovered by following the sound of their hammering. Legends say that if you come upon a leprechaun unawares, it must lead you to treasure. If you take your eye off of the leprechaun, however, it vanishes.

Some leprechauns are known to have stolen human babies, but in general they're more playful and mischievous than evil. They are very fond of music and dancing, especially to a jig played on a fiddle. They are said to dance in great numbers within fairy circles under the full moon. Leprechauns young and old tend to resemble older men, and there are few reports or stories of females of the race. It has been speculated that leprechauns are nothing more than male fairies, since there are equally few mentions of male fairies.

The favorite color of the leprechaun is green, and its symbol and charm is the shamrock. In Daventry, however, the little green folk also revere the four-leaf clover.

Lion (KQ3) The king of beasts and the ultimate guard over Valanice as she was kept prisoner by Hagatha in the Crystal Tower. King Graham has written that the beast itself was a prisoner of the witch, held in bondage by a powerful spell. Before returning to Daventry, he and Valanice traveled through the magic doors to the enchanted isle and freed the great golden lion from its chains. He claims to have taken it to its jungle home and released it, but he doesn't say just where that jungle is. Graham writes that just before the lion disappeared into the foliage, it was joined by a tall man wearing nothing but a loincloth. Both the lion and man roared to the heavens, the man beating his chest, and then they were gone.

Locket (KQ5) In his brief captivity in a Roc's nest high in the mountains of Serenia, Graham found a small gold locket amongst the twigs and grass. Inside were the portraits of two people. These were the parents of Princess Cassima, and when Graham gave the locket to her, she gave him her trust. Given all the horrors and hardships and threats Cassima must have suffered at the hands of Mordack, this was not an inconsiderable giving.

Cassima says that she lost the locket when Mordack kidnapped her in the Green Isles. She and the wizard flew to his castle in the wings of a giant bird. It must have been a Roc, and the same one who captured Graham—perhaps still under the influence and control of the evil sorcerer.

Lolotte (KQ4) The evil witch who was the great enemy of the good Fairy Queen Genesta. Lolotte stole Genesta's magic Talisman, which Rosella had to recover in order to save the lives of both her father and Genesta. She lived in a twin-towered castle on a crag high in the Impossible Mountains with her son Edgar, guarded by an army of winged monkeys. Lolotte was skeletally thin and greenish in complexion; her voice was more akin to a serpent's than a human's.

Rosella mentioned in a short interview in the *Bruce Banner* that she still wonders if she really did kill the witch and says she has unsettling dreams at times where the crone recovered from her apparently fatal wound. In the dreams, Lolotte points a blood-covered finger at Rosella and cackles, "I'll get you, my pretty! I'll get you!" repeating it over and over.

Madame Mushka (KQ5) The gypsy fortune teller who showed Graham what had become of his family after they had been captured by Mordack.

Mushka, her husband Vladic, and her three daughters appear often at carnivals and public celebrations throughout Daventry. Since the story of her meeting with Graham became widespread, her crystal ball and Tarot card readings have become much in demand. Success for Mushka has also led to successes for the rest of her family. Vladic's impassioned violin-playing elicits sighs from women everywhere; their daughters' dancing has the same effect on men. The family now travels in three wagons; one for Mushka and Vladic, one for their teenage girls, and the third for all the silver and gold that has crossed their palms.

An Encyclopedia of Daventry

Magic Beans (KQ1) Used to grow the beanstalk that took Graham up to the Land of the Clouds. To obtain them, Graham had to guess the gnome's name within three tries.

See also Beanstalk.

Magic Carpet (KQ2) The first time King Graham rubbed the brass lamp, the imprisoned djinn gave him a persian carpet with the power of flight. He used this to scale the cliffs of Kolyma in order to gain the second key to the magic doors.

In our world, magic carpets appear in many stories that come out of the Middle East. There is a story in the *Arabian Nights* of three princes—brothers—who wished to marry the same princess. They were each to travel the world for a year, and the one who returned with the greatest rarity would win the maiden's hand. One of the three treasures was a piece of tapestry that if you sat on it would instantly transport you anywhere you wished.

There is also a magic carpet mentioned in the Koran. It belonged to King Solomon and was made of green silk. It was large enough to carry Solomon, his throne, his army, his spirits, and his attendants wherever he wished to go.

Magic Doors (KQ2) In order to rescue Valanice, King Graham was required to find three keys that opened three magic doors—the last of which brought him to a strange, enchanted realm. The doors were surrounded by steep cliffs and a deep chasm and could only be reached by crossing a frayed rope bridge.

After he won Valanice's heart, Graham married her in the monastery in Kolyma not far from the destroyed bridge. As a wedding gift, the monks repaired the crossing in order that Graham and Valanice could return to the Crystal Tower and free the golden lion.

Magic Fruit (KQ4) In the middle of the joyous celebration welcoming the return of Prince Alexander and the rescue of Rosella, King Graham collapsed onto the throne room floor. To save her father from death, Rosella was offered the chance to go to Tamir where there grows a magic tree that bears but one fruit every one hundred years. The tree is hidden in a swamp within the Impossible Mountains. To reach the swamp, Rosella had to enter a waterfall, pass through a troll-infested cave, and cross a hidden abyss. Then she had to cross the deadly swamp and get by the king cobra that protected the fruit tree. One bite of the fruit cured her father and restored his vigor.

In the *Arabian Nights* story of the three brothers attempting to win the hand of the same princess (see Magic Carpet), one of them discovers a magic fruit that cured sick people of most mortal diseases. One sniff was enough to do the job. The prince was able to save the princess's life with it, having been transported to the fruit on his brother's magic carpet.

Magic map (KQ3) Alexander-Gwydion found a blank parchment in Manannan's wardrobe. As he traveled, the parchment slowly became a map, revealing where he had been. More remarkably, if the prince wanted to return to any place shown on the map, all he had to do was point to the area on the map and be teleported there in an instant. The teleportation was never so exact that it would move him to something as specific as, say, the flower garden in front of the Three Bears' house, but it would get him close enough. Also, it would never take him back to Manannan's house, just to the foot of the mountain path that he had to walk up. At sea, the map showed how close Alexander was to Daventry, and after he got there it showed where he had been in his travels through that land. The map is now on display in the Royal Library of Daventry.

Magic Staff (KQ5) When Graham spied the desert bandits opening the door to the temple, they waved a staff and shouted a magical phrase. Graham liberated the staff from a snoring cutthroat's tent so he might enter the temple himself. Interestingly, the 40 thieves that Ali Baba had to deal with used the same magic incantation, "Open, Sesame!" In order to enter that particular lair, though, they weren't required to use a magic staff.

Magic wands (KQ3, KQ5) One of the three pieces of paraphernalia that no sorcerer is without, the other two being robes and a pointed hat. The wands are made of some powerful wood, harvested at a special time, and are usually carved with magical runes and decorations. The wand is thought to be the conduit through which the magical forces are transmitted from the spell caster to its target.

Alexander was able to discover where Manannan had hidden his wand—the cabinet in his study—and used it to prepare the spells that allowed him to escape, return to Daventry, and destroy the three-headed dragon. He had to be careful with the wand; if he ever forgot to put it back in its place before the wizard returned, he surely would have been killed for his transgression. The wand of Manannan now belongs to the prince, and he uses it in the preparation of all major spells.

To be useful, magic wands need to be charged. There are many ways to do this; Manannan's cabinet was a chamber that tapped the magical energy fields and transmitted power through the aether to his wand. This had to be done on a regular basis or the wand would run out of power. Like a dead battery in our world, if this happened to the wand, it would be unable to be charged again. The wand that Crispin gave to King Graham was in such a state, whether through Crispin's forgetfulness, or his upgrading to better, or more modern, equipment.

However, with the right paraphernalia, new magical power can be transferred from a potent wand to an impotent one, depleting the charged wand in the process. This was how Graham was able to finally get Crispin's magic wand to work.

See also Power-transfer machine.

Magicians' Guild Guilds are organizations of people who practice the same craft, and they have the purpose of protecting and advancing that particular craft. In Daventry, wandering magicians have formed a loose organization called the Magicians' Guild, and its members are easily recognized by their distinctive black and purple pointed hats decorated with the image of a crescent moon—the same shape we see carved in the doors of out-buildings in this world. The guild passes on information about different spells to its members, along with magical gossip. As magicians become powerful enough to be considered sorcerers, necromancers, or thamaturgists, they tend to leave the guild, thereby amplifying the notion that the guild is just a collection of amateurs.

See also Society of Wizards

Manannan (KQ3, KQ5) The evil wizard who kidnapped Prince Alexander and kept him as a slave for 17 years. Manannan is the brother of both Mordack, and the evil witch Hagatha (sometimes known as Dame Hagatha). Manannan is said to have kidnapped the infant Alexander in revenge for King Graham's rescue of Valanice from his sister.

Manannan taught Alexander-Gwydion to read and write, and by doing so led to his own downfall. The prince was able to find the wizard's book of magic and cast a spell that turned Manannan into a cat. Nobody knows what became of Manannan after that point. Derek Karlavaegen, who lives now in the wizard's house, says that the place was totally deserted when he arrived there a few months at Alexander's escape. There was no cat and no remains of a dead cat. It is probable that Manannan fled the house in his feline form, wandering the world until finally making the connection with his brother Mordack. Graham encountered Manannan the cat in Mordack's castle and tied him inside a cloth sack. He was left behind in the castle when Graham, his family, and Castle Daventry were joyously returned home. It is quite possible that the sack is still there containing the remains of a cat. It is also possible that the cat, Manannan, was able to escape by clawing his way out. It is even possible that he has been able to effect a cure for his feline condition. And, if this is true, then Manannan may well be hiding someplace plotting new revenge.

In our world, there are many stories about a most powerful weather wizard by the name of Manannan Mac Lir, after whom the Island of Man in the Irish Sea is named. It is said that Manannan had a magic horse that could travel easily across both the land and the waves, had a magic ship that could take him anywhere without the use of sail or oar, raised storms at will, wore armor, which shone as bright as the sun and which could not be pierced, and possessed a cloak of invisibility—and these are just some of the wonders that surrounded him. It is also said that Manannan had a special fondness for the Irish. There are even stories that link Manannan with a Welsh hero by the name of Gwydion.

Curiously, he is said to be a most happy and generous wizard who brought happiness to all around him. This is quite unlike Daventry's Manannan.

Manannan's Clock (KQ3) The wizard kept a magical device in his house that recorded the passing of time. Alexander says that the time it kept was different from the time normally recognized in Daventry. From this evidence, it is safe to assume that time runs differently in that universe, slower than it flows here. If Manannan's clock were some sort of clock from our world, then we must wonder how he obtained it. Of course, we have not solved the mystery of the Eye Between the Worlds, either; it apparently is

Manannan's computer. There seems to be much truth in the Daventry saying that "Any magic, sufficiently advanced, is indistinguishable from technology."

Marionette (KQ5) A puppet that is manipulated by strings. Graham, who has an eye and an appreciation of first-rate workmanship, was given a hand-made marionette by a gnome in Serenia in exchange for a magic spinning-wheel. Later he used the marionette to buy a sled for his trip through the mountains.

Maylie (KQ1) Wife of King Edward the Benevolent and the beloved person after whom Lake Maylie was named.
See also King Edward.

Maze (KQ5) Mordack had a number of defenses in order to prevent intruders from getting into, or out of, his castle. One of these was the way in which he constructed his dungeon. This maze served to frustrate any escape by the prisoners that were kept in the dungeon cells. It also did the same thing to anyone who entered the castle there. Mazes are built to befuddle and confuse all who enter them without either a map or knowledge of the way through. Mordack's maze also had a creature—Dink, for want of a better name— patrolling and protecting it. Dink was trained by the wizard to let no one leave the maze alive. Dink, however, is more stupid than deadly; although, to attract him is fatal enough. Princess Cassima was able to befriend Dink and his brother Sam. This warm human contact probably had much to do with Graham's opportunity to survive his encounter with the deadly beast.

Medusa (KQ3) As he roamed the great desert of Llewdor, Alexander-Gwydion was attacked by this grotesque monster. One glance at her face would have turned him to stone. He averted his face, though, and let the creature see her own awful reflection in Manannan's hand mirror, turning herself into a statue instead.

Although the desert of Llewdor is apparently home to many creatures known as medusas, in our world there was only one Medusa. Medusa was one of three gorgons, creatures with snakes for hair, boarlike tusks, claws of bronze, and golden wings. The other gorgons were named Stheno and Euryale. It was Medusa's flashing eyes that could turn both mortals and immortals to stone.

Medusa was destroyed by Perseus, who cut off her head while she slept, using a polished shield to guide his blow so he would not have to look directly at the monster's face. Medusa was remarkable even after death; from her neck was born the winged horse Pegasus, the blood from her left side was a poison, and the blood from her right could restore the dead to life.

Another story says that Medusa was originally a beautiful girl who thought she was as lovely as the goddess Athena, especially her hair. As punishment, the goddess turned the girl's hair into snakes.

Merlin's Mirror (KQ1, KQ2, KQ3) One of the three great treasures of Daventry, along with the Shield of Achille and the Chest of Gold. The mirror has the power to foretell the future. Edward and the rulers before him used it mostly for weather and crop forecasting, but Edward and Maylie did use it at least once to look upon the image of Daventry's next king. The mirror was stolen from Edward and Maylie by a sorcerer, and the thief hid it in a cave guarded by a fire-breathing dragon. Graham was able to reach the dragon by climbing down a well and dousing the dragon's flame.

The legend in Daventry is that the mirror was first found in a cave beneath the earth, next to the crystal coffin of a great necromancer who was thought to be Merlin himself. The Merlin we know was a great magician and the advisor to King Arthur and a number of other kings. It is said that it was

Merlin who created the Round Table for his monarch, and perhaps even Stonehenge. Merlin possessed a wondrous mirror with which he was able look into the future or gaze upon anyone or any place he wished. He used it often to help Arthur become victorious in battle.

Graham used the mirror while he was searching for a wife. It was within its mahogany frame that he first saw the image of Valanice, imprisoned in the Crystal Tower. This is similar to a story in our world where a fair prince was eager to find a bride. He looked into a magic mirror and saw the loveliest of women, but he did not know who or where she was. Often he looked upon her and once saw that she was looking into her own magic glass, and in it was his own image. He was looking at her looking at him. This sent him into the world where he finally found her and they lived happily ever after.

Mermaids (KQ2, KQ5) Graham met a mermaid who was sitting on a rock along the west coast of Kolyma. He gave her a bouquet of flowers in acknowledgment of her beauty, and she called forth a sea horse to carry Graham to King Neptune. Neptune gave Graham the key to the first of the magic doors. When Graham made his final crossing of the Northern Sea to Mordack's castle, he was escorted and led by another mermaid. Her name was Pearl.

There are legends about mermaids everywhere in our world. They are semihuman beings that are human from the head to the waist and fish below, but at times the mermaid is allowed to take the entire form of a human being. There are many stories of mermaids—all of whom are said to be beautiful—marrying human men. Sometimes the mermaid remains on land with her husband, thus losing her magical powers. At other times the mermaid is able to bring the man to live with her under the sea, preserving his life with her magic.

An Encyclopedia of Daventry

There are also similar stories about mermen.

Minstrel (KQ4) In her adventures in Tamir, Rosella met a wandering minstrel by the name of Frankie of Avalon. He played the lute and sang, both with little skill. Rosella gave a book of Shakespeare's plays to the man and in return was given his lute. When last seen, Frankie was emoting loudly to the world and declaring that he had found his true profession—that of actor. I'm not sure how long he kept that vow; in one of the *Bruce Banner* transcripts that Derek Karlavaegen has sent, there is an advertisement for "a musically comedic adaptation of the Bard's masterpiece, *Hamlet*—a world premier by the one and only Frankie of Avalon!"

Monastery (KQ2) The Monastery of the Blessed Wilbury is a resting place and haven for weary travelers in western Kolyma. Its great bell is chimed a half hour before sundown each night to warn all that hear it of the time—after sundown, the Prince of Vampires hunts for food. There King Graham stopped to pray for a bit while he was searching for Valanice, and was given a silver cross by one of the monks, Brother Fragola. With this cross worn about his neck, Graham was able to enter Dracula's castle safely.

Graham and Valanice were married in the chapel of the monastery by Brother Fragola. He is now the royal chaplain to the court of Daventry.

Monkey soldiers (KQ4) Lolotte's soldiers and bodyguards, these winged monkeys served the wicked witch only because of a spell of blind obedience she had cast over them. They were freed of the enchantment after Rosella shot Lolotte with Cupid's arrow. There is a great resemblance between Lolotte's former goons and the monkey soldiers Dorothy encountered in Oz. Those creatures, however, were only bound to serve the witch there three times, a much different situation than their counterparts in Daventry. Although they had their freedom to leave after Rosella's victory, Derek mentions that many stayed on to serve Edgar, whom they thought wasn't such a bad soul at all.

Mordack (KQ5) The brother of Manannan and the witch Hagatha. Mordack was an extremely powerful sorcerer, but his mastery of the magical arts wasn't enough to return Manannan to his human form. For this reason, and to revenge his brother, Mordack was able to capture King Graham's family—and Castle Daventry!— then shrink and transport them to his laboratory on an island far away from Daventry. This was not an insignificant feat. He was finally beaten and extinguished by Graham in a monumental magical battle.

Derek Karlavaegen speculates that a powerful evil family must exist in their universe in order to balance the presence of the powerful and good royal family of Daventry. He feels that such conflict is part of the order of any universe, not just to balance forces, but to give purpose to existence. If he is correct then this means that good and evil (or whatever one wants to call the two) *must* exist—*just to keep things interesting!* Now, *that's* an interesting theory.

Mordack's Henchman (KQ5) Mordack seems to have had but one guard in the living and working areas of his castle. This nameless henchman was incredibly strong, tireless, and loyal. It was also incredibly clumsy. Cassima says that the henchman was related somehow to Dink, although whether he was made from parts of Dink or his tissue is not clear. Whatever its true origin, the henchman roamed the halls and rooms of the castle without the need of sleep or food, relying on its strength and speed to capture all intruders.

Mordack's Island (KQ5) Mordack's island is a powerful and mysterious place situated somewhere in the Northern Sea, east of Serenia. It consists of a few sheer vertical peaks, with almost no level areas. At its summit is Mordack's castle, the only path to which passes between the lethal gaze of a pair of stone cobra dragons. Occasional stories told by mariners say that the island seems suspended in the air, floating its mass above the waves as if hanging from an invisible string. One or two of these mariners say they have sailed under the island, and have seen the dungeons of hell hanging above their masts. As has been noted before, stories like this are often told when sailors and strong drink share a table.

Mummy (KQ4) The last task Lolotte set upon Rosella was that of finding Pandora's Box. Rosella located it in a crypt built into the side of the Impossible Mountains. The magic box was inside the place, guarded by an undead Egyptian mummy. The princess was carrying a black scarab charm at the time and was thus protected from the creature.

Almost all cultures, at one time or another have attempted to preserve their dead. Technically, a mummy is simply the preserved remains of a corpse, regardless of whether the preservation was assured by artificial means or natural ones. The mummy Rosella encountered is similar to the ones many people are familiar with in films—shuffling around slowly, constrained by its wrappings. The most popular story is of an Egyptian priest who was in love with the pharaoh's daughter. He was wrapped like a mummy and buried alive for his insolence. He returned to life thousands of years later when his tomb was finally opened, and he searched for Tana leaves in order to bring his beloved back to life alongside him. Kharis—that was the poor priest's name—was not evil at all, but all thought of him as a monster, and he ended up acting accordingly. Such is forever the misfortune of the undead.

Mushroom (KQ1) When the condor dropped Graham by the hole leading to the land of the leprechauns, he found a mushroom growing nearby. As it turned out, Graham needed to eat the fungus in order to return to the world above ground. This solution to his predicament is much like the one Alice used in her famous adventures. At one point in Wonderland she met a hookah-smoking caterpillar sitting on a mushroom. Between puffs, the creature told Alice the mushroom was what she needed to change her size—one side to make her taller, the other side to make her shorter. Since the girl had already been stretched and shrunk by a variety of cakes and potions, she had no trouble at all believing what the caterpillar said.

In another adventure underground, the caterpillar showed Alice a mushroom and said that if she ate the top of the mushroom, it would make her taller, and the stalk would make her shrink.

Needle in the Haystack (KQ5) Following his father's advice—"Check carefully into, under, above, below, and behind things"— Graham went searching through a haystack outside of Serenia's Swarthy Hog Inn. With the help of King Antony, he found a golden needle which had been lost by or, more likely, stolen from the town's tailor. When Graham returned the needle, he was given a cloak to warm him on his journey through the mountains.

The phrase "Needle in a haystack" connotes something which is very hard to find or locate. While we might assume that the saying has been around forever, written records of it only go back about 500 years. In Don Quixote, Cervantes writes about looking "...for a needle in a bottle (bundle) of hay". Thomas More refers to "...a nedle in a medow", and Melville to a "...needle in a hay-mow." James Fenimore Cooper in the "Pathfinder" has a character complain, "I might make up to pick out a single needle on this deck...but I much doubt if I could pick one out of a haystack." Come to think of it, just finding any specific reference to "...finding a needle in a haystack" is somewhat like finding a needle in a haystack.

An Encyclopedia of Daventry

Neptune (KQ2) Lord of the sea. Graham received the first key to the magic doors from him after he returned Neptune's trident to him in his throne room under the sea. In our world, Neptune is the Roman name for Poseidon, the Greek god of sea and water. One of the three sons of Cronus, he and his brothers, Zeus and Pluto, killed their father and divided the world between them—Poseidon getting the fluid part. He lived in a golden palace beneath the waves, where he caused both storms and favoring winds. Sailors, naturally, worshipped him, and he was thought of as the god of navigation. His trident was used to lash the sea to fury, cause springs to gush from the ground, and cause earthquakes. For this last reason, one of his descriptive names was *enosichthon,* which translates to something like "a real earth shaker!"

Nightingale (KQ2) When King Graham entered Hagatha's cave, he found a nightingale in an ornate cage. While the nightingale is a somewhat plain bird in appearance, its song is thought by many to be beyond compare. Graham rescued the creature from the witch after first covering the cage with a cloth to muffle any sound it might make as they were leaving. When the king eventually arrived at Milvia's Olde Antique Shoppe, he discovered that the bird had been stolen from the woman by the witch. For returning the bird to her, Milvia gave Graham the brass lamp he needed to obtain the second key to the magic doors.

There is a story of an emperor who so admired the song of the nightingale that he had one captured and caged for his enjoyment. So much did he like the song, and so much did he dislike the bird's plain appearance, that the ruler had a jeweled, mechanical nightingale constructed—one with a song as lovely as the real thing. In time, the emperor grew ill and was told that only the song of a nightingale might save him. Alas! The song of the jeweled bird didn't, so he sent for the plain bird he had rejected. The nightingale agreed to sing for the emperor in return for a promise never to be caged again.

The emperor agreed, and the bird's marvelous song, the most beautiful in the world, saved his life, and the bird was set forever free.

Ogre (KQ1, KQ4)   Ogres are large, human-eating creatures of humanlike appearance. Often mistaken for giants, ogres range in size from 9 to 12 feet tall, with strength to match. They have prominent tusks growing out of their jaws and large talons on their feet—both quite suitable for tearing their prey open. Some ogres are reported to also have small horns growing out of their hard, thick skulls; their skins are various dirty, dark yellowy shades and covered with warts. Their tempers range from bad to worse. Ogres live in dark places, mostly underground, but often deep in some dark hollow or forest. They tend to live in pairs, male with female, and both are equally fearsome.

Graham stumbled across one in his exploration of Daventry; he was invisible at the time, so the ogre didn't see him. It probably smelled Graham, as that sense is well developed in their kind. Rosella had to enter the house of an ogre couple in order to steal the hen that laid golden eggs. She waited in a closet until the male finished counting his treasure and fell asleep, then dashed out and took the bird. The ogre woke before she could get out of the house, and she was barely able to outrun it to safety (ogres have long legs; they're not fast but can cover a lot of ground quickly). Rosella, like her father before her, was lucky to get away.

See also Beanstalk.

Oracle (KQ3)   An oracle is someone who divines the future by special means in a special place. In a manner of speaking it is both the person and the place, each inseparable from the other. To confuse things further, the prophecy itself is also known as an oracle. The most famous oracle was in Delphi in ancient Greece, and people came from all over the Mediterranean world to seek its advice. It even became common practice for cities to seek counsel with the oracle there before undertaking an action of any magnitude. An elected ruler often sought advice before taking office. By tradition, the oracles were female, either virgins or married women over the age of fifty.

There were many methods by which oracles read the future—the entrails of certain animals, the rustling of tree limbs, smoke, water—the list is long. No matter how it was done, the pronouncements of the oracles were, at best, obscure, confusing, and open to various interpretations. Getting a prophecy was the easy part; knowing just what it meant was another matter altogether. Alexander-Gwydion was lucky—the oracle he encountered spoke to him plain and clear, more like a gypsy fortune-teller than a seer.

Organ (KQ4, KQ5) At the top of the secret tower in the haunted house—sometimes known as Whateley Manor—there is a fine pipe organ. Rosella discovered this when she first visited the house, but found nothing unusual about it other than the fact that it was hidden. However, when she played the sheet music she found in the trunk in the house's attic, a secret compartment opened in the organ to reveal a key to the crypt in the mountain. The secret drawer would only open if that certain tune were played. While there is no apparent relationship at all, one cannot help imagining a masked phantom playing eerie melodies in a chamber hidden in the sewers of Paris.

There is another organ in Mordack's castle. Graham admires it for its fine, if somewhat macabre, workmanship. Its tone is another matter. Graham dared not try it out while he was there. He was sure that if he did, he would alert Mordack of his presence on the island. I'm sure Graham was correct in his decision to keep his hands off of the instrument.

Pan (KQ4) After receiving the lute from the minstrel, Rosella encountered the demi-god Pan, who was dancing and playing a flute. Rosella joined the half-man half-beast by playing a tune on her lute. After she gave the lute to Pan, he gave the girl his flute and fled. Rosella used the flute to charm the snake guarding the magic fruit.

Pan is sometimes confused with a satyr, who is a Panlike creature with the head and torso of a human and the legs, horns, and ears of a goat. Pan was more beast than man and was thought by some to be the god of fertility and the protector of herds and flocks. He played the pipes and could make beasts stampede; it is from this that we get our word "panic." The satyrs, on the other hand, were playful rogues, lovers of wine, women, song, and dance. Their instrument was the flute, and they delighted in playing it while dancing with nymphs in the forest.

Pandora's Box (KQ4) The object of Rosella's final quest from Lolotte, she found it hidden in the crypt in the mountain, guarded by a walking mummy. After defeating the wicked witch, Rosella returned the box and relocked the crypt.

Pandora was supposed to be the first woman, bestowed with all the choicest gifts of the gods. She was created by Zeus as part of his revenge against Prometheus, who stole fire from heaven and gave it to us mortals. Pandora's Box was actually a jar given to her by Zeus; it contained all of the evil and misery the god could conceive.

Pandora was given to the brother of Prometheus who fell in love with her and made her his wife. To satisfy her husband's curiosity, Pandora opened the jar, just as Zeus had planned. Out flew all the evil, pain, and misery that had been bottled up inside. Perhaps some evil was still caught within after the distraught Pandora hastily closed the jar; that would explain why Lolotte wanted it so badly.

An Encyclopedia of Daventry

Pegasus (KQ2) The great, white, winged horse that was born from Medusa when her head was cut off by Perseus. Pegasus could only be captured and tamed by use of a golden bridle. Athena gave this bridle to Bellerophon to help him in his task of killing the Chimaera—a fire-breathing beast with the head of a lion, the body of a goat, and the tail of a great serpent. Later, Bellerophon tried to ride Pegasus up Mount Olympus, but the winged horse threw him off down the mountain and escaped. Bellerophon did not live happily ever after. He was doomed to spend the rest of his life wandering the world as an outcast, lame and shunned by all.

Graham encountered Pegasus after he accidently threw the djinn's bridle on the great snake in the cliffs above Kolyma.

See also Bridles.

Pirates (KQ3) The pirates of the western sea are the ones who took Alexander-Gwydion's gold for passage to Daventry and then imprisoned him in the hold of their ship. What they planned to finally do to him is unknown, as the prince escaped by casting a sleep spell on them as they approached landfall. Alexander was able to recover their buried treasure, and he took it home with him to Daventry.

As far as Derek Karlavaegen knows, all of the pirates but one are now dead, the victims of a great storm spell cast upon them by Prince Alexander some weeks after his return home. The lone survivor washed up on the coast of Llewdor babbling of shipmates being consumed by sharks and others swallowed by a great squid after being crushed in its tentacles. The unfortunate man also kept whimpering a word that sounded something like "Cthulhu," but his mind had been shattered by the experience and he only continued to chatter incoherently.

Power-Transfer Machine (KQ5) From the point of view of the Daventry universe, Mordack's power-transfer machine is a key indicator as to just how evil that sorcerer had become. Technology is looked on as evil by many in Daventry, and Mordack's cheesy-looking contraption of steam and wheels and levers would make many there shudder. It is organically powered, which is a small consolation to its critics.

The power-transfer machine was kept on the balcony above the main part of Mordack's laboratory. Its purpose, as far as anyone has been able to determine, is to siphon magical power from a fully charged magic wand to another, one from which most or all of the power had been drained. While Graham is no advocate or apologist for technology, he holds little prejudice for the few in Daventry that do. Because of this open-mindedness, he was able to bring himself to use the machine to charge Crispin's magic wand. In a way it's ironic that the Kingdom of Daventry, founded upon and embedded in the magics of its universe, was saved by such a device.

See also Magic Wands.

Queen Icebella (KQ5) The Ice Queen that Graham met in the high mountains of Serenia. Icebella, attended only by her army of wolves, rules the frigid peaks and icy wastes of that world. Her consort is the changeling and werewolf, Sir Greywolf.

Icebella values her isolation and privacy and enforces a policy of capital punishment for all who enter her realms without invitation. She never issues invitations. One small kiss from her will chill a man's soul; the second is cold death.

It is said that Icebella once had a warmer heart, but it was pierced by a shard from a magic mirror. That mirror had the malevolent power of reflecting all good and beautiful things as ugly and deformed. One day the mirror was dropped and pieces of it, most as tiny as the smallest grains of fine sand, were scattered by the winds throughout the world. If a grain entered someone's eye, they would see the world as an ugly place. If one entered a person's body, their heart would turn as cold and as solid as the hardest ice. And this is just what happened to Icebella.

It is also said that music has the power to thaw such a cold heart for a short time, and this quirk alone is what save the lives of Graham and Cedric. Love alone can melt the hardness, and until Icebella finds love her heart is doomed to be as frigid as her kiss.

Rat   (KQ5)   King Graham and his family are not much enamored of cats. How one's heart could not go out to such intelligent, furry, and somewhat vain creatures is a universal mystery; one whose only answer can be, "There's no accounting for taste". The royal family of Daventry is far from perfect, and their lack of fondness for felines is just one of their shortcomings.

How, you may ask, does this have to do with rats? While adventuring in Serenia, Graham spied a rat being chased by a large and mangy cat. Although the king's heart usually goes out to all beings in distress, it went out especially so that day to a rodent that most folk react to with revulsion. The old shoe that Graham hurled at the cat helped save the lives of the king's family. Without that nameless rat's gratitude and aid, Graham's quest would have either ended in a dank basement in Serenia or beneath an unclimbable cliff in the mountains. It is through small kindnesses that great monarchs are made.

Riding Hood   (KQ2)   Graham met the little girl as he walked through the woods of Kolyma. She told Graham that a wolf had stolen her basket of goodies and begged him to help her find it. The goodies were hidden in the mailbox outside Grandma's house, and when he gave them to the girl, she handed him her bouquet of wildflowers. Graham gave the flowers to the mermaid he met.

In the story about Little Red, the girl was warned by her parents that she must never stray from the path through the woods for any reason. As she took a basket of goodies (cake and wine) through the woods to Grandma's house, Red met a wolf, although she didn't know what one was. The wolf asked where she was going, and Red told him. They strolled together for a time until furry-face decided it was time to dine. He suggested that Red leave the path and pick some wildflowers for her grandmother. Disobeying her parents, Red left the path to do some picking. While she was doing this, the wolf ran ahead to the house, pretended to be the girl, and when he got inside, gobbled Granny whole. A little later Little Red arrived and noticed what big eyes, ears, hands, and teeth "Grandma" had. Of course it was the wolf in disguise, and he gobbled up the girl whole also.

After such a meal, the big, bad wolf fell asleep and began to snore loudly. The sound was heard by a hunter, who rushed inside the house thinking Grandma was ill. The hunter recognized the wolf for what it was and shot the creature dead through the head. He then heard noises from inside the wolf, and cutting the body open, found Grandma and Red alive. The girl still had the flowers clutched in her hand.

Why the wolf in Kolyma hid the basket of goodies in the mailbox we may never know. But we do know why Riding Hood was carrying flowers when she met Graham.

Ring of invisibility (KQ1) As Graham walked through Daventry on his quest for the crown, he came across an elf with whom he stopped to chat. This so surprised the small elf that he gave Graham a gold ring embedded with a tiger's eye stone. The ring was magic and, if rubbed, had the ability to turn the wearer invisible for a while. Graham used the ring accidently, but the accident saved his life.

The ring is quite similar to the enchanted ring given Rosimond by a fairy. This ring was gold with a diamond in its center; if the diamond were turned, it would render the ring's wearer invisible. The ring also had the power to give its wearer the shape of the king's son. At first the ring seemed a great gift, but grief and sorrow followed it everywhere. In the end, Rosimond returned the ring to the fairy, saying that it is dangerous to have more power than the rest of the world.

Roc (KQ5) A giant, carnivorous bird that captured Graham in the high mountains between Serenia and Daventry. On one of his voyages, the sailor Sinbad found himself carried off by a giant bird, called a roc, to a deep valley with walls too tall and steep to climb. The floor of the valley was covered with diamonds, a point not lost on Sinbad. He despaired, however, because without a way out, he would die amongst the riches. On the next day, large chunks of meat began falling out of the sky, thrown by people who collected the precious stones. It seems that eagles nested in the area and had to feed their young. When the meat landed at the bottom of the valley, the sharp points of the diamonds would stick to them. The eagles would carry the flesh—and diamonds—to their nests. The hunters would follow them and collect the gems.

Sinbad had heard of this before, but thought it was just a tall tale. Not so! Sinbad concealed himself under the largest piece of meat and held on tight. He was carried—along with plenty of diamonds—to safety, much to the amazement of the diamond hunters above.

Roman pool (KQ4) A structure in northern Tamir where Rosella discovered Cupid bathing. As she approached him, Cupid flew away startled, leaving his magic bow and arrows of love behind. Rosella used the bow and arrows to capture the unicorn, and also to defeat Lolotte.

See also Cupid.

Rose (KQ4)   After Rosella completed the last task Lolotte had demanded, she was imprisoned in Edgar's tower bedroom to wait for dawn—at which time she was to marry the witch's ugly son against her will. Worse, if she did not escape before then and recover Genesta's Talisman, then the Queen of the Fairies would die, and so too her father. Rosella was imprisoned but a few minutes when she heard a sound by the door and saw a red rose slipped under to her. When she examined it, she discovered a small gold key that allowed her to escape the room. The key also unlocked the door to Lolotte's chamber, and that is how Rosella was able to conquer the wicked witch. Because of his act on behalf of Rosella, Genesta transformed Edgar into a handsome prince, but Rosella still declined his offer of marriage.

The name Rosella, by the way, means "little rose."

See also Rosella.

Rosella (KQ2, KQ3, KQ5)   Daughter of King Graham and Queen Valanice of Daventry and twin sister of Prince Alexander. In the space of two days, just before her eighteenth birthday, Rosella was tied to a stake and left as sacrifice to a dragon, was rescued by the brother she had never met and had thought dead, watched her father collapse into a near-death coma, was taken to Tamir to find the magic fruit that would save him, kidnapped by a witch, swallowed by a whale, chased by an ogre, escaped a troll, and a few other things.

There is a curious story about a princess by the name of Rosanella, the daughter of a queen named Balanice. Balanice was extremely bright and charming, and this intelligence was passed on to her daughter, who was given the name Rosanella because of the tiny, perfect, pink rose birthmark on her neck. Rosanella, however, was kidnapped from her bed one night, and no matter how much the king and queen searched, she could not be found.

One day, twelve peasant-girls approached Balanice, each with a wicker basket, each basket containing a little girl of about the same age as Rosanella.

Each of the little girls had a pink rose in the same place as the lost princess. Balanice and her husband raised the girls as their own, and they all grew up to be beautiful, but each had a totally different disposition—gay, sweet, grave, joyful, loving, etc. They became known to all as the Rose Maidens. One day, when they were all together at a garden party, enormous bees buzzed out of the skies and flew off with the all of the Rose Maidens.

Several days later, a crystal chariot drawn by fairies flew out of the sky and came to rest outside of the palace. In the chariot, accompanied by another fairy, was the most beautiful princess anyone had ever seen. The fairy introduced the girl to the joyous king and queen as their long-lost daughter Rosanella, whom she had stolen years before. The fairy had divided the girl's character into 12 parts so that each would develop to perfection—these were the Rose Maidens, all single aspects of Rosanella.

Royal University (KQ1) After he had put his kingdom in order and before the great troubles connected with losing the magic treasures of the realm, King Edward the Benevolent founded the Royal University of Daventry. One of Edward's beliefs was that a kingdom is only as strong as its weakest minds, and he intended that Daventry would train the keenest, sharpest minds in the world. Graham was one of the university's prize pupils, and it might be said that it was only the sharpness of his mind that saved the kingdom from ruin. This more than anything else bore out the wisdom of Edward's philosophy.

Prince Alexander teaches magic now at the university, and his mother Queen Valanice is considered its best historian.

Rumplestiltskin (KQ1, KQ5) The true name of the gnome who posed the riddle to Graham, although why he insisted on it being spelled IFNK-OVHGROGHPRM is anybody's guess. Gnomes are not normally known to be pranksters, and his subsequent behavior suggests that there were motives behind the incident that we may never know.

We know Mr. R. from the story about a miller who had a beautiful daughter—a daughter so beautiful that he pridefully thought she should be the bride of the king. One day the miller was delivering flour to the castle and, noticing the king nearby, began to boast about his daughter. The king listened politely, but everyone tells kings that their daughters are the fairest in the universe. "Ah," invented the miller, "but my daughter can spin straw into gold!" Now this got the monarch's attention, and he commanded that the girl be brought to him.

The next day the king put the poor girl in a large room full of straw and commanded her to turn it to gold. The miller's daughter didn't know what he was talking about, for her father had not told her of his lie. Angry, the king threatened her, telling her that she had till dawn to change the straw or she would be killed. Try as she could, the task was impossible. The girl could not do what her father had promised, and began to weep loudly.

As she cried, a little man appeared and told her he could do the chore—if she would give him a gift. He took her necklace, turned all of the straw into gold, and then disappeared. The king was astonished, but demanded more proof of her skill. He took her to a larger room and filled it with straw, promising the same punishment if she failed. Again the little man came; this time he accepted her ring for the service and again left.

When the king saw all the gold the next day, his heart did not soften towards her; instead, he filled his largest hall with straw and demanded one last magical transformation. If she succeeded, she would become his queen. This time, she had nothing to give the little man, so he demanded she give him her firstborn child in return for saving her life. She agreed, but planned never to have a child.

The queen did have a child, however, and one night the little man came to claim it as his own. In tears the queen offered the man anything if he would not take her child. He replied that he would not, but only if she could guess his name within three days.

For two days she guessed, but she was always wrong. In desperation, she sent her servants throughout the land to discover the little man's true identity. One was successful; he said he had discovered the man dancing and laughing by a fire. He called himself Rumplestiltskin.

When he came back that night to claim the child, the queen pretended still not to know the proper name. Reaching for the baby, the little man gave her one final guess. He was so mad when she told him "Rumplestiltskin" that he stomped his foot hard enough to send him right through the floor, and he was never seen again.

At least when Graham got the answer right, the gnome was a more gracious loser.

While there is no doubt that the gnome who helped Graham in his quest for the throne of Daventry was Rumplestiltskin, there is much confusion as to the identity of the gnome he met in Serenia. He was an old gnome to be sure, and while he looked familiar to Graham, he acted as if he had never seen the monarch before in his life. However, the spinning wheel which Graham returned to him could turn straw to gold and this could only belong to one gnome. Perhaps the years had clouded both Graham and Rumplestiltskin's memories and they merely didn't recognize each other.

This is possible, but the king is fabled for his memory. Was it then that the gnome did not want to be recognized and had cast a mild befuddlement spell over Graham? Finally, mayhaps the gnome was the son (or even the grandson) of Rumplestitlskin himself; the spinning wheel having been handed down to him. Gnomes are known to live ancient lives and it does not stretch possibility too far for this to be the case. Family resemblance alone might account for Graham's sense of familiarity with the gnome. Whatever the case, it is a mystery still in wait of a solution.

Sapphire Jewels (KQ2) As King Graham adventured through the land of Kolyma in quest of Valanice, he discovered a number of pieces of fabulous jewelry—a diamond and sapphire bracelet, brooch, necklace, earrings, and tiara. He called them the Sapphire Jewels and presented them as a gift of love to his bride on the day of their wedding. Queen Valanice treasures the jewels as her dearest possessions, and as a symbol of her love for Graham and Daventry. No one in Daventry seems to know how they came to be scattered about Kolyma, but since one of the pieces—the tiara—was found in Dracula's castle, some speculate that they were dropped by one of the vampire's victims as the poor woman was flown to join the count's Legion of the Undead. Valanice smiles and dismisses this theory. She says that she has dreamed they are actually the jewels of Scheherazade, given to her by her caliph as a gift of love at the end of a thousand and one nights of storytelling. Valanice might be right.

Serenia (KQ5) The name Serenia actually refers to three distinct places. The largest is the continent of Serenia, a vast land of towering mountains, deep forests, and endless deserts. While the world of Daventry is far from fully explored, it seems likely that Serenia is the largest landmass there. It was in Serenia where folk arrived when they *withdrew* from our world to Daventry.

This continent is broken up into many kingdoms and principalities, with two of the most significant ones being the Kingdom of Daventry, and the Sovereignty of Serenia. Thus, Serenia is also the name of a nation or political state. There is also a town that goes by the name Serenia, and while it is not a city in the sense we think of them, it is an important center. There folks can buy, sell and trade essential goods, and deal with fine craftspeople for that which they cannot make for themselves. In Serenia, one can also find industry, entertainment, libraries, theaters, and many of the other trappings of urban life, Daventry style.

According to Derek Karlavaegen, it is somewhat peaceful in Serenia now. This has not always been so. Not so many years ago, the Soverignty's present Queen was abducted by a wizard named Harlin and imprisoned in Harlin's castle. Serenia's King at the time, George IV, was able to convince a wandering barbarian to attempt rescuing her. The man accomplished that quest but, since he had much more brawn than brain, walked away from the offered marriage and kingdom. He walked off into the endless desert with a bloody broadsword in one hand, and a few gold coins in the other. He neglected to carry any water. Caravan drivers who travel that deadly desert say that the warrior is there still, his bones bleached white, with only one lone boot and a few scorpions for company.

Priscilla and her husband, Kenneth the Huge, rule now. They have legislated peace and love and harmony between all. The penalties for breaching those laws is severe.

In our world, the first computer adventure game with graphics as part of it was titled "The Wizard and the Princess". It was written by Roberta Williams, and was set in Serenia.

Scarab (KQ4) The scarab is a type of beetle that was venerated by the ancient Egyptians and was associated with the sun. It is noted for pushing balls of dung before it on the ground, and it was said that likewise was the sun pushed across the sky by a giant scarab beetle. Pieces of stone were carved into the likeness of the beetle and used as charms. Since the scarab represented the sun, the charms were thought to ward off the undead. The obsidian scarab that Rosella was given by the three sister witches, therefore, was able to protect her from the mummy and zombies she encountered during her night of grave-robbing in Tamir.

Seven dwarfs (KQ4) Miners in the land of Tamir whom Rosella helped by cleaning their house. In return they gave her a bag of diamonds, which they insisted she keep. When she tried to give the diamonds back to them in their mine, they gave her a lantern to add to her loot. Rosella used the lantern to light her way through the troll's cave behind the waterfall, and she gave the diamonds to the fisherman and his wife.

In the story of Little Snow White, the girl was the child of a queen who had wished for a daughter with skin as white as snow, lips as red as blood, and hair as black as ebony. The queen died shortly after Snow White was born, and the king remarried. His new wife, Snow's stepmother, was a wicked woman who played around with the blacker forms of magic. She had a magic mirror; its power was to tell who was the fairest woman in the land. For years, the new queen asked the same question:

> Looking glass, mirror, on the wall,
> Who's the fairest one of all?

Always the answer was the queen; always, that is, until Snow White started becoming a woman. From then on the answer was always her stepdaughter, Snow White. This enraged the queen more and more until, one day, she called in the king's huntsman and commanded him to take the girl into the forest and kill her. Then he was to bring back her lungs and liver as proof of the deed. Snow White was able to talk the reluctant man out of the foul deed; she promised she would hide deep in the forest forever if he would spare her. He did, she ran, and the huntsman brought the heart and lungs of a boar to the queen, saying they were Snow White's. The woman accepted the man's story and ate the innards, thinking she was done with Snow White forever.

Snow, however, went deeper and deeper into the woods until she could go no farther. She found a small house, and when there was no answer at the door, entered to find a messy home with only cold food in the kitchen. There were seven chairs, seven bowls, seven mugs, seven pipes, and seven beds in the house. Snow White tested them all and then fell asleep. When she awoke, she was surrounded by the seven dwarfs. They took pity on her when she told them her story and said that she could live with them and they would protect her, if she would clean house and cook for them. Thus they lived happily until the evil queen asked the mirror yet again who was the fairest in the land. The mirror told her it was Snow White in the dwarfs' house. The evil stepmother was not at all pleased.

Three times did the queen try to kill Snow White. She would dress as an old woman and go to the house in the woods and give the sweet girl something fatal. The first time it was ribbons to choke her, the second, a poisoned comb. Both times though the dwarfs returned in time to save the girl. On the third occasion Snow White was given a poisoned apple, which she bit into and died. The grieving dwarfs placed her body in a glass coffin and put the coffin in the prettiest part of the woods. The coffin was found by a young prince, who was smitten by the dead girl's beauty. He told his servants to carry the coffin back to his palace, but as they picked it up, one of them stumbled and jarred the coffin. The shock dislodged the piece of poisoned apple from Snow White's throat, and she came back to life. Then they journeyed to his palace and were married.

There are two versions of what happened to the wicked stepmother. Some time after giving the girl the poisoned apple, she asks the mirror her customary question and is informed Snow White is still alive. In a rage, she throws the mirror against a wall, and one of its shards flies through the air and pierces her heart. That is one way she dies. In the other version, she is invited to attend a wedding. When she gets there the queen is shocked to discover the bride is Snow White. The wicked stepmother is captured, has her feet placed in white-hot iron slippers, and dances herself to death in them.

By the way, the dwarfs are never named in the story. Names have been given to them in the Walt Disney animated version, however, and they are Happy, Sleepy, Sneezy, Grumpy, Dopey, Doc, and Bashful.

Shakespeare (KQ4) English poet and playwright: 1564-1616. He is sometimes called the Bard of Avon, or simply the Bard. Rosella found a copy of his plays in the haunted house and gave the book to the minstrel, hoping he would stop playing and singing. Daventry is mentioned in one of his plays—Henry IV, Part III—by its ancient name "Daintry"; however, the Daventry he refers to is in our world.

Shield of Achille (KQ1) One of the three great treasures of Daventry, the shield is titanium set with emeralds, and it's believed that whoever carries the shield into battle will always be victorious. King Edward lost the shield when he gave it to a dwarf in return for a root to cure Queen Maylie's final illness. It was all a sham, and the lovely queen died, plunging Edward into his final despair. Graham was able to recover the shield from where it was hidden in the throne room of the King of the Leprechauns.

The shield was named after Achilles, a Greek hero of the Trojan War. He was said to be invulnerable because he had been dipped into the waters of the river Styx as a baby. The only way to wound Achilles was by striking his heel—the only part of his body that did not go in the water. It was an arrow wound to the heel that finally led to his death. Some believed that his shield would bestow Achilles' invulnerability on its bearer, but it was supposed lost after being placed upon the hero's chest as his body burned on its funeral pyre.

Shoeshop (KQ5) The Corner Cobbler is a prominent shop in Serenia specializing in fine hand-crafted footwear. Its proprietor, Sonny Cincinatus, uses only the finest leathers, and spends weeks making sure that each pair of shoes or boots he crafts fits perfectly and meets his high standard of quality. As a result, he and his wife were among the less prosperous merchants in town, most potential customers preferring less of a wait for their merchandise.

Graham was given a fine pair of shoes with golden buckles by the elves of the Dark Forest. Since they were too small for Graham's feet, he gave them to the poor couple at the shoeshop. He received Sonny's cobbler's hammer in return. At the time, the shoemaker and his wife declared they would retire on the money they'd get for selling the elven shoes, but later changed their minds. Their business is still meager, but it does provide them with a substantial tax write-off.

Silver cross (KQ2) This small cross on a chain was given to Graham at the monastery in Kolyma. By wearing it, he was protected against the undead, especially Count Dracula. Derek Karlavaegen writes that the king still wears the cross as a reminder of his love for Valanice, and in case he ever runs into another vampire, or "similarly unpleasant creature."

Silver whistle (KQ4) While stranded on a desert island, Rosella discovered she had a dead fish still in her pocket, which she threw at a pelican in frustration. The bird dove and caught the fish, but dropped a silver whistle from its beak as it did so. By tooting on the whistle, Rosella was able to summon a dolphin, which rescued her and returned her to the mainland of Tamir. Where the bird obtained the whistle is unknown. However, when the wicked witch was sending her minions to attack Dorothy and her friends traveling to the Emerald City, she summoned them by blowing on a silver whistle. Silver whistles are not that uncommon, though, so it is doubtful that this was the same whistle that Rosella found. On the other hand, you never know.

Slingshot (KQ1)   While in the Land of the Clouds, Graham discovered a slingshot hidden inside a tree. He had the option of using it—along with the pebbles he collected on the bank of the River Fools—to kill the giant that was protecting the Chest of Gold. He didn't, but he could have.

See also Giants.

Snakes (KQ4, KQ5)   It is said that in some parts of our world, fakirs can charm the king cobra and make it do the fakir's bidding, merely by playing a mystical tune for it on a flute. This may be true; however, it is said by more skeptical scientists who claim to have studied the phenomenon that the snake is just following the swaying motion of the person playing the music and not the music itself. The cobras in the world of Daventry don't seem to have heard of this pronouncement.

On the other hand, the snake Graham encountered in the mountains of Serenia did know something about getting spooked. Snakes, like most creatures in Daventry will startle, then flee, at sudden and unexpected noises. This particular snake took that particular pronouncement seriously.

Snow leopard (KQ4)   When Rosella visited Genesta in her bedchamber, she saw a snow leopard sitting by the side of the bed, apparently guarding the fairy queen. In her short interview in *Daventry People,* Rosella speculates that the leopard might be more than just a bodyguard. It seems that fairies must spend a day each week in the form of some animal. Rosella thinks Genesta becomes a female snow leopard and the regal beast she saw in Genesta's Ivory Tower is her animal husband.

Society of Wizards (KQ5) A professional and academic organization of the best magical minds in Daventry. It was founded in the earliest days of Daventry, immediately after the first great *withdrawal* there, by the Grand Wizard Crispinophur. The identity of the Society's leader is kept secret, but rumor has it to be Crispinophur himself, and always has been.

Made up of the leading adepts, sorcerers, magicians, wizards and necromancers in the world of Daventry, it is dedicated to advancing the state of the magical Arts, historical and thaumaturgical research, and maintaining a strict set of ethical standards. One does not apply to join the Society—one is invited, and then only after the application is proposed by a current member in good standing. That application must be approved unanimously. The Society of Wizards is not to be confused with the Magicians Guild, a collection of amateurs.

See also Magicians Guild.

Spinning Wheel (KQ5) In the house of the witch of the Dark Forest, Graham found a small spinning wheel. He took it, of course, and later gave it to a gnome he met. The gnome said that the spinning wheel had been stolen from him by the witch, and that it was magic. It had the ability to spin gold from straw.

Obviously this was the spinning wheel of Rumplestiltskin, something that is quite well-known in our world. This fact, though, has raised some serious questions as to the identity of the gnome Graham met in Serenia, since he or Alexander had encountered Rumplestiltskin on at least two prior occasions—years earlier in Daventry. I suppose some form of time warp must be considered in this matter because anything seems possible in that magical land. In that case, Graham's second meeting with the gnome could very well have been the gnome's first meeting with Graham. This is a paradox of a high order.

See also Rumplestiltskin.

Sugar cube (KQ2) After King Graham threw the bridle on the snake in the cliffs above Kolyma, it was transformed into the winged horse Pegasus. Pegasus gave Graham a sugar cube to protect him from the poison brambles that entirely cover the island on which Dracula's castle stands. It is well known that sugar cubes are a favorite treat for all horses, which is probably why Pegasus bestowed his magic gift in this form.

Sword (KQ2) One of the gifts given Graham by the djinn in the brass lamp. It had a snake carved on its handle, giving Graham the impression that it had special powers against serpents. Graham was reaching for the sword to kill the snake, when he mistakenly grabbed the bridle and tossed it on the snake. If he had killed the snake, he would never have received the sugar cube, and he would have killed Pegasus. That would have been a tragedy.

Tailorshop (KQ5) The trendiest clothing emporium in Serenia, the prices are quite high but the colors are guaranteed to be the year's most popular. Graham visited the shop while he was in Serenia, returning the golden needle he had found, and getting a much-needed warm cloak in return. Without that protection from the cold of the high mountains, Graham surely would not have survived long there. The shop's owners, the Fey brothers, put the needle on display each year in conjunction with their annual clearance sale. It is mounted on a plaque telling the saga of how the needle was stolen and then returned by a king. Beneath the plaque is another prominent sign stating:

KING GRAHAM OF DAVENTRY STEPPED HERE!

This is apparently considered effective marketing in Serenia.

An Encyclopedia of Daventry

Talisman (KQ4) The magic medallion stolen from Genesta by her arch-enemy Lolotte. The Talisman is Genesta's emblem as queen of the fairies. It contains great powers and is able to focus those forces to do the magical bidding of its wearer. The relationship between the Talisman and the fairy queen, though, is more intimate than just a person wearing a powerful ornament. The Talisman is attuned to the fairy queen's life energies; in a sense, the Talisman and the queen become one. If the Talisman is lost or stolen, it is as if part of the queen is lost. Death follows shortly, and only restoration of the Talisman can prevent it. If the Talisman were destroyed, it would bring destruction to the entire fairy race.

Tambourine (KQ5) A shallow, one-headed drum with rattles attached to the outside. It is played by shaking, hitting, or tapping.

Along with the guitar and violin, the tambourine is a favorite instrument of gypsies. Derek says that Graham prefers string and wind instruments over percussion, but the king has a fine sense of rhythm and can shake the skins with the best of them. Whether this is true or not, Graham used the tambourine left behind by Madame Mushka and her family to entertain his way through a pair of dangerous encounters as he searched for his family. The tambourine in question is now the property of a strange beast who resides on Mordack's island. I doubt if anyone will contest the creature for ownership of the instrument.

Telescope (KQ3) In the tower of Manannan's house, there is a small observatory containing a telescope. Alexander-Gwydion says that Manannan could look through it and spy on anyone or any place he wished. Derek Karlavaegen, who lives in that house now, confirms this report. In the *Arabian Nights* story about the three brothers wanting to marry the same princess, one of the princes came upon just such a telescope, and it was through its power that they were able to discover their princess near death. They then flew the magic carpet to her side and cured her with the magic fruit.

Teleportation (KQ3) The ability to be instantly transported from one place to another. Alexander-Gwydion was able to teleport around in his adventures both by the power of the magic map and the specially prepared amber stone. Teleportation is not a quiet activity; when a person's body instantly leaves its location, it creates a momentary vacuum. Air immediately rushes to fill the spot, creating an implosion, the opposite of an explosion. The sound is a loud "POOF!" and resembles a muffled explosion. When the person instantly appears in the new location, the air is forced out in a loud "WHOOSH!" accompanied by a sudden gust of wind. This is the way it should work—in theory anyway. It is possible that teleportation by a magical spell adds a secondary sound-reduction element, but short of visiting Daventry, we have no way of testing the theory.

Temple in Desert (KQ5) Hidden amongst the cliffs on the northern edge of Serenia's endless desert is a deserted temple to an nameless god. It was used by the bandits that prowl the sands as a treasure house, the door of which could only be opened by the waving of a magic staff and the voicing the words, "Open, Sesame!" Graham was able to steal the staff and enter the temple. Once inside, he discovered that the door would quickly close behind him, and he wasn't sure that the words for opening it from inside were the same as opening from outside. He got out quick, taking only a brass bottle and one gold coin.

Once the forgotten god had a name, and the endless desert was a fertile plain teeming with people. In the name of their deity, they practiced technology. Neither the plain, the people, nor their god survived the experience.

The Objurgation of Souls (KQ5)   The book of magic that Graham found in the library of Mordack's castle. It detailed the magical Art of Iconomancy, a magic that can be cast without words. Using it, and the fact that Mordack's Wand of Magic had been nearly drained dry of power, King Graham was able to defeat the evil wizard who had kidnapped his family.
   See also Chapter 9, Prince Alexander's treatise on Iconomancy.

The Sorcery of Old (KQ3)   The ancient book of magic that Alexander-Gwydion discovered and used in Manannan's secret laboratory. It is most important that all instructions be followed perfectly, and to the exact letter.
   See also Chapter 5, Prince Alexander's treatise on Magic.

Three Bears (KQ4)   Mama Bear, Papa Bear, and Baby Bear lived in a tidy cottage in southern Llewdor. Alexander-Gwydion stole porridge from their table in order to feed the cat cookie to Manannan. He also stole a silver thimble from their bedroom to collect dew from the flowers in their garden. Derek Karlavaegen, who lives not far from them now, says that the prince gave him gold to give to the Bear family as payment for Alexander's deeds. Upon hearing the story of the prince's trials and adventures, they forgave him and gladly took the offered gold.
   In the tale we know of the Three Bears, Goldilocks was a spoiled, ill-mannered little girl who let herself into the house, and basically ransacked around. She saw three bowls of porridge on the table and tried them all until she found the one that was just right. She bounced around all three chairs until she found the one that was just right, and then broke it. Finally, in a snit for falling when the chair broke, she mussed up all the beds before she fell asleep in Baby Bear's. Imagine how you would feel if you came home and found your home the way Goldilocks left it. After checking out the damage, and calming Baby Bear down, the bears stomped upstairs and confronted the

intruder. The sound of their approach awakened Goldilocks, and as they entered the bedroom, she tried to escape by jumping out out the window. She broke her neck and died from the fall.

Three sisters (three witches) (KQ4) Rosella discovered a cave in the form of a skull, and inside met three witches, blind except for one glass eye that they passed among them. They would have eaten Rosella except that she was able to steal their lone eye from them. The witches gave Rosella a black scarab charm and begged her to return the eye. She did, but she made sure she had plenty of room and time to escape before the sisters picked it up. The charm protected Rosella from the undead that she encountered later that night.

The ancient Greeks knew of three women who they called the "Graeae," or sometimes "Phorcides." These weird sisters had only one eye and one tooth to share among them, and Perseus stole both of them from the old women. They are the sisters of the gorgons and were born as old women. Their names are Enyo, Phephredo, and Dino, and they live in the far, far west, in a place where the sun never shines.

Toyshop (KQ5) The toy shop in Serenia, owned by an aged craftsman by the name of Gepeppo and his son Gepeppito, is reputed to make the finest anatomically correct dolls in all of Daventry. While dolls are their specialty, they also make fine doll furniture, wooden swords, snow sleds, and yo-yos. It was at this shop that Graham was able to trade the gnome's hand-made marionette for one of Gepeppo's small sleds. At the time, the proprietor told Graham that he thought he, not the king, was getting the better part of the deal by far.

As fate would have it, Graham would have been unable to cross the mountains without the sled. In effect, Graham exchanged a fine puppet for a child's sled and his family. I suspect Graham feels that Gepeppo didn't get the best part of the deal at all.

Trees (KQ4)   Trees are the proof of Graham's father's adage that "Nothing is as it appears!" In Daventry, trees double as homes, hideouts, treasure repositories, places to hide weapons, and monsters. Rosella met the latter after her escape from the ogre in Tamir. While she was in the ogre's house, she took a sharp ax and was carrying it as she fled into the scary forest. The trees there are endowed with a rudimentary kind of life, and they like to snatch up anyone who comes within the grasp of their limbs. Death comes crushingly to the trees' victims.

Rosella was able to escape their clutches by swinging the ax at them. She gained their dim respect, and they left her alone afterwards. Derek Karlavaegen writes that that is the way with those trees; if you stand up to them, they get scared and back down. Indeed, one might say that their bark is worse than their bite, but I won't.

The trees in the scary forest are not at all like the trees in the Land of Oz. There, in Gilliken country, is a grove of willows that bother people by laughing at them as they pass by. They are cousins, of course, to the weeping willows. There are also stories of trees that throw their apples at you if you try to pick them, but I suspect you've seen the movie.

Trolls (KQ1, KQ2)   Trolls are cousins to ogres, slightly shorter and more slender, but uglier, dirtier, nastier, and more primitive. They never live in houses, for instance; they seek out the darkest parts of caves or the darkest parts of a forest. Trolls are greenish in color, have large talons on hands and feet, and large pointed teeth. People are their favorite food.

Rosella had to journey through a troll's cave on her way to the island of the magic fruit in Tamir. A large pile of bones decorated the inside of the cave, but it was only much later that the girl realized that it was a human bone that she took from there. No wonder the ogre's dog liked it so much!

The troll Graham encountered guarding the bridges in Daventry was a forest troll. The brightest of these creatures are sometimes known to live beneath bridges, hopping up to demand treasure from all who try to cross over their self-appointed domain. In these creatures, the appetite for treasure overpowers their appetite for human flesh; the places where they keep guard are known as troll bridges.

Unicorns (KQ4) These are thought by many to be the rarest and most magical of beasts. The unicorn has the head and body of a horse, but with a long, sharp, twisted horn in the middle of its forehead. They are very shy beasts, intelligent, and inhabiting open woodlands. It is said that only a pure, virgin maiden may touch or ride the fabulous beast, and that none can ever tame it. For these reasons it is a symbol of freedom and purity. The unicorn's horn is held to have magic properties, and people have hunted them for millennia to obtain the horns. This is perhaps the main reason they are so rare today.

Rosella was given the task by Lolotte of bringing a unicorn to her—something she obviously could not do for herself. Rosella did this by shooting the magic beast with one of Cupid's arrows of love, and then placing a golden bridle (which she had found on the desert island) about its neck. After she had defeated the wicked witch, Rosella freed the unicorn from Lolotte's stable.

Universe Interpreter (KQ5) An unusual device that stands in front of Crispin's house in Serenia. Crispin says that he has forgotten for what purpose he originally built it, but that it does do an adequate job as a wind chime. It seems that Crispin has many explanations as to what the Universe

Interpreter does or does not do. They have the odor of being invented on the spot.

Cedric told Graham that the device keeps the stars aligned. Local legend has it that it is used somehow in the act of *withdrawing* from our world to Daventry. It is quite possible that all of the above—and more—are true.

Valanice (KQ2, KQ3, KQ4, KQ5) Queen of Daventry, wife of King Graham, and mother of Alexander and Rosella. Graham rescued Valanice from the Crystal Tower, where she had been held prisoner by Hagatha after her kidnapping. Valanice is a scholar and a teacher in Daventry, and is the author of the court chronicle detailing Rosella's adventures in Tamir. The kidnapping of her son Alexander from his cradle was a massive blow to her, not just because of the loss, but because it reopened memories of her own kidnapping. Valanice attempted to submerge her grief through hard work—first by studying the histories of the world, and then by opening a school to teach the brightest children of the kingdom. When the three-headed dragon demanded the sacrifice of a young maiden, she fiercely fought against the decision to comply, and when it became time to offer her daughter to the beast, she refused, standing guard by Rosella's room with a drawn sword.

Weeping Willow (KQ5) Near the Dark Forest of Serenia, Graham discovered a graceful weeping willow tree. A harp was cradled in its branches, and at its base was a small pond formed by the tree's tears. The tree was really a princess named Alicia who had been transformed into a willow by a jealous witch who had also stolen her heart. In this light, it is somewhat understandable why Alicia was weeping.

Graham was able to find Alicia's heart and return it to her. At once she returned to her womanly form and was soon reunited with Prince Herbert.

The lovers went off together, never to be seen by Graham again. Presumably they are living happily ever after.

For his efforts, Graham got Alicia's harp, which later helped him out of a couple of tight situations, but not even a "Thank you!" from the happy couple. Isn't young love wonderful?

The willow tree, with its drooping branches, has traditionally symbolized grief, melancholy, and suffering. It was once customary for a woman who had been jilted by a lover, or who had lost one, to wear a garland of willow leaves or flowers. The Jews in captivity in Babylon hung harps on the branches of willow trees in sorrow over their exile. The willow can also represent death. Orpheus carried a willow branch with him into the underworld, the land of the dead, and Circe hung corpses in a willow grove.

However, the willow trees of European tradition are not the same as the weeping willow. The weeping willow tree actually come from China. Those trees though have the same sort of sorrowful significance there, and in Japan, as do the willows of western culture.

Well (KQ1, KQ3) Not far from Castle Daventry stands an old, covered well. Derek says it is in use again, restored by King Graham after having been nearly destroyed by the dragon. It is said that the sweetest water in the land can be drawn from the well, and that folks have been doing so since the first time any being *withdrew* from the Other World—our world. Graham climbed down the rope into it and then swam into a cave concealed beneath the water. There he recovered the mirror of Merlin that was guarded by a fire-breathing dragon, although it was not the same one that later ravaged the land.

Whale (KQ4) Rosella was swallowed whole by a whale—the species of which was not noticed in the panic of the moment—while she was swimming back to Tamir from Genesta's isle. She escaped by tickling the inside of its throat with a peacock feather she had found on the beach at Genesta's. In her interview in *Daventry People,* which evidently took place some time after she recovered from her harrowing adventures, Rosella recalled unimaginable stench and stomach fluids that burned the bare parts of her legs—much like a sunburn, but without the fresh air and cool breeze. She said that she was able to see because of a fluorescence that clung to much of the debris that was dissolving in the stomach acid, perhaps as a by-product of digestion.

Witch of the Dark Forest (KQ5) King Graham seems to have developed the bad habit of having run-ins with particularly nasty witches. Dahlia would have imprisoned him for life or baked him into a Graham cracker; Hagatha would have stewed him (perhaps serving the dish with a hearty green maggot wine); and the nameless hag of the Dark Forest, I'm sure, would have added him to her collection of slime toads.

That she followed the dark path, we have little doubt. She lusted after Prince Herbert, turned Alicia into a tree, stole her heart, and tried to steal her man. She apparently even stole Rumplestiltskin's magic spinning wheel. I would even bet that she didn't brush her pointed teeth or gargle after every meal, and I don't want to know what comprised her diet. Since she's bottled up for the next half millennium, most of us will not be around to find out that answer.

When Graham searched the inside of the witch's house he found a bag of gems, Rumplestiltskin's spinning wheel, and the key to Alicia's heart. He passed on the witch's recipe book.

Woodcutter and his wife (KQ1) Graham met these people during his first quest; they were hungry and had nothing to eat. Graham gave them the bowl that filled with food magically, and they insisted he take their fiddle as a gift. Graham played a merry tune on the instrument for the leprechauns and their king, and was able to recover the Shield of Achille.

The couple that Graham met strongly resemble the people who abandoned Hansel and Gretel in the forest. They, too, were a woodcutter and wife who didn't have enough to eat. Nah, they couldn't be the same people, could they?

Zombies (KQ4)   In the legion of the undead, zombies are the opposite of ghosts. Ghosts have distinct personalities, but no bodies; zombies have bodies, decaying though they may be, and no personalities at all. Zombies are animated corpses—walking appetites for human flesh, especially brains. The only way to stop a zombie is to destroy its own brain, or whatever is left of it. The rule is "Kill the brain, kill the ghoul," and it's a good one to keep in mind—so to speak. If you ignore this rule, you could hack a zombie to pieces, but the pieces would still move on their own. Rosella had to dig up five graves that night in the cemetery; all the time she was doing this she was surrounded by the walking, eating dead. If she had not been protected by the black scarab charm...well, it's just too ghastly to think about!

13

The Final Score

*P*erhaps the greatest mystery in the King's Quest game universe revolves around the word "SCORE" or, in some versions, "STATUS." Nowhere in any of the games' booklets and instructions are the words even mentioned. Yet when the game is being played, that magic word takes its comfortable place on the screen and stays there, moving upward every once in a while. It is understood, since it does exist, that we get rewards in the form of points for doing certain things successfully. It is even somewhat obvious just what might score points: rescuing Valanice, defeating Lolotte, finding the magic fruit, guessing the gnome's name, finding Mordack's island, completing subquests, and finding treasure or other items. What is not so obvious, however, is why a score is tallied. If the object of the game is to complete a specific quest, why score the game at all? We're dealing with a simple win/no-win situation here, aren't we?

Likewise, if the game is being scored, is there a perfect score? If there is, what is it? Can I complete the quest and the game with less than a perfect score? And finally, will somebody please give me a list of what I can get points for in the games?

We're asking a lot, aren't we?

Yes!

In no particular order, yes, there is such a thing as a perfect score, and it's different in each game. Yes, you can complete a game successfully without earning all of the available points. And yes, I will list all the ways you can score in the King's Quest games.

The ability to score points gives many computer game players a feeling of accomplishment, a second measure of achievement. It's a way to mark one's progress and can create a personal standard, a personal best, against which to strive the next time you play. Also, perfection can be a goal in itself; almost everybody wants to be perfect. Winning a competition is not always enough if you only scored a 9.9 out of a perfect score of 10.0.

527
The Final Score

The people of Daventry, whose real-life adventures constitute the basis for the King's Quest games, overcame their particular challenges in their own individual ways. In the game universe, on the other hand, there is often more than one way to successfully solve a problem. Occasionally you will score more points by not doing things the same way the characters did. That's OK, it's only a game, not real life.

If you're into King's Quest for the adventures and puzzles, the following list of scores will give you some ideas as to alternate solutions and nudge you a little to notice things you may have missed. If you're into maximizing your score, feast your eyes, it's all here.

One last reminder: *all* is revealed here; no game mysteries remain uncovered and every problem is solved. This may be too much for many mortal minds to bear. Like strong drink, use it in moderation. If you're the impatient type, beware! Too much knowledge is dangerous; it can take all the fun out of life.

KING'S QUEST:
QUEST FOR THE CROWN

Note: It is impossible to get all of the points listed below. For example, if you guess the gnome's name, you will not get the gold key, or be able to unlock the door in the mountain from the outside. Also, if an item is marked with an asterisk (∗), it means the point total is different than that given by Sierra-On-Line.

The way points are scored differs somewhat between the classic and the *SCI Version*. Both version are listed here, but the final totals remain the same.

What to Do	**Points**	
	Classic	SCI Version
Enter Castle Daventry (beginning of game)	1	0
Bow to King Edward (beginning of game)	3	0
Fairy Godmother's spell	0	0
Get carrot from garden	2	2
Talk to Elf (get ring)	3	3
Use ring to escape wolf/witch/sorcerer	lose 2	0
Get bowl on ground	3	3
Read the bowl	1	1
Get pebbles	1	1
Get walnut from gound under tree	3	3
Open walnut (find gold inside)	3	3
Climb big oak tree (west of garden)	2	2
Get golden egg	6	6
Move rock (west of castle)	2	2
Get dagger from hole under rock	5	5

The Final Score

What to Do   **Points**

	Classic	SCI Version
Looking into rotting stump	1	1
Getting pouch from stump	3	3
Looking inside pouch (diamonds)	3	3
At witch's cottage:		
Get note	2	1
Read note	1	2
Push witch into fireplace	7	7
Open cupboard (cabinet)	2	2
Take cheese	2	2
Eat house	2	2
At woodcutter's cottage:		
Fill bowl	0	2
Give filled bowl	3	3
Get fiddle (play fiddle)	3	3
At well:		
Cut rope with knife (gets bucket)	2	2
Climb down rope	1	2
Fill bucket	2	2
Dive (without filling bucket)	4	4
Dive (after filling bucket)	2	0
Enter dragon's cave	1	1
Throw water on dragon	5	5
Get magic mirror	8	8
Throw dagger at dragon (kill)	lose 2	3
Leave by swimming (after killing)*	4	0
Leave by swimming (without killing)	2	0
Leave via cave	0	2

King's Quest

What to Do   **Points**

What to Do	Classic	SCI Version
Pick clover	2	2
Get picked-up by condor	3	3
Pick mushroom	1	1
Down hole:		
Give cheese to rat	2	2
Give treasure to rat	lose value of treasure	
Play fiddle to guards	3	3
Get magic shield	8	8
Get Leprechaun King's scepter	6	6
Eat mushroom	2	3
Leave through tiny hole	1	0
Troll:		
Show carrot to goat (goat follows)	5	5
Goat butts troll	4	4
Give treasure to troll	lose value of treasure	
Gnome:		
Get gold key (don't guess name)	3	3
Unlock door in mountain	2	2
Guess gnome's name	5	9
Get magic beans	4	0
Plant beans	2	2
Climb beanstalk	0	2
Land of the Clouds:		
Get sling	2	2
Kill giant (with sling & pebbles)	2	3
Wait for giant to sleep	5	7
Get magic chest	8	8

The Final Score

What to Do	Points	
	Classic	SCI Version
Return to Castle Daventry (open gate)	1	3
Bow to King Edward (upon return)	3	0
Highest possible score	**158**	**158**

KING'S QUEST 2: ROMANCING THE THRONE

Note: It is impossible to get all of the points listed below. For example, if you kill the snake, you won't be able to get the sugar cube or throw a bridle over the snake, for that matter.

What to Do	Points
At Grandma's house:	
Open mailbox	1
Get basket of goodies	2
Give basket to Riding Hood	4
Give chicken soup to Grandma	2
Find black cloak and ruby ring	4
Wear black cloak and ring	3
Fairy's spell	0
At monastery:	
Pray	2
Get silver cross	2
Wear silver cross	2
Look in hole in rock (south of monastery)	1
Get brooch	7
Cross bridge (maximum 7 trips)	1 point per trip
In the woods:	
Get stake	2
Get mallet	2
Get necklace	7
Take chicken soup	2
Get earrings	7

The Final Score

What to Do   **Points**

    Lose treasure to dwarf   Lose value of treasure
    Retrieve treasure   Regain value of treasure
On the beach:
    Get trident   3
    Get bracelet   7
    Give flowers to mermaid   2
    Give treasure to mermaid   Lose value of treasure
    Ride sea horse   2
Under the waves:
    Get bottle   4
    Get key to door #1   5
Unlock door #1   7
Get cloth from bottle   2
Cover birdcage with cloth   2
Take birdcage (with bird)   2
Give birdcage to woman   6
Trade 2 treasures for lamp   Lose value of treasure
Rub lamp (carpet)   2
Rub lamp second time (sword)   2
Rub lamp third time (bridle)   2
Top of cliffs:
    Fly carpet   4
    Kill snake   2
    Throw bridle on snake   5
    Get sugar cube   2
    Get key to door #2   5
Unlock door #2   7
At Dracula's Castle:

King's Quest

What to Do	Points
Give treasure to boatman	Lose value of treasure
Eat sugar cube	1
Take candle	2
Light candle	1
Take ham	2
Kill Dracula (in coffin)	7
Get silver key	2
Unlock chest in tower	1
Get tiara	7
Get key to door #3	5
Unlock door #3	7
Get net	1
Catch golden fish	2
Throw fish back	3
Ride fish	1
Enchanted Isle:	
Get amulet	3
Kill lion	2
Feed lion	4
Enter room at top of quartz tower	5
Say "HOME"	3
Highest possible score	**185**

KING'S QUEST 3: TO HEIR IS HUMAN

What to Do	Points
In Manannan's house:	
Get mutton	1
Get fruit	1
Get bread	1
Get bowl	1
Get spoon	1
Get cup	1
Get knife	1
Get small mirror	1
Get fly wings	1
Get cat hair	1
Get rose petal essence	1
Find brass key	3
Find magic map	7
Find magic wand	4
Find hidden lever	5
Hide stuff under bed (one time)	4
Get chicken feather	1
In secret laboratory:	
Get saffron	1
Get mandrake root	1
Get nightshade juice	1
Get fish bone powder	1
Get toad spittle	1
Get toadstool powder	1

What to Do	Points
Spells:	
Prepare "Fly Like an Eagle or a Fly"	10
Prepare cat cookie	10
Prepare "Understanding the Language of Creatures"	10
Prepare teleportation stone	10
Prepare "Causing a Deep Sleep"	10
Prepare "Brewing a Storm"	10
Prepare invisibility ointment	10
Change Manannan into a cat	12
Around Llewdor:	
Get mistletoe	1
Get acorns	1
Get spoonful of mud	1
Get eagle feather	2
Get cup of ocean water	1
Kill spider	4
Get amber stone	3
Fly into oak tree hole (as fly)	5
Pull rope	3
Find bandit's hideout	2
Find coin purse	4
Get cactus	1
Get snakeskin	1
Turn Medusa to stone	5

The Final Score

What to Do	Points
At three bears' house:	
Get porridge	2
Get thimble	1
Get dew	1
In tavern:	
Overhear bandits (as fly)	3
Give money to captain	3
In store:	
Get dog fur	1
Buy lard	1
Buy salt	1
Buy empty pouch	1
Buy fish oil	1
On pirate ship:	
Board ship	2
Leave hold	2
Find stolen possessions	3
Get shovel	1
Escape ship	5
In Daventry:	
Find treasure	7
Get past Abominable Snowman	4
Kill dragon	7
Untie Rosella	3
Enter Castle Daventry	4
Highest possible score	210

KING'S QUEST 4:
THE PERILS OF ROSELLA

What to Do	Points
Around Tamir:	
Get book of Shakespeare	2
Flip latch	4
Get shovel	2
Give book to minstrel (get lute)	3
Give lute to Pan (after playing lute)	3
Clean dwarfs' house	5
Get pouch (diamonds)	2
Return diamonds (get lantern)	3
Get worm	2
Quest for magic fruit:	
Get gold ball	2
Kiss frog	3
Get gold crown	2
Swim under waterfall (as frog)	5
Get bone	2
Get board	2
Cross chasm (first time)	2
Cross to swamp island (using board)	2
Play flute to cobra	4
Get magic fruit	10
Cross chasm (second time)	2
Quest for unicorn:	
Give diamonds to fisherman	3
Put worm on hook	1

The Final Score

What to Do	Points
Catch fish	3
Get peacock feather	2
Tickle whale's throat	5
Get gold bridle	3
Throw fish to bird	4
Get whistle	2
Blow whistle	2
Ride dolphin	2
Get bow and arrows	2
Shoot unicorn	4
Bridle unicorn	3
Take unicorn to Lolotte	7

Quest for hen:

What to Do	Points
Give bone to dog	4
Get ax	2
Get hen	4
Take hen to Lolotte	7

Quest for Pandora's box:

What to Do	Points
Use ax on scary trees	4
Get eye	3
Get scarab	2
Return eye	3
Get baby rattle	3
Give rattle to baby ghost	2
Get bag of gold	3
Give bag of coins to ghost	2
Get locket	3
Give locket to ghost	2

King's Quest

What to Do	Points
Get medal of honor	3
Give medal to ghost	2
Get toy horse	3
Give toy to boy ghost	2
Get sheet music	2
Play organ (using sheet music)	4
Get skeleton key	2
Open crypt	3
Drop ladder	2
Get Pandora's box	4
Take box to Lolotte	7
At Lolotte's castle:	
Get gold key	2
Unlock door	2
Retrieve possessions	4
Unlock Lolotte's door	2
Shoot Lolotte	8
Get talisman	5
Get hen	2
Get Pandora's box	2
Free unicorn	4
Return box to crypt	2
Lock crypt (after returning box)	2
Give talisman to Genesta	10
Given hen to Genesta	2
Highest possible score	**230**

KING'S QUEST 5:
ABSENCE MAKES THE HEART GO YONDER

What to Do	Points
Around Serenia:	
Throw fish at bear	4
Get honeycomb	2
Get stick	2
Throw stick at dog	4
Get gold needle	2
Give gold coin to gypsy	3
Get amulet	2
Get tambourine	2
Give heart to tree	4
Get harp	2
Get marionette	4
Desert:	
Drink at oasis (first time)	2
Find temple (first time)	3
See bandits open temple door	2
Find bandits' tents	3
Get staff	2
Open temple door	2
Get brass bottle	2
Get gold coin	2
Get old shoe	2
Dark Forest:	
Enter Dark Forest (first time)	2
Give brass bottle to witch	4

King's Quest

What to Do	Points
Get pouch of emeralds	2
Get spinning wheel	2
Get gold key	2
Unlock door in tree	3
Get gold heart	2
Squeeze honey on ground	4
Throw 1st. emerald	2
Throw 2nd. emerald	2
Drop 3rd. emerald	2
Follow elf through hole	2
Get shoes	2

Around Town:

Get fish	2
Get silver coin	2
Throw shoe at cat	4
Buy custard pie	2
Get cobbler's hammer	4
Get sled	4
Get cloak	4
Get rope	2
Break lock in cellar	4
Get leg of lamb	2

Mountains:

Scare snake	3
Use rope to climb	5
Cross waterfall	2
Wear cloak	4
Eat 1/2 of lamb	4

The Final Score

What to Do	Points
Cross chasm	5
Give 1/2 of lamb to eagle	3
Captured by wolves	2
Play harp for Ice Queen	4
Throw pie at Yeti	4
Get crystal	4
Captured by Roc	2
Get gold locket	2
Beach and Ocean:	
Get iron bar	2
Plug hole in boat	5
Find Harpy's island (first time)	3
Play harp for harpies	4
Get fishhook	2
Get conch shell	2
Pick up Cedric	3
Give shell to hermit	4
Wizard's Island:	
Arrive on island	3
Get dead fish	2
Explode Serpent Gate	5
Open grate	4
Play tambourine for Dink	3
Get hairpin	2
Unlock labyrinth door	4
Get dried peas	2
Throw dried peas at henchman	3
Give locket to Cassima	4

King's Quest

What to Do	Points
Captured by henchman (first time)	2
Get cheese	4
Bag Manannan	2
Get Mordack's wand	3
Read spell book	3
Put Mordack's wand in machine	4
Put Crispin's wand in machine	4
Put cheese in machine	5
Use Crispin's wand	4
Casting spells (at the right time):	
Tiger transformation	4
Rabbit transformation	4
Mongoose transformation	4
Rain	4
Highest Possible Score	**260**